A Life of My Own

OTHER BOOKS AND BOOKS ON CASSETTE
BY LISA MCKENDRICK:

On a Whim

A Life of My Own

a novel

Lisa McKendrick

Covenant Communications, Inc.

To Ada Green,
my grandmother and friend

Sincere thanks to the guy with the fetching smile,
Rich. It would be impossible for me to write
anything more daring than a grocery list without
your love and support.

chapter 1

Elder Matt Hollingsworth
MTC Box 210
CHI-SAS 1010
2005 North 900 East
Provo, UT 84604-1793

Dear Matt,

Are you sure you didn't rob a Quick Mart or something? I'm joking. Well, sort of. It's just that the MTC is so strict! My guess is it's really a minimum-security prison, and you used your one phone call to order pizza. What were you thinking? Anyway, if you need a lawyer, just let me know. Sadly, I know a few. Speaking of lawyers . . . Mom and Keppler's wedding is in two weeks, which stinks entirely. Not that I don't want them to get married. Keppler is nice enough. I'm just sad you're less than a mile away and can't attend. I know, you're getting ready to go to Chile and every minute counts, but cake and punch and wishing the newlyweds well, according to my estimations, would only take 3 minutes and 12.9 seconds if you take big bites and don't try to practice your Spanish on anyone. At least run it by the warden.

This whole wedding thing has gotten out of hand. I mean, originally they were going to have a small wedding and reception in Keppler's back-yard, but then Mom went over to inspect and said it wouldn't work. Too many pigeons. They looked around for a while and decided the country club was the perfect place, I think because they figured if the reception got boring, they could grab a golf cart and still get in nine holes. But that was before they found out that a local yodeling club (some people have too much *time on their hands) would be meeting there as well, and the country club couldn't guarantee Mom and Keppler a yodel-free reception. So to make a long story short, now the reception is going to be at the Museum of Art on campus, the guest list has ballooned from 50 to 250 guests, and a harpist, valet parking, and lobster bisque have all been added. At this point it wouldn't surprise me if they decided to televise the dang thing.*

But anyway, I've been saving the worst for last. Now they've decided to get married in the temple. I was barely comfortable with the country club idea. I can't even tell you what it does to my insides to have my mom getting married to someone other than my dad in the temple, even if it is just for time. It's like Cub Scouts are learning how to tie granny knots with my intestines. I don't even fully understand it, but the thought of it just freaks me out. Of course, they asked me if I was okay with the wedding taking place in the temple, and I told them sure, whatever. I mean, what else could I have said? No, you have to hang with the pigeons? At least Jill will be there to coach me through it. Dang! You're missing your chance to meet Jill. You'd like her. She's the best. Okay, you're both tied for best. Well, gotta go. Love, Whims

* * *

Jill Nicholson was no baby-sitter. Sure, she was the oldest of seven children, but that hadn't done much to morph her into Mary Poppins. So you can imagine how thrilled she was to have Melanie and Steve, our upstairs neighbors the year my mom and I lived at Wymount, show up at the Provo temple for my mom's wedding with Tyson and McKenner in tow. I don't know how Mel and Steve pulled it off. I mean, it kinda felt like they were on one of those moving sidewalks you see at airports, because almost without breaking stride they handed us their kids and walked inside the temple, turning around just long enough to thank us in advance for "keeping an eye" on their "all-stars."

For a moment we all stood there staring at each other, not really sure what to do next, and then McKenner broke the ice. Remembering he preferred to be held, he raised his arms to Jill and began to cry.

Jill folded her arms. "Whims, no way am I holding beef-o-baby. He looks like he weighs as much as I do."

Feeling sorry for the little guy, I said, "He's not that huge." I then picked him up, instantly feeling the strain in my back.

"You got a hernia wish or something?" Jill scolded. "That kid's as solid as a slab of concrete, and you didn't even bend your knees."

I hoisted him a little higher onto my hip, trying to get comfortable. "I'm all right," I said. McKenner looked at me as if he knew otherwise, then contentedly stuck his thumb in his mouth.

"So what am I supposed to do with Captain America?" she asked, referring to Tyson's red, white, and blue T-shirt.

Tyson answered her question. "Try and catch me. Beep! Beep! I'm a car!" he said, and ran out into the parking lot.

As she ran after him she said, "Whims, check the diaper bag for a stun gun!"

"You're dreaming. They don't have a—"

"Candy then!" she shouted. "Check it for candy!"

Years of gymnastics training had done little to teach Jill how to run in stiletto heels, and it showed. She moved slowly and awkwardly, as if each step were as much fun as walking on hot coals, which, of course, gave Tyson quite the advantage.

"Just take your shoes off," I told her as she hobbled back, holding Tyson's hand.

"No. You know I hate to get my feet dirty. Speaking of dirty . . ." she said, sniffing the air.

We both looked at McKenner, who seemed quite pleased with himself. "You change it," we said, pointing at each other.

I couldn't remember the last time I'd changed a dirty diaper, no doubt because it was one of those painful experiences my mind had found a way to repress. Feeling a little desperate, I said, "Come on, Jill. You've got more experience with this sort of thing than I do."

"So?" said Jill. "He's your boyfriend's nephew."

I took a deep breath, pretending that such a statement was hard to tolerate. "For the bazillionth time," I huffed, "Matt's not my boyfriend. I mean, sure, we get along great and sort of dated each other exclusively during the summer, but, like I've told you, Matt and I had a long talk before he started his mish and . . ." The thorough explanation of my relationship with Matt Hollingsworth slowed to a standstill as I saw a stupid smirk spread across Jill's face. "What?" I asked Jill.

"Nothing," she said. "It's just that I'm so interested in what you're saying, I feel like applauding." She let go of Tyson's hand to do just that.

"Beep! Beep!" said Tyson as he zoomed away.

"Right behind you, pal," shouted Jill as she hobbled after him.

"Some friend you are," I mumbled, and then got to work changing McKenner's pants.

Wincing with every step, Jill finally returned with Tyson. "I was telling Tyson about the candy in the diaper bag."

"Give me candy!" Tyson demanded.

McKenner, who still insisted on being held, appeared to understand the word *candy* and jumped with anticipation in my arms.

"Sorry," I said. "There isn't any. Just smashed saltine crackers and diapers."

McKenner appeared to also understand the word *sorry* and began to wail in disappointment.

Tyson muttered a couple of slow and sorrowful *beep beeps* and sped away.

Not that Jill ever swears (at least on the temple grounds), but as she watched Tyson run farther and farther away from her, it seemed like it was all she could do to keep herself from uttering a string of choice, four-letter words. She took several deep breaths, like the kind she takes before sprinting toward the vault, then finally said, "What's the matter with these people? He's in law school, not dental school. What kind of parent doesn't keep a freakin' lollipop in their diaper bag? Can you tell me?"

Jill glared at McKenner, half challenging the thirteen-month-old to give a reasonable answer, but McKenner just stuck his thumb in his mouth and thwacked his head down against my shoulder. What I would've given to have been able to sit down, but every time I tried, McKenner fussed. He made it clear he wanted to be up, and he wanted me to do the standing for him.

I was so busy watching Jill chase after Tyson that for a moment I forgot why I was outside the temple in the first place. Spotting a wedding couple exit the front doors, I looked at my watch and felt a chill go through me. It was 2:15. Mom and Keppler's wedding had already started. In fact, there was a good chance that they were already married. I don't know how Jill knows this, but she told me that temple weddings are pretty darn speedy as far as wedding ceremonies go.

Joan *Keppler* instead of *Waterman.* The thought caused my knees to buckle and McKenner to nervously grab ahold of my hair. "Jill!" I said as she limped toward me, firmly gripping Tyson's wrist.

She looked like she would rather have changed a hundred dirty diapers than watch Tyson one second longer. "Okay, could you explain to me how we got stuck with Mel's kids?"

"Let me go! Let me go!" Tyson howled as he tried to pull free, but Jill didn't budge.

"I don't know. I guess their baby-sitter canceled at the last minute," I said, my back and arms aching as I moved McKenner to my other hip. "But Jill, it's—"

Trying to break free from her grip, Tyson dropped to the ground. "So how did we become their backup plan?" Jill asked, barely managing to stay atop her three-inch heels.

"I don't know," I said, growing a tad impatient with my best friend. "Maybe it has something to do with the fact that they can go in the temple and we can't."

"Whims, one back handspring into a back layout and we would have been past that front desk," she huffed. Jill likes to forget that, unlike herself, I can barely manage a cartwheel.

"Girl," I said, ignoring the whole back-handspring-back-layout comment, "will you just listen to me for a minute? It's past two. My mom is a married woman."

"Dang it!" yelled Jill.

Whether she was referring to my mom or Tyson was anybody's guess. After all, he had wiggled free again and was racing toward the fountain. This time, however, Jill didn't follow after him. Instead, she cupped her hands around her mouth and yelled, "Tyson! It's been nice knowing you. I'll tell your parents you said good-bye before you died."

A bride posing in front of a bunch of geraniums nearby heard Jill and turned in shock to her husband just as the photographer took the picture.

Leaning toward Jill, I whispered, "Girl, what are you doing?"

"I've had it with that kid. Coach worked us hard this morning, my shoes are killing me, and I am not chasing after him anymore."

"But why tell him—"

Tyson, who was just a few feet from the fountain, turned to face us. It was obvious Jill had his attention. "I'm not dead," he said defiantly, putting his fists on his hips.

"No, but you will be. The temple is a dangerous place. You stick your hand in that fountain and your fingers are gonna get chewed off. That fountain is filled with piranhas."

Out of the corner of my eye, I saw the same bride fold her arms in disgust and whisper something in her groom's ear. It was hard not to look at her. She was practically perfect with her empire-waist wedding dress accentuating her slender frame and her bright blonde hair cascading into curls that gently hung around her scowling face. I'm telling you, except for the frown and the finger pointing, she looked like a page from *Bride* magazine.

Tyson gave Jill a skeptical look and walked over to the fountain, his fingers hovering above the water's edge. "I don't see any errana," he said boldly.

Instead of walking over to the fountain to talk to Tyson, Jill sat on the grass and continued to yell. "Of course you can't see them. They're invisible this time of year. But they're in there, swimming around, waiting to eat some pudgy little fingers. That's their favorite food, you know—four-year-old-kid fingers. So go ahead, put your hand in the fountain, but chances are we won't be able to stop the bleeding once your fingers get bitten off."

Tyson looked down for a long while at the clear water gurgling in the fountain, then slowly pulled his hand away from the water and started to run down the sidewalk, heading behind the temple.

"I wouldn't go there if I were you," yelled Jill. "Behind the temple is more dangerous. I mean, you might as well put your fingers in the fountain if you're thinking of running behind the temple."

Tyson's eyes were wide now with fear. "What's back there?"

"Mostly mountain lions and brown recluse spiders, but there's other stuff too. I probably shouldn't say."

Tyson gulped. "What?"

"Well, for starters . . . the sidewalk people."

"Who?"

"The people who live in the sidewalk. You can't see them 'cause they're gray and flat, so they blend in pretty well, and for the most part they're nice . . . unless you step on them. Then they get real mad and shove you into the grass, which is covered with pesticides. And I don't need to tell you how dangerous those are, do I?"

Tyson shook his head and slowly curled up in a ball where he had been standing. Newly married couples walked around him as they made their way here and there taking wedding pictures.

"You should be ashamed of yourself!" said a shrill voice. It was the practically perfect bride who had been standing near the geraniums.

Jill took off her shoes and began rubbing her feet. "Beat it, Barbie," she said, squinting as she looked at her.

The bride stormed off to her groom, and they finished their pictures by the geraniums, her smile looking more like a grimace.

"She looks pretty mad," I said once the bride and groom had moved on.

"Yeah, well, until she's walked a mile in my dang stiletto heels, I don't really want to hear about it."

Just then Mel and Steve came out of the temple along with my Aunt Helen and Uncle Pete. Both Melanie and Helen were wiping away tears, sorta making it look like they'd just been to a funeral.

"Mom!" shouted Tyson. "Get me out of here!"

Melanie smiled at her son, who was still sitting in the center of the sidewalk. Though pregnant, she effortlessly scooped Tyson off the ground and brought him to rest in her arms.

Jill put her shoes back on her aching (but clean) feet. "How'd it go?" said Steve as he walked toward us, making McKenner cry because he wasn't coming fast enough.

I handed McKenner to his dad and felt so much lighter I wondered for a moment if I might lift off the sidewalk. "Uh, fine," I said. Jill shot me a look that said, "liar."

We walked over to Melanie and Helen, who were standing in front of the temple talking with their heads close together, like schoolgirls sharing a secret. When Mel saw me, she put Tyson down and gave me a hug.

Ignoring Tyson, who was shouting at the top of his lungs for her to pick him up and that he didn't want to die, Melanie said, "Oh Whimsy, I wish you could have been in there."

I thought of how much fun it had been to hold McKenner for an hour and said, "Yeah, me too."

Tearing up again, Melanie choked on her words as she said, "It was such a beautiful wedding, and Professor Keppler was so sweet. It almost made me wish I were the one marrying him. No offense, hon." Steve smiled in a way that made me think quirky comments like that were part of the reason he was so crazy about Mel. "But I can't say any more. Your mom wants to tell you about it herself."

This seemed weird. I mean, what was there to tell? They went in the temple two single people and, after signing some papers and saying a few "I do's," were going to come out of the temple a couple. Still, something about what Mel said made me nervous, and as soon as I could, I planned to pull Mom aside and find out what was so special about her wedding.

"Let's get out of here!" shouted Tyson.

"Tyson's right," said Melanie. "We'd better scoot. But we'll see you at the reception."

As the Johnsons walked back toward Wymount, Tyson turned and gave Jill a long, hard look. What the look meant I wasn't sure, but it made me wonder if unfinished business lay between them.

Aunt Helen went back inside the temple and a few minutes later came out to tell us Mom and Keppler would be out soon.

"Oh," I said, suddenly feeling panicked.

Aunt Helen gave me a hug, then asked, "Are you doing all right?"

"I think so. It's just weird to think Mom is married. And let's be honest, she may have just made a big mistake. After all, they haven't known each other that long. I mean, it's entirely possible he leaves his nail clippings in the sink, and never bothers to put the cap back on the toothpaste, and—"

"Whimsy," she said, cutting short my list of Keppler's possible faults, "you can relax. He's perfect for her."

As Aunt Helen walked over to Uncle Pete, I frowned and thought, *Yeah, but is he perfect for me?*

"They're perfect for each other," said Jill in a dreamy voice. "And besides, just the other day your mom was saying she's always wanted a backyard full of pigeons."

Pushing Jill just hard enough to make her grab ahold of my arm to keep her balance, I said, "You are such a liar."

Jill let go of my arm. "Whims," she said, suddenly sounding like a concerned parent, "don't say the L-word. We're at the temple."

I was just about to push Jill again when suddenly there they were—Mr. and Mrs. Keppler, walking hand in hand out of the temple doors. A chill went through me as I looked at my mom, slender and stylish in her powder-blue suit, with a rock on her hand the size of Texas. Let's face it, she was radiant. In fact, when it came to the glowing-bride thing, she beat the other brides on the temple grounds hands down (especially Scowl Barbie), and she did so without the help of a bouquet, veil, or white, flowing dress.

Mom glanced at me, then whispered something to Keppler. He nodded in agreement, then gave her hand a kiss before letting go. As Mom walked toward me, I couldn't help noticing that though her makeup was flawless and her eyes bright, it looked as if she, like Melanie, had shed a few (okay, probably more than a few) tears during the wedding. She gave me a hug, and as she did, I whispered in her ear, "Mrs. Keppler."

Mom whispered back, "Darling, how does that make you feel?"

The truth was it made me feel lonely, but now didn't seem like the right time for the truth. Forcing a smile, I said, "I'm all right with it, but if it's okay with you, I think I'll just keep calling you Mom."

Mom took my face in her hands. "You'd better," she warned with a smile.

Leaning closer to her, I said in a low voice, "But quick, tell me the secret!"

Mom looked at me as if I'd just spoken to her in French (learning a second language is still on her to-do list) and then carefully scratched her head with one of her manicured nails. "What are you talking about?" she asked.

"Mel said there was something about your wedding she couldn't tell me—something you wanted to tell me yourself. What was it? Did Keppler cry like a baby when he saw you all decked out for the wedding? Or was it that somebody mistook you for his daughter?"

Mom straightened her jacket and squirmed a little in her pumps. "No. It wasn't anything like that, but you're right, there is something I'd like to tell you—"

"Joanie," Helen said as she walked toward us with a camera, "we need you for pictures, and you too, Whimsy."

Looking concerned, Mom asked, "Would it be all right if we talked later? Maybe after the reception—once everything has settled down a bit."

Patience isn't a virtue I've cornered the market on, but somehow I managed to keep from complaining. "Sure," I said, and smiled weakly. "But right after the reception, we talk."

"Deal," she said, and kissed me on the cheek.

I watched Mom as she walked toward Keppler and slid her arm through his. "Mrs. Keppler," I whispered, trying to get used to the idea.

Jill, who had taken a moment to sit down on a bench, now stood beside me, wobbling again on her tenuous heels. "So she didn't say anything?" asked Jill.

Still looking at Mom and Keppler, I said, "Nope. We're gonna talk later—that is, if she can pry herself loose from him for a minute. Geez, you'd think he's afraid she's gonna make a run for it the way he's holding on to her."

Jill assessed the situation. "No, it looks more like a game of tag and she's base. But why the huffy, angry tone? I thought you said you liked him."

"I do, sort of anyway. I mean, as far as evil stepfathers go, he's all . . . oh . . . my . . . gosh," I said, my voice trailing off as I began to feel that a problem of gigantic proportions had just plunked down in front of me.

"What?"

"What the heck am I going to call him?"

"I thought you called him Keppler."

"Yeah, but not to his face. When I've got something to say to him, I just clear my throat or say 'um' until I get his attention."

"Why not call him *Father?*"

I looked at Jill as if she had lost her mind.

"I'm joking!" she said. "I think you should call him . . . *Daddy.*" She burst out laughing.

"You're zero help, as usual," I whined.

"All right," she said, barely managing to speak she was laughing so hard, "*Pa* then."

While waiting for Jill to quit cracking up at her own joke, I looked over at Mr. and Mrs. Keppler smiling by the piranha-filled fountain as Helen and others took their picture. Keppler was standing behind Mom with his arms tight around her, stooping a little to get in as close as he could to her. His smile surprised me—shocked me even. There was an intensity to it that made it seem like at any moment he might throw his head back and laugh triumphantly into the blue sky. *No,* I told myself. *That's what evil villains do after tying young, ringleted females to railroad tracks. Keppler's just . . . happy. Fiercely happy.*

Keppler. The thought of his name brought me back to my problem. What was I going to call him? Any minute now I'd have to go over there and talk to him. I couldn't do the "uh" thing forever. I had to decide, and I knew I should start right away, sort of to get the awkwardness over with. "Come on, Jill," I said. "I need your help. What should I call him?"

"Why not call him by his first name?"

I shook my head. "Stanley? No, it'd be too weird—like I was trying to be his bud."

"Then keep calling him Keppler."

"Whimsy!" Helen cried. "We need you."

I waved to tell them I was on my way, then turned to Jill and took a deep breath. "Okay," I said, "I'm gonna go over there and call him . . . Keppler."

Jill gave me a thumbs-up and as I walked away, I could hear her softly chanting my name, making me feel as if I were about to enter a wrestling ring. Wrestling, especially professional wrestling, makes me gag, but as I walked toward the newlyweds, it was thoughts of professional wrestling (more specifically, thoughts of Keppler as a professional wrestler) that made me smile and momentarily forget about my what-to-call-Keppler crisis.

Sure, outside the ring he might have been Stanley Keppler, your average, cranky law professor, but inside the ring he was affectionately known to his tattooed, Harley-riding fans as The Litigator. Oiled down and wearing black biker shorts, a muscle shirt, and a bow tie speckled with the scales of justice, Keppler shouted insults at his fans as he waited for the chance to pulverize, or rather, pretend to pulverize, his opponent. He was, after all, a professional wrestler. The Litigator had just started bouncing from one side of the ring to another when I heard, "Hello, Whimsy!"

Snapping out of my daze, I looked to see Keppler walking towards me with his arms outstretched, ready to give me—horror of horrors—a hug. On the list of things I had never done before in my life, which included stuff like calling Keppler "Keppler" and bungee jumping off the Ratazupe Bridge in Zaire, was also giving Keppler a hug. Anything—a headlock, body slam, half nelson—anything would have been better than a hug from Keppler.

It's not like I thought, *Gee, what can I do to hurt Keppler's feelings on his wedding day?* It was practically reflexive. The Litigator, I mean, Keppler came toward me for a hug, and I ducked.

Keppler stepped back a little. "Very well," he said with a smile that hardly hid his disappointment.

As I straightened up, Keppler extended his hand to me for what I sensed was meant to be a goodwill handshake—sort of his way of letting me know he didn't hate me for not hugging him. *This is it,* I thought. The perfect time to make myself clear, to establish a precedent, to start calling him what I wanted to call him. Not *Stanley,* or *Dad,* or even worse, *Father.* But *Keppler,* plain and simple. And I was going to do it, but as I held out my hand, I made the mistake of glancing to see if anyone was watching us, and they were. Mom, Aunt Helen and Uncle Pete, Jill, Keppler's two oldest sons and their wives, a couple of brides and grooms, and even the maintenance guy fixing sprinkler heads—all of them were watching to see what I was going to do next.

We shook hands, and Keppler said, "You couldn't look more lovely, Whimsy."

My mouth went dry, and I hoped he hadn't noticed that my hands felt like I had thrown caution to the wind and stuck them in the temple fountain. As he squeezed my wet sponge of a hand, I said, "Thanks a lot . . . uh . . . Kep, uh . . . I mean, I *kept* hoping someone would say that." Feeling like a total dork, I added, "I spent a lot of time on my hair."

It could have been my imagination, but I thought I heard Jill make chicken noises.

Keppler clasped his other hand around mine and said, "I guarantee you it was worth the effort. The end result is stunning."

He released my hand, almost imperceptibly wiped his hands on his pant legs, and walked back over to Mom.

Jill walked over and leaned on me for balance. "Way to go," she said.

Watching Mom and Keppler smile once again for the camera, I said, "Everyone was watching."

"And you rose to the challenge."

"I'll do it next time."

"And I believe you. The next time your mom gets married, you'll call the guy Keppler."

I looked at Jill, wincing and wobbling about. "You know what I meant. I'm gonna do it, just later."

Pressing down on me even harder to take the weight off her aching feet, she said, "Whims, I got two words for you."

"What?"

"Cluck cluck."

chapter 2

The wedding invitations clearly stated the reception started at four. I ought to know, I had to stuff all the envelopes and lick them shut. However, when Jill and I walked into the Museum of Art with fifteen minutes to spare (we would have been there sooner but, for some reason, Jill wanted to change her shoes), it looked like the reception was practically in full swing. Many of the tables were already taken and at them sat distinguished-looking couples so engaged in conversation they barely seemed to notice the confused harpist playing "Danny Boy" (she sounded great, but the way she kept her eyes half closed and her face scrunched up made it look like she was trying to remember where she put her car keys), or the waiters in black tuxedos striding across the marble floor to bring them their drinks. In fact, if Mom and Keppler did a no-show, my guess was that most of their guests would have paused their clever chit-chat just long enough to shrug their shoulders and grab some refreshments.

"What's with all the punctual people?" whispered Jill as we stood in the museum's entrance, unsure of where to go.

"Who knows? Maybe Keppler's giving out demerits to anyone who's tardy."

Jill grabbed onto my arm. "That's funny, and I'd laugh but my feet are still killing me."

"Then let's sit down."

"Are you kidding? I'm not going near those people. They look like they solve math problems for fun—the word kind."

Just then I felt a hand on my shoulder. I turned to see Melanie standing behind me holding Steve's hand. "Isn't this exciting!" she said. "I just knew your mom's reception was going to be a swanky, A-list event. Look at all those important people, and to think we were invited too! I'm telling you, it pays to be neighborly."

Steve leaned toward us and, with the cautious enthusiasm of an avid bird-watcher, pointed out the people he recognized, which included two General Authorities, an appellate court judge, the president of BYU and his wife, the dean of the law school, and a member of the Utah State Supreme Court who at nineteen was one of the five finalists in the Miss America pageant. "Not many people know this," he said smugly, "but she is quite accomplished on the accordion."

Mel nudged Steve. "You should go talk to her. Tell her my uncle plays the accordion, and then casually mention you got an A last semester in Biblical Law."

Steve's mouth went slack at the suggestion.

Mel nudged Steve again. "Oh, come on, honey. It's perfectly okay to toot your own horn. I'm sure any one of these people here would be interested to know you made a very fine paper maché bust of Orrin Hatch over Christmas break."

Steve's slack jaw sagged a little lower. He looked desperate to think of an argument against "horn-tooting" that would satisfy his wife when—and I'm sure he said a silent prayer of thanks—he spotted one of his law professors waving for them to come sit at their table. Ignoring his wife's question of whether this was the same law professor who had told him to never ask a question again in his class, Steve took Mel by the hand and led the way over to his professor's table. But before they could sit down, suddenly everyone rose to their feet as one of the waiters announced the wedding couple had just arrived.

The room went quiet as all eyes suddenly focused on Jill and me, standing in the entryway. (Now the harpist was really looking confused.) Time dragged as a wave of embarrassment swept over me, leaving me feeling strangely as if all anyone at the reception had been discussing was the grade I got in Spanish my freshman year of high school. I could almost hear them saying things like, "She simply didn't apply herself," and "She spent more time waxing her legs that year than hitting the books." I stood there with my feet bolted to the floor, staring back at them like Tyson to any cartoon, until Jill grabbed me by the arm and pulled me to the side, something for which I'll forever be grateful.

Genteel applause filled the air as Mom and Keppler walked hand in hand into the room, waving at their guests. And when the harpist spontaneously started playing "Here Comes the Bride," Mom in her powder-blue suit and without a bouquet good-naturedly turned around to see if someone looking more like a bride was heading their way. This made the guests break into a most refined laughter—except, of course, for Melanie, who preferred to give a two-fingered whistle.

As much as Jill wanted to sit down, she wanted to be first in line for refreshments more. So when I spotted an empty table tucked behind a large bronze statue of a UPC symbol, we decided I'd head for the table to save our seats and Jill would make a beeline for the yet untouched stack of glass plates. We were just about to walk off in different directions when Jill grabbed ahold of my arm in much the same way she had been doing all day, but this time it wasn't to gain her balance. "Just look at her, Whims," Jill said, pointing to my mom. "She's amazing—so poised, which you know is a word I rarely if ever use to describe anyone, and classy. She's already won over the entire room. You should be proud of her."

I watched Mom as she gave Chief Justice Accordion Player a hug. "Yeah," I said, knowing I should feel happy for her, but hard as I tried, the only feeling I seemed capable of mustering was annoyance. I sat down at the table and continued watching my mom through the slits in the larger-than-life UPC symbol in front of me. It wasn't like I regularly equated my mother with an apple pie at Thanksgiving, but as I watched her—the new Mrs. Keppler—meeting and greeting so many people, I couldn't help but feel by the time she got over to me, there wouldn't be a sliver of her left.

If it were just a new husband and new friends Mom was getting, I wouldn't have been stressed (well, as stressed), but in addition to all the other changes taking place, Mom was getting a change of residence. I guess BYU has its reasons for not wanting professors who own homes just three minutes from campus to live at Wymount Terrace, but still, I was completely bummed when Mom told me they were going to live at his house. "And we both want you to think of it as your home," she had said. "I know you'll be busy having fun at the dorms, but during holidays or times when you just need to get away—whenever, it will be home for you."

I could see how much Mom wanted me to accept the idea of us living at Keppler's, so at the time, I made a joke of it. "All right," I had said, "but tell the pigeons they get the lower bunk."

When I finally saw Keppler's house, I would have gladly given the pigeons the upper bunk too. Not that it was in a bad neighborhood. All the lawns were well manicured, and many of the houses on the street, though old, were pretty. But if there were a way to shoot a house to put it out of its misery, that's what I would have done with Keppler's. Inside and out, the place was a sunlight-deprived disaster. Large trees surrounding the house gave the feel of perpetual early evening, and inside the house all the windows were draped with what looked like curtains yanked from an old opera house—they were so dark, heavy, and dusty.

Why some people want to make sure their couches outlive them I'll never know. But it appeared that Keppler was one of those people. All of his furniture was wrapped in plastic (and probably had been since he bought it in the early seventies), except for one lumpy storybook chair and ottoman. This was obviously the place Keppler spent most of his time. Law books and old newspapers were stacked all about, and a large set of scriptures lay open on the ottoman. It was easy to imagine Keppler spending hours on end sitting in that lumpy chair, and the thought of it made me feel sorry for him. Don't get me wrong. Had it been Whimsy-Gets-Her-Wish Day, I probably would have wished for Mom to call off her wedding. But still, the thought of him sitting there alone—it didn't seem right.

Throughout the house, the color scheme was uninviting orange and gag-me avocado. I take that back. The guest bathroom was vomit violet (okay, it was just violet, but I don't like that color). But all of it in its own gross way might have been bearable were it not for the oil painting of Edna over the fireplace. I'm not sure how Edna Keppler died, but I do know that had she not died, my mom wouldn't have been giving me the grand tour. The whole thing creeped me out—the situation and the portrait. No, it's not like Edna's eyes followed me as I walked across the carpet, but her expression clearly said to me,

"What the heck are you doing in my house?" And if no one had been around to hear me, my answer would've been simply, "I wish I knew."

Of course, when it had come to feeling welcome at Keppler's, Jill wasn't exactly helpful. I had called her to tell her the dreary details. "It's the ugliest house I've ever seen, but my mom says it has good bones, whatever that means."

"Forget about the house."

"Huh?"

"I think the best thing you could do would be to consider yourself an orphan—at least for the next six months. Look, I don't want to gross you or me out, but they're gonna be newlyweds . . . and, well, that's all I'm gonna say, other than the Preamble to the Constitution."

I didn't need to ask Jill to explain what she meant by that. Reciting patriotic stuff had always been her way of stamping out unwanted visuals.

* * *

Newlyweds—that's exactly what they were now. I looked at the two of them laughing pleasantly at something one of their guests had said and tried my best to not think about what the rest of the evening held for my mother. "We, the people of the United States," I mumbled.

But before I could utter another word, someone said in a loud, smug voice, "I give it six months, how 'bout yourself?"

I looked up to see a twenty-something man with a deep tan and blue eyes standing in front me. Plain and simple, whoever he was, he was good-looking. Sure, his nose looked like it had been broken once or twice, and a thin scar ran across his chin, but that just gave him a ruggedness which only enhanced his good looks. And then there was his smile. In addition to showcasing his glacier-white teeth all perfectly aligned like good soldiers, his smile infused his face with merriment—making it almost impossible to not like him.

"Excuse me?" I asked, unsure if he meant to talk to me.

He sat down across from me and held out his hand, his gold watch shining on his wrist. "I'm Hudson. Hudson Keppler—the object of countless fasts and prayers, the black sheep, or better said, the *inactive* one in the family."

As we shook hands all I could think to say was, "Oh." So much for poise and class.

Hudson pointed a twirling finger at me. "And you're Whimsy. The red hair and freckles gave it away. I was going to say I tried to make it to the wedding breakfast this morning, but the truth is I really didn't," he said, and smiled, a smile that somehow altered his confession from rude to clever. Hudson leaned back in his chair and put his hand to his chin. "So tell me, sis, what did you think of Johnny and Dave? Quite the pillars of the community, aren't they?"

Sis. As an only child, I had obviously never been called that before, and to be honest, I sorta liked the sound of it, even if Hudson's tone made me wonder if he had meant it as an insult. And Johnny and Dave? I had to think for a second who he was talking about. "You mean John and David, your older brothers? They seem nice, I guess."

"Nice is a good way to put it. The two of them are always involved in some saintly endeavor or another. In fact, when I first moved to Park City, they made a few calls and got me set up with a home teacher." Hudson laughed at the thought of what he was about to say. "And so the next thing I know, I've got this old guy with an oxygen tank—Brother Cluff, I think it was—shuffling up my brick path to read me a magazine article. I'm telling you, sis, it was agony. Every month he'd come over, remind me that he'd grown potatoes for the war, fumble around in his pocket for his glasses, and then read to me at a tortuously slow rate. Finally one day I pulled out my checkbook and said to him, 'Listen, why don't I just buy the magazine and save you the trouble of coming over here?' The look of bewilderment on his face was classic."

"So did he ever come back?" I asked.

"No, but I can't take the credit. It wasn't long after that I saw his name in the obits, the poor guy. The last year of his life my *nice* brothers get him roped into walking the three blocks from his home to mine to read me a magazine article."

I had never met Brother Cluff, but somehow felt like I had. "I'm sure he wanted to do it," I said.

"I wouldn't be surprised if you were right. But I'll tell you one thing, if all I've got is one year left, you can bet I'm going to find something better to do than home teaching."

I felt uneasy with the things Hudson was saying and figured I'd better change the subject. "So you live in Park City. Do you ski?"

"Never tried."

"Hudson, you're horrible," said a professional-looking blonde in a voice that oozed IQ points. She sat down next to him and placed her plate of fruit and cheese on the table. Without bothering to introduce herself, she said, "Yes, he skis. It's the one thing that cracks his rough exterior. He's moved on the slopes. One time I saw him shedding tears just looking at the mountains, snow, and whatnot," she said, and then bit off the head of a strawberry.

It was clear to me by the way Hudson tugged at his gold cuff links and shifted in his seat that he was uncomfortable with what Blonde Gal had disclosed. Less clear to me was whether she had meant to do it—to make him feel as exposed as a shaved lamb.

Blonde Gal wiped her fingers on her cream-colored napkin and said in a low voice, "Hudson, don't be ill-mannered."

At first he looked a bit indignant, as if what she were referring to were his elbows, which were nowhere near resting on the table. Then it dawned on him. "Right. You two haven't been introduced. Merriwether, this is Whimsy Waterman, my new redheaded kid sister, if you can believe that. And Whimsy, this is Merriwether Huff, my *girlfriend*."

Merriwether wiped her fingers once more before shaking my hand. "Nice to meet you. Hudson emphasized the word *girlfriend* to annoy me. He knows I prefer to be called his meaningful companion."

I laughed until I realized she was serious. "Um, yeah, I can see how that sounds better."

Just then Jill appeared with a plate piled high with food. "Don't let anyone ever tell you the governor isn't greedy," she said as she unfolded her napkin. "He took all the meatballs." Preferring to wave instead of shake hands, she said, "And hi. I'm Jill, Whimsy's best friend. Who are you guys?" Then she took a heaping bite of chicken salad.

After I introduced her to Hudson and Merriwether, Jill said, "So, Hudson, what do you do in Park City?"

"I'm a land developer."

"When he's not skiing," said Merriwether in a disapproving tone.

Merriwether cringed as Jill took another heaping bite and said with her mouth full, "So did your dad teach you how to ski?"

Hudson smiled. "Pop taking time to ski? That's funny. I'll have to write that down. No, he didn't teach me how to ski, but then again, teaching has never been one of his strong points."

I could tell Hudson's smile had left Jill confused. Was he trying to insult his professor father, or was that meant as a joke? But before Jill had a chance to ask, Merriwether offered her own explanation. "Hudson and his father aren't particularly close. In the nine months we've been together, this is the first time I've met him."

With a wave of his hand Hudson dismissed her assertions. "Not seeing Dad just reminds me of my childhood. You can't blame me for being sentimental, can you?" he said, and then flashed that mischievous smile

"You're hopeless," said Merriwether and stuck her fork in a slice of Swiss cheese and placed it on a wheat cracker.

"No, actually I'm hungry," he said, rising to his feet. "Whimsy, we've watched them eat long enough. Let's go see what we can find at the buffet."

When he mentioned it, I realized I was kinda hungry. "Sure," I said as I stood up.

You have to understand that's all I was prepared for—just going over to the buffet and taking heaps of everything, especially the stuff in the large stainless steel serving dishes with the little burners beneath. So when Hudson, just as we were about to walk away, said, "Besides, from what Johnny and Dave tell me, our parents were welded today, so I guess it's only fitting we stick together," my mouth went dry.

"Welded? What are you talking about?" I asked, and gripped the back of my chair.

Hudson, who had taken a few steps toward the buffet, walked back to our table. "Right. Well, I suppose the official word is *sealed,* but I think *welded* sounds better, don't you? Sealed makes me think of leftovers in Tupperware, not marriage. Of course, bonded sounds all right, and fused—"

"Shut up!" shouted Jill as she stood up. "Just shut up. Can't you see what you're doing to her?"

I hardly heard Hudson's apology or Merriwether pointing out that "be quiet" would have sufficed; I was too stunned. In fact, I was so stunned that Jill feared I might pass out. Leaning on her as we headed for the door, she kept saying things like, "There's no give in this marble floor, Whims. Think about your teeth. Keep it together for your teeth. I don't want you starting college looking like a pro boxer."

I didn't faint, even though for a moment the room had started to spin horribly like a ride I tend to avoid at the state fair. I did, however, cry. We walked outside, found a soft patch of grass, and sat down. It wasn't the most secluded of places, but I didn't care. Stopping only long enough at times to wipe my nose on my silk sleeve, I sobbed with abandon. This may sound weird, but even I was surprised by how much I was crying and how little I cared about what those passing by might think of me. It was as if a place inside of me that I had yet to fully understand had been wounded, and the only thing to be done was to cry harder.

Trying to comfort me, Jill said, "He's wrong, that's all there is to it. Hudson doesn't know what he's talking about."

In between sobs, I croaked, "How can you be so sure?"

"Well, for starters, he wasn't even there."

"Neither were we, but his brothers were," I said, and then burst into tears again. Jill opened her mouth to say something, but nothing came out. With my chest heaving like I'd just sprinted across the parking lot, I said, "That's what's freaking me out. I can't say he's wrong because I wasn't there. I was outside giving myself back problems holding McKenner."

Jill kicked off her shoes and ran a hand through her short brown hair. "But sealed?" she asked. "Your mom wouldn't do that, would she?"

That question brought forth a whole new wave of tears, and so it took awhile before I was able to speak. "I don't know. A month ago she came into my room with a sweater on."

"Wow," Jill said, obviously thinking I was losing my mind.

"No, you don't get it. It was a hot day, but when Mom's nervous she gets cold. Anyway, she sat on the edge of my desk and asked me what I'd think if she and Keppler got sealed someday."

"What'd you tell her?"

I wiped my nose again on my multipurpose sleeve. "That I was fine with it," I said.

Jill looked genuinely concerned. "Whims, how many fingers am I holding up?" she asked.

"She said *someday,* and isn't that just another word for never? People are always saying stuff like 'Yeah, we should get together someday' or 'Someday we should do lunch,' when what they're really thinking is 'I'd rather eat glass shards for breakfast than spend fifteen minutes with you!'"

Just saying all that stuff about the word *someday* made me feel encouraged until Jill, while staring at the grass, said, "Not to frighten you, but what if when your mom said *someday,* she meant . . . someday. Um . . . she did say there was something she needed to talk to you about."

I felt panic flood back into my heart. "Why did you have to bring that up? I was almost better and then you bring that up!" Now my crying was nearly uncontrollable.

Jill scrambled to think of something to comfort me. "Don't worry, don't worry. Whims, we're jumping to conclusions. All we know is that something happened during the wedding that made Melanie cry—something that your mom wants to tell you about herself. And that Hudson is saying his brothers, who attended the wedding, have told him his dad and your mom were hot glued, or whatever. I mean, it could all easily add up to mean a lot of . . . stuff." Jill, who clearly hadn't believed a word of what she'd just said, shook her head and sighed.

The grass beneath me swayed a little as I stood up. "Well, I'm going in there right now to ask her what happened."

Jill grabbed my wrist and forced me back to grass, which didn't take much effort. "You can't do that—not yet."

"Why not? She's my mom, and I've got a question for her," I said, but made no attempt to stand up.

"You know why," Jill said. "If you go in there right now with your eyes swollen from crying and ask her if her marriage to Keppler is one of those forever deals, the party will be over. I mean, you might as well take an ax to the ice sculpture because she will no longer be able to enjoy herself. And I know you well enough, Whims, to know that you don't want to do that to her. Let her enjoy her wedding reception."

Jill was right—going back into the reception right now would be a disaster, so I took a deep breath and tried to calm down. Grasping at straws, I said, "Maybe they can switch it."

"Switch what?"

"Their marriage," I sniffled. "Maybe they can tell the people at the temple they've made a mistake and need to switch to a till-death-do-us-part marriage."

"Whims, honey," she said softly, "the temple isn't the Gap. I don't think they do exchanges."

"Well, you never know until you ask," I said. "You just never know."

chapter 3

Elder Matt Hollingsworth
MTC Box 210
CHI-SAS 1010
2005 North 900 East
Provo, UT 84604-1793

Dear Matt,

Please don't tell me the MTC has rules against missionaries starting teensy fires, because after you read this letter, you have to promise to burn it! I hate my mother, I really do, and I'm positive I always will. Even if eighty years from now I have trouble remembering my name and tend to wear my shirts inside out, I won't ever forget what she did to me today, and I'll never forgive her! She got sealed to Keppler, and without asking me first! Apparently just a few minutes before the wedding was set to start, "Salt Lake" called the Provo Temple to say Mom and Keppler had "clearance" to get sealed. So instead of taking a moment to walk outside the temple and ask me what I thought of the idea, the two of them just went for it.

And the worst of it is that when Hudson, my new stepbrother (he's another letter altogether) spilled the beans, I was in a room filled with tuxedo-clad BYU waiters, and you weren't one of them. I wish you had been there, even though you would have been dead wrong about everything! I can practically hear you saying stuff like, "You shouldn't be upset, Wilhelmina. This doesn't mean your mom loves Keppler more than you, Wilhelmina." All I can say is, how would you know? Come to think of it, both you and Jill have a lot of nerve telling me to calm down when your families are rock solid. You have no idea what it feels like to have a bow-tie wearing, pigeon-loving law professor suddenly proclaimed to be not only your stepdad but your mom's eternal companion. How can I help but panic? I mean, where does this leave me? I still don't know. Mom's schedule was a bit cramped for such a discussion.

The reception ran late, and by the time my mom was available to talk, it was time for them to head to the airport to catch a flight to Hawaii. She came outside to find me, all excited, looking at her watch, and asked me if perhaps we could talk when she got back in a week, but that was before she saw my tearstained face. "Go," I told her. "He's the one you want to be with FOREVER. Just go. I'll be fine without you." She kept saying how sorry she was that she hadn't been the one to tell me and that I shouldn't think that her sealing to Keppler changed in any way her sealing to me. I couldn't take it anymore. I said, "If being sealed to you means I'm stuck with him too, forget it. I don't want the package deal."

And that's where it ended. We didn't have time to say more because Keppler came looking for her tapping his wrist. She tried to touch me, but I stepped away. She tried to tell me when she got back, we'd talk. I told her she was mistaken. She wanted Keppler—she could have him, and him alone. I told her if I wanted to talk to her I'd let her know, but for now I didn't even want to look at her, and I turned and walked away. I half expected her to come after me, but she didn't. Talk about feeling abandoned. But hey, that's okay. She wasn't that great of a mom anyway. I'm lying. I'm completely devastated. More than anything I want her to rush in here and hug me, then tell me everything is all right, and that she got her marriage switched from eternal to noneternal. Fat chance.

Sorry about the tearstains. I've been crying all day, and yet the tears keep coming. Hopefully I'll be able to get a grip by the time I get back from Lake Powell. Jill and I are driving down there with her aunt and uncle to meet her family. I know I should be happy for Jill that she has such an awesome family, but sometimes I'm flat-out jealous. I mean, why did I have to be the only child to two people who weren't meant for each other? And to think that all these years I assumed that my mom and even my dad loved me. But maybe, I mean it's possible, that I've just been an obligation. After all, the minute I'm ready to head to college, presto, she's on with her life.

I'm too tired to write more. Make sure that if you can't burn this letter, you at least tear it into such tiny pieces it looks like a pile of ashes. Thanks for reading all of this. I'll write you again when I get back. Love, W

* * *

Jill was right, I told myself as I resisted the urge to call my mom, the best thing I could do was consider myself an orphan. Trouble was, I was accustomed to talking to her—especially when I was about to do something that frightened me, and trust me, the night before entering the dorms, I was plenty frightened. Jill tried to relate to it, but when you're accustomed to doing back flips on a four-inch beam, there isn't much that frightens you. "Just think of the dorms as one big sleep-over," she told me, "but be sure not to wear your pajamas to class."

That night, I lay awake staring at the sparkles on Jill's aunt's front room ceiling, thinking of everything that had gone wrong and what seemed destined to head in that same direction. Our week at Lake Powell had been fun, at least during the moments I was able to forget my life was ruined, or *blown apart*, as Jill liked to put it. But now, back in Provo, with a cool breeze coming through an open window and the sound of Jill snoring on the other couch, I didn't try to forget anymore.

I thought it fair to blame the Utah Valley Yodeling Society for the way things had turned out. If they could've just promised to put a cork in it for a few hours, I was certain Mom and Keppler's reception wouldn't have swelled to the size that it did, and then Mom would have had time to talk to me, to tell me she loved me, and to help me untangle the wad of emotions her sealing had thrown on my lap. You'd think I'd be used to my parents being apart, and I am. But even after their divorce was final and they were living thousands of miles from each other, their temple marriage, I mean the fact that they were still sealed together, comforted me. It gave me hope that in spite of everything, maybe the end of their story—and I'm talking end, like, next-life end—would still read, "And they lived happily ever after."

I didn't bother to wipe away the tears that rolled down my face. Why, I wondered, did I feel like someone had died? I guess in a way, it was like a death for me—Mom getting sealed to Keppler. Any chance of Mom, Dad, and me eventually becoming a forever family was officially over, and I couldn't help mourning. Sure, Dad had done his part long ago to make impossible such a possibility, but as long as they were still sealed, I don't know, I guess I figured we had a fighting chance.

The grandfather clock in the front entry chimed, announcing it was three in the morning. I sunk my head deeper into my pillow and tried not to think about how tired I was going to be in the morning. I wasn't sure what time it was in Hawaii, but I guessed Mom was asleep with her new husband beside her . . . hogging the sheets. (Is it okay if somebody besides me is miserable for a change?)

Hawaii. I wondered what it must've looked like outside my mom's window and could almost hear the waves crashing on the dark and empty beach, see the moon glowing as restless clouds drifted past, and feel the salty breeze rustling through palm fronds and causing the curtain in my mother's room to swell with air like the sail of a ship. She was in paradise and I, well, I was in a front room with sparkles on the ceiling. And to think they had me to thank for them being in Hawaii.

When everything was still in the planning stage, Mom had fretted endlessly about the Hawaiian honeymoon Keppler had arranged. Not so much because she'd have to miss the first week of her second year of law school, but because she wouldn't be back before I moved into the dorms. Finally, one evening as they sat in our tiny kitchen looking at the calender and trying to make their schedules jive, she had said, "I'm sorry, but Hawaii is out of the question. We need to stick closer to home, sweetheart."

Keppler's jaw tightened the way it usually did when his fiancée— my mom—suggested something disagreeable to him, like going to the mall or watching his fat grams. It was clear Keppler wanted this Hawaiian honeymoon, so really, there was only one thing to do. I got up from the sofa and on my way to grab a soda from the fridge said, "Well, I hear Ogden is nice this time of year."

"Honestly, Whimsy," Mom said as she continued to pore over the calendar.

I sat down at the table. "Look," I said, "I don't know what you think you're gonna do for me by sticking around. I mean, if I had a sofa to lug upstairs that'd be one thing, but Mom, it's gonna be no big deal, and besides, Jill will be with me."

"Yes, but what about the roommate crisis? I want to make sure whoever blundered by not assigning you and Jill as roommates will be willing to set it right."

What's the deal with my competitive nature? There my mom was wanting to stay and help me sort out something that was stressing me out big-time, and yet, in the interest of winning the argument, I downplayed my concern. "Mom, it's more like a roommate snag than a crisis, and yes, it needs to be figured out, but Jill and I can do it. Go to Hawaii. You'll be back before school starts. And besides, I want a muumuu."

That had been enough to persuade her. "We'll drop by as soon as we get back," Mom had said, her voice already tinged with excitement. Keppler was so excited he took Mom's face in his hand and kissed her, and when he looked at me, his eyes were full of gratitude.

* * *

I closed my eyes and sighed. "She was right," I whispered. "This is a crisis." Fears of whether Jill and I would end up as roommates started crowding my thoughts. After all, wasn't rooming with your best friend one of the reasons they invented college? Okay, maybe not. But still, it was going to be for me one of the great fringe benefits, or at least I hoped. Jill and I had been assigned to the same floor, just different rooms. She had ended up three doors down from me with a girl named Chloe Wescott from San Diego, and I had been assigned Prudence McKinley from Coalville, Utah.

"Chloe and Prudence," Jill had said, sounding like she'd just downed a tall glass of curdled milk. "Did they look at our applications at all or just throw darts?"

"I'm not living with Prudence," I had said. "There's no way I'm living with Prudence."

* * *

I opened my eyes as the kind of panic I usually reserved for chemistry exams washed over me. I didn't want to live with a girl named Prudence who probably liked having a chance to wear a bonnet and didn't own a pair of pants. Her suitcases were most likely packed with doilies, Hummel figurines, and a big cross-stitch that said, *I love milking cows.* I gulped hard. "No way am I living with her," I whispered to the ceiling. "It'd be pure torture."

"Hey!" yelled Jill as she bolted straight up. "What's the matter with you? We need more cheese balls!" While lying back down, she muttered again and again, "And don't forget the relish tray! People, the relish tray!"

Why in Jill's dreams she was usually a caterer I wasn't sure, but I said, "I'll get right on it," which seemed to satisfy her.

I worried about everything for a while more: Mom's sealing to Keppler, the roommate crisis, whether I had remembered to floss (dentures aren't in my game plan), but as I neared sleep, my worries subsided as a picture began to take shape in my mind—a picture of my mother sitting beside me, brushing a few of my unruly curls behind my ear, telling me not to worry, telling me it would all work out in the end, telling me to slice the pineapple. I opened my eyes long enough to see Jill propped up on her elbows. "I'm slicing, I'm slicing," I said with a yawn, and then drifted to sleep.

* * *

There are some things you can count on: the sun coming up in the morning, the winter migration of the black-throated dickcissel (I've been watching The Learning Channel a lot), and me being cranky when I haven't had enough sleep. However, by the time Jill and I started hauling our stuff up to Stover Hall's third floor, I was slipping past cranky into the belligerent zone.

"Watch it, watch it," Jill said. "There's one more step."

"I know there's one more step," I grumbled. "What I don't know is why you thought you needed to bring a forty-pound—"

"Thirty-five."

"Whatever. A thirty-five-pound, almost-as-large-as-life stuffed kangaroo!"

Girls edged by us at the top of the stairs as Jill paused (her trademark) for dramatic effect. "Whims," she said as she leaned past the kangaroo's head to look at me, "since you've never won anything at a state fair, I can't expect you to understand."

"You didn't win. The guy thought you were cute and bumped the table to knock the last pin over."

Jill has never minded rewriting history. "The pin was already wobbling. Gravity was on my side before the bump. But you of all people shouldn't question my need to bring Spot, especially if I'm going to stick my landings this year."

I grunted, not wanting to admit she was right, but I knew she was—there was no way to separate Jill from Spot. Jill had "won" Spot a few years ago at the state fair and had somehow turned him into the world's largest good-luck charm. Before her gymnastic meets, she nearly always slugged Spot a few times in the stomach. "Hey," she had told me one day when she caught me rolling my eyes at the Spot-punching-bag thing, "this is no more weird than my dad wearing the same shirt for the past twenty years to the Phoenix Sun's games."

"Maybe that's been the Sun's problem all along—your dad's shirt. It's possible the hex shirts at Wal-Mart got mixed together with the good-luck shirts and your dad's been the reason they can never make their free throws."

"You can say what you want, but my guess is if you had to do a full twisting mount onto the balance beam, you'd want to slug Spot too."

"You're probably right," I had told her. "But still, wouldn't a rabbit's foot have been, I don't know, more compact?"

We dragged Spot down to the end of the hall, placing him (according to Jill, Spot's a boy) outside the room where Jill had been assigned. Jill checked to make sure no one was around, then said, "You know I love you, but right now, on a scale of one to ten, you're a negative two on my like list, which normally wouldn't be a big deal. However, seeing as how the hall advisor, Sister Whatever—"

"Wauteever," I corrected.

Jill shrugged. "Whatever."

"Wau . . . never mind," I said as Jill's eyes narrowed on me and her hands moved to her hips.

"You're edging toward negative three," she said. "Can I continue?"

Had I had a decent night's sleep, I would have said, "Sure, go for it." But as sleep deprived as I was, sarcasm seemed the right choice. So I leaned against Spot and said, "Whatever."

Jill took a deep breath and with clenched fists said, "Okay, for the sake of moving on, I'm gonna call her Clipboard Lady. Since Clipboard Lady said we can make the switch if our roommates agree to it, we need to be persuasive. In fact, we need to be more than persuasive. We need to be . . . what's more than persuasive?"

"I don't know, violent?" I offered, trying to be zero help.

Jill pressed her fingers to her temples, took a deep breath, then looked at me. "Whims, it's pretty obvious you didn't get your required eight hours, so here's the deal. Once we go in there, just let me handle it. Chew on one of Spot's legs for all I care, just don't open your cheerful mouth. While violence might be persuasive in, let's say, federal prison, Clipboard Lady made it clear that we can't *force* them to switch. All we can do is tell them our situation and see if they'll be willing to help us out. I'll be sure to mention the big stuff, like, we've been best friends since the third grade, we both like to sleep with the window open, and I gave you a kidney."

"You didn't give me a kidney."

"Well, I would have if you'd asked. The point is that we let them know in a nice way that we're inseparable."

I zipped my lip, and with that she knocked on the door and we walked in.

At first I thought the room was empty, mainly because the lights were off and the curtains drawn. Two things surprised me once we turned on the light: how small the room was (it made Wymount look spacious), and that a girl was sitting cross-legged on one of the beds. "Dang," said Jill, "you scared me. So what's the deal, are you part bat, or did you just get your eyes dilated? Heh heh. Uh, that was a joke. Heh heh heh." I made a mental note to tell Jill her laugh sounded like her lemon-yellow Corolla trying to start.

"No, just working on a song," said the girl, who then pointed to a pad of paper beside her with a bunch of words scribbled on it. "It's easier for me to hone in, you know, get to a really creative place when it's dark."

Jill tries to not say everything that comes into her head, but it doesn't always work. "That's sort of weird," she said, "but in a good way . . . weird good—that's what I meant. So anyway, you must be Chloe. I'm Jill, and this is Whimsy, who isn't going to be saying anything. She's shy . . . and has laryngitis."

I glared at Jill, then waved.

Chloe took a moment to scribble something else down on her pad of paper, then said, "Yeah, I'm Chloe. So which one of you is my roommate?"

I'm usually pretty good at guessing what a person is going to look like, but when it came to Chloe, I couldn't have been more wrong. Sure, I got tall, tan, and blonde right, but what I hadn't counted on was the military haircut and the gloom to spare. Her ultrashort haircut would have been disastrous on most girls, but not on Chloe. She had one of those amazingly beautiful faces that didn't really depend on hair. As for me finding her gloomy, that might have initially had something to do with her T-shirt, which was black and had the word *Torment* written in small print on the front. However, the more she spoke, the more clear it was to me that she chose to view life through mud-colored glasses.

Jill and I sat down on the other bed as Jill cleared her throat, sounding more than a little like Brother Hack (that's what Jill used to call him, anyway) before he sang a musical number in church. "Actually," she said, "we wanted to talk to you about the roommate-assignment thing. You see, and I need to find the right way to put this . . ."

While Jill was still searching for the right words, someone rapped on the open door and said, "Hi, sorry to interrupt, but is anyone in here named Wilhelmina?"

I turned around and started to say something, but before I could, Jill flipped off a sandal and threw it just inches from my head, making a loud thwack against the wall. "Yeah, her name is Wilhelmina," she said, her other sandal in hand ready to launch, "but she goes by Whimsy."

I mustered a smile and waved hello.

The girl, who had long, brown hair as thick as rope and eyes the color of chocolate, happened to be wearing (though in a larger size) the very shirt I'd been longing to buy at the mall. She said, "That is so great—we both have nicknames. I'm Prudence. Prudence McKinley, but my friends call me Pudge." She gave the sides of her legs a slap and said with a smile, "That's me—pretty face, pudgy thighs. But anyway, I'm glad I found you. I wanted to say hi since we're going to be roommates and all. I've already put up my stuff, but if you want to switch sides it's no biggie; I can take it all down. I like plants. I hope you don't mind that I brought my needle-point ivy and African violet. If they bug you or you're allergic or anything, I can take them back home. You name it and I'll do it, except for laundry. Dirty laundry creeps me out. But if you're really in a bind, I could always grin and bear it." She snorted with laughter.

"Could you turn down the happiness? I'm trying to write a song," said Chloe as she jotted something down.

A look of confusion appeared on Prudence's, or rather, Pudge's face, and Jill tried her best to take control of the situation. She introduced everyone to Pudge, then said, "Look, why don't we sit down, because as it turns out, there's something we all need to talk about in a no-pressure, hassle-free sort of way."

Pudge giggled, then remembering Chloe's comment, covered her mouth. "Sorry, it's just that you sounded so much like a car dealer. Anyway, sure, I can sit," she said, and sat down on Chloe's bed.

"I wouldn't want you to take this personally," Chloe said as she continued to write, "but I'd rather you not sit on my bed."

"Oh, sorry," said Pudge, who moved without protest from Chloe's bed to a chair.

Jill rolled her eyes. "Geez Louise," she mumbled. "Talk about your personal bubbles." I don't think anyone heard it but me because just as she said it someone sang in a clear, piercing voice, "Good morning!"

A slender, blue-eyed brunette with a haircut stuck in the eighties stood in the doorway. "I'm Kay Swindle, your resident assistant," she said, "and my guess is you're Wilhelmina and you're Jill." We nodded as she continued. "I was just downstairs talking to Sister Wauteever, who explained to me your situation—so sorry to hear about everything that's happened lately to Wilhelmina: the amnesia, the heart, lung, and kidney trouble, and the sudden fear of lined paper that's gripped her. But I think it's so sweet that you, Wilhelmina, have such a good friend in Jill. She's really there for you. That's so special. Anyhoo, I was just wondering if everything was fine. Have your roommates agreed to the switch?"

"What switch?" said Pudge. "I can switch. Just tell me what to switch."

"How do you spell annoyingly compliant?" asked Chloe, firmly gripping her pencil.

"That's easy," sang Kay, "a-n-n—"

"Stop, stop, stop! We haven't asked them yet, and you've completely wrecked my intro!" yelled Jill.

"Sorry, sorry, sorry," said, or rather, sang Kay, who then put her hand to her mouth as if to say "oops" and hurried away. I'd never met someone who sang when they spoke as Kay did, so until that moment I didn't fully understand how lucky I had been. It wasn't that her voice was bad. To be honest, it sounded sorta pretty. Still, had I wanted to hear someone sing in a conversation, I would have gone to the opera.

Once Kay was gone, Chloe was the first to say something. "I think I speak for everyone," she said, "when I say she needs to die."

Pudge giggled until Chloe stared her down. "Uh, that was funny . . . um, never mind," she whispered.

Jill took a deep breath, then said, "Look you guys, I was gonna give you a bunch of background info, but here's the deal: Whimsy and I want, make that, *need*, to be roommates. We're best friends and have been since forever. We made it clear on our applications that we wanted to room together, but it got messed up somehow. This has been a dream of ours for a long time—not that we want to pressure you. We're completely casual here, but if it's not too much to ask, we'd like one of you to hightail it to the other room."

"Uh, sure," said Pudge without a trace of enthusiasm. "We can switch. I'll just go and empty my drawers, and take my stuff down, and—"

"UCLA," said Chloe.

"What?" asked Jill.

"You said it's been your dream to room together. My dream was UCLA. I wanted to study film there, but then my parents told me the only school they'd pay for was BYU. So here I am," she said, not hiding her anger.

"But hey, you don't have to be *here*," Jill said. "You can be three doors down."

"Or I can move three doors up," said Pudge. "Really, it's no big deal for me to unpin my posters and—"

"Keep your plants and your potpourri where they are," said Chloe. "There is no way I am living with a too-happy-too-chatty-can't-say-no Pudge!"

It was obvious that when it came to dealing with insults, Pudge was an experienced professional. She showed no sign that Chloe's words had wounded her, only smiled and with a shrug told Chloe she was entitled to her opinion.

Jill looked exasperated. "Okay," she said, "let's give three cheers for tact."

I noticed Chloe had written the word *no* on her paper and was tracing over it again and again, making it as black as possible. "Look," Chloe said, "I'm emotionally at a place where I crave honesty from others and myself. It's not like I'm trying to hurt anyone's feelings. I'm just telling it like it is. And the truth is, as bad as I don't want to be at BYU, I don't want to be Prudence's roommate even more. She's too happy for me."

"Well, why don't you sing her some of your songs," grumbled Jill. "That ought to help her tone it down."

An argument erupted between Jill and Chloe, and I felt like I had to do something, so after getting their attention I said, "Guys, we can talk about this calmly. I mean, yeah, Jill and I do want to live together, but that is only because we're best friends. Chloe, you need to realize that no one in their right mind would want to live with Jill." I pulled Spot over till he filled the doorway. "First of all, she brought this monstrosity with her."

Chloe grinned as she looked at Spot. "I won't mind having a kangaroo around. My uncle is an animal-rights activist, and besides, we've always had a membership to the zoo."

Jill looked pleased to have found someone else who shared her taste for large stuffed animals. "His name is Spot," she whispered.

"Spot," said Chloe. "I like that."

"Whoa, whoa," I said. "Hold off on all the kangaroo happy feelings because there's more. Jill talks and, at times, yells in her sleep—it all depends on how well things are going that night in the kitchen. I'm not talking about an occasional moan or lip smack. What I'm talking about here are loud, complete sentences jarring you out of a deep sleep every night."

Chloe chewed on her pencil as she thought. I was certain I had her convinced, but then she said, "Though I crave solitude, this could be a new source for lyrics. I can't pass it up."

We all just sat there for a moment looking at each other with Pudge all the while whispering "sorry." Then Jill stood up, dragged Spot over to the window, and crammed him onto the ledge, making his head press tight against the ceiling. "You should have let me handle it," she said afterward as we walked into the hallway, making it sound like she'd been seconds from clinching the deal.

I rolled my eyes and said, "Whatever."

chapter 4

Some people have a hard time saying they're sorry. Pudge isn't one of them. In fact, *sorry* rolls off her tongue as effortlessly as *um* does for most people. As soon as I started moving my stuff into our room, Pudge was on a sorry rampage: sorry you have to be my roommate, sorry they haven't fixed that drawer yet for you, sorry you forgot your hangers, etc. It was all I could do to keep from wringing her sorry neck. Not that it's bad to say you're sorry, but if that's all you're saying, all I'm saying is it gets old. And besides (not that I planned to tell Pudge this), in a way I was glad we were roommates. Sure, had it been possible to room with Jill I would have chucked Pudge in a heartbeat, but Jill was just three doors down, so it wasn't like we were never going to see each other. And besides, I liked the way Pudge had decorated our room. It reminded me of my home. More to the point, it reminded me of my mom.

"You made curtains and pillows and a chair cover?" I asked, marveling at how perfectly put together everything looked.

"Sorry," said Pudge. "The only thing I love more than chocolate is fabric, and lately I've been nuts about blue and yellow plaids and florals. I can't get enough of them, as you can tell. But if you hate it—"

"No," I said, "I don't hate it at all. In fact, I was thinking it's too bad my stuff is going to clash."

Pudge bit her lip. "Promise you won't think I'm weird?"

"Uh, sure," I said, and braced myself for her to show me something like a used Band-Aid collection or worse.

Pudge opened her closet and pulled out a large paper bag. "Please don't think I'm expecting you to use this stuff, but on the off chance my roommate wanted to color coordinate, I whipped together a few things." Pudge started taking items out of the bag. "Let me see," she said, "a duvet cover, some pillowcases, a small topiary for your desk or wherever, and then I found this desk organizer in the same fabric on clearance, so, uh, I got it too . . . just in case."

"You made all of this?" I asked, touching the duvet, which was so perfectly pressed and folded it looked ready for a store shelf.

"Except the desk organizer," she confessed, sounding like she'd just admitted to cheating on an exam. "Sorry to, I mean, don't feel like you have to use any of it."

"Pudge," I said (why did I feel guilty saying her name?), "I don't mind it at all. In fact, I like it."

Pudge smiled. "You do? Oh, that's great. Sorry I was so stressed," she said.

"You don't—"

"I just didn't want to appear pushy, you know?"

"Pudge, don't—"

"After all, it was entirely possible that you wouldn't like blue and yellow. I mean they are a bit bright and—"

"Pudge!"

"Sorry, you were going to say something and I cut you off. So sorry."

QUIT SAYING YOU'RE SORRY! That's what I wanted to tell her. I wanted to shout it in her ear with a megaphone, repeat it in Spanish, French, and Japanese, and just in case she still hadn't gotten the point, rent a plane to drag a sign saying "Don't apologize for everything" through the sky. My instincts, however, told me that doing so would only make her apologize more. So instead I said, "Don't, I mean . . . you didn't say how much I owe you."

Pudge's face went red. "Pay me?" she said. "Don't feel like you have do that. I mean, I didn't—"

I felt another "sorry" coming on, so I quickly said, "Or I could just borrow this stuff and at the end of the year you could use the material to start, I don't know, a loud tie company?"

Pudge laughed. "Ties, out of this? The sad thing is it'd probably work. Fashion is, after all, about standing out in a crowd."

We unfolded the duvet cover and started stuffing my comforter inside it. "Ooh, I know. We could name the tie company after something loud. Heavy Metal Ties? No, people would expect them to be black and dreary, but that's an idea we might want to pass on to Chloe." We both giggled, and Pudge turned to make sure the door was shut. "Thunder Ties? Jackhammer Ties? Sonic Boom Ties?"

"I like that one," Pudge said. "Boom Ties. It's catchy."

"Okay, then it's settled. If I don't drool too much during the school year, we'll take this material and start a tie empire. Deal?"

Pudge laughed. "Deal."

* * *

There's nothing like fast Sunday to help me catch up on sleep. I figure if I have to be hungry, I want to be oblivious to it as long as possible, which explains why just twenty minutes before my first Sunday meetings with my new ward, I got out of bed, threw on a dress, and went to find Jill.

After knocking several times, Jill finally came to the door. The room was as dark as it had been the first time I saw it. "You're still sleeping," I said.

Jill yawned and rubbed her eyes. "No," she said. "We were just writing a couple songs."

I flicked on the light, and Chloe instantly hid her face beneath the pillow. "Go away," she said. "All night we made melon balls."

Jill lay back down. "Why don't you go and take notes? Maybe grab a few extra pieces of bread, and we'll wait right here."

This was standard procedure for Jill. She never went to church without a fight. I opened her closet. "Which skirt do you want to wear: the blue one or the one with little flowers?"

"Flowers," Jill said with her eyes closed and her face pressed hard against her pillow.

I wasn't sure how Chloe would react, but I opened her closet, took out the one dress she had in there, and threw it on the bed. "I'm not going," she said.

"Sure you are," said Jill as she sat up and stretched. "It's either that or we send Kay down here to—"

Chloe took the pillow from her face and sat up. "You're forcing me to go to church. How is that Christian?"

As Jill put on her skirt and a white T-shirt she said, "It's the whole staff thing."

"What?" asked Chloe.

"We're supposed to be shepherds. Shepherds have staffs. Staffs, in addition to helping the shepherd look more shepherdy, are great for whacking sheep, especially the ones who don't want to go to church."

"And?" Chloe asked.

Grabbing her toothbrush, Jill said, "We'll talk about it on our way to church."

We didn't talk about shepherd staffs on the way to church. Instead, we talked about dresses and how oppressive they are—at least to Chloe.

"I really don't get why we have to wear dresses to church. I've spent a lot of time thinking about dresses, and I think they're a form of oppression. An attempt to mold us into docile little housewives who bake cakes and fetch slippers."

"My dog fetches slippers," said Jill, "and she's never worn a dress."

"You don't have a dog," I said.

"But when I do, she'll fetch slippers."

When I heard that our church meetings took place in the Harris Fine Arts Center, I didn't think anything of it. Not for a second did I stop to consider that on my way to church I'd have to pass right by the Museum of Art and the shady spot where I had cried my eyes out—not, that is, until those two places were right in front of me. A lump grew in my throat as my mind replayed everything that had so recently taken place there: the reception, meeting Hudson, and then him telling me what Mom (supposedly) was going to tell me herself. The right moment, she had said, was all she had been waiting for—a peaceful time when the two of us could talk. "As if," I whispered, and rolled my eyes. Mom knew—she must have known—there was never going to be such a moment. She and Keppler were always together, and now that the summer was over, it was just a matter of time before she'd be swallowed whole by her second year of law school. For all I knew she had been thinking, "After Whimsy's dead and I see her in heaven, that's when I'll tell her."

Jill gave me a knowing nudge as we walked inside the Harris Fine Arts Center. I took a deep breath, like the kind Jill takes before sprinting toward the vault, and forced myself to smile. *Whatever you do,* I told myself as we walked downstairs to the main level, *don't cry. It would be too lame if the first time people in your new ward see you you're a mess. Just stay calm and don't do anything stupid.*

"Aaahhh!" screamed Jill as we walked inside the de Jong Concert Hall lobby on our way to sacrament meeting. Normally when Jill walks into church she doesn't scream like she's trying out for a part in a horror movie. But then again, normally when she walks into church she doesn't see Tyson standing in front of her with his hands on his hips.

Grabbing ahold of my sleeve, Jill said, "Whims, apparently I'm more stressed than I realized about adding that double lay to my floor routine and have started to hallucinate nightmarish stuff, so I'm going to close my—"

"You lied to me," said the three-foot-tall hallucination.

"That's all childhood is," said Chloe. "One big lie: fairies that pay top dollar for used teeth, a rabbit that doles out anything made of refined sugar, and a big happy guy in a red suit who likes to give away—"

"Chloe!" I said. "Go away . . . um, and find Pudge."

Chloe folded her arms and looked like she was about to say she wasn't going anywhere when Tyson said to her, "Why is your hair as short as my dad's?"

"I'll tell her you're here," said Chloe, and turned on her heel and walked inside the concert hall.

"You lied to me," said Tyson again, his little fists clenched tight.

"Uh, well, that all depends on how you define *lie,*" said Jill.

"There are not any eranna and sidewalk people and pesty-cides at the temple. I know 'cause I asked my mom and she told me there are not."

"Right, well, uh—"

"She told me they're at the baseball field."

"She did?"

"That's why I can't play down there."

"No kidding," said Jill, looking quite relieved. "Well, nice talking to you, Tyson. But we've got to—"

"There you are!" said Melanie as she ambled toward us with McKenner propped somehow atop her ever-swelling stomach and contentedly chewing the end of a large white bow sewn to the front of his mother's dress. "It's amazing how things work out," she said. "Steve got the call to serve in the bishopric—oops, don't say anything—and I had a hunch it was going to be your ward. I just knew it, and here we are! Isn't that terrific?"

"Not really," mumbled Jill, but Mel didn't hear her. She was too busy telling us everything we didn't want to know. "A nice Korean family moved into your apartment, Whimsy. Now the apartment smells of ginger. When you and your mom lived there it smelled like cinnamon sticks. I always notice smells. I walk into someone's apartment, and my nose instantly goes to work, except when it comes to my apartment, which is just as well. I'm sure most of the time it smells like dirty diapers. So, how are the dorms? Did you two end up together? Joan said she was worried about it not working out."

Joan. Just hearing my mom's name made me miss her even more. "No, it didn't work out, but it's okay," I said. "We're just a few doors down from each other."

"Too bad," said Melanie as she pushed McKenner onto her shoulder like a sack of potatoes, something he didn't appear to mind. "My uncle works for BYU, but he manages the laundry service, so I don't think he'd be able to pull many strings for you. I could ask, though."

"Thanks, but—"

"So, what have you heard from the newlyweds? I still cry every time I think of their wedding. It was so romantic, especially the moment when Professor Keppler kissed Joan's hand after the ring exchange, then pressed it to his cheek before kissing it again. He looked like he could hardly believe she was his wife—so touching. In fact, since then I've made Steve kiss my hand that way essentially every other day! Isn't that right, honey?" she said to Steve, who was walking quickly toward us.

Tyson jumped into his daddy's arms. "Daddy, let's go. They're boring."

Disregarding both his wife's and his son's comments, Steve said a quick hello and told us that sacrament meeting was about to start. Normally Steve is a pretty easygoing guy, but at that moment he looked like it was all he could do to keep from shoving us in the right direction.

Before walking into the concert hall, Mel dabbed Steve's forehead with her slobber-soaked bow and gave him a sympathetic look. "Will yourself not to perspire," she said, then held out her hand for him to kiss.

A dopey grin spread across Steve's face as he took his wife's hand and kissed it. It was much too obvious that Steve would have liked, were sacrament meeting not about to start, to have kissed his wife some more.

Jill, who has never been able to stomach public displays of affection, leaned toward me as Steve and Mel walked inside and said, "Remind me to become a nun."

"But you're not Catholic," I said, scanning the concert hall for Chloe and Pudge.

Jill shivered. "Just don't mention that when you remind me."

* * *

Jill knows I hate it when she falls asleep in church (I figure, if I've gotta listen, she's gotta listen), but when she attempted to fluff a hymn book, I figured the best thing to do was ignore her—most likely glares or nudging would have just made things worse. So for a while, Jill and Chloe enjoyed a little sacrament meeting nappy time . . . until, that is, Tyson decided to relocate. After Steve was sustained as the new second counselor, he went to sit on the stage with the other members of the bishopric. This, of course, left Melanie alone with the kids, and it wasn't long before Tyson was out of his seat and wandering. Sure, at first Melanie did a little finger snapping, trying to coax him back. However, when he didn't obey, she just turned around, and with McKenner on her lap, listened to the rest of the meeting.

Considering that Tyson could have pretty much gone anywhere in the concert hall, I thought it interesting (not to mention amusing) he ended up at the one place he was definitely not wanted—next to Jill. "Hey," he whispered as he poked her in the arm with the eraser on his pencil. "Draw me some pesty-cides."

Jill opened one eye. "Beat it," she whispered.

"They have purple skin, don't they?" he whispered back.

"Scram."

"And poison squirts out of their eyes."

"One, two . . ."

Apparently not fazed by the threat of her getting to three, Tyson placed his pad of paper on Jill's lap and held out his pencil for her. "But what are feelers?" he asked. "Larry says they have feelers."

In all the years I've known Jill, the most I can remember her doing for her little brothers and sisters in church was flicking them on the head when they got too loud. Guaranteed she never drew them a picture. Taking the pencil, Jill thumbed through the pad in search of an unused piece of paper. After finding one, she leaned close to Tyson and said, "I just remembered, we're not supposed to draw pesty-whatevers on Sunday. It's worse than waterskiing." Tyson didn't say anything, just pushed the pad of paper closer to her. "Fine," she grumbled. "We'll pretend it's Monday."

For the rest of sacrament meeting, Jill drew pictures as Tyson whispered to her things she needed to fix. A couple of times she tried to hand him the pencil, telling him that since he knew so much about this particular kind of monster, he should draw them himself. Tyson just looked at Jill, his lower lip pouting, and waited for her to begin drawing again, which she did, but not without a lot of grumbling. By the time sacrament meeting was over, Tyson had exactly what he wanted: lots of pesty-cide pictures. He didn't say thank-you, or at least he didn't say it directly. Instead, as the bishop made the closing remarks, Tyson took his pad of paper, flipped until he got to a certain page and, showing it to Jill, said, "This one's sorta good. I'm gonna show it to Larry when I get home. See ya."

"Let's hope not," Jill said as she watched him walk back to his mom. She waited until just after the closing prayer to say, "That's it. I'm never coming to church again."

Chloe yawned. "Count me in."

"I'm sorry he wouldn't let me draw for him," said Pudge. "I tried."

Ignoring for the moment Chloe and Pudge, I focused on Jill. "Let me get this straight. You're going to go inactive, chuck your baptismal covenants, and possibly get kicked out of BYU all because of a four-year-old kid?" I asked, trying to spell out the stupidity of what she was saying.

"You got a problem with that?"

"It just seems, what's that special word I'm searching for . . . extreme," I said, knowing Jill wasn't serious but still feeling like I needed to be a voice of reason.

Not that she would have ever admitted it, but it kinda seemed like the whole Tyson thing was threatening to make her laugh. "Did you see how he poked me when I stopped for a second to rub my nose?" she huffed.

"Well, you weren't done drawing the goo oozing from its mouth."

"That wasn't a mouth," said Jill. "It was clearly a third ear."

Chloe stretched and stood up. "You were drawing pictures of gooey third ears," she said. "Did I miss something?"

"Ladies!" sang a voice from a few rows below us. It was Kay, and though Chloe is a good five inches taller than Jill, it didn't stop her from trying to hide behind her roommate. "We'll see you in Sunday School!"

I forced a smile. "Yeah, we'll see you in there," I said.

Kay crinkled her eyes in a way that seemed to say, "I sure appreciate ya!" and started off for Sunday School.

"What's the deal with Kay squinting?" asked Jill.

"It was crinkling, not squinting, and I think she was trying to make us feel special," I said.

"That makes sense," said Jill. "I mean, after all, she is . . . Special Kay." From then on, that was exactly what we called her . . . well, except to her face.

As we made our way to Sunday School, Chloe said, "If the Church is true, why are there so many weird people in it?"

I could tell by Chloe's tone she wasn't joking. She had asked a straightforward question and wanted an honest answer, but what she got was Jill saying, "You realize that most of the people in *Ripley's Believe It or Not* are Mormon. In fact, that guy with the world's longest fingernails is our ward clerk back home."

"She's lying," I said.

"I'm sure they're related though—cousins maybe. But seriously, I think the reason is Jell-O; Mormons eat too much of it, which everyone knows is bad for the brain."

We walked into a large room with paint-splattered easels stacked against a wall and sat down in the back. Kay, who was sitting near the front, turned around and waved at us until Pudge and I waved back.

"We just saw her," complained Chloe. "You shouldn't say hello to people you've just seen. It's impolite."

That seemed like a strange rule of etiquette, but rather than ask where she had heard such a thing, I said, "Getting back to your question about weird people, I think it has something to do with Him," and I pointed to the ceiling, "wanting us to stretch. You know, learn to get along with all sorts of people. Does that make sense?"

Chloe slouched down in her chair. "Hmm," she mulled, moving her palms back and forth like the scales of justice. "Chance to stretch or Jell-O overload."

Just then, a young man with hair redder than mine stood at the front of the room and welcomed everyone to Sunday School. As he did, someone from behind me squeezed my shoulder. It was Mel, crouched down behind my chair with McKenner in her arms. Leaning close enough to me for McKenner to grab a chunk of my hair, she said in a loud whisper, "I forgot to tell you earlier that I got a letter from Matt yesterday. He sounded great—so excited about his mission. Anyway, he wanted me to tell you he needs your new address, and there was something else . . . what was it? My bunions are killing me. I knew I shouldn't have worn these shoes. They're a little too small, but I thought they were cute. I found them at a garage sale yesterday. Two bucks!" She reached down to take one off to show me, which, since McKenner hadn't loosened his grip, caused my head to wrench backward. "Can you believe what a great deal?"

Several hands went up as the young man asked for a volunteer to say the opening prayer. Melanie put back on her deal of a shoe and started to get up to find a seat when she realized McKenner was planning to take my head with them. Crouching down again, she said, "No, McKenny," and began prying his fleshy fingers from my hair. "Don't grab Whimsy's . . . oh!" She suddenly sat up and leaned closer to me. "I know what the other thing was Matt wanted me to tell you. He said no mountain climbing and was so emphatic about it—must have used three exclamation points. My brother is such a worry-wart—always has been. He was the only Boy Scout in our ward who carried three canteens. Don't listen to him, Whimsy. You go out there and climb every—oops," she said just as everyone else in the room said "Amen."

"Excuse me," asked Chloe as she turned around to face Mel, "but you wouldn't happen to like Jell-O?"

Mel licked her lips. "Love it," said Mel. "Tangy lime is my favorite. Gotta scoot."

"Warning labels," said Chloe. "That's what Jell-O needs."

As Mel walked away with McKenner clutched to her side like a rolled-up sleeping bag, Jill leaned forward and stuck her tongue out at me in triumph, which I shielded from my sight with my triple combination.

* * *

It takes Jill awhile to get off the gloat wagon. So on the way home from church, it didn't surprise me at all that she sang her own version of the national anthem. "Oh say that I'm right!" she howled.

"Never," I said. "You're so far from right that I'm lumping you together with the people who used to think the world was flat."

"I don't mind," she said. "They're a nice bunch."

According to Jill, fasting has nothing to do with candy, so even though she had been popping the occasional Starburst during church, she was starving and insisted we go straight to the cafeteria. We walked up the path to the Cannon Center and were about to go inside when all at once an annoyingly melodious voice shouted my name. "Whimsy!"

I turned around and saw Kay rushing toward me with a piece of paper in hand. "I was hoping I'd find you," she said as Chloe—obviously trying to dodge yet another "rude" hello—dashed toward the lunch line with Pudge following close behind. "Your mom just called," said Kay. "She said to tell you her flight has been delayed and that she won't be back until late tonight." Handing me the piece of paper she'd been holding, Kay said, "She sounded super worried about you, especially when I told her Jill wasn't your roommate—must have said, 'Oh dear,' a hundred times. Anyway, she left three different numbers where you could reach her and made me repeat each one. I told her not to worry, that I'd make sure you got the information myself, and I have, which I think counts as my good deed for the day." She then gave us the official Special Kay eye-crinkle and headed back to Stover Hall.

As we walked into the Cannon Center, I crumpled up the piece of paper and threw it in the trash. "So I take it you don't want to talk to your mom right now," said Jill as we got in line for lunch.

"You got that much right."

Jill said, "So, um, when?"

"When what?"

"Are you planning on talking to your mom again?"

"Never."

"Never as in I-really-mean-in-a-few-days never or never ever?"

"Never ever," I said, annoyed to spell out the obvious. "Why?"

"I don't know. It's just that she's your mom."

"And?"

"And you love her."

"And?"

"And she loves you."

"And?"

"And never speaking to her again seems, what's that special word I'm searching for . . . extreme."

The part of my head that stays logical in crisis situations was telling me Jill was right. Even though I had been surprised and hurt by Mom's decision to get sealed to Keppler, she was still my mom and I loved her, and what's more, I needed her. Unfortunately, however, the part of my head that tends to freak out in crisis situations beat the tar out of the logical side of my head that day, and I refused to back down. "What's extreme is getting sealed when you already have a family!" I said, my words carrying over the din in the lunchroom as clearly as if I had shouted them through a megaphone.

"What?" said Jill to the people who had turned around to look at me. "We're in a lunch line, not the library. She can yell if she wants to." She glared at them until one after another they sheepishly turned back around. The only way to explain Jill is to say she thinks she's six-foot-seven and three hundred pounds. She's absolutely fearless, and when it comes to defending her friends and family (including her little brothers and sisters, although she likes to maintain a spirit of crankiness toward them), she is a frothing pit bull.

"Thanks," I said.

Jill smiled. "Don't mention it. Listen, we'll talk more later, but right now let's just sit down and enjoy some Jell-O."

I took a deep breath and said, "Wauteever."

chapter 5

Elder Matt Hollingsworth
MTC Box 210
CHI-SAS 1010
2005 North 900 East
Provo, UT 84604-1793

Dear Matt,

Got your message via Mel about no mountain climbing, and I've just got one question for you. What makes you think that every time my life falls apart I'm gonna climb a mountain? True, I climbed to the Y one night several months ago when things were beyond dismal, but that doesn't mean every time I face catastrophe I'm going to head to higher ground. I mean, I like the mountains well enough, but it's not like I own a goat and want to change my name to Heidi. Besides, if I were wanting to climb a mountain right now to try and figure out my life, it wouldn't be a simple hike to the Y. I'm talking grab the air tanks and a couple of native guides 'cause it's Everest time.

How is it that I know when I finally hear from you about my mom getting sealed to Keppler you're gonna be on their side? I know you're going to try to lull me into seeing things their way, and I've got news for you: I will not be lulled! What they did was inconsiderate to me, let alone my dad and Edna, Keppler's first wife. In fact, this morning in Relief Society (so weird) we sang "Families Can Be Together Forever," and I started to panic. Who in the world is my family? Who am I going to be together forever with? As much as I love my mom, if she's just signed me up for an eternal quilting bee with Edna, then I'm for sure not interested in the celestial kingdom.

And then, of course, there are Keppler's sons. Hudson is off the deep end pretty much, so, chances are I'm not going to have to worry about him. But what about the other two? We hardly know each other, and now we're linked forever. If long awkward pauses don't already exist in heaven, they will when I'm up there hanging out with my stepbrothers. Jill says I shouldn't worry about celestial life. She's planning on ditching her little brothers and sisters (they get on her nerves) when she gets up there, but then again, she's also planning on beaming up her stuffed kangaroo, Spot.

I'd write more but I'm bone tired and have my first class, biology, in the morning. Yikes! Suddenly I'm getting nervous about the whole college thing. Make sure you write soon. With love, W

* * *

It wasn't the worst night's sleep I had ever had because, after all, Jill was three doors down. Still, the night before my first day of college I didn't sleep much, mainly because I couldn't turn off my head. Staring at the ceiling, I cataloged my concerns, arranging them from least to greatest, listing them in alphabetical order, and even conducting a random survey, which, according to my research, indicated eighty-three percent of the population agreed I had every right to feel sorry for myself. Not that I'm generally swayed by public opinion, but in this case I thought they were right and gave myself the go-ahead to wallow in self-pity.

* * *

The next morning, yawning and rubbing my eyes (I wear smudge-proof mascara), I headed out Stover Hall's front entrance for my eight o'clock class. Generally speaking, I don't have to worry about dark circles under my eyes. Freckles on my nose, yes. Dark circles under my eyes, no. But having had practically zero sleep, not only did I have dark circles, I had the mother of all dark circles, and no amount of makeup that morning was able to hide them. *Just keep your eyes to the sidewalk,* I told myself, *and later, after class, you'll find some cucumber slices and—*

"Hey, Whimsy," said an all-too-familiar voice in front of me.

Without looking up I knew who it was: Josh Iverson, my former crush, the guy who just by walking into a room used to cause my head to tilt stupidly to one side and my mouth to curl into a drowsy grin. The guy whom I had spent the better part of my senior year hating after our one date together detonated. But all of that was in the past, wasn't it? Sure, every now and again what happened between us would roll through my brain and leave me grumbling. But Josh and I were friends now, really we were. And besides, with him and Jill dating (or "hanging out" as she called it), we had to be. So Josh was a friend, but still, as I looked up to say hello to him, I couldn't help wishing I had dark sunglasses on to hide behind, or better yet, a welding helmet. "Uh, hey, Josh," I said, trying to sound casual.

Josh took a good look at me. "Geez, are you sick or something?"

I ran a hand through my hair in a way that I hoped looked carefree. "Not really," I said.

"Good," said Josh, "'cause if you felt the way you looked, you'd be in big trouble right now," he said, and slugged me softly in the arm.

I laughed to show I was a good sport. "Yeah," I said, "when I haven't had enough sleep, I tend to look . . . "

"Dead?" Josh offered, and slugged me again.

I wasn't at a loss for words. Well, not exactly. It was just that at that moment I spotted Keppler walking toward us, and my mouth dropped open wide enough for a dental exam. I was shocked to see Keppler, and for a lot of reasons: his normally fish-belly-white skin was lightly bronzed, his ridiculous comb-over that used to stand at attention in the wind was gone, replaced by a short cut that didn't hide his hair loss and, as a result, made him look more contemporary and distinguished. But most shocking of all, especially considering Keppler and I had spent zero time alone together, was that he had come to see me . . . and without my mom.

"Good morning, Whimsy," said Keppler. "I was hoping I'd find you."

"Uh, hi," I said, though what I really wanted to say was, "Where the heck is my mom?" I mean, sure, I was officially still fuming and hurt, but it wasn't like I wanted to hear she'd poked her nose too close to a smoldering volcano or that the rope tethering her parasail to a boat had snapped and last reports had her flying over the Polynesian Cultural Center.

However, I didn't have a chance to say anything because, as it turned out, Josh and Keppler needed no introduction. They already knew each other. Lucky me.

Josh and Keppler shook hands.

"Mr. Iverson," said Keppler.

"Professor Keppler," said Josh.

"Stunning victory you led our team to on Saturday. The Seminoles really thought they had us."

"Thank you, sir. The Noles are a powerhouse, no doubt about it, but things really came together for us in the second half."

"Well, congratulations."

"Thanks, and congratulations to you. It seems like when we met at the president's luncheon, Whimsy's mom said the wedding was set for August, so you two must be married now."

Keppler glanced at me. "Yes, er, just barely."

I wanted to say, "Just barely? There was nothing 'just barely' about their wedding. The two of them got sealed, or as some like to call it, *welded,* and without my permission!" But instead, I just stood there saying nothing.

"Well," said Josh as he reached out to shake Keppler's hand again, "it's good to see you, Professor." Then, slapping me on the backpack, he added, "And you too, Whims. Well, I've gotta get moving if I'm going to catch Jill. We said we were gonna walk up to campus together, but you know how she is . . . she's not exactly one to wait around."

As Josh walked away, Keppler and I looked at each other and both rubbed our foreheads in the same nervous way and at the exact same time. It was freaky. I mean, aside from him not being eighteen, redheaded, or a girl, I swear it was like looking into a mirror. And yes, when he cleared his throat and folded his arms, I made sure I did not do the same. "Speaking of walking up to campus," he said, "I was hoping to do so with you. Would you mind?"

Would I mind? I wondered if the word *yes* was straightforward enough for him. "Well," I said, figuring I should opt for a more subtle approach, "it's just that I've got biology in twenty minutes, and—"

"Perfect. I enjoy a brisk pace."

No, I thought. *Perfect would be you at home feeding your pigeons, completely unaware there was a woman in the world named Joan*

Waterman. Perfect would be a life like Jill's, where a guy like Josh (on the outside anyway, but more like Matt on the inside) wants to walk with you up to campus and is even stressed you might leave without him. Perfect is not a brisk walk with my mom's new husband. "Okay," I said, and as we started off together, I mumbled something I probably hadn't said since the fourth grade. "Opposite day."

I took off in a hurry. I figured I'd walk as fast as I could without looking like one of those goofy speed walkers you see in the Olympics, and if he couldn't keep up, too bad. Unfortunately, Keppler works out regularly, and didn't have any trouble keeping pace. In fact, as we climbed the hill toward campus, he said, and without a hint of fatigue, "So how was Lake Powell?"

"Fine," I said, keeping my answer as short as possible.

"Glad to hear it," he said, and clasped his hands together with enthusiasm. "And freshman orientation?"

Remembering our cute Y group leader, I said, "Great."

What's the deal? I thought. *I've been with the guy for over five minutes now, and he still hasn't said a word about Mom. Ten bucks says he wants me to ask about her so he can blab about how much fun she had on their honeymoon. Honeymoon.* The word alone was threatening to conjure up freak-me-out visuals. There was no way I was asking him anything about Hawaii, but thankfully, before it was necessary for me to start reciting the Declaration of Independence, Keppler asked, "And what about things with your roommate?"

"Fine too."

"So you're happy?"

His question took me by surprise, and I froze in the middle of the crosswalk, which on the first day of the school year isn't the smartest thing to do.

An anxious driver laid on the horn. Keppler glared at him, and the driver, through the use of exaggerated hand gestures, began apologizing like crazy. Then, as if we hadn't already gotten the message, the guy rolled down his window and said, "Very sorry, Professor Keppler. Got a little impatient there."

Keppler forced a smile. "Good morning, Mr. Davis," he said as we finished crossing the road.

"It's Davison," said the young man. "Uh . . . not that it matters."

But it's good to see you, and I'll see you in Crim-D on Wednesday—
or is it Thursday?"

A few cars honked their horns. "I suggest you move your foot to
the accelerator," said Keppler.

Davis, I mean, Davison nodded in agreement and hurriedly rolled
up his window. Clearly he was a guy who was done talking and ready
to drive, and even his tie getting caught in the window wasn't going
to detract him from his objective. Rather than fix the problem,
Davison drove off, his head leaning to the side and the end of his tie
dancing in the wind.

As we stepped onto the sidewalk, Keppler mumbled to himself,
"Insufferable boob."

I'm not a fan of hair-trigger horn honkers. Generally speaking, I
find them obnoxious. Still, I thought Keppler had come down too hard
on this Davison guy, and I wanted to ask him about it. I mean, it was
common knowledge Keppler wasn't a nice teacher. He had even made
my mom cry when she was his student. Still, I wondered why Keppler
had been so gruff. Was Davison the type of student whose hand was
drained of blood at the end of class from constantly being raised? Or
was he an ordinary student and Keppler was just treating him as such?
But asking questions meant having a conversation with Keppler, and
that was something I was determined not to do. In fact, when Keppler
asked me if my class was in the MARB, I responded with only a nod.

As we walked along the busy sidewalk, I tightly gripped my backpack straps as I thought, *This is as bizarre as it gets. Keppler's walking
me to class. I must look like the president's daughter with my own security
detail. Okay, maybe just the vice president's daughter. Keppler's not that
intimidating. But would someone please tell me why he got up this
morning and hightailed it over to my dorm? I mean, he's not talking to
me, which actually works out well since I don't want to talk to him. In
fact, I don't want to walk with him. Why, then, am I letting him stride
alongside me? It's not like I have to be nice to him. He's not my husband.
We don't have to make this work. And he's not my professor, so whether I
tick him off or not isn't going to impact my GPA.* I waited until we were
near the Kimball Tower and the stream of students had thinned a bit,
then I stopped and said (making sure to avoid the whole name thing),
"Look, is there something you want?"

Keppler looked surprised. "Want? No, I just thought it might be nice since we've—I mean, your mother and I—have been gone, if one of us saw you before you started school today."

I couldn't stand it any longer. I just flat-out asked, "So where is she?"

Keppler looked at the trees behind me, his jaw tightening the way it does when he's irritated. "She's at Law Review," he said. "They had a mandatory meeting this morning at six-thirty."

I could have handled jet lag. Had he said she was still in bed, dead to the world, I would have been all right. But hearing she had gone to law school before coming to see me was too much, and my eyes—despite my best efforts not to let it happen—filled with tears.

Keppler obviously didn't know what to do. He put his hand on my shoulder, but then took it back. "I'm sorry," he said.

I lowered my head as I wiped the tears away. *Whatever you do,* I thought, *don't hug me.*

Keppler didn't try to hug me. He did, however, put his hand on my shoulder again, giving me hesitant little pats of comfort until I shrugged it off.

If doing so angered him, he didn't show it. In fact, when he spoke, his voice was softer than usual and packed with sympathy. I hated him for it. I mean, it was one thing for *me* to feel sorry for me, but no way in the world did I want Keppler's pity. "We arrived home from the airport late last night," he said, "and several messages were waiting for her from Mr. Spessard detailing the urgency of this meeting."

"You mean Henry?" I asked, momentarily too stunned to cry. After all, Henry had been the goofball (granted, a very intelligent goofball) who, in spite of Mom consistently telling him "no," had remained absolutely convinced it was just a matter of time before she'd agree to marry him. When Mom told Henry she was engaged to Keppler, he flew home to his parents' ranch in Texas and, from all reports, spent the next month writing sad country songs, attaching the lyrics to clay pigeons, and blowing them to smithereens with his shotgun. I think you could say he took the news well.

"Yes," said Keppler through gritted teeth, "Henry Spessard. It appears he takes his involvement in Law Review very seriously."

Trying to stomp out the compassion attempting to surface inside me, I dismissed thoughts like, *The poor guy. Just home from his honeymoon and bam, his wife is hanging out with the guy who wanted to marry her*, and chose instead to dwell on thoughts like, *No, not poor guy—poor me! I'm the one who has gotten the shaft, first from my dad and now my mom. I'm the poor person here, not him!* The two of us stood there, both miserable, both wanting my mom . . . but not necessarily each other.

"Whims!" shouted a voice from behind me. It was Phil Fitzsimmons, a friend of mine from high school I hadn't seen since graduation. He had spent the summer working in Alaska at a fish cannery, and I swear, though it could have been my imagination, he sorta smelled like a tuna fish sandwich. Phil gave me a hug, took one look at my puffy, red eyes ringed with dark circles, and said, "Talk about your allergy attacks. How've you been? You don't look so— whoa," said Phil suddenly noticing Keppler. "Aren't you Professor Keppler?"

Keppler cleared his throat. "Yes, I am."

"Man, I saw you on Court TV when you helped out in that Diablo thing. You were awesome. If you had a trading card, no lie, I'd buy it. So Whims, where are you headed?"

"Uh." I had to think. "Biology."

"Get out! Me too. Come on, I'll walk you there, unless you two got stuff to—"

"No stuff," I said, cutting him off. "We don't have stuff. Let's go." Without looking at Keppler, I walked off and, just so Phil wouldn't think I was rude, said, "See ya."

As we walked away, Phil turned around and said, "Nice meeting you!"

I heard Keppler say good-bye and tried not to notice the disappointment in his voice. And why should he be disappointed anyway? I mean, if what he wanted was to walk me to the MARB, he had taken me more than halfway there. Mission accomplished.

"So," said Phil as we headed to class, "what's the deal with you and the prof?"

"Nothing and everything."

"That narrows it down."

"He married my mom."

"Eureka!"

"Usually people say congratulations—not that I really want to hear that either."

"Whims, I don't think you understand what you've got here. I mean, you've got Professor Keppler. When it comes to networking and letters of recommendation, he's the man."

"Yip, yip, yahoo."

"It's who you know, Whims. It's all about who you know."

I rolled my eyes and thought, *No, when it comes to my life, it's more about who you know and wished you didn't.* However, not wanting to talk anymore about Keppler, I changed the subject. "So," I asked, "how's Chiara?"

Phil's face broke into a smile. "She's awesome. Just spoke to her last night on the phone. I'll probably have to get a job just to pay for that one phone call, but she's worth it."

I had met Chiara while she and her family were living at Wymount. Her dad, a professor of engineering, had moved his family from Italy to Provo for one year while he taught at BYU. Chiara was the only other Laurel in our ward, and at first we didn't really hit if off, mainly because she couldn't speak English. But eventually we became friends, and so did she and Phil. But their friendship turned a tad gooey graduation night. Anyway, I smiled at the thought of Chiara. "If you talk to her again, tell her I've been meaning to e-mail her."

"She'll be glad to hear it. She's kinda lonely right now, what with being the only member at her university and living a couple of hours from home."

"Poor Chiara."

"More like poor Phil," he corrected. "After all, I'm the one who's got to pay for that phone call."

I sighed as I opened the door to our class. Phil had a lot to learn.

* * *

At the end of my first day of college I was relieved . . . and a wreck. Relieved because even though I had always planned on going to college, a part of me had wondered if I was really college material. However, sitting next to Phil in biology, I don't know, it just felt right—me being in college, I mean. Sure it was kind of intimidating having so many students in one class, but, and this might sound strange, it was comforting to look around and realize that everyone looked pretty normal. I don't know what I had been expecting, maybe a room full of Einstein look-alikes, but it was a relief to know my classmates were just a bunch of people my age. Sure, some were going to be smarter than me, but I figured if I didn't get behind, if I just did my best, I'd be fine. And it was weird how quickly a weight (think midsize European acrobat atop my shoulders) lifted once I came to that conclusion.

As for being a wreck . . . well, who wouldn't be after finding out your mom is back from her Hawaiian honeymoon and hasn't bothered to see you? It was just one of those things I couldn't help putting in my Mom-could-care-less-about-me file. But as I walked back to the dorms, I looked at the sun setting in the horizon and said, "Big whoop." I waited until a group of students walking up to campus passed me so they wouldn't think I was losing it, then said to myself, "So you've been shoved, or more to the point, crowded out of the nest. It's a common enough occurrence. No big deal. Of course, I'm assuming in most cases the nest, even after you've left it, is still there for stuff like doing laundry or crashing on the couch when you've got a cold or are creeped out by a scary movie. A homestead, really. I'm not talking about a get-the-cattle-'cause-it's-branding-time kind of homestead, just something permanent . . . with a pool . . . and possibly a weight room, because my arms are starting to look scrawny. A place where you never have to knock, or ask before you open the refrigerator, and you don't have to avoid the living room to steer clear of Edna, or at least a painting of her."

I stopped mumbling to myself long enough to cross the street leading to Helaman Halls and then picked up where I had left off. "But, like I said, no nest is no biggie. After all, I'm eighteen. I'm old enough to join the army or pierce something—not that I want to do either. But the point is, I'm a big girl now. Not girl . . . woman . . . no, that sounds like I've got two kids and a husband who commutes. I'd say young woman, but that smacks of church. What I am is a youngish female. Make that a mature youngish female, and nest or no nest, I'm gonna make it after all. I should have a hat to throw in the air. Oh well."

I climbed the stairs to my dorm, tired and ready to kick back.

"Hey," said Pudge with a hand over her mouth. She was eating a Tar Bar—an ice cream bar made from a blend of dark chocolate ice cream and a box of Swiss chocolates—and from the look on her face, she seemed a little embarrassed to have been caught doing so. Throwing her half-eaten Tar Bar in the garbage, she said, "Your mom stopped by twice today looking for you, and she's phoned a lot too. In fact, she just called maybe two minutes ago. She wants you to call her as soon as you get in. Oh, and she left you this," she said as she pointed at the small box on my bed.

"That's an awfully small muumuu," I said, examining the box.

"You told them to get you a muumuu? Geez, if I had your body I wouldn't wear anything that couldn't be tucked in. You're so lucky," she said, and sighed.

No one had ever told me I was lucky because I can tuck in my shirts, and I wondered if Tar Bars were as bad for your brain as Jell-O. Still, I figured I should try to make her feel better. "Really, tucking isn't all it's cracked up to be," I said as I ripped the brown paper from the small box. "And besides, tucking leads to untucking, which leads to wrinkles, which forces you to tuck again, and—"

I was speechless as I looked at what was in the box.

"Wow," said Pudge as she leaned over to take a better peek. "That's tons better than a muumuu."

I gulped. "I have to agree," I said, and carefully pulled a small, intricate gold pineapple pendant and its delicate chain from the box.

"My parents usually bring us back T-shirts or maybe a paper-weight," said Pudge. "But that's all right, because Sophie always brings me back something great. She's my aunt. You'd love her. She's the opposite of me, which is not to say I'm bad, just that Sophie has tons of confidence. She doesn't let anything stop her. I, on the other hand, let everything stop me."

If she lets everything stop her, I wondered, *why then did she just pick up the phone when I said, "Don't answer it"?*

She stood there for a second with the phone to her ear, then said, "Hello," after which she mouthed me the words, "I'm sorry."

Looking like an overenthused umpire, I used hand gestures to make it clear I did not, under any circumstances, want her to say I was there.

"Uh, hi, Mrs. Keppler. Um, is Whimsy here? Right, you just asked me that. Um, well, uh . . . sort of."

I rolled my eyes. Pudge hadn't told me what she was planning to do after college, but I vowed that if she tried to work for the CIA, I'd do everything in my power to stop her. I figured it was the least I could do for my country.

Mouthing silent sorry after silent sorry, she handed me the phone. I waited until she left the room, then took a deep breath and said, "Hello?"

chapter 6

I thought it was universally understood, especially by mothers, that when someone says, "I don't want to talk about it," what they really mean is, "Not only do I want to talk about it, I need to talk about it, because the things I have to tell you are buzzing in my brain like a swarm of bees (the killer kind) and if we don't talk, chances are I'm gonna lose it!"

Apparently I was wrong.

When I told my mom on the phone I didn't want to talk about her perma-nuptials with Keppler, she said, "Well, please let me know when you're ready." Before I explain what happened next, I just want to point out that I think it's pretty big of me to be able to admit (now) I was wrong. I know I shouldn't have assumed my mom was trying to insult me. Still, I don't think I'm the only person on the planet who would have taken what she said as a slam. Maybe it was her tone, or possibly my unwillingness to think of the word *ready* as anything but a gentler way of saying *mature*. But whatever it was, I could have sworn what she was trying to say was "When you're *mature* enough to talk about it, let me know." Mature? I'd give her mature. In fact, I vowed right then that my maturity was gonna blow hers out of the water, that when it came to maturity, I would be the undisputed winner—the first to cross the finish line and hoist high the silver cup. Mature, not Lavinia, was going to be my middle name.

It's weird how the walls inside you shoot up so quickly. I mean, if they were built with bricks and mortar, one brick after another, and a couple permits had to be granted, and financing approved, well, let's just say I probably would have had the time to, you know, figure things out. And as a result, I probably—no, I *definitely*—would have had a happier freshman year. But as it was, a wall more impenetrable than that one in China surged upward inside me, shutting me off from my mom.

"It's not a question of being ready," I said, determined to sound courteous yet apathetic, or in other words, mature. "I've just come to realize that you should be able to do what you want. I mean, after all, you're an adult."

"Sweetheart," said Mom, her voice strained with what was probably frustration. "No one could have been more surprised about our sealing than Stanley and myself." "You want to make a bet" was tottering at the tip of my tongue, coming dangerously close to falling out of my mouth. But that, I reminded myself, would have sounded immature, so I bit my lip and let Mom continue. "The news we could be sealed came minutes—just minutes—before our wedding was set to start, and swept us up in what was the most wonderful whirlwind. But had I known it was going to upset you this much, I never would have—"

Okay, that was enough maturity for one day. "Mom," I said, cutting her off, "I'm not upset," knowing full well I sounded upset. But I couldn't help it. The whirlwind comment got to me. I mean, yeah, I didn't doubt they got caught up in a whirlwind, but from where I sat, there was nothing "wonderful" about it. It was just a whirlwind, plain and simple—the kind of thing that turns farmhouses to kindling and cars to cruise missiles. It was destructive, not wonderful, and had she had that much figured out, I wouldn't have cut her off.

"But you were upset, and I rushed off to the airport," she said, sounding like she might cry.

Usually the slightest quiver in Mom's voice sends me running to her side, but not this time. The wall inside me stood the test. "Well," I said, sounding even more aloof, "I'm not upset anymore. You should be able to do what you want without checking with me first. Like I said, you're an adult. In fact, we both are. Besides, I'm sure eventually I'm going to make a decision that you're not going to necessarily like, but that's okay, that's just the way it goes."

Mom was silent on the other end of the phone. I could practically see her face, weary and joyless, and hear her wish she could talk to her daughter again and not this of-age mature youngish female waving the I-can-do-what-I-want flag. Mom took a deep breath. "Well, why don't we plan on dinner together on Sunday."

I had nothing going on Sunday. In fact, my calender for that day was completely empty, except for the giant question mark I had written there. But this was a chance to assert my independence—a chance to let my mom know I was a grown-up, because, after all, I had plans on Sunday that didn't include her. "I can't," I said, and closed my eyes as guilt rushed over me.

"You can't," said Mom, her voice jam-packed with disappointment.

"Nope," I said, my eyes still shut tight as I forced myself to not engage in any type of wall demolition.

Mom cleared her throat, but it still sounded croaky. "Well," she said, "can you at least come," she paused for a second, choking on her tears, "um, downstairs so I can give you a hug?"

I looked out the window and immediately saw my mom's car parked in front of the dumpster. "You're here," I said.

Still sounding pretty croaky, she said, "Where else would I be?"

I didn't bother to hang up the phone. I just flung the door open and ran downstairs, nearly knocking over Jill on the landing.

"Hey, where are you going?" shouted Jill.

The wall inside me, for all intents and purposes, was surrounded by dynamite. "My mom's outside!"

"I'm gonna want a play-by-play," yelled Jill.

"You'll get your play-by-play!" I yelled back, and then raced down the rest of the way to the parking lot.

I walked outside and there she was. In fact, there *we* were—just the two of us, the way it had nearly always been, and I might have been inclined to believe the way it still was had the whopping diamond on her left hand not caught the fading sunlight.

But at the moment, huge diamonds and perma-vows didn't matter. All that mattered was my mom walking over to give me a hug. Her eyes were puffy from crying, but still, she looked beautiful. Her blonde bob curled perfectly under, and her rust-colored twin set and tan skirt both accentuated her slender frame. Of course, Mom looking terrific was nothing new. I mean, Mom primps even to grab the newspaper off the front lawn. Still, my ego couldn't help getting cranked up a notch as I looked at her and thought, *I've got one classy mom.*

It was one of those hugs where, even though you've been hugging for a long time, your mom doesn't want to let go of you. Actually, she starts to let go, but then while pulling away she looks into your face, and bam, starts hugging all over again. Not that I minded our extendo-hug. I mean, sure, with anyone else it would have been majorly uncomfortable. But this was my mom, and it felt good to be hugged by her. The one downside, however, was the tears. I didn't want to cry, but what I wanted didn't seem to matter. Maybe crying is like yawning. You see someone doing it and the next thing you know, you're stuck doing it too. At any rate, there we were, the two of us crying and hugging, looking the way we did the day I got lost in the mall . . . except, of course, back then Mom was taller than me.

"You seem thinner," Mom said as she finally pulled away, a look of concern stamped on her face. "Are they feeding you enough?"

"Are you kidding? The lunch ladies stand ready to whack us with spatulas if we don't finish our milk. It's just like home."

Mom smiled. "I never whacked you with a spatula."

"Sorry, wooden spoon."

"Whimsy!" Mom said with laughter, though tears continued to fall.

Mom reached for my hand. "So did you have a good time in Hawaii?" I asked. "Don't say it was terrific 'cause then I'll be jealous, and don't say it was horrible 'cause then I'll feel guilty."

"It was water and sky and I missed you."

Dang, I love it when my mom says exactly the right thing. "I missed you too," I said. The wall inside me was primed for leveling.

Mom put a hand to my face. "I should have missed that flight. I should have stayed and talked with you." *Well, yeah,* I thought, *that pretty much sums it up in a nutshell,* but forced myself to keep from saying anything. After all, Mom was on a roll. "And Jill not ending up as your roommate. I'm sick I wasn't here to do something about that."

"It's okay, Mom," I said. "I mean, yeah, we wanted to be together, but we're on the same floor, and besides, it's sorta nice not to have to reassure Jill at three in the morning I didn't forget to tenderize the meat or whatever."

Mom, well acquainted with Jill's nocturnal catering business, smiled. "But your new roommate, is she likable?"

"She goes out of her way to be likable."

A look of relief crept over Mom's face, making the lines between her eyes disappear. "I'm so glad to hear that," she said. "I've just had images of you with a cheerless, unsociable sort of girl—"

"No, that would be Chloe, Jill's roommate." The lines between her eyes reappeared. "But it's okay," I said. "They get along well enough."

Mom smiled as she reached out and tucked a few of my unruly curls behind my ear. "Can we count on you for dinner next Sunday then?"

"No problem," I said.

Mom grinned. "Terrific."

Yeah, I thought, *"terrific" says it all for me too. I mean, my mom's hugging me and telling me she missed me and . . . looking at her watch.*

"Goodness," said Mom, "it's getting late. I need to hustle."

Okay, that much didn't bug me. After all, I was sorta used to her harried school schedule: a kiss hello at the end of the day when she walked through the door, a quick mom-daughter convo, and then back to the books. But what did bug me was when she said, "Stanley will be wondering what's become of me. I promised him I wouldn't be late for family home evening."

Attention all personnel, remove all dynamite from wall. I repeat, remove dynamite from wall. I folded my arms and moved ever so slightly away from her.

"That's cool," I said.

"Whimsy, what's wrong?" Mom asked, her voice filled with concern.

"I'm fine. Go."

"Yah," screeched a voice from behind us. "You go!" It was Sister Wauteever, our house resident, and in the short time that I had lived in the dorms, I had come to realize two things about her: yelling was just her normal way of speaking, and secondly, she couldn't care less that her English was sketchy because to her it was an inferior language to her native Finnish. "This is not one park-king spot. You go-ing!"

"Oh dear," said Mom, completely unprepared for Wauteever's outburst.

I didn't bother to give her a heads-up. "You'd better go," I said.

"Go-ing!"

Apparently not trusting their ability to communicate via the English language, Mom jangled her keys and smiled at Wauteever, letting her know she was about to leave. Sister Wauteever made a shoving motion and walked back inside.

I wanted to say, "Go. I wouldn't want you to be late for YOUR family home evening!" but didn't. I had a hunch it wouldn't be mature. So I casually tossed my hair over my shoulder and said, "What time Sunday?" as if I were talking to someone's receptionist.

"Four," Mom said, sounding and looking deflated.

"See you then," I said, and walked inside, leaving her just standing there.

chapter 7

Jill didn't get her play-by-play, mainly because after one look at me she knew exactly how my conversation with my mom had gone.

"Let's go," she said, taking me by the hand and pulling me off of her bed.

"I don't feel like going anywhere. I've just started wallowing," I said.

"Which is exactly why we're out of here."

"Where are you going?" asked Chloe as she looked up from her calculus textbook. She was wearing a black T-shirt with *Pulled from the Wreckage* written on it.

"We're gonna get creamed," said Jill as she grabbed her wallet. "Wanna come?"

Chloe slid her funky rectangular glasses back on the bridge of her nose. Her glasses were so trendy (make that ugly) that only the prettiest of people could look good wearing them. And let's just say I didn't bother asking her where I could get a pair. "And where you come from, 'getting creamed' is code for? . . ." she asked.

"Ice cream. We're going to the Creamery."

"Oh," said Chloe as she returned to her book, obviously not interested.

Jill said, "I know, you're thinking ice cream with the girls sounds too peppy." Chloe shrugged and continued to look at her book. "And, as you've told me, pep's bad when you're a serious songwriter. But here's what's good, or rather bad, about the whole thing—we're taking Whimsy." Jill had her attention, and mine. "I mean, the girl has just had a level 4 argument with her mom, and remember, level 5 is the worst."

"Wow," said Chloe. "You only ranked my argument with my mom a 2.5, and that was intense enough—I threw my cereal spoon at the wall."

"We didn't even argue," I complained.

"Whims scored higher because hers is a cold war, and those are the worst—big-time tension and lots left unsaid." I would have told her she was wrong but she wasn't, and the realization that I was at war, hot or cold, with my mom made me slump back down on Jill's bed. But at even at five feet four inches, Jill's a powerhouse, and she instantly yanked me back to my feet. "When you think about it, right now Whims is no better off than a stray cat. I mean, she's written off her mom, which is just as well since if she did hang out with her it might become obvious the only thing she feels comfortable calling her new stepdad to his face is 'Um.'"

"Wow," said Chloe, marveling at my wretched life.

But Jill wasn't done. "And then there's her dad. He's the guy they were thinking about when they made those *Where's Waldo?* books. She never knows where he is since he only gets in touch every other leap year. So essentially what we've got here is a homeless, parentless girl we're going to hang out with while we eat ice cream. And what is ice cream but a cold, sticky way to slap fat on your thighs?"

"Well," said Chloe, closing her book, "when you put it that way."

By the way, when we asked Pudge if she wanted to come, she put down her tole painting and said, "Sure." Who got the better room-mate? You do the math.

* * *

The line for ice cream at the Creamery was beyond long. It twisted through aisles of candy, past freezers packed with cartons of ice cream, and practically went out the entrance. Though dark outside, as soon as we walked indoors Chloe put on her cat-eye sunglasses. As she walked over to look at the pretzels, I said to Jill, "Did she swipe those off her grandmother?"

"Probably. She's into vintage."

"And where she comes from, vintage is code for grandma stuff?"

"Pretty much," said Jill.

Discreetly pointing at Chloe, who was now talking to three way cute guys, Pudge said, "If wearing grandma glasses can attract guys like that, then count me in."

I couldn't have agreed with her more. I mean, how cool would it be to have guys like that want to talk to you? *Just once,* I thought, *I'd like to have some gorgeous guy tap me on the shoulder and start saying stuff like, "Don't I know you?"*

Just then, no lie, someone tapped me on the shoulder. But before my heart could race and my expectations even kind of soar, I heard, "Evenin', kiddo," from a familiar, southern-twanged voice. I turned around and there he was—Henry Spessard, the guy who had thought if there was one thing more certain than the sun setting at the end of the day, it was that sooner or later he was going to marry my mom. I decided the best way to handle running into Henry was to be cheerful, say hello, and pretend as though I had no memory of him doing things like serenading my mom outside her window. (He only did the serenade thing once. I don't think he liked Mel harmonizing with him from her upstairs window.) However, before I could say anything, Henry said, "I'd like to have a word with you."

Jill shot me a look that said, *Who the heck is he?* And I shot her one back that said I'd tell her later. "Uh, sure, Henry. That'd be fine."

As soon as we walked outside, he folded his arms, looked past me to the dimly lit parking lot with a look so serious I half wondered if he was going to tell me he had six months to live, and said, "I saw Joan today."

I was pretty sure Henry had more he wanted to tell me, but instead of getting on with it, he just kept staring at the parking lot, almost looking like he was replaying something in his mind. Hoping to snap him out of his daze, I cleared my throat and said, "Wow, me too."

It seemed to work. Henry looked at me and, with both his index fingers pressing in at his temples, said, "As you know, Joan and I had a good thing going there for a while . . . "

"Okay, you're delusional," just about came out of my mouth.

"However, she decided to hook her wagon to old Keppler's star . . ."

As freaked out as I was about my mom's marriage to Keppler, there was something in Henry's tone that ticked me off and made me want to say, "Trust me, you were never a serious contender for my mom's heart. Keppler from the get-go was the only man for her. In fact, even if it had come down to her choosing who to marry out of a few different guys, I guarantee you wouldn't have been eeny, meeny, miney, or mo."

"She wanted security . . . "

No, actually she wanted Keppler.

"And social standing . . ."

And, FYI, you're officially whacked out of your mind.

"But what it all comes down to in the end is money . . ."

No, what it comes down to is she didn't give you the boot from the start out of sheer kindness.

"Old Keppler has more of it than me . . . but only for the time being. Too bad she wasn't smart enough to see that." Henry forced a smile. "But there's fish, kiddo. Lots of fish out there. If you breathe real deep, you can practically smell them, yes, sir! Well, listen, I'm glad we had this talk."

"Uh, me too."

"You take care, kiddo," said Henry as he pointed his hand at me like a gun and with a wink pulled the trigger.

Forcing a smile, I fired back as he got in his truck. And as soon as he started to drive out of the parking lot, I pulled the pin on a pretend hand grenade and launched it in his general direction. After all, who was he to call my mom stupid? (Okay, he didn't say stupid, but it was implied.) I mean, sure Henry was smart when it came to legal stuff, but a no-brainer like why Mom married Keppler had him arriving at bonehead conclusions. I laughed (well, started to anyway) as I thought about what Henry had said clinched the deal for Keppler: his money. Seriously, it was such an absurd thought that I really could have been doubled over in laughter had the whole subject of money not made me reach for my wallet.

I guess I'm one of those the-glass-is-half-empty sort of people, because instead of thinking, *Whew, I've still got twenty bucks,* I thought, *Get me a paper bag and put it over my head, I've only got twenty bucks in the entire world!* Sure, I had realized I was getting low on cash, but I could have sworn there was another twenty in my wallet, or at least a ten. I tried to tell myself the money crunch wasn't my fault, and that I was merely a victim of a conspiracy against all the trusting, non-change-counting people in the world. It was clear that the only way I had gone through so much cash so fast was that a network of evil salesclerks had made a point of pinpointing all the people in the world who don't count their change back, and I had been found out. So when the lady at McDonald's with the shifty eyes (her eyes hadn't seemed shifty at the time, but in retrospect they were) said she was handing me a ten and two ones, it was really just three ones. It's amazing how some people can sleep at night.

But before I could call the police and make a report, that nag, Miss Reality Check, whispered in the back of my mind, "You have been spending a lot of money lately—paying to eat at restaurants when you could have eaten for free at the Cannon Center."

"So," I said, trying to shove her to an unlit corner of my brain (that would be the corner where my science abilities are located), "it's not like we've been heading to Magelby's. Sure I've spent money, but no more than anyone else."

And this is why reality checks are nags. Just when you think you've got a good point, they roll through your head and break to pieces your logic. "Admit it," said my reality check. "What you really mean is you haven't been spending any more money than Jill. Well, I've got news for you. Jill has more money to spend than you do. Lots more."

It was true. I knew it.

I took a deep, cleansing breath (you know you're bored on Saturday when you watch yoga on TV) and said to myself, "Okay, this isn't a problem. I'll just e-mail Dad and tell him I'm down to a twenty. He's paying for college, and college, as I'm sure he knows, is more than just tuition and books. It's clothes and French nails and shakes at the Creamery. I just need to let him know my situation, that's all."

By the time I walked back inside, the line for ice cream had moved along considerably, and it was nearly our turn to order. Chloe was still talking to that group of good-looking guys, and Pudge had slipped out of line to get a better look at the ice cream. So it was just Jill and me for a moment, and I guess I must have looked stressed because the first thing Jill said to me was, "Any guy who looks like he uses a ruler to part his hair should not be listened to, trusted, or in any way believed."

"I know," I said.

"Then what's with the weighed-down look?"

"Money. It just hit me I'm running out."

The line edged up a little. "So ask your mom for some—" I shot her a look, and she said, "Okay, maybe that would be awkward right now. Then talk to your dad." I guess once again the look on my face said it all because she leaned toward me and said, "And if worse comes to worst, you could always try to get on the gymnastics team. Coach might give you a scholarship. Of course, you'll have to learn how to do back flips and front flips. Plus, overcoming your fear of the uneven bars wouldn't hurt."

"Every time you reach for that lower bar I close my eyes."

"Me too," she said, and socked me softly in the arm. We both laughed. Jill had a way of forcing me into a better mood, and to be honest I was glad for it. "But in the meantime," she said, "if you're looking for a way to earn some money, I'll give you five bucks if you speak with a British accent when you order your ice cream."

I thought of the lone twenty in my wallet and without hesitation looked at the guy behind the counter and said, "Jolly good, might I try the vanilla?"

chapter 8

Wilhelmina Waterman
D-3209
Stover Hall
Provo, UT 84604

Dear W,

Every time I see a letter from you in my mailbox I smile. Your letters are great, and when I read them it feels like you're here, standing beside me, talking. This may explain why lately I've found myself wanting, especially while reading your last two letters, to reach out with my hand and cover your mouth. I know I earn no brownie points for saying this, but Wilhelmina, you need to relax. Please, before you toss this letter, hear me out. I completely understand that you were surprised—really surprised— to find out your mom and Prof. Keppler got sealed. But what I don't understand is why you're not happy for her. You're so worried about how her decision is going to impact your life, or more to the point, your after- life, that you're not seeing how great this is for your mom.

She has someone who loves her so much that he's not willing to settle for a lifetime of happiness. He's not saying, "Joan, I love you a lot, but a lot doesn't include forever." I can't think you'd want her to be married to someone who wasn't willing to give her an eternal commitment. Be happy for your mom, and what's more, let her be happy. I know your mom well enough to realize that she's going to be miserable until she knows you're okay.

I know a sugar-coated letter would have been more enjoyable for you, and who knows, maybe, if I got lucky, would have ended up in your backpack for you to pull out and reread on occasion. Wilhelmina, if I thought such a letter would help you, trust me, I'd write it. I'm trying to tell you what I think you need to hear, and for the sole purpose of helping you. Your mom and Professor Keppler getting sealed is a good thing. Don't try and concoct sorrow out of what should be joy.

You made a few predictions about me in your last few letters, and now, I'm going to make one about you: I predict that after you read this letter, if you ever write me again on my mission, it will be months from now. I'm not sure if you know how much letters mean to missionaries, but plain and simple, they mean the world. Still, I'm willing to risk never hearing from you again if through this letter I can in some way help you.

I haven't tried to reassure you about what heaven is going to be like for you, mainly because I really don't know what to say. (I guess there's nothing thin about my veil of forgetfulness.) However, this I can tell you: everything I read in the scriptures—and trust me, I've been reading the scriptures a lot lately—makes it clear that Heavenly Father is fair. Trust Him, even though it's weird right now to think that your mom and Prof. Keppler are sealed. He'll make it all right in the end.

Sincerely, Elder Hollingsworth

When reading a letter like the one Matt sent me, it is always wise to be alone at the Grand Canyon so you have ample space and privacy to scream your lungs out. (Plus, the echo adds a nice, dramatic effect.) Be that as it may, there wasn't time for a jaunt to the north rim before my nine o'clock class, so I read Matt's letter at the Cannon Center and did my best to control myself. "Augh!" I groaned as I wadded up Matt's letter and threw it in my backpack.

"What?" said Jill, her mouth full of cereal. Jill could eat cereal for breakfast, lunch, and dinner as long as no one tried to slip her Grape Nuts or any other cereal whose first ingredient wasn't refined sugar.

"I just read Matt's letter," I said, and stabbed my pancakes with my fork.

"And?"

"Let's just say that if he didn't predict that I'd never write him again . . . well, I'd never write him again."

"Uh-huh, sure," said Jill, continuing to munch her cereal.

"I never write anyone; I don't trust words," said Chloe, not bothering to look up from her newspaper.

"It's the guy's reaction to my words that *I* don't trust, especially Clayton's," said Pudge, licking the syrup off her fingers. "Which explains the stack of never-mailed letters to him on my desk at home."

Ignoring Chloe and Pudge, I focused on Jill. "You don't think I'm serious?" I asked.

Jill shoveled more cereal into her mouth. "Oh, I think you're serious," she said. "You absolutely believe what you're saying, but what you don't realize is Matt is home plate, or, at least, home-plate material."

"How long have we been friends?"

"Long."

"And not once have I ever heard you refer to a guy as home plate."

"That's because I just made it up."

"No way," I said, oozing sarcasm.

"Way," said Jill, sounding as confident as one can with a mouth full of cereal. "Here's the concept. Dating is a game, sort of like baseball, except instead of three bases to run around, you could, if you're Chloe, have something like fifty."

Chloe looked up from her newspaper. "Why do I get so many?"

"How many guys asked for your phone number last night?" Returning to her paper, Chloe held up four fingers.

Jill gave me a smug look. "Okay, the point of the dating game is to eventually get to home plate. Some people get there fast, others get there slow, and—"

"Others never get there at all," said Pudge glumly.

"And some people choke to death on hot dogs, but very few, so it's not even worth mentioning," said Jill, obviously annoyed to have anyone point out a flaw in her theory. "At any rate," she said, turning to me, "everything points to Matt being a home plate candidate. So my guess is, even though he ticks you off, you'll keep writing and he'll keep writing, and in a couple of years, it'll be da da-da da." It was the flattest version of the wedding march I'd ever heard.

Sure, I had spoken to Jill about Matt a lot, but never had I told her, "I think he's the one." Yes, we got along great, and he made me laugh, but he was . . . just Matt. I mean, nothing knee weakening. "Matt is just a guy I know," I said.

"Da da-da da."

"You can sing all you want," I said, trying not to laugh, "but I'm telling you, Matt's not home plate for me. I mean, that's ridiculous, especially since—"

"What?" asked Jill as she grabbed ahold of my arm. "You're holding something back. Does he have a spare toe?"

I hadn't really counted Matt's toes, but I said, "Of course not!"

"Then he sings show tunes in the car, and expects you to join in? Stuff like 'Oklahoma.' That's it, isn't it?"

Chloe folded her paper and put it on top of her books. "Show tunes are a bourgeois monstrosity."

Ordinarily, what Chloe had said about show tunes was a guaranteed way to make someone say, "What the heck are you talking about?" But Jill's focus on me didn't waver. "Well, what is it? Did he tell you he wants to be a magician? That would definitely bite. I wouldn't want my husband levitating the bed or bending the utensils."

"No."

"A ventriloquist then."

"No."

"Good, 'cause those puppets freak me out. Ooh, I know what it is. He wants to be a farmer, and since you've killed every plant I've ever given you, I'd have to agree, it's not gonna work out. Too bad. I mean, just when you think you've got your best friend's life figured out, bam, everything changes."

Jill's knack for exaggerating was kicking in big-time. "You've only ever given me one plant."

"But you killed it."

"I was ten."

"All I'm saying is, the next thing I knew, it was in your trash."

I didn't try to defend my plant-tending skills any further. Some things just aren't worth arguing. "Okay, are you done?" I asked. Jill did her best to nod while drinking the milk from her cereal bowl. "What I was going to say is, the whole idea of Matt as my home plate, or whatever you call it, is ridiculous since . . . we haven't known each other all that long." This wasn't what I was going to say, not really. But at the last second I didn't feel like finishing that statement with the truth, which was, how could Matt be the one for me when we decided before he left he wasn't even my boyfriend?

During the summer we did spend a lot of time together, but it wasn't like we went out on one bona fide date after another. For the most part we just hung out, watching TV at my apartment (until Mel got in the habit of coming downstairs and asking if we'd baby-sit while she ran a "quick" errand), or hiking Rock Canyon, or biking down to Utah Lake—pretty much anything as long as it didn't cost much, because Matt is . . . well, I wouldn't say he's a penny pincher; it's more like he's a penny observer. He tracks the cost of everything, making sure he's got money for his mission and beyond. I asked him once how he could stand living like he was broke when he had money in the bank, and he just made a joke of it, only saying, "After awhile you get so you love saltines and water for dinner."

Don't get me wrong, we had a lot of fun together. We just didn't date. I take that back. We did go out on one date. In fact, that was the night he told me I wasn't his girlfriend. Just one of those romantic things you say over a candlelit dinner, I guess. Anyway, it was our last night together because the next morning I was leaving for Arizona to spend a few weeks with Jill (not to mention get away from all the wedding-planning stress), and by the time I'd get back, Matt would be in the MTC.

Matt wanted to take me on a date that was "Whimsy worthy," as he put it. So he borrowed Mel and Steve's Gremlin and took me to the top of the Joseph Smith Memorial Building (the expensive side) for dinner.

* * *

"Are you sure you want to do this?" I had said as we walked into the restaurant. "There's a McDonald's across the street."

"I didn't drive you to Salt Lake to eat a cheeseburger."

"I just know how attached you are to your money. It's like each dollar is a close friend of yours, someone you can't bear to say good-bye to. Um, you don't happen to give your money names, do you?"

Pulling a quarter out of his pocket, he said, "Right down to my loose change. Fred, how ya doing, buddy?"

I slugged him softly in the arm, and when I say softly, I mean I hardly touched the guy.

However, knowing that the lady behind the reservation booth was watching us, Matt walked up to her rubbing his arm like he'd just been kicked by a horse, and said while wincing, "Hi, reservations for Hollingsworth."

The lady smiled at us, obviously pleased to see two people enjoying themselves. "Right this way," she said.

Matt held out his arm to escort me to our table. As the lady led the way, I took his arm and dug my nails into his skin. He, of course, took this as a cue to tickle me. We must have looked like two people with a serious case of ants in the pants, but no one seemed to notice.

Dinner was yum, and since it was a buffet, there was tons of it. I had just gone back for my third dinner roll (okay, fourth) when I noticed Matt looked deep in thought. As I sat back down I said, "What's up? Are you stressed about the tip or something?"

"Nope, just thinking."

"About what?"

"About how much I like being with you."

"Well," I said, "you'd better soak tonight for all it's worth because by the time I get back to Utah, you'll be in the MTC, and I won't be able to visit you because once you're in there, I'm lumped together with all the stuff you're supposed to avoid, like swimming and side-burns."

"I guess that's one way of looking at it," he said, grinning.

"But that's okay. I didn't want to see you for two years anyway. I've got a lot of . . . stuff to do."

Raising his glass of ice water, he said, "Here's hoping that 'stuff' doesn't include you getting married."

I threw a part of my dinner roll at Matt. (I know you generally shouldn't throw food in nice restaurants, but it was a small, butter-free piece of roll.) "No way am I going to be matrimonized anytime soon."

"How about homogenized?"

"Ha." I tore off another chunk of my roll and threw it at him.

"Pasteurized then?"

"Ha ha." I launched what was left of my roll at him, and he caught it in midair.

"I know you're not planning to get married," he said, and took a bite of my roll, "but you're going to be dating, and who knows what will happen."

"Who says I'm going to be dating?"

"Why wouldn't you date?"

"I don't know. You tell me."

"Wilhelmina, there's no question you're going to date, and you should date. Two years is a long time. I'd just prefer that you go out with guys with names like Frankenstein."

"So, let me see if I've got this straight. You want me to date while you're gone, but just guys made out of dead body parts."

"More or less."

It was time to ask the question that had been bouncing around in my head all summer. "So what exactly would you say we are?"

Matt was moving his finger over the side of his glass, spelling something in the precipitation that I couldn't see. "We are," he said, his eyes focused on his glass, "Matt and Wilhelmina having dinner and talking about your future dates in Transylvania."

I waited until he was looking at me, then said, "So you're not my boyfriend."

"Define *boyfriend*."

"Look, I'm all out of dinner roll over here, but I've got plenty of utensils. You know what a boyfriend is, so answer the question."

"All right, I'll answer your question. Just keep your hands on the table where I can see them."

"What? You think I'm armed?" I joked.

"No, I just like looking at your hands," he said, making me blush in spite of my best efforts not to. "Okay, the question was, am I your boyfriend? Well, I'm of the opinion that boyfriends should be around to open doors and pick up the tab. And—"

"You're going to be a couple thousand miles away."

"Which complicates getting the door for you. My arms are long, but they're not that long," he said, and then stretched his arms out as far as he could to illustrate his point.

Matt looked at me hoping to see that his goofball joke had made me smile, and I—because I am, after all, just a titch competitive— tried like crazy to keep my mouth from curling up at the edges. But it was no use. He'd won, and I covered my mouth with my hand to hide my grin. "Dork," I said.

"Fork," he said eagerly, as if we were playing some sort of rhyme game.

I rolled my eyes and started to laugh. "Matt, this is supposed to be a serious conversation. I mean, for all intents and purposes, we're breaking up."

"I like to think of it as breaking off."

"And there's a difference?"

"Big one," said Matt as the waiter handed him the bill. "Breaking up is final. It's an I-never-want-to-see-you-again situation. Breaking off is temporary. No one is saying good-bye forever, just good-bye for now—"

"And here's hoping I have fun dating guys with bolts in their necks."

"Exactly," said Matt, and laid down the money for the bill.

"So non-boyfriend, what else are we doing this evening?"

"Well," he said, "I thought we could take a carriage ride around—"

"No way are we taking a carriage ride," I interrupted. "You've parted with too much of your hard-earned cash as it is tonight. Those rides are expensive, and you wouldn't even be able to enjoy it because you'd be too busy calculating how much each clomp of the horse's hooves is costing you."

Standing up and walking around to get my chair, Matt said, "I promise I won't calculate clomps."

So, of course, the first thing he did once we were in the carriage and riding around Temple Square was begin to mumble, "Two-fifty, two-seventy-five."

I nudged him with my elbow. "Hey, you promised!" I said, knowing he was just joking.

It was a beautiful night—the sky clear and dark, and the street lights glowing brightly, making the stars in the distance as hard to see as the future. Matt leaned back next to me and put his feet up on the opposite seat. He took my hand in his, and it just seemed natural to put my head on his shoulder. "So non-boyfriend," I said, "what are you thinking?"

"One day I'll tell you, non-girlfriend. One day I'll tell you."

* * *

There are people in this world who think after reading a few chapters of their Psychology 111 book, they're ready for a guest spot on *Oprah*. Jill happens to be one of them. "You can deny it all you want . . . right now," she said. "In fact, denial at this point might even be therapeutic since he's long gone for the next two years. But believe me when I tell you, the table washer is very possibly home plate."

I didn't wince, at least not like I do when flipping channels I catch a glimpse of a surgeon whistling while he works. (I'm not a big fan of blood.) Still, hearing Jill refer to Matt as the table washer bothered me. She had called him that before. Heck, I had called him that before. But now, I don't know, it just sounded like she was pegging him. As if she were saying that the only thing he'd ever be able to do with his life was wash tables. But was I going to tell her this? No way. Jill would just say it was proof positive she was right about Matt and me.

"I don't ever want to talk to Matt again," I said, "and you've got him picked out as my future husband."

"I wish she had someone picked out as my future husband," said Pudge. "Someone cute, that is." Pudge snorted with laughter, but there was a concern in her voice that was unmistakable.

"*Husband* is just another word for *boredom*," said Chloe, and laid her head down on her backpack.

"And *thesaurus* is just another word for *Go buy one*," said Jill.

"Whatever Matt and I are for each other, it's not home plate," I said. Jill, losing patience, rolled her eyes the way Mrs. White, my piano teacher, used to. (I never did like her or her horehound candy.) "Sure, there's a chance I could be wrong, but—"

"That's the thing that scares me the most: choosing the wrong guy. Well, actually that's not true—it's no guy choosing me." Pudge smiled, but her face was drained of its usual merriment. "Being thin is sort of a requirement for getting guys to notice you."

"Not as much as beating them in arm wrestling," I said, trying to make her laugh. It sort of worked, but she was still stressed.

"But even if I were as thin as you guys, isn't it possible I could mistake the right guy for a wrong guy and then move on to date other guys who for sure are all wrong for me because I was just with the right guy, only I didn't realize it, and chances are I won't realize it until it's too late—until I'm married to the wrong guy and we've got a mortgage and a minivan?"

I wanted to say that things like that never happened, that couples (especially those sealed in the temple) were meant to be together, and that nobody mistook a run-of-the-mill base for home plate. But how could I? I mean, considering what happened to my parents' marriage.

"She's right, you know," said Chloe to me as she stood up, grabbing her backpack with one hand and her tray with the other. "The odds are stacked against happiness."

"Alex, I'll take gloomy freshmen for five hundred," said Jill, and hoisted her backpack onto her back.

"I didn't mean to mope," said Pudge, forcing a smile. "But it's just so stressful. This," she said, her arms out wide, "is the happy hunting ground."

"Dang!" said Jill. "And I forgot to pack my rifle and one of those duck-caller thingies and that green face paint for blending into the scenery."

"I know I sound pathetic. But think about it. We're only here for four years, and in that amount of time, we're supposed to figure out who we want to spend the rest of our lives with, not to mention forever."

"I feel so stupid," said Jill. "I thought we were supposed to graduate."

"Well, that too. But now's the time to scope out prospects, because once you leave BYU, no joke, you'll never find anyone."

"Which explains how my parents met in the Air Force," said Jill.

"All I know," said Pudge, "is my Aunt Sophie is gorgeous and smart, but she didn't get married while she was at BYU, and she's still not married."

"How old is she?" asked Chloe.

"Twenty-nine," said Pudge. "She's still beautiful, but she's sorta old."

"Look," I said, "you're getting stressed for no reason. We're eighteen. We've got tons of time to figure out who we're going to marry. Pudge, you're acting like we just started some sort of race."

"It *is* a race . . . for me, anyway," she said, trying to sound cheerful. "I've got four years to find the one guy on this campus who isn't looking for, well . . . Chloe."

Chloe let out a deep breath. "They're all silly boys," she said. "Anyway, I've got to go."

I looked at my watch. It was quarter to nine. "Me too," I said as I stood up.

"Me size three," Pudge said, and giggled. "Sorry, just wishful thinking on my part."

Standing up and grabbing her tray, Jill said, "Then what are we waiting for? On your mark, get set, go."

* * *

As Jill and I walked up the hill to campus, we talked—after checking several times to make sure the coast was clear—about Pudge. "Geez," said Jill, "that girl needs to get a freakin' prescription. I've never seen anyone so stressed out about finding a husband."

"I know, but I have to admit she has a point about guys. They generally don't ask out girls that are, uh, well insulated."

"So get on a diet."

"I think she is on one."

"She ate four pieces of bacon at breakfast. What diet in the world has you do that?"

"You got a point there. I think I'm going to try to talk to her later today. Not about getting on a diet—"

"Why not? Whims, that's the first thing you should tell her."

"But it will hurt her feelings."

"So will never getting married."

"True."

"All you have to do is nicely let her know that doctors have determined that overeating has a direct impact on the size of your thighs, and from the looks of her thighs, she needs to put down the ham sandwich."

"That ought to make her feel great."

"Think of it as tough love, Whims."

"I'll talk to her. I don't know what I'll tell her, but I'll talk to her. Anyway, speaking of roommates, how are things with Chloe?"

"Fine. She's still getting used to me turning on the light and opening the curtains. I should call her Bat Girl. And, of course, she's still ticked about being here. You should see Spot. She's punched him so much to let out aggression that I swear he's afraid of her."

"Jill, we're talking about a stuffed animal."

"Hey, all I'm saying is, she walks in the room and that's the vibe I get from him. But I think it's funny she's here. I mean, people from all over the planet want to get into BYU and can't. She's in and she hates it."

"Because her parents forced her into it?"

"Well, there's that. But her testimony isn't the strongest."

"What's she hung up on?"

"Well, for starters, Noah. She thinks if the whole ark thing really happened, the beavers and the woodpeckers would have shredded it."

"She actually spends time contemplating the ark?"

"The girl analyzes everything. She's way too . . . thinky." Jill's never had a problem tossing the dictionary aside when a word of her making fits the situation better. "Oh, and guess why she likes the loser she left behind in SD?"

"Um, because he's thinky?"

"You got it."

"So why do you think he's a loser?"

"For starters, the guy is taking a year off of college to think, which I know sorta sounds like they're made for each other. But isn't that what college is for, to make you think? So that's bizarre to me. Plus, he looks like he takes down carnival tents for a living. No offense to carnies, but they tend to pierce and tattoo a little more than the rest of society."

"Gross. Why in the world would she even like him? Oh yeah, thinky."

"Dang, I've got to run, but it's been fun talking to you, Whims. We haven't done this for a while."

I smiled. "I know. It sort of makes me mad all over again that we're not roommates."

"Yeah, but there's no way Chloe and Pudge would have worked. I mean, it would have been like, 'Do you think I'll ever get married?' 'Sure, if you move to India and get somebody to arrange one for you. Now go away. In fact, couldn't you just live in the lobby or something?'"

I smiled. "You got a point there."

"Oh, and I didn't mean to bug about Matt."

"You didn't. I was just surprised. I mean, you've never met him—"

"All I'm gonna say is, I have my reasons. Hey, I'm gonna have to run, literally. You want to meet for lunch?"

"That'd be great."

"Josh is gonna be there. Just want to make sure that's okay."

"Of course," I said, trying my hardest not to look bummed. Like I said, Josh and I get along fine, but he can monopolize Jill's time. That's the way he was in high school too. When he dated a girl, he dated her and her alone. However, Jill's not one to go with anyone's flow but her own. And if he calls her too much, she has been known to tell him stuff like, "Don't call for a week 'cause you're getting on my nerves." Just the sort of thing I used to tell him last year. Ha!

"Meet me at one outside of my Spanish class in the JKHB, and we'll head over from there. See ya!" I watched Jill's backpack bounce up and down on her back as she ran to class. I should have been running too, but I was having a thinky (lame word) moment. As I walked to class, I thought about how glad I was that in life you learn from your mistakes. Last year, for example, I shouldn't have spent so much time obsessing over one guy. How stupid was that? Sure, I finally got out and had a lot of fun with Matt, but a big chunk of my time was wasted dwelling on Josh.

This year, I promised myself, was going to be different. My game plan was going to be to get out there and have fun: no serious relationships, no head-over-heels emotions for anyone in particular. If a guy called, no big deal, and if he didn't call, even smaller deal. Mine, I told myself, was going to be a perfectly carefree freshman year, and as I took my seat in American Heritage, I promised myself that whatever else I learned during the year, I was not going to relearn how stupid it is to have a crush.

And for the next three hours, I was true to my word.

chapter 9

To: Chiarissima@italnet.com
From: Whims1@byu.edu

Cara Chiara,

Buon giorno, amica mia! (Don't be too impressed with my bilingual skills. I'm sitting in the library with an Italian dictionary beside me.) So sorry it's taken me forever to write. Lately, my life has been a barrel of monkeys (a weird American expression meaning "a good time," except when you're trying to be sarcastic, like me). However, I'm going to spare you the gory details and instead tell you some good news: I have a class with Phil! Is that amazing or what? We ran into each other on the way to class (meaning we saw each other unexpectedly, not that we crashed into each other while sprinting down the sidewalk). It's so nice having him in there. It's a big class, which sort of intimidates me. I knew college classes were going to be big, but I guess I wasn't prepared for how unimportant it was going to make me feel. I'm used to teachers knowing my name and asking why I was absent if I haven't been around. In that class, I could ditch (not go) all semester and no one—besides Phil— would even notice.

Speaking of Phil . . . you should have seen his face light up when I asked about you. I know you're trying to be practical, seeing as how there's an ocean between the two of you, but it's so obvious he's whipped (in deep like). It totally wouldn't surprise me if after his mission, he decides to do a little sightseeing in Italy. Dang, why did you have to go to college in Italy? I know your dad worked hard to get you a slot in that university, but it would be so fun to have you in the dorms. You'd totally like Jill, Pudge *(her real name is Prudence), and maybe even Chloe (she's a little weird, kinda gloomy, and big into music). Anyway, I know you'd love it here.*

The one thing Phil said that bummed me out is that you're kind of stuck at that university of yours on your own. He made it sound like there weren't any other Church members for miles. That would be weird, especially since I currently find myself surrounded by members of the Church. I like it, but some of them get on my nerves—the special ones, like our resident assistant, Kay. She's such a cornball you would die (a person who bugs everyone because they try too hard to appear happy and helpful). Hang in there, Chiara, and hopefully some nice, non-cornballish Mormons will pick up and move to Padova, or the missionaries will get on a roll and start baptizing all sorts of cool people.

Anyway, write soon.

Sinceramente,

Your amica, Capricciosa (I like my name in Italian.)

* * *

To: Whims1@byu.edu
From: Dentking@goodlife.com

Dearest Whimsy,

Got your letter, and am truly sorry to hear you're low on funds. Would love to help you out, honey, but my money is tied up right now in the market and other investments. Feel real bad about it. Perhaps your mother could help you cover the cost of incidentals. Hope all is well. Enjoy yourself, sweetie, and I'll write you again when I get back from Vienna. Your dad

P.S. Will be sending off tuition and housing checks today. I hope BYU educates as efficiently as they issue fines. They certainly are merciless about financial deadlines. Anyway, good luck!

* * *

I sat on the floor outside Jill's Spanish class wishing my last name were Onassis or Vanderbilt—something that would guarantee I'd be dripping with spare cash. Okay, maybe "dripping" was overstating it.

After all, it wasn't like I wanted to buy a helicopter or a summer beach house. I just wanted to have enough money so that when I bought something at the bookstore, I wouldn't half expect the cashier to say, "You know you can't afford this. What in the world are you thinking? Go put that back on the shelf and don't bother coming in here until you have more than twelve dollars to your name!"

I watched as a group of students all wearing that overpriced grunge look walked down the hallway, laughing and talking about a movie they had recently seen. No doubt *their* wallets were bulging with excess tens and twenties, and it seemed as if by instinct they could tell mine wasn't. In fact, as they walked past me I got the distinct impression that if I had an overturned baseball cap next to me, they would have thrown me some quarters. I wanted to say, "Hey, don't think I'm poor. Okay, I'm poor now, but I wasn't poor that long ago. Really, I'm just like you guys . . . except I'm currently out of cash."

It was weird to feel my self-esteem shrivel like my third grade plastic art in my mom's oven simply over the amount of money I had, or rather didn't have, in my wallet. I mean, money had never been that big a deal to me before, mainly because I always seemed to have enough. But now, I don't know, I somehow felt people were (and I know this is stupid) better than me because they could buy things I couldn't. Of course, the obvious solution was to get a job, but one thing was making me drag my feet—I had zero experience.

It was one of those vicious circles in life: in order to get a good job you needed experience, but you couldn't get experience without a job. I mean, I knew I was just the person to do something homework-friendly like sit behind a desk in the library and look official, but with no prior experience, my chances of getting such a job seemed slim. Life can be so unfair. More than likely, the only job I was qualified to do was something like picking up the garbage on campus strewn about by rich kids plastered with expensive labels who knew there was no need to aim for the trash can because other students poorer than themselves were paid to pick up after them. A chill of defiance went through me. "Never," I mumbled. "I'll stay broke before I—"

"Hello, hello," I heard someone say in a friendly voice as he tapped the bottom of my shoe with the tip of his.

I looked up and gulped. It was Colin (that was his name, wasn't it?), my Y group leader, the cute Canadian who pronounced *sorry* like it was supposed to rhyme with *gorey*. "Hey," I said with a smile as I sat up a little straighter and did my best to look trouble-free.

"It's Whimsy, isn't it?"

"Right. Good memory." *Act breezy, Whims,* I thought. *Don't let him know he's making your heart race right now like it did when you thought you'd sprint the last mile of your first ever (and last ever) 5K.*

"Well, it's hard to forget a name like yours."

"And it's hard to forget you too." Embarrassment the consistency of granite came crashing down on top of me. "Er, I mean, your name is hard to forget. It's not every day you meet a Colin."

"My name's Jeff."

Again, colossal embarrassment.

"I'm joking," he said with a smile. "You got it right. I'm Colin."

I giggled, but it wasn't just a regular giggle. It was one of those I'm-so-feminine giggles, and I was very glad Jill wasn't there to see it. After all, she and I roll our eyes in gag-me disgust when we see a girl trying to pour on the girly charm by laughing that way. "You're too funny," I squealed, instantly making me wonder who it was I was reminding myself of, and certain only that, whoever it was, it wasn't me.

It was nearly time for the bell to ring, and the hallway that before had been mostly empty was beginning to fill with students. Even in an empty hallway, my long legs get in the way. (I refuse to sit criss-cross applesauce. It makes me feel like I'm in kindergarten.) Colin held out his hand, and as he helped me off the ground he said, "I'm so glad you're here, really."

"Really?" There was an intensity to his words that surprised me. I mean, he sorta sounded like someone who'd been stuck in a cave for days and had just spotted the glare of the search party's flashlights.

"I know, I know," he said as he ran his hand through his thick blonde hair. "I shouldn't be terrified. It's just a freshman English class, but writing doesn't come easy for me."

"Really?" I said once again. So much for my ability to create sparkling conversation.

Colin shook his head and smiled, and I tried my best not to melt. "It's embarrassing that I've put off English 115 this long," he said.

"But things work out, eh? After all, now we're in the same class, and though I'm not sure why, just knowing you're going to be in there is making me breathe easier."

My "huh?" was drowned out by the sound of the bell, and I swear there wasn't time to say something like, "Whoa, back up. You think I'm sitting here waiting for a noon 115 class to start? Well, I'm sort of . . . what's the word? . . . *done* with my freshman English requirement. I finished that in high school. No offense meant toward you or your writing phobia. I mean, really, I wish you the best of luck, but I'm not signed up for this class. I've just been sitting here waiting for Jill, my best friend, to get out of Spanish class. We're going to lunch together, and, by the way . . . your eyes are gorgeous . . . and though I've never really been a fan of guys in cable sweaters, suddenly I am."

But there wasn't time to set the record straight because the next thing I knew, Jill was walking toward me saying, "Hey, *chica*. Ready to *comer*?"

"Jill, hey, wow, you're here. What a surprise! Um, you remember Colin, our Y group leader?"

Scarcely bothering to look at Colin, Jill said, "Hey," then turned to me and said, "So let's *andar*, babe. I don't know why, but I'm in the mood for nachos . . . or maybe a burrito. Anyway—"

Before we get into what happened next, I'd like to say in my defense that BYU is a big school—make that a very big school—and it just didn't seem likely that I'd ever spend any time with Colin again if I didn't, uh, well . . . do something stupid. "Actually," I said, begging her through mental telepathy to go along with what I was about to say, "I wish I could go with you, but I have class right now. I thought you knew."

Jill read the situation perfectly. "That's right, but remind me again what *clase* you're taking."

"Oh nothing," I said as I desperately tried to now send Colin a message via brain waves. "Whatever you do," I said in my head, "don't tell her!"

"English 115," he offered. "And Whimsy and I are in the same class. Pretty amazing, eh?"

"Very," said Jill in a completely casual tone, which had me thinking for a moment that disaster had somehow been dodged. But, of course, that was before Jill put her hands on her hips, and while glaring at me said, "Do either of you know how to say in *español*, 'Oh my gosh, my best friend has completely lost her mind'?"

The hallway was crowded enough before Jill decided to fill it with tension. Colin obviously felt uncomfortable. He shifted back and forth for a moment, then said while Jill continued to glare, "Well, it sounds like you two might need to . . . talk. So, uh, I'm going to go find a seat. I'll see you in there, Whimsy. And Jill, it was nice seeing you again."

My eyes followed Colin as he walked into class. Jill's eyes were still glaring when I looked back.

Jill didn't bother to wait until Colin was out of earshot, but quickly said, "At exactly what time today did you say, 'Hey, here's a thought. Why don't I take a class I already have credit for?'"

"Ballparking it, I'd say 12:51. But here's the deal: I told you I thought he was cute, and then, wham, I see him here while I'm waiting for you, only he thinks I'm just waiting for class to start—"

"So you let him believe it?"

"Sort of."

Jill let out a deep sigh of disappointment. "It's time for a story."

"No, it's not time for a story," I said just as a lady carrying a large stack of papers walked past us and into the classroom. She gave me a persnickety look, as if instantly perceiving I was the sort of person that bugged her. *Right back at you, babe,* I thought.

I was in the middle of thinking about persnickety gal and how the weight of her head—not to mention the big bow knotted at her neck—seemed to be causing her to lean slightly forward like a walking Tower of Pisa, when Jill, determined to have my attention, poked me in the arm. "Ouch!" I said.

"Stay with me. Like I was saying, it's officially time for a story. There once was a smart yet stupid redheaded girl who ran into this nondescript guy outside, we'll say, a tattoo parlor. He said, 'Hi,' then she said, 'Hi,' and then he said, 'I'm so glad you're here. Needles scare me, and just knowing you're going to be in there, sitting beside me, getting the picture of a book branded into your arm—'"

"Why a book?"

"What else would you get?"

"True."

The bell rang, and Jill gripped my arms (her subtle way of letting me know she wasn't finished telling her story, I guess). "So anyway," said Jill, "instead of telling nondescript guy, 'Sorry, you've misunderstood. I'm just here to pick up a friend—'"

"So why am I in a tattoo parlor? I hate tattoos."

"Could you, for once, stay focused?"

"Sorry."

"So the redhead, for the sake of spending time with the guy, walks in, sits down, and gets a tattoo."

"How do you equate taking a class with getting a tattoo?"

"It's a class you don't have to take. So taking it is obviously like getting some stupid picture drilled into your arm. It's avoidable pain, Whims."

"But you're the one who's always saying, 'no pain, no gain.'" Jill's eyes narrowed on me. "I'm joking. Okay, you're right, this is completely stupid. Thanks for pointing that out to me, really. And could you do me one more favor?"

"Sure, anything for a best friend."

"Could you get out of here? I'm late for class."

Jill folded her arms in disgust, and as I opened the door and walked in class, she shouted loud and clear, *"Loca, stupida chica!"*

"Find a seat," said the Leaning Tower of Pisa, "and I wouldn't, if I were you, be late again."

There were plenty of empty seats in the classroom, but Colin motioned for me to take the one next to him, and well, I didn't argue. Leaning Tower turned to the chalkboard and wrote *Miss Snell* on the board.

"I do not," she said, "answer to Sister or Mrs." Then she fixed her eyes on us as if trying to detect who among us would dare such impertinence. "This class is designed to not only improve writing skills, but—and take this down—to help you become critical thinkers." She paused until all eyes were back on her, and then said, "What, I ask you, is a critical thinker?"

Basically anyone like yourself, I thought, *who thinks they've cornered the market on intelligence.* In the classroom there was plenty of sighing and squirming, but no hand raising. Colin gave me an anxious look that seemed to say, "I'd appreciate it, eh, if you'd put your hand up before she has a chance to call on me." So, out of concern for Colin and a vague (okay, so there was nothing vague about it) desire to show off, I raised my hand. Helpful hint: when showing off in class, it helps if you actually know the answer to the question.

"Yes?" said Snell's bells.

"Would that be learning to analyze a text through certain critical approaches, namely, historical, psychological, mytho—"

"That is incorrect," said Miss Snell. I felt like there should have been some of that loser music they play on game shows to emphasize the contestant's wrong answer. "What you're referring to is literary criticism. The question I asked was, what does it mean to be a critical thinker? Write this down: 'Words are tools.'"

I wrote, *Miss Snell eats gruel.*

"Every day," she said, "we are glutted with messages that desire to persuade us, that desire to have us realign our thinking with theirs. These messages are found in books, newspapers, and even menacing neon signs blaring the words *hot doughnuts.*" Had it not been for the earnest look on her face, I would have thought she was joking.

"If," she said, holding her index finger high, "we are not going to be swayed by every message that comes before us, we must understand the assorted ways words are employed to persuade us, enrage us, and even call us to arms." Except for the scratching of pencils on paper, the room was quiet as Miss Snell paused for effect. "Such discernment involves, and write this down, thinking . . . , " she waited until all eyes were on her and then finished her sentence, "critically. Learning to not just read a text, but to analyze it, observe in it the various tools of language being put to work, and then coming to our own sound conclusions. Write this down: 'There's more to reading than reading.'"

I wrote, *Snell's knees are scraped and bleeding.*

So after "analyzing" Snell's little spiel, I came to the sound conclusion that I was definitely out of there. No guy—even one as cute as Colin—was worth having to deal with Essence of Snell for a whole semester. Still (and I'd have to blame it on the three summers I spent at Miss Adele's Ettiquette Camp), I knew it would be rude to disrupt the class by walking out, and couldn't bring myself to do it. That, and well, I liked sitting next to Colin.

"We will be doing a lot of reading and writing," said Snells like Teen Spirit, "perhaps even more than is expected, because I'm of the opinion that the university experience is too valuable to let oneself become concerned with minimum requirements. And those who have no stomach for the class, let them depart," she said, suddenly acquiring an English accent. "We would not write in that man's company."

It's weird how a bazillion thoughts can fly through your mind in just a few seconds. Thoughts like, *Hello, Whimsy! This is your cue, your moment to leave. No longer will leaving be rude or disruptive. After all, Scratch and Snell is pausing, waiting for people to walk out, and look, there go two people—now three—out the door. Be strong, girl. Get up and be the fourth. You can do it. Four's your lucky number, and it's the number of migraines a week you'll be avoiding by chucking this class, and it just might be the number of adorable children you and Colin will have. No! Think migraines, Snelly migraines, and get up and . . . wouldn't it be nice if all four had his green eyes?*

Miss Snell walked over to the door, opened it one last time, and said, "Anyone else?"

I reached for my backpack, and as I turned to Colin to mouth the word *sorry,* he smiled, making the cutest dimples appear in his cheeks. Suddenly, all I could think about were the odds our children would have his dimples too. So, needless to say, instead of getting up and leaving, I unzipped my backpack and whispered to Colin, "It's always nice to have two pencils handy."

Colin winked at me and handed me his own brand-new, number two Ticonderoga. "It's the least I can do for you," he said.

I wanted to say, "If only the same could be said about me taking this class! But this is going to be a major pain, and all for the sake of helping you out . . . not to mention our adorable posterity." But instead, I took the pencil, placed my backpack back on the floor, and said, "Thanks."

After it was clear that no one else was leaving, Miss Snell said, "We few, we enlightened few," and then snickered. "I've been giving you modified quotes of Shakespeare," she said. "That's my area of expertise—Shakespeare."

That and dressing like you're stuck in the eighties, rolled through my mind, but I didn't say a word.

"In fact, I spent my summer in London researching Shakespeare. What a magical city. *He who is tired of London is tired of life*," she said with a faraway look that lingered until the person behind me had the good sense to sneeze. "But anyway," she said, "returning to the purpose of this class . . . I will do all that I can to make sure our time together is not a waste of time."

I wasn't aware that I had laughed out loud until I noticed Snell glaring at me. I uttered a quiet "sorry" and she continued. "Our first section this semester is going to be the narrative. We will be learning about what constitutes a narrative and how to go about the process of writing one. Though it would be simplest to allow you to use your own lives as the subject matter of your narrative papers, I'm not going to do that."

"Figures," I mumbled to my lined paper.

"I want to go beyond you. You know who you are. There's nothing to be discovered there. Instead, I want the narratives that you write this semester to be the cumulative effort of interviewing and researching the life of someone else. Someone who is still alive, but barely."

I would have laughed, but the look on Snell's face told me she was dead serious.

"I want you to find someone whom you don't know, someone quite elderly, and interview them. Find out all you can, and then write a narrative about them regarding this topic: Regret. Have the individual, in the course of your interviewing, relay to you an experience that left them burdened, mired down with regret. This will not only create meaningful narratives, but might prove useful for my thesis, which will be a postmodern look at Shakespeare's treatment of regret in his early works.

"As for next time, bring in a short essay, just two pages typed, on what you expect to get out of this class, and be sure to read the first fifty pages of the novel mentioned in your syllabus. That is all for now."

I was beginning to hear Jill in my head saying stuff like, "It's not too late to bail. All you have to do is walk out the door and toss the syllabus in the trash as you tell Colin you just remembered you already have AP credits that cover this class. It's no big deal," just as

Colin stood up from his desk and brushed back his hair with his hand. "Do you think," he said, instantly making me hit the mute button on Jill's voice in my head, "we could get together tomorrow, maybe for lunch, and you could take a look at my essay?"

Jill was still banging around in my head trying to get my attention, but I shoved her aside (after all, it's my head) and said, "Sure, that'd be great."

"Uh, well, how does Chinese food sound?"

"Great," I said, preferring to ignore that I don't like Chinese food. Too many vegetables.

"And no worries about lunch. I won't try to pay for you. I know how you girls like your independence."

I wanted to say, "Not when we girls have $12.75 to our name," but instead I complimented him on his uncanny insight into the workings of the female mind.

"The Cougareat then, tomorrow at noon."

"Sounds great," I said while smiling so big it was nearly hampering my ability to talk.

"Bye," said Colin.

"Bye," I said, still smiling and beginning to feel the first signs of face cramp.

I hadn't been speaking to the Snellminator, but she thought I had. Looking up quickly from a group of students who had gathered to ask her questions, she said, "Good-bye to you too."

I waited until I was nearly out of the doorway, then mumbled to myself, *"Loca, stupida chica. Loca, stupida chica."*

chapter 10

Elder Matt Hollingsworth
MTC Box 210
CHI-SAS 1010
2005 North 900 East
Provo, UT 84604-1793

Annoying Elder H,
I was going to write "Dear Elder H," but I figured since you're a missionary you wouldn't want me to lie. Your last letter, quite simply, made me want to break things and take up swearing, but other than that it was good to hear from you. Seriously though, what is it with you and your ability to tick me off? Don't get me wrong, it's not like I was wanting you to write me a you-poor-thing letter, but was it really necessary to send me one so jam-packed with stuff guaranteed to make my blood boil?

The real gem (and by that I mean the part where I wanted to slug you) was when you said I was concocting sorrow out of joy. Since when is having Keppler's creep of a son announce my mom and his dad are sealed a joyful experience? You made it sound like I've been a big party pooper, determined to ruin their wedding bliss. That is not only a big, fat lie, it's a big, fat, unfair lie. I was—and you know this—the first to congratulate them when they got engaged, the first to insist my mom have a bridal shower, and when Keppler started turning purple because my mom was thinking it might be wise to wait to get married until after her second year of law school, I was the first to tell her she was nuts.

All along I've supported them and their little happy world. But excuse me if when my mom tells me, in our one conversation about the "possi-

bility" of her getting sealed to Keppler, that it's something that won't take place for a long time, I happen to believe her. You want me to be Miss Joy Gal about everything, ignore my true feelings the way your sister does housework, and yet you don't even take the time to consider my side of the situation.

Listen, I know it's a good thing for my mom to be loved. And yes, Keppler wanting to be sealed to her does say a lot about how much he cares for her. But if only instead of preaching, (could you save it for the Chileans!) you had just told me you understood where I was coming from and felt sorry things had played out the way they did, I don't know, it would've helped me. Do me a favor and let's just drop the whole subject. There's lots of other things for us to write about: the joys (there's that word again) of wearing white shirts practically 24/7, MTC food and whether it's better or worse than the stuff they give us at the Cannon Center, and what the odds are you'll be as good about writing me as I'm going to be about writing you. Not that you deserve it.

That's it for now. Sort of take care. W

* * *

To be honest, I was glad to see another Sunday roll around. Usually (and I know I'll probably get demerits in heaven for saying this) Sundays are hard for me. I like going to church well enough, but the rest of the day I tend to feel stuck. And it's not like I really want to do stuff like shop, but just knowing I shouldn't makes me feel boxed in. I guess it's just hard for me to switch gears and slow down. However, by the end of my first week of college, slowing down sounded fine by me.

After my lunch date (in my book it was a date) with Colin, I was down to my last dime. Okay, $1.75, but it felt like a dime. After all, $1.75 was never meant to buy anything. It's merely what slides between the sofa cushions or gets thrown in the car ashtray. Suddenly, however, $1.75 was all the money I had in the world, and I found myself wishing I had been a little more careful with all the previous $1.75s in my life. It was easy to imagine a much more money conscious and less stylish me (I'm thinking if I'm a tightwad, I'm accessorizing at the dollar store) putting nearly every dollar that ever came my way into a savings account for college. And though my purse, which I've made from old Levis, is an eyesore, inside it my plastic wallet is loaded down with cash, cash that I wisely spend only on bare essentials, like the ingredients to make my own soap and toilet paper. About as likely a scenario as Jill starting a day care.

Don't get me wrong. I didn't mind spending money to go to lunch with Colin. We had a great time, got some work done (okay, so it was work I shouldn't have had to do in the first place, but it still felt productive), and got to know each other better. Well, sort of anyway. The problem wasn't him, it was me. Aside from his puka-shell necklace, Colin couldn't have been cuter. I, on the other hand, was a mess. What I mean is, I just couldn't relax. I was so worried that silence might crop up between us and leave us staring at our sweet-and-sour chicken that I turned into (not to be rude) Melanie, or at least someone as chatty as her.

I yammered on and on as Colin sat back and listened with this amused look on his face that made him appear as though he were watching adorable circus poodles jump through hoops. Not exactly the look I hope to inspire in men. But at least I didn't bore him, and he didn't bore me. I mean, I laughed really hard when he said he'd "spring" for my napkin and straw.

After our "date" though, it was time to face reality. So with $1.75 jangling in my pocket, I hauled bootie over to the employment office and quickly discovered that nearly every student on campus had hauled bootie there before me, snagging the best jobs. Needless to say, cleaning toilets in the Bean Museum at four in the morning was not high on my list of things to do in life, but considering my current cash flow (none), I figured I'd better gulp back pride and take the job. After all, cleaning toilets was honest enough work. And how many people actually visited the Bean Museum a day? Two, possibly three max, and if BYU wanted to pay me to clean toilets that were hardly ever used, well, that was fine with me. So, of course, just as I was getting comfortable with the idea of my new job, I ran into Jill, told her about it, and she said, "Cleaning toilets! That's disgusting! Dang, girl, don't you have any pride?"

"Apparently not," was the only thing I could think to say.

So, as I was saying, suddenly Sunday wasn't looking too bad to me. After all, when you don't have any money to spend anyway, not shopping on Sunday isn't that big of a deal. And besides, after a week as stressful as the one I'd just had, the only thing I was interested in doing was kicking back and taking the time to count my non-blessings. Weird, I know, but sometimes listing all the things that are going wrong in my life can boost my spirits. I guess it makes me feel like it's my turn to finally have something go right. I call it optimism. Jill calls it proof that falling off the monkey bars in the third grade and landing on my head took its toll.

Anyway, I was just to non-blessing number thirty-four (having a best friend who I have to drag to church) when I walked into sacrament meeting and our bishop shook my hand and said, "You must be Whimsy."

"I must," I said stupidly, sounding more like I was asking a question than making a statement. I can't help it. Bishops make me nervous. They remind me of principals, and principals remind me of wardens. Do you see where I'm going with this?

"Would it be possible for you to meet me in my office after church?"

"Uh, sure," I said, feeling strangely like I'd just been caught.

"Busted," whispered Jill as we walked into the concert hall.

"There you are!" said Melanie as she came bustling toward us with Tyson by the hand and McKenner on her hip.

"Speaking of busted," I whispered back.

Melanie entirely skipped hello and said, "Never wear pantyhose when you're pregnant. All they do is roll down and make you feel like an oiled-down flagpole on the Fourth of July."

Letting go of Tyson's hand, she took her pantyhose by the waist and gave them a good yank. "You're just the girls I was looking for. I'm speaking in sacrament today, so can Tyson sit with you?"

"No," mumbled Jill, which I quickly followed up with, "problem."

"No problem," I said. "That's what we meant."

"How great that you can finish each other's sentences like that. I try to do that with Steve, but I'm hardly ever right. Thanks so much. Be good, Tyson. Bye now."

Tyson didn't bother answering his mom. Instead, he looked at Jill and pulled a pen out of his pocket. Jill rolled her eyes, took Tyson by the hand, and said, "Let's get this over with."

Chloe lowered her sunglasses and said, "Amen to that." She was still mad at Jill for dragging her—almost literally—to church. Of course, I had been the one to drag Jill to church, which left me wondering who, if anyone, was there to drag me to church if I needed it. One thing was sure, it wouldn't be Pudge. I looked over to see her apologizing to a rather snooty-looking girl who had stepped on her foot, and mumbled, "Bring me breakfast in bed, maybe. Force me to wake up and get moving, never."

Melanie opened her talk by saying, "It is so wonderful to look out and see so many prospective baby-sitters," and closed by assuring everyone they could count on her, particularly for their Tupperware and scrapbooking needs, something which appeared to make the bishop get a serious case of ants in the pants.

Sunday School and Relief Society flew by, and before I knew it, I was sitting outside the bishop's office trying to tell myself I had nothing to worry about. After all, Bishop Hawkins looked more like a professional rock climber than he did a bishop. Sure, his blonde hair was short, but it stood on end like he'd just encountered a fierce wind on the north face of Dead Man's Bluff. And although he looked quite respectable in his white shirt and dark suit, his nose, which had obviously been broken a few times, and his deep tan made me wonder if it had even been a full week since the last time he slept strapped to the edge of a cliff.

One thing, however, that was easy to figure out about him was that he didn't like to waste time. I had barely sat down in his office when all at once he said, "Let's have a prayer." I was barely finished saying the prayer when he said, "Let's have a talk."

"All right," I stammered.

"We'd like to call you to be the new compassionate service leader."

"Huh?" I asked, not because I hadn't heard him, but because I couldn't believe he'd actually meant to say that to me.

"Compassionate service leader, which is, as I like to think of it, sort of like a designated good Samaritan," Bishop Hawkins said as he leaned back in his chair in a way that implied I had nothing to worry about. "You'll work closely with our Relief Society president, Sister Kay Swindle—"

Special Kay! You want me to work with that cheese ball! I thought.

"And together, the two of you will look out for the needs of the sisters in our ward. So, how does that sound?" he said, and clapped his hands together as if we'd already struck a deal.

"Um, bad," I said before I could stop myself.

Bishop Hawkins leaned even closer toward me, and I sunk as far as I could into my chair without falling on the carpet. "Is there anything," he said with his eyes fixed on mine, "regarding your personal conduct that would keep you from accepting this calling?"

My face turned a shade or two redder than my hair. "No," I said, as humiliated as if that question were a strip search. "It's just that I'm not a . . . huggy person." I instantly thought of my mom and her knack for comforting people.

The bishop smiled. "Don't worry," he said. "That's just one of those weak things about yourself that needs to be made strong. And in the meantime, if anyone needs a hug, you can always send them to Sister Swindle."

I let out a sigh of defeat. "I'll do that," I said. "I'll definitely do that."

* * *

If I had been expecting a boatload of sympathy from Jill about being called as the compassionate service leader, I'd have been just a titch disappointed. "You think that's bad," she said as she shoved me over so she could sit on my bed too, "you haven't heard what happened to me today. Mel's husband pulled me aside and asked me if I'd teach—are you ready for this—Tyson's Primary class!"

"Whoa," I said.

Pudge, who had been sitting at her desk writing in her journal and nibbling at a bar of chocolate, said, "Oh, but he seems like a sweet little boy."

"Little boys aren't sweet," Jill growled. "They're right up there with rodents and speed bumps and other little but obnoxious things in life."

"But what about Fly Boy?" I asked, referring to the pet hamster she had solemnly buried (and yes, Fly Boy was dead at the time of burial) in their backyard.

"That was different. That was Fly Boy, and it doesn't change the fact that I am the one who deserves some pity here. Besides, you're the new compassion girl," she said as she took a hunk of Pudge's chocolate without asking, "so get busy and show me some dang compassion."

I flicked her on the side of her head, and she said with her mouth full of chocolate, "You're gonna need some practice."

"Yoo hoo!" said a sugary voice as our door opened. It was Special Kay. "Hope I'm not interrupting." She didn't pause to get an answer on that. "I'm just going around handing out visiting teaching assignments. I would have done it in church today, but the copier was being a stinker." Jill looked at me and rolled her eyes, something which Kay noticed but ignored. She handed Jill and me each a pink envelope covered in cutesy hearts. "Your assignment is inside. I thought it'd be easiest to just assign roommates as companions. Hope that's okay. Gotta run. Oh, and Whimsy," she said as she edged out the door, "thanks so much. Sure 'preciate ya!" She crinkled her eyes up in that way of hers that's supposed to convey friendship and caring, but only conveys to me it's time to gag.

As she shut the door, Jill leaned toward me, her eyes crinkled to the point of practically being closed, and said, "We all 'preciate ya, Whims, our grand queen of compassion."

"Say what you want, Primary Gal," I said as I tore open the pink envelope. "At least I'm not going to be singing that snowman song."

"If they didn't make him melt to oblivion, I wouldn't mind it so much!"

I pulled the card from the envelope and, completely ignoring the snowman-song complaint, said, "So who's Athena Croward?"

Pudge stopped cold breaking off a piece of chocolate. "We have her?" she said in a tone that said, "Please tell me it's not true."

"Looks like it. Her and a Stephanie Reese, who I guess is her roommate—"

"More like her number-one fan," Jill piped up.

"What are you talking about?"

"Athena Croward," said Jill. "Haven't you heard of Croward Pickles? They supply pickles for eighty percent of the restaurants in the nation. "

"How would I have heard of Croward Pickles?" I asked, amazed to hear Jill quoting pickle statistics.

"From Athena Croward, of course. She's like a walking ad. Just the other day she brandished a pickle in the Cannon Center—"

"You can't brandish a pickle."

"She did," said Jill. "Okay, maybe she didn't. But she did hold it up for everyone at her table to see and said, 'You can tell this is a Croward by how crisp it is.'"

"She stepped on my foot today," said Pudge.

"That was Athena!" I said, and looked back at the paper in the hopes that I had read it wrong.

"Her family's not rich," said Jill with just a hint of enthusiasm. "They're massively wealthy, and there's a difference."

"Ya think?" I said just to bug her.

Jill ignored me. "They've got summer homes, winter homes—"

"All stocked with pickles, I hope."

"—a yacht, and from what I hear, they even own part of an island."

"Just a part? Well, whoop-dee-doo."

"I don't think she likes me," said Pudge, crumbling up the wrapper and strangely trying to hide it in the garbage can.

"She doesn't have to like you. She's a bazillionaire," Jill said as she ripped open her envelope.

"Thanks, Dear Abby," I said, and whacked her with my pillow.

"Ouch," she said. "That hurt, but it's okay because that's what visiting teachers are for!"

"You got us? That's not fair," I moaned. "You gotta get some island-owning prima donna too."

Jill got off the bed, and as she opened the door said, "I think we can count this as our visit, don't you? See ya!" And non-blessing number 120 for the day was that she bolted from the room and shut the door before my pillow hit her. So much for it being my turn to have something go right.

"Do me a favor," I said to Pudge, "and tell me it's my turn."

"Sorry, for what?"

"I'll explain later," I said.

"Okay, it's your turn," she said.

I let out a sigh. "I hope you're right."

chapter 11

To: Whims1@byu.edu
From: Chiarissima@italnet.com

Carissima Whimsy!

Ciao bella! Thank you for the e-mail you send me. Your italiano is molto buono (very good). Phil wants to learn, but is hard because speaking italiano makes him hungry for pizza. Poor boy. I am happy you have class with Phil. He is so cute. I try to tell myself not think about him, but is not easy. I miss my American boyfriend! I hope his mission call is Italy. That would be fantastico. I know I cannot see him when he is missionary, but to have him in my country would make me miss him less—and he would have to learn italiano!

It is hard now to be back in Italy. At first it is not bad because I am with my family and we are busy biking and camping and enjoying good weather. But now I am here in Rimini at university, and my family is at home in Siena, and you and Phil are in Provo, and it is very lonely. I am the only mormone at my school. It is very good school and I am happy (little lie) to be student here. Is difficult to become veterinaria in Italy, and so it is good that I am here. But I do miss everyone, especially Phil.

The Church here is small. We are forty-five on Sunday, and there is no one my age. The members are so good, and our presidente of branch makes me laugh. He is a taxi driver and likes to talk! They are very proud of me to study at university, which makes me work hard. Of course, there is nothing else to do here but work hard! But, I do not mean to sound sad. I am happy, especially when I hear from you and Phil.

If I can ask a favor, when you see Phil, could you ask him if something is wrong with his e-mail? I sent him message three days ago and have not had message from him. I hope he is fine. Must go now. Ti voglio moltissimo bene! Chiara

One more thing. Luca called yesterday. It was good to talk to him. He is still in Roma studying the law. He asked if he could come to visit me, and I tell him I must study. I think he was sad, but I said what is true. It is also true, however, that if Phil called to ask same question, I would say I am not busy. This makes me feel bad. Luca is so nice, but as you say, he is no mormone.

* * *

To: Chiarissima@italnet.com
From: Whims1@byu.edu

Dear Chiara,

That's it, I'm going to have to dust enough dead animals to buy you a ticket back here. You're just missing out on too much! In fact, it sorta makes me feel guilty, especially when I'm in the Marriott Center with thousands of other students attending a devotional (a big churchlike meeting that takes place every Tuesday). This week's devotional was awesome. It was all about the BYU motto, "Enter to Learn, Go Forth to Serve," and I left wanting to become a doctor/rocket scientist/inventor who figures out a cure for something or another. Silly, I know, but the whole idea of making a contribution to society really struck me. Anyway, it just seems like you should be here for stuff like that. You'd appreciate it, unlike Chloe, who rolls her eyes when we ask her to come with us. Well, I've gotta get going. Be sure and write soon. Ciao, W

P.S. Spoke to Phil, and apparently the boy has been so busy he hasn't had time to look at his e-mails. I told him to get with it and write you back, and I'm sure he will soon.

* * *

It was a stupid thought, but it rolled through my mind all the same when I noticed my favorite jeans felt a little snug. Was it possible, I wondered, that living with Pudge was going to make me chunk out? Did her clothes—even her pajamas—have the subliminal message, "Let's have seconds" written on them? After all, it seemed possible—especially with my top button nearly refusing to button— that she worked for a weight loss clinic, making people fat to help drum up new business. No wonder she was always saying sorry! It just took me awhile to put two and two together.

Okay, so I didn't exactly believe my Pudge theory. Still, it was nice while it lasted to not accept blame for my uncomfortably snug jeans, and, trust me, I tried to put off doing so for as long as I could. After accepting that Pudge wasn't working undercover for Weight Watchers, I started to blame the washer, and then I blamed the dryer. And when I had to rule those two out, I moved on to the laundry soap and fabric softener, and even the shortage of fresh air in college classrooms. The last thing I wanted to admit was that I needed to put down the jelly doughnuts.

But jelly doughnuts for me had become a part of survival. I don't know about the rest of you, but if I've got to get up before the crack of dawn to clean toilets, I need a carrot, make that a doughnut, dangled in front of me. Besides, with the rest of groggy America downing kegs (those little cups add up) of caffeine-packed coffee, a jelly doughnut seemed like a harmless enough alternative. That, of course, was before I noticed my thighs were beginning to resemble lumpy marmalade.

It wouldn't have been so bad if we were further into the school year. After all, lots of people had told me they had gained weight their freshman year. Not a ton, maybe ten pounds that they quickly lost during the summer. But it was barely the end of September, and already I felt I was puffing up like a bag of microwave popcorn. But who knows how long I would have put off facing reality (after all, jelly doughnuts are tasty) if Tyson hadn't socked me in the stomach with the truth (not to be confused with the time he kicked me in the shin) one day during church.

I had popped into his classroom to hand Jill a sign-up sheet for Relief Society and found the two of them facing each other in little chairs as if in the middle of some sort of interrogation. "What does it mean to be thankful?" asked Jill in a voice that took me back to Mr. McWaydid's I-talk-like-I'm-cremated driver's ed class.

"What's a thank?" asked Tyson and tipped his chair back.

Jill brought his chair back down with a thunk. She took a deep breath as if to keep from losing her patience and said, "Tyson, I'm shutting my eyes, and when I open them I'm gonna expect you to be a lot smarter." Jill's gentle approach to nurturing children.

"All right," said Tyson, and rubbed the top of his head as if to rev his brain.

When she opened her eyes, Tyson said, "I think I know it," and tipped back in his chair until Jill gave him one of her looks. "Thankful," he said with all four chair legs on the ground, "is when you're full of this stuff called thank . . ."

Jill smiled. "You're on the right track."

"And your buttons pop off like hers," he said, pointing at me.

I looked down to see that the button on my skirt was missing, obviously the work of my new and not-so-improved waistline. And that was all I needed—that and Jill's oinking noises—to make me decide then and there it was time to start running or at least walking briskly.

So the next day around three in the afternoon, the time I usually fell asleep doing homework, I put on sweats and running shoes and headed out the door. Not to sound antisocial, but I was glad no one wanted to come with me. I needed the time to think about a lot of things, but mostly about my mom. Since our dismal conversation in the parking lot, we had only seen each other a handful of times, and each time (the Sunday afternoon dinner I had been invited to had been as memorable as a head cold) it seemed like the tension between us—which I admit was mainly from me to her—got worse instead of better. And it wasn't just because of the sealing, although that certainly was a part of it. The problem was how happy she looked. She radiated happiness, and that, plain and simple, ticked me off.

Not that I wasn't happy. For the most part I was, and on any given day I could be spotted laughing with friends or flashing Colin a winning smile as we studied for English. Still, I wasn't as happy (or as thin!) as my mom. I mean, everything in the past year had fallen into place for Joan Keppler, especially if you didn't count that her daughter (me) was acting aloof and that her new husband's jaw tightened pretty much any time she mentioned Law Review.

As I jogged past the Carillon Tower panting heavily (apparently this was going to take some getting used to), I did everything I could—even na-na-na-ing—to drown out the sound of my conscience trying to put in its two-cents' worth. *You shouldn't be so unkind to your mother.* "Camp town ladies blah blah blah, do dah, do dah!" I sang, lowering my voice on the last 'do dah' as a mom with a stroller full of kids walked out of the Bean Museum. (And by the way, why are so many people interested in seeing dead animals? You wouldn't believe how dirty those bathrooms get!)

And not returning her phone calls.

"All the do dah dee!"

And not hugging her back when she hugs you.

"All the do dah day!"

She's not the one who's doing the neglecting. You are.

"It would really help," I continued to sing, "if I knew the words to this song, all the do dah day!"

So much for having time to think! My run had turned into one massive guilt trip, and let's face it, if I had wanted a guilt trip, I could have just reread one of Matt's letters. But the traffic on 900 East sort of cleared my head (weird, I know), and as I waited for a chance to cross, my thoughts turned to less stressful subjects, like Colin and the cute way he sometimes rubs the bridge of his nose when he's talking. But practically the moment I crossed to the other side of the street, stressful thoughts started rolling around in my head again, and I decided it was time to start belting out "Ninety-Nine Bottles of Beer on the Wall."

By bottle thirty-six (I admit, I glossed over a few bottles), my jog had become a shuffle, and I was seriously considering turning that shuffle into a walk when all of a sudden I saw in the distance what I immediately understood to be opportunity knocking. You see, unlike the rest of Snell's class, I didn't really know any people so old they could kick it at any time. I mean, my mom was as close to a senior citizen as we got at Wymount, and even my grandparents didn't fit that description, what with their weekly tennis games and rounds of golf. But on the other side of the street and directly in front of me, I saw a lady in a pink knit suit with hat to match who definitely had the I-could-kick-it-anytime thing going on.

Small and frail, she was obviously trying to step onto the sidewalk, but for some reason couldn't. As I got closer, I could see the problem was her cane. It was stuck in a drain on the edge of the road. I was afraid of startling her (she was clutching her purse tightly), so as I crossed the road to help her I said, "Excuse me, but it looks like you could use some help."

"Dear Mother of Pete!" she exclaimed as I kneeled down to help her with the cane. "I have mace in my purse somewhere, and I shall remember your face and notify the police if you dare take my handbag!"

Maybe I should have said "excuse me" louder? "No, I'm not trying to rob you. It just looked like you needed help."

"I'm perfectly fine," she huffed, and I noticed that her eyes, though a sharp blue, seemed unable to focus on me.

I'm usually a pretty compliant person. I mean, if someone tells me they don't need my help, I'm out of there. But her cane was one of those hand-carved jobbers with a brass top, and the bottom of it was getting all covered in mud, and, well, let's face it, she was lying. She did need help. I put my hand near the bottom of her cane, carefully pried it free, and as soon as I had done so, she said, "And now I suppose you'll be wanting something?"

"Huh?" I asked. Were all old people this mean?

"For wrenching me free and—without doubt—ruining my cane, I suppose you'll be wanting some sort of payment."

As much as I wanted to say, "No, you old bat, I was just trying to be nice and help you out, that's all. Now I'm going to leave and you'll never see me again," I did sort of have something I wanted to ask her.

"Well, um," I said, trying to think of how to say it.

"Get on with it," she said. "Quit dawdling."

"Uh, well it'd be great if I could . . . I mean, I'm taking—"

"Speak up and in complete sentences," she said, shaking her head at the sidewalk, "or I shall be on my way. I haven't time for—"

"Could I interview you?" I nearly shouted, figuring that I'd better get to the point before she whacked me over the head with her cane.

The old lady pressed her lips together hard and humphed. "Who are you with?" she said, sounding so irritated you would have thought I'd asked her to fork over her precious handbag and everything in it.

"Excuse me?"

"Oh, come on, girl, don't be a ninny. Tell me who you represent."

It seemed like a weird question, but hey, if she wanted to know, I'd tell her. "Miss Olivia Q. (I made up the Q) Snell's freshman English class," I said loud and clear.

She burst out laughing and quickly covered her mouth with a gnarled hand until she had recovered her frown. "That," she said as she leaned on her cane in a stately manner, "was not what I expected to hear."

"It's a three-credit class," I said, as if that were supposed to be some sort of selling point.

"That doesn't impress me whatsoever. As if what life has to teach is found in a class."

"So you won't do it?" I asked.

"I didn't say that."

"Then you will do it?"

She pressed her lips together again and didn't say anything for a moment. "My policy is no interviews," she finally said. I felt like saying, "No kidding, mine too!" but I bit my lip and she continued. "However, as it appears you think I owe you a debt of gratitude for destroying my cane—"

"Huh?"

"I will agree to have you interview me."

"Oh. Well then, great."

"But on my terms."

"Your terms. Sounds good."

"I'll expect you on Saturdays at four until your assignment is done, and if for whatever reason you fail to show—"

"You'll hunt me down?"

It looked like she was doing her best to keep from smiling. "No," she said, "but that will be the end of the interview."

"Sounds fair enough."

"You'll need to know where I live, so I suppose you'll have to walk this way."

I quietly mouthed the words, "Don't sound so happy about it," and then followed her as she slowly made her way down a sidewalk cracked and bulging with roots. More than once I reached out to catch her, fearful that the unpredictable pavement was going to send her flying, but it didn't. Somehow and without even really looking down, she knew how to avoid what needed to be avoided.

We stopped in front of a white, two-story house with dormer windows and a picket fence, and I couldn't help noticing a man across the street lean on his rake and take in the sight of us as if we were some sort of lunar eclipse. "I like your house."

"You can't have it," she said in a matter-of-fact tone.

"Then what about your cat?" I asked, causing her mouth to fall open. "I was joking."

"I should hope so."

We walked up the path to her front door, and though she hadn't asked for help, I took her by the arm—the man with the rake still intently watching—and helped her slowly climb the three brick steps to her door. And she seemed glad enough for my help until, that was, we got to the door. "I'm all right," she said as she shrugged off my arm. "Enough nonsense."

"Okay, so I'll see you on Saturday," I said, and started to walk away.

She humphed in agreement but quickly added, "You haven't told me your name."

"Oh, sorry. It's Whimsy. Whimsy Waterman," I said. "And what's yours?"

Again she looked like she had barely managed to stop herself from laughing. "My name," she said, "is Sable Thompson Greer. And yes, I'll expect you on Saturday."

"Four o'clock, I'll be there," I said, sounding way too peppy.

Sable Thompson Greer fumbled for her key in her purse, opened her front door, and without another word, walked inside. "Cranky old goat," I mumbled, then turned around, gave the man with the rake a friendly wave, and headed back to the dorms.

chapter 12

Wilhelmina Waterman
D-3209
Stover Hall
Provo, UT 84604

Dear W,

I'm sitting in the laundry room waiting for my clothes to dry, and thought I'd write you before I run out of time again. P-day—better known to you as Monday—always zooms by. It's the one day we have as missionaries for doing things like writing letters, and the last few P-days I've been so busy running errands and taking my companion to the dentist (he has cavities, but, then again, he eats licorice for breakfast) that I haven't been able to write you back. So if I've appeared to be, as you would put it, a "stinkin' ingrate," please forgive me. I really have wanted to get a letter off to you.

Life in the MTC is good. No, it's great. I love being here. It's an awesome feeling to know I'm doing the right thing at the right time, especially since in life there aren't many moments when you can unequivocally say that. I was thinking about this the other night while falling asleep, how going on a mission is one of the rare no-brainers life will, as a priesthood holder, throw my way. It's the right choice, I know it, end of story. For the most part, however, decisions in life are far more complicated. Sometimes it's not a choice between right and wrong, but one between two rights. Trouble is, which of the two is the most right? Does that make any sense? So anyway, it's great to be here doing the right thing.

I can hardly believe that in two weeks I'll be flying to Chile. Mel, last time I heard, was planning on disregarding the Church's request that fami-

lies and friends not go to the airport, and—as if armed General Authorities will be standing at the entrance—plans to wear a trench coat and dark glasses, and only wave to me from a distance. My guess is she'll be fairly easy to spot. I wish it were possible to see you before I go. But, since I was talking about choices earlier, I'd have to say that if given the choice between seeing you in two weeks at the airport or in two years, hands down, I'd take two years. Well, my laundry is hot and ready to fold, so I'd better go. Be good, and know I'm thinking of you. Sincerely, Elder H

* * *

The air was beginning to turn that bitter cold Provo is known and hated for, at least by me. Leaves, which had just recently burst into color, painting the mountainsides in reds and golds so gorgeous I almost didn't mind winter coming, were now brittle and brown and zero compensation for having to put up with snow. I walked outside Stover Hall on my way to my morning biology class and, as usual, nervously scanned the scene for a tall, stiff law professor.

In spite of the arctic vibes I consistently sent his way, Keppler couldn't seem to grasp that I was wanting him to hit the high road, and so my Monday morning walk to campus had become about as pleasant a part of my life as my Saturday afternoon chats with Sable Thompson Greer.

However, this particular Monday, Keppler wasn't there to meet me (I could have kicked myself for feeling vaguely disappointed), and I rushed up to biology a little faster than usual. I figured it would be a good thing to get to class early since we were having a quiz, and I wanted a chance to look over my notes and talk "photosynthesis" with Phil. Well, interestingly enough, when I got there someone was already talking with Phil, but the hot topic wasn't the quiz. A short brunette with a leather backpack (I didn't like her, but couldn't help liking her backpack) sat next to Phil, her hand pressed against his as the two of them cooed over the differences.

"Yours is so big."

"No, yours is so small."

"Yours is so rough."

"And yours is so soft."

She had just started to say something about his fingernails when Phil looked up and saw me. "Hey!" he said, quickly taking back his hand. "Didn't see ya there."

I gave him an icy, you're-busted look and said, "I'll bet you didn't."

Phil quickly and nervously introduced me to Donna. "It's Fauna," she said with a pout of disappointment.

"D-E-F," he said. "They're so close they're practically the same letter. A simple mistake."

Fauna didn't appear to see it that way, and she and her small, soft hand left in a huff.

"Heh heh." Phil laughed the laugh of the guilty.

"Well that looked cozy."

"Not cozy, friendly," he said. "Just keeping it friendly. Besides, Donna's just a friend."

I didn't bother to correct him and hoped the next time he spoke to her he'd up the ante and call her Shauna. "I'm sure she's a real pal," I said.

I wanted to say more. In fact, I wanted to tell him, "Be careful, dang it. You've got this great girl in Italy who's totally crazy about you. Don't do anything to break her heart." But there wasn't time. The teacher walked into the auditorium, and it was time to start class. I did, however, look over at Fauna, whose lips were still set in a pout, and while giving her the meanest look I could muster whispered, "Stay away from my friend's boyfriend."

It was bad enough to see Chiara's boyfriend flirting, let alone mine. Okay, so Colin wasn't my boyfriend . . . yet. Still, it was something I was working toward, and spotting him in the library with some cheap blonde (no offense, but her roots were showing) was not a part of my game plan. I know what you're thinking, that the whole Colin thing was just another Whimsy Waterman pulverization (I would have said crush, but it didn't seem strong enough). However, nothing could be more untrue. After all, when it came to boys, I was more mature now, really. I know on the surface taking English 115 just to spend time with Colin may have appeared immature, but if you consider how much dumber it would have been for me to sign up for Advanced Japanese (I happened to look up his schedule), then

115 doesn't seem so bad. And I'd just like to say that I really don't have an answer for why the new, calmer, more mature me wanted to sneak over to their cozy table and sound an air horn in her ear. All I can say is, it's a good thing I don't carry one in my backpack.

So it's not like I was waxing (some words stick with you from scripture study) desperate when I decided to invite Colin to the LSU game. It was a big game, and I happened to have an extra ticket, that's all. Besides, just a few weeks before, he had mentioned (in that way people mention stuff when they want a favor) that he didn't have football tickets, and I thought for sure he'd jump at the chance. But when I asked, he said, "Thanks, but I'm more of a hockey guy."

"Oh," I said, trying not to sound disappointed. "Well, it's no big deal. I'm not into football either. In fact, you could say there was a time in my life when I hated football—despised it even." Do all the stupid things that are said on this planet have to come out of my mouth?

"Wow," said Colin with a laugh, making me feel even more moronic.

Still, I couldn't seem to keep my mouth shut. "But hockey's great, just great," I said, trying to keep the conversation going. "I really like that Wayne guy."

"You mean Wayne Gretsky?"

"That's the one."

"He's retired."

"Well, you can't have everything."

The conversation was going nowhere, and I had a boulder in my stomach telling me it was time to throw in the towel. No doubt he was whipped on Peroxide Gal, and I didn't stand a chance. She was probably from some town called Frozen Lake and was playing hockey before she could talk. I could practically see the two of them on the ice giving loving looks to each other through their hockey masks as they passed the puck back and forth and socked it to the opponent with the occasional swift elbow. I mean, who could compete with that?

Then a miracle occurred, or at least it seemed like one at the time. "Well," said Colin, "if you're not really interested in football, why don't you come fishing with me? I've got some extra gear. We could make a day of it, unless you don't like that kind of thing."

I didn't intend to lie, but my competitive spirit got the best of me. Trying to knock Peroxide Gal off her hockey skates, I said, "I love fishing." The truth was, I could barely stand to open a can of tuna.

"Really?" said Colin, his voiced filled with both surprise and satisfaction—a lethal combo when it came to my normal resolve to tell the truth.

"Absolutely," I said and, knowing full well I deserved to be thrown in the penalty box, added, "I am quite the angler." *Angler* was just a word I'd remembered from a bumper sticker, but suddenly knowing it gave me clout, and I felt a rush of gratitude to Angler's Paradise Bait and Jerky in Lake Havasu, Arizona.

* * *

We made plans for Colin to pick me up at six (apparently fish are morning people), and I was so happy I could barely keep from skipping, something Jill took care of as soon as I told her. "You're not going to the game?" she growled.

"No, but maybe I'll bring my radio, and we can—"

"You know Josh is stressing about this game," she huffed. "He's your friend, and you should be there to support him. He'd do the same for you."

Though Jill was my best friend, there was one thing I knew she'd never understand: it was still sometimes hard for me to be around Josh. Not that I didn't like him—I did, and I was glad he liked me. But it was just too easy when I was around him for a wave of humiliation to overtake me as memory after memory of my Josh-mania year would seem determined to resurface. According to Jill, however, that stuff (and, of course, she didn't know the half of my Josh-inspired stupidity) was in the past. We were old high school buds, and when one of your buds has a big game, you show up, and preferably with something painted on your face.

"Jill," I said as she glared at me, "the stadium is going to be pretty packed. I really don't think he'll miss me."

"I'll miss you," she said, and shoved me.

That was nice to hear, even with the shove. Trying to reassure her, I said, "But Chloe's going and Pudge—"

Jill rolled her eyes. "But not you. You're going fishing with Colon." She had recently started to call him that to bug me, and to bug her more, I didn't get mad.

"I'll bring you a trout," I said.

Jill cracked a smile. "You're supposed to be the head honcho of compassion," she said, referring to my calling in the Relief Society, "and yet you won't even go to a football game to support your friend."

"Jill," I said in a soothing voice, "every game I've gone to, Josh has gotten sacked. I think it's got something to do with me—some sort of energy I send out. So really, by not going, I am supporting him."

"He is just such a piece of cardboard!"

"Josh?"

"No, Colon. I mean, it'd be one thing to skip the game to do something way fun, but to go fishing with Canada boy? Whims, studying sounds more fun."

"That's because you don't really know him yet, Jill."

"What's there to know? He's a Canadian with a cute face and zero personality."

"He's got personality," I said, not sounding very convincing.

"No," said Jill, "the truth is, you've got personality, maybe even enough for the two of you. But I'm not joking, Whims. Your Colon is cardboard. A nice, flat piece of cardboard. Just think about that while you're out there fishing for conversation."

Jill's words stuck with me in the same pesky way gum does to your shoe, but I said to her, "You've got it all wrong, girl. I'm telling you, you've got it all wrong."

* * *

And she did have it all wrong. Colin not talking much had nothing to do with his personality and everything to do with fish temperament. Fish, as he explained, do not like noise. I guess it makes them think there are hooks in the water, which makes it seem all the more wrong to catch one. After all, they are pretty smart. But I wasn't there to assess fish IQ, I was there to end their sorry little wet lives, and if that was what it took to impress Colin, well then that was what I was going to do . . . or so I thought.

I knew about the worms, and the hooks, and the standing around forever by a river when you could've been at the mall or hiking on a nice dry trail, but I didn't know about the LIVE worms, and the squish, and the worm smell, and the ice-cold water. Oh, by the way, what idiot thought up waders? I mean, I was envisioning sitting on the bank of the river, like Huck Finn minus the corncob pipe, and waiting for a tug on the line. But apparently some brilliant man (couldn't have been a woman) thought he needed to get closer to the fish, so he invented waders—rubber pants that keep the river out but let the chill in.

Had someone told me, "Whims, let's put on rubber pants and boots and stand in a cold river," I would have said, "Even pretty please with sugar on top isn't going to pry me from my warm, soft bed." But there I was, on a cold October morning, up to my waist in river, and shivering, though whether it was from the river or the thought of squishing that worm on the hook, I wasn't really sure. Speaking of squish, who knew the bottom of the river was so squishy? The mud held to my rubber boots, which were several sizes too big, as if by magnetic force, making it hard to move. But of course, as Colin pointed out, moving was right up there with talking. Dumb fish. Why did their needs have to come first?

Tired of standing in cold water and watching Colin reel in fish after fish while I reeled in twigs and an old shoe, I finally decided it was time to get out of the water. "Hey," I said softly through chattering teeth, "I think I'm going to get out for a while."

Colin's line was tugging, and the lean muscles of his arms were taut in response. Gulp. "Do you need help?" he asked, glancing at me and then quickly looking back to his line.

In spite of the magnetic pull of the river bottom and the difficulty involved in walking in larger-than-life rubber boots, I said, "No, I'm fine," with a big, super-happy smile. "Don't worry about me." Fake, I know. But hey, I was trying to troop. And I was fine, at first. I was only ten feet from where we had laid our stuff on the riverbank, and I figured all I needed to do was take it nice and slow. Trouble was, I was taking it nice and slow into a deeper part of the river, and unlike Tyson's sippy cups, waders do not have lids.

Colin was too busy reeling in his line to notice that the river water was coming precariously close to spilling into my waders, and, to be honest, I was too busy watching him to care. Not to sound like a cornball, but with the sight of him standing there in the middle of the river, the sun reflecting off the water, his fishing pole arched tight like a hunter's bow, and every muscle in his body—even the firmly clenched ones in his jaw—engaged in the fight, all I could do was sigh and say so quietly that even the fish wouldn't mind, "You, right now, are the perfect screen saver."

If I were to write a book about the joys of fishing, it would begin like this: "While wearing waders in a muddy river, it is recommended that one not raise their hands in victory at the moment a mambo fish is caught by a fellow angler. This tends to sink one ever so slightly farther down into the mud, thus allowing one's waders to fill with ice-cold, make that iceberg-cold, water and consequently cause one to squeal like a freakin' banshee." Just a little something I thought I'd share.

You would think that my waders filling with water would have been enough to guarantee I had a bad time. And if it didn't, having to nail the fish to a tree so as to make skinning a breeze would pretty much have dealt the day a death blow. But it didn't either. Even entrails flopping on my shoe and having to eat the catch of the day couldn't cloud my mood. I was with Colin, and all the rest of it didn't seem to matter. "You're a real good sport, eh," said Colin as we drove down the canyon.

I had Colin's scarf around my neck and his jacket on my legs, the heater was blasting, but still my teeth refused to stop chattering. "O-oh, n-not r-really. A g-good attitude is j-just p-p-part of being in the g-great outdoors."

"Well, I don't think most girls would be willing to stay and have lunch after getting soaked in the river on a cold day like this. Come to think of it, I doubt most guys would."

I smiled weakly, my teeth still chattering like one of those stupid wind-up toys. I'm sure Colin hadn't intended to make me cringe, but he did. It was just too obvious to me that the so-called new and improved Whimsy, the one with maturity to spare, was, when it came to Colin, trying way too hard. I knew that under normal circumstances—meaning I wasn't with a guy I was trying to impress—if my waders filled with cold river water and whoever I was with didn't instantly drive me home, I would have stuck out my thumb and hitched.

I didn't know what to say. My face burned with embarrassment at the thought of him knowing the truth, but how do you explain away your happy-go-lucky approach to hypothermia? I thought about lying, telling him I came from pioneer stock and barely found it necessary to wear shoes in the wintertime, so ice-cold river water was no big deal, but it seemed like a stretch, so I said, "W-well, I d-did listen to J-John Denver a lot as a kid. My m-mom likes his m-music."

"Aw, Whimsy," he said with a laugh, "you do say the darndest things."

There was something about what he said and the way he laughed that made me feel seven, or rather, that Colin thought of me as nothing more than an adorable seven-year-old, and I could practically see Peroxide Gal fold her arms in satisfaction and give me a smug smile. As I looked out the window and tried to figure out what to say to keep the conversation going, a thought flashed through my mind in the same vague, dim way headlights shine on a foggy night. Maybe, just maybe, I should let Peroxide Princess have him. Somehow, this wasn't going to be worth it.

chapter 13

To: Chiarissima@italnet.com
From: Whims1@byu.edu

Dear Chiara,

That was very rude and inconsiderate of your branch to go to that castle for an activity. How is that supposed to make me feel about the bowling nights and ice cream socials we have here for ward activities? Highly inconsiderate :) But honestly, I am so glad to hear you are doing better. It sounds like, if nothing else, you're too busy to feel homesick.

Speaking of keeping busy, I cannot believe you've been assigned TWELVE people to visit teach, and the fact that you actually do it—especially considering some of your people are an hour away—completely amazes me. I'm embarrassed to think in my last e-mail that I complained to you about what a hassle visiting teaching is for me! I was comparing my situation to Jill's. She's my visiting teacher, and on the last day of the month, she pops her head in our door and reads something like the side of a box of crackers. The message she gave us last month was, "Hydrogenated cottonseed oil, brown sugar, and wheat," which, I admit, made me laugh, but it bugs me that it's so easy for her and such a stressor for me.

Part of the problem is that Athena, the girl we visit teach, intimidates me. It's stupid, but she's from a VERY wealthy family and nearly always has this look of disgust on her face when I talk to her, as if it is a trial for her to speak with someone so below her income bracket. And maybe she does have a legitimate complaint there. After all, her world is completely different from my own.

For example, the last time I talked to her, she had on these enormous diamond earrings. You remember my mom's engagement ring? Well, the stones in her earrings were even bigger than that. We're talking unbelievably big diamonds. Anyway, I told her I thought they were beautiful, which went over all right. She nearly smiled and seemed glad to have someone compliment her, but when, out of genuine curiosity, I asked if they were real, she looked at me in that sour way of hers and said, "You think I'd actually wear fake jewelry?" as if she were a tiara-sporting European princess.

Since I'm on such a roll writing you about church stuff (weird, maybe I'm sick), let me ask you this: is it ever okay not to help someone? Here's the situation, our Relief Society president has asked me to find a way to activate Chloe, Jill's roommate. I've told you about Chloe. She's the one who's drop-dead gorgeous, writes songs about everything going wrong, and though she can be surprisingly fun to be around, tries—I think, anyway—to come across as gloomy. (By the way, guys seem to like it, so she may be on to something.) Anyway, I don't know what to do, and would probably do nothing if Special Kay, our Relief Society president, would just leave it alone! Let me know though if you can think of anything.

Well, I'd better get going. Oh, one more thing, and by the way, I have definitely saved the best for last—Phil told me that he called you! He said you weren't there (darn!), but that he was going to try again soon. Anyway, I was really glad to hear he did that, especially since that boy isn't the best about staying in touch. Ciao for now, W

* * *

To: Whims1@byu.edu
From: Chiarissima@italnet.com

Cara Whimsy,
Just got e-mail and I want to write back quickly because I have idea for Chloe. She love the music, no? So I think maybe you can ask her to sing in church, and she will say yes. Just an idea. When you see Phil, tell him I love it the teddy bear he send me. He is so sweet! Ciao bella, Chiara

* * *

If Olivia Q. Snell had a brain in her head, she knew I didn't like her. It was nothing personal, I just didn't like the way that leaning tower of knowledge taught, dressed, spoke, or stood, and I made a point of letting her know it through, um, mental telepathy. Okay, so maybe she wasn't aware of how much she bugged me, and, yes, maybe I was Princess Pleasant in her presence (yet another tongue twister courtesy of Whimsy Waterman). All I can say is it's easier to compliment your teacher on her leg warmers (a few pairs survived the eighties and Snell has them) when you keep in mind she has the power to impact your grade point average.

The only way my Snell aversion really manifested itself was through the quality of my note taking, especially when she prefaced information with, "Write this down," a phrase I found about as enjoyable as a roach crawling inside my cast (hands down the worst thing that happened to me in the fifth grade). But it wasn't really the phrase itself that made me want to snap my pencil in two, it was more the way she said it. Her tone sent the message loud and clear that she considered herself a vast lake of knowledge and her students a value pack of kitchen sponges all in desperate need of what she could teach them. And so when she (after, of course, ceremoniously telling us to "Write this down") would give us some precious drop of info like "Literature is the best that has been thought or said," I would (after giving her a grateful look) write something like, *Literally Snell's dress looks smeared with tire tread.* What can I say, it helped let off steam.

The one good thing, however, about having to put up with Her Royal Snellness was that it was going to give Colin and me something to laugh about later. I love hearing the stories of how couples meet and am always amazed at how the retelling of "their story" has the power to slip a person back to that euphoric moment in their history, when clouds sailed quickly off the horizon, sleep was a nuisance, and the only thing that mattered was being near each other. Even after my dad left, my mom, on those rare occasions she felt like talking about it, would still get that hint of bliss in her eye as she explained about Camp Minnehaha and that night by the campfire when Bill Waterman, a cute senior from McClintock High, asked her out.

Of course, Colin was not yet my boyfriend, but as I walked out of the library to get some lunch at the Cougareat, I couldn't help smiling as I thought of how it might be one day, the two of us walking hand in hand, playing the remember game. "Remember," he'd say, "how glad I was to see you in that hallway, how terrified I was to take that class?"

We would both laugh and swing our interlocked hands high, as if in practice for the day when there would be a child between us, clutching our hands and shouting, "One, two, three!" "But remember," I'd say to him, "how I didn't need to take that class, but only took it to spend time with you."

Obviously touched by my thoughtful and giving nature, Colin would reach out and touch my cheek, then say with a laugh, "And remember Miss Snell?"

"How could I forget?" I'd say, then roll my eyes and smile.

"And the obnoxious way she'd say, 'Class, write this down'?"

And shrugging my shoulders, I'd tease him and say, "Miss Snell? Are you sure? I don't remember her ever saying that," which, of course, would make him laugh, marvel at my resilience, and kiss me.

I swung the door open to the Wilkinson Center, and all I can say is, I shouldn't have felt responsible, but I did. I mean, the fact that I had been thinking about kissing Colin did in no cosmic way compel Phil to lean forward as I walked toward him and kiss the girl next to him. There was no correlation. Still, I was mad at myself and even madder at Phil, so I guess it's not surprising that the first thing I said to him was, "What are you thinking?"

Phil abruptly ended that little kisseroo and sprang up from the table where they were sitting. "Hey, ho, Whims!" he said, followed by a surprisingly long, "Uhhhhhhhh."

Completely ignoring the girl, I said to Phil, "We need to talk," and then headed back out the door and waited for him to follow.

I could see him through the glass door, talking to that girl, imploring her to stay, probably telling her everything was fine and that he'd be back in a moment to pick up where they had left off, but it looked like she wasn't willing to buy it, and she grabbed her backpack and left. He watched her for a second as she sped off in the direction of the bookstore, then headed outside to talk to me with an I-can-explain-this look on his face. As if.

The look bugged me so much I started walking away from him before he even had a chance to get near me. "Hey!" he said as he ran up to me. "Don't worry, Whims. Everything's cool."

This made me stop cold. Looking straight ahead to avoid that stupid look on his face, I asked as calmly as I could, "How do you figure everything's cool?"

He shrugged and said what he must have thought was so obvious. "What I'm saying is, I can explain—"

Finishing his sentence for him, I said, "Why you were kissing that girl? Who is she? What's her name?"

Still sporting the I-can-explain-this look, he said, "Well, I don't know. I was just going to ask her that when you walked up."

Had he tried, he couldn't have said something that would have bugged me more, and I growled at the sky and stormed off again.

"Wait!" said Phil, rushing after me. "Whims, all I've got is ninety-six days, ninety-seven max!"

That, as you can imagine, persuaded me to stop. That and the big crowd in front of us gathered to hear some guy on a box making some stupid point. "To live?" I asked.

"Um, define *live*." I glared at Phil, and he decided to skip the definition. "Okay, this is the situation. I sent in my mission papers last week, which means I'm going on a mission."

"You're kidding," I said, my voice dripping with sarcasm.

"You got to hear me out on this one. A mission is like a freakin' desert. You've got to get ready before you try to cross it. You know what I mean?"

I let out a deep breath in an effort to stay calm. "And how does kissing Jane Doe help you prepare to cross that desert?"

"Well, let me put it to you this way. Chiara's awesome, really awesome, but she's clear over there in Italy, and I'm clear over here, and in the meantime—and don't walk off again—I've got a canteen to fill before I cross that two-year desert."

"Okay, I'm filing that under one of the stupidest things I've ever heard."

"If you were going on a mish, I think you'd understand."

"Well," I said, noticing that the guy on the box had stepped down, "since you think you're making a ton of sense, why not share your theory with everyone here?"

Showing zero sign of embarrassment, Phil said, "Whatever," and went to stand on the box.

Still hoping that the stupidity of what he was about to say would make him lose his nerve, I moved to the front of the crowd to hear Mr. Logic give his spiel. "Before you go into the desert," he said without hesitation, "you fill your canteen, am I right?" A guy near me applauded, and I gave him a cold stare. "Whether we like to admit it or not, entering a mission is no different than entering Death Valley, and there are certain things you gotta stockpile if you're gonna make it through. I'm of the opinion that some *quality* time with the ladies is one of those things. I'm not talking anything you gotta go bang on the bish's door for, but just some female interaction, a few, okay, maybe more than a few nice, sweet kisses to tide you over until you reach the other side." The blasé crowd was suddenly pumped, and though there were a few boos to be heard, for the most part, they were cheering.

"I'm a man with a canteen!" yelled Phil.

"Yes, you are!" shouted someone.

"Dude!" shouted another.

As many of the guys in the crowd started chanting, "Canteen! Canteen!" Phil said over their roar, "And I intend to fill that canteen as high as I can before I report for my two-year stint of duty, sir!"

The cheering was more than I could take, and all I wanted was to get out of there. But before leaving, I walked over to Phil, who was still standing on the box, soaking up the applause, and I said to him, "Well, Chiara thought you were more than that. She definitely thought you were more than that," and stayed just long enough to watch the smile drain from his face.

* * *

Elder Matt Hollingsworth
Casilla 28, Las Condes
Santiago 10, Chile

Hey Elder H,

I know I should ask how you're doing, but I sort of want to cut to the chase. Not to get your mind off doing missionary work, but I've got a question for you. Phil just explained to me about how before a guy leaves on his mission, he needs to make sure that in addition to packing enough socks and white shirts, he has to cram as many kisses as he can into some stupid imaginary canteen. He said it's because the mission, at least when it comes to female affection, is nothing but sand dunes and spitting camels, and so if a missionary is going to survive for two years in this kind of desert, he's gotta make sure his canteen is overflowing. So the question I have for you is this: since you never bothered to kiss me before you entered the desert, where exactly were you filling your canteen? Just curious. W

P.S. Keep up the good work.

chapter 14

To: Chiarissima@italnet.com
From: Whims1@byu.edu

Hey Girlie,

Just got a call from Colin! No lie, every time the phone rings I hope it's him, and this time it really was. He wants me to meet him tomorrow afternoon to look at his paper. Jill's gonna kill me because we're supposed to go find her a cornucopia (this horn-shaped thing you stuff vegetables in at Thanksgiving time). Don't ask me why she wants one; she just does, and I promised her I'd go. But hey, I'm sure Josh won't mind if I'm not there. Anyway, just wanted to tell you the good news! See ya, W

* * *

The dance at the Wilkinson Center had been more fun than I expected, and even though I had to get up early the next morning to make those toilets shine, I didn't mind Chloe and Jill following us into our room to hang out for a while. It felt like we needed a moment to wind down, and besides, I was getting to the point where sleep was becoming optional. Well, almost.

"Geez," said Chloe as she sat down on my bed and glanced at the scriptures lying open on Pudge's desk, "why not highlight what *isn't* important and save yourself some trouble?"

Pudge laughed, but I could tell she felt embarrassed. "I do tend to treat them like a coloring book," she said, and reached over to shut them.

"Hey, at least you're reading them, Pudge," said Jill as she shoved Chloe with her foot. "I've been trying to help my wanna-be apostate roommate here by reading the scriptures at night together, but we've been on 'My father dwelt in a tent' for what, five or six weeks now?"

"Feels like seven," mumbled Chloe.

"But then again," said Jill, "it is a deep scripture. There's lots to ponder. Plus, it usually gets us talking about camping and how much we hate everything about it."

"Especially the way dirt always seems to get in your food," said Chloe.

"Wow," I said to them both, "sounds spiritual," which made Jill feel justified in pelting me in the head with a few M&Ms off of Pudge's desk.

"Ten-second rule," I announced, and picked the M&Ms off the ground and popped them in my mouth.

"What are you talking about?" asked Jill. "It's a five-second rule, and you took way too long, so my guess is you're gonna die from something like candy botulism any second now."

"Well," I said, "then it was nice knowing you."

"Ooh," said Jill with excitement, "speaking of funerals, I just remembered something I wanted to tell you guys. Can I, Chloe?" Chloe shrugged a "whatever," and Jill said, "Chloe, despite her hostility toward skirts and dresses—"

"I'm not hostile. I just question conformity."

"Whatever. Anyway, Chloe here is going to sing in church this Sunday."

"Whoa," I said, completely surprised. I mean, sure, I had told Kay about Chiara's idea, but I never thought in a million, make that a trillion, years Chloe would say yes to it. As I thought of the key behind-the-scenes role I had played in the whole thing, a leafy vine of pride began to sprout inside me, and I couldn't help but consider how good it felt to have made a difference.

Pudge's eyes looked as if they'd been dipped in red Jell-O, which left little doubt she was bone tired. Still, she was as upbeat as ever. "Oh my heck!" she cried.

"We gotta somehow cure you of saying that," mumbled Jill. "It not only grates, it makes me feel like I'm hanging with Donny and Marie."

I shook my head as if to say that though I had known Jill my whole life, there were still things about her even I couldn't explain, and Pudge continued her squealing. "That is so incredibly awesome," she said stifling a yawn. "I can't wait to hear you sing."

"Yeah, me too," I said with loads of enthusiasm.

It almost looked like a smile was threatening to appear on Chloe's face, but she was quick to downplay her church gig. "It's no big deal," she said. "I sang all the time in the garage with my band and even at a couple of gigs at bowling alleys before coming up here. It's been a long time, though, since I've sung in church. I don't know, maybe since Primary, and honestly, at first when they asked me, I wasn't going to do it. I mean, essentially I find hymns trite."

"Don't we all," said Jill as she lay down and put her head on my pillow. "Nothing but 'Do the right thing, blah, blah, blah.'"

"But then, you know, I started thinking about it being the Sunday before Thanksgiving, and the pilgrims and—"

"I told her I'd pay her twenty-five bucks if she did it," said Jill, her head snuggled down into my pillow and her eyes closed.

"Well, that too," whispered Chloe.

"So typical," I said as I shoved Jill for making my pride vine wither and die. "Why do you think everything has a price?"

Jill opened one eye. "Because it nearly always does. But hey," she said, "don't be mad at me. I mean, if Special Kay hadn't butted in and insisted on making it a duet, I wouldn't have had to cough up a quarter."

"Kay's singing too?" I asked. Considering how much Kay bugged Chloe, I was suddenly surprised she settled for twenty-five.

Pudge's head was now propped in her hands. "Kay does have a beautiful voice," she said, her eyes halfway closed. "And it carries so well."

"So would yours if you kept a cordless microphone in your pocket," said Jill, making us laugh. Even though it was obvious she was joking, she said as emphatically as she could, "You guys, I'm totally serious," which made us laugh more.

I looked at the clock then, and without saying anything, slid Jill's feet over to the ground and pulled her up. "I take it that's your subtle way of telling me it's time to go," she said as she rubbed her eyes.

"I think I'm just gonna sleep here tonight," said Chloe, grabbing one of Pudge's floral pillows and snuggling down in.

Pudge laughed, but it sounded more like she was on the edge of tears. "Uh, sure, if that's what you want," she said, obviously trying to be a good sport.

Chloe sat up and stretched. "I'm just joking. Girl, you're way too nice. I need to teach you how to say no."

"I know," said Jill as I opened the door and pushed her out. "We could do a joint oh-my-heck detox and just-say-no seminar. What do you think?"

Knowing somehow Pudge was with me, I slammed the door shut and we both shouted, "No!"

* * *

Even Jill thought Chloe did it on purpose. In fact, she was convinced of it.

"She never planned to sing a single note," said Jill as she jammed one last pair of jeans into her bulging duffle bag. "From the get-go she looked at it as a chance to protest."

"Protest what?" I asked, trying to squeeze the zipper together so she could zip.

"Who knows, maybe that the sacrament cups aren't biodegradable? The girl's got a bone to pick with just about everything," she said, and gave the zipper an enormous tug.

"I'm telling you, Jill, you weren't looking at her eyes," I said, still wrestling with that zipper. "Something happened, I don't know what, but I swear she didn't do it on purpose, and do you really need to take this much stuff to go home for Thanksgiving?"

One last tug and the zipper was zipped. "Hey, I am packing light. Spot's staying here."

I looked over at Jill's enormous stuffed lucky kangaroo crammed next to the window and said, "Are you sure you can handle that?"

She hefted her duffle bag onto her shoulder and said, "It's just a long weekend, Whims. Besides, Meals on Wheels are going to be in the back." She meant Nils and Wills Skousen, twins from our ward back home whose greatest hope was to one day take the professional wrestling world by storm, and needless to say, they had the bulk to do it. With a hint of real concern, she said, "Just make sure no one steals him."

"I'll be on the lookout for stuffed-kangaroo thieves."

I looked outside and saw Josh's Mustang pull into the parking lot. "He's here," I said.

She gave Spot a lucky punch and said, "Walk slow. He's told me one too many times he wants to make it to Page, Arizona, by noon."

After Jill checked a couple times to make sure the door was locked, we headed (slowly) for the stairs. Returning back to what we had originally been talking about, Jill said, "I still say she did it on purpose."

"Maybe she—"

"I don't know what you thought you saw, but from where I sat, and come to think of it I was sitting right next to you, her look was defiant."

"I see where you're coming from, but isn't it possible that—"

"Whims, she was just being belligerent. By the way, I like that word. I have to admit it though, it was kind of worth it to have Special Kay up there singing the alto part to . . ."

"Um, 'For the Beauty of the Earth.'"

"That's right, and getting so mad," Jill said, and smiled as she relived the moment. "I'd never seen a person simultaneously sing and grit their teeth. It was classic. But I'm glad she didn't ask me about the cash, because I wouldn't have given it to her. Well, maybe $12.50 for ticking off Kay, but that would have been it."

"All I'm saying is, it looked to me like she was taken by surprise."

Even walking as slow as we could, we had already arrived at the first-floor exit. Jill stopped and, with her hand on the stairwell door, said, "You actually think she had stage fright? Girl, we need to get your eyes checked. There's no way that's it. Her fists were clenched, her eyes were fierce. She was just being, as they say in Utah, *ignernt.*"

There wasn't time to say any more. Jill pushed the door open and there was Josh, rubbing his hands together as if in an effort to make Jill hustle. As soon as he saw us, he gave Jill a huge smile and took her bulging-beyond-normal-capacity duffle bag. "Hey, Jet," he said, a nickname he'd given Jill after seeing her fly toward the vault in practice.

Jill skipped hi and thanks and said, "Don't mention you want to be to Page by noon or I swear I'll buy the largest drink they sell and the whole trip will be nothing but pit stops."

Josh put his hands in the air as if in surrender, and we walked (slowly) outside.

The twins were already squashed into the backseat, and to just look at them made me feel claustrophobic. There was definitely no room for Spot. Meals on Wheels nodded hello and contentedly continued downing Doritos.

"Be careful," I said, and gave Jill a hug.

"We'll try," she said, "but we gotta be to Page by noon or, who knows, maybe the universe will explode." She looked over at Josh, who wisely said nothing. "You're the one I'm worried about, stuck here with your mom and Keppy."

"It's just as well I'm sticking around," I said. "Mom really wanted me to stay, and besides, I'll be able to finish interviewing that lady I was telling you about."

"Madam Cranky Pants?"

"That's the one."

"Sounds like you're in for a loser holiday. But hey, if you look mopey enough, ten bucks says your mom will take you shopping." I gave Jill my mopiest look, and she said, "A little more lip, maybe." Josh cleared his throat, his gentle way of telling Jill it was time to go. Jill rolled her eyes, hugged me, and said in my ear before climbing into the car, "First gas station we stop at, I'm getting a seventy-two ouncer."

"Bye, Josh," I said as we hugged. Strange, I thought, how a year ago hugging Josh would have left my head spinning, and now it was like hugging my brother—if I had one, I mean.

"Take care, Whims."

"Good luck playing Arizona State this weekend."

"That I'm not worried about," he said as he walked over to his side of the car. "It's getting out of the doghouse with you-know-who that's got me sweatin'."

I crossed my fingers to wish him luck, then stayed in the parking lot waving until they were gone.

* * *

To: Chiarissima@italnet.com
From: Whims1@byu.edu

Chiara,

The fumes from the sink cleanser I use at the museum must be starting to get to me. I was just about to ask what you're doing for Thanksgiving break. Duh. Plymouth Rock is over here. Anyway, I thought I'd write you before I headed over to Mom and Keppler's for a not *fun-filled weekend. I'm such a complainer. I mean, I know they both go out of their way to make me feel at home. But still, it's just awkward for me to be there. That's okay though. I can handle it for a few days anyway. :)*

I know you've been wondering how things went with Chloe. Trouble is, I don't really know what to tell you because she didn't sing. Yes, she agreed to do it and even stood in front of the entire ward, but when it came time to actually sing, she didn't. She just stood there. Jill thinks she did it on purpose, that she was just being a jerk. I'm not so sure. I guess it's possible that's what happened, but I swear she looked like she was ready to sing and then, bam, something took her by surprise—like they switched hymns on her at the last second.

But Jill's most likely right; Chloe did probably mean to do it. I guess the important thing is we at least tried. Who knew she'd be so hard to reach? Take care, Whimsy

* * *

To: anglertomax@mapleleaf.com
From: Whims1@byu.edu

Have fun ice fishing with your dad and brothers over Thanksgiving break. Sounds like a blast. We'll dive into the research paper when you get back. Whimsy.

* * *

"Mom, Whimsy's looking at me," Hudson said, and poked me in the knee.

Mom laughed a little, but Merriwether was not amused. She was sitting between Hudson and me in the back of Keppler's spacious Lincoln Continental, but the way she was behaving, you would have thought she was sandwiched between Meals on Wheels. "Hudson, please put a stop to the dull-witted humor, and would it kill you to open the window like I asked?"

"Only if I crawl through it," mumbled Hudson as the window went down, letting in a burst of cold air.

The chill made Mom curl up a little more in the front seat, and I watched as Keppler again and again glanced over at her, a look of concern on his face.

"Would you like me to turn on the air conditioning?" asked Keppler.

"Actually, I doubt that would help, Stanley," said Merriwether, talking to him as if she were his bud. "I'm just feeling a bit cooped up."

Mom put her limp head on Keppler's shoulder, and I watched as he leaned over and kissed it, a still semi-weird sight. Of course, going to the country club for Thanksgiving dinner was not the original plan. Mom had wanted to orchestrate one of her Thanksgiving extravaganzas for all of us (major yum) and had even done most of the shopping for it when she got hit by the flu. Mom is hardly ever sick, and so she really doesn't have any experience with slowing down. Keppler tried to get her to stay home and rest, but she wouldn't hear of it. "I'll be all right," she had said. "Really, once we get there, I'll be fine."

Keppler had had enough of cold air pouring in on his sick wife, and without apology closed the window. This, of course, Merriwether took as her cue to complain about other things. "Your feet are too large, Hudson."

"I'll get right on it."

"And why must you jangle your keys? It only reminds me we could have followed behind in your car."

"But you wanted Thanksgiving togetherness."

"What I wanted was the window down," she mumbled so quietly I could barely hear her. Merriwether then leaned forward and in a bright but edgy voice said, "Stanley, I really can't think of any other way to put this, but are we there yet?"

"We'll be there soon enough," said Keppler as he glared at Merriwether in the rearview mirror. *If you were his student, he'd be turning you into scrap metal right now,* I thought, *which, come to think of it, might be just what you need.*

"So sis—" said Hudson.

"Please, Hudson, don't talk directly into my ear," interrupted Merriwether.

Leaning forward, Hudson continued. "You should come up sometime and go skiing."

"Thanks, but I don't think so. I mean, I've never done it before, and—"

"Whoa, back up," said Hudson. "You've never skied before? Ever?"

Why was he acting like I'd just confessed something major, like I'd never learned to write my name? "Never," I said. "It didn't snow much in Phoenix while I was growing up."

Mom turned her head, and it startled me to see how pale she looked. "That was something I always meant to do with you but never did. Sorry about that, sweetie," she said, and sunk back down onto Keppler's shoulder.

"Well," said Hudson, "you're going to have to come up, and I'll teach you. In fact, a few of the runs are open already. You could drive up with us and stay the weekend."

"Hudson," scolded Merriwether, "you're forgetting we have plans."

"But this is a family emergency," said Hudson with that wry smile of his. "I have a sister who doesn't know how to ski."

As much as I wanted to throw a wrench into whatever Merriwether had cooked up for the weekend, the truth was I was busy. "I wish I could take you up on it," I said, "but I've got an interview on Saturday with this lady, Sable Thompson Greer, and—"

Merriwether's laughter cut me off. "You're interviewing Sable Thompson Greer. That's hysterical, really."

Okay, I thought, *so her name isn't the best, but it's nowhere near as bad as yours. And why in the world are you acting like I said I'm interviewing the Queen of England?* "It's no big deal. She's just an old lady I'm interviewing for my freshman English class."

"You're interviewing Sable Thompson Greer for a freshman English class?" spat out Merriwether. "Journalists from every major paper have tried for ages to get her to talk, and yet you say she's spilling the beans for a college undergrad. It's too ridiculous."

I had a feeling that if I said, "Why is it so unbelievable that I'm interviewing her? All she talks about is her garden," Merriwether would have thrown her head back and laughed. Obviously, Sable Thompson Greer had more to say than what time of year to plant turnips, and the fact that she hadn't was just one of those details Merriwether didn't need to know. "But I am interviewing her," I said, a little louder than necessary and directly into her ear.

"Whimsy," said Merriwether, sounding quite smug, "I don't doubt you're interviewing someone claiming to be Sable Thompson Greer, but, darling, the poor dear must be delusional. Today, she says she's Sable Thompson Greer. Perhaps tomorrow she'll introduce herself as Cleopatra. It's the only logical answer, because Sable Thompson Greer has a strict policy of—"

"Not giving interviews," I said. "I know. She told me that when we first met, but she said she'd make an exception for me." Merriwether clucked her tongue, no doubt thinking that was exactly what all the sham Sable Thompson Greers say.

"Sweetie," said Mom, turning slowly around, "Sable Thompson Greer is internationally famous."

"There are places in the world that celebrate her birthday," said Keppler, taking a quick look at me as if trying to detect from my expression if I was telling the truth.

"Her portrait is hanging in the Smithsonian," offered Hudson. "Don't ask me who told me that," he added.

"Well," said Merriwether, "whoever told you that was wrong. Her portrait is in the National Gallery. It's called *The Cane Picture.*"

It was almost like I spoke when I just meant to think. "She still uses that cane today," I said, and when I noticed all eyes were on me, even Mom's sick, droopy ones, I decided to say more. "It's beautiful, with lots of stuff carved on it. At the top it's mostly animals, the kind you'd find in Africa, and as you go down, there's a pagoda, which just in case you don't know," I said while glancing at Hudson's know-it-all girlfriend, "is one of those funky Far Eastern towers, and there are other things too, like the Eiffel Tower, and airplanes, lots of them, and paratroopers, and at the very bottom is, I don't know what you'd call it, I guess a motto, but it says, 'This burden lifted.'"

It was a beautiful thing, the stunned look on Merriwether's face. "Captain Lawrence Glengarry's cane," she said.

"Yep," I said as we pulled into the country club's parking lot, "the very one. You know, I can't wait to see what this lady comes up with when she decides to be Cleopatra," then gave her a ha!-I'm-right grin and got out of the car.

chapter 15

Elder Matt Hollingsworth
Casilla 28, Las Condes
Santiago 10, Chile

Elder H,

How was I to know that the canteen theory wasn't a universal guy thing? You should have seen all the guys cheering Phil on. Every time I see him, he mentions that afternoon and how good it felt to be up there making his point as the crowd went wild. He says it's made him realize that his calling in life is politics, which, according to Phil, means my catching him kissing what's-her-name was meant to be, and consequently a good thing. He only gets flustered when I ask if he thinks Chiara would see it that way. I didn't tell Chiara about that whole smoochy afternoon. I was going to, but then Phil came over to my dorm begging me not to say anything, and I figured since there isn't anyone for her to date in Italy anyway, I'd cut him some slack. But I can't help wondering if by doing so I'm being a bad friend to Chiara. This is definitely one of those situations where it feels like you can't win. Anyway, thanks for clarifying that not all guys fill a canteen before the mish, which is not to say that you weren't free to do a little canteen filling before you marched into that dateless horizon. After all, you made it clear before you left we shouldn't consider ourselves an item. So, for the record, I'd like to say I've never enjoyed myself more spending time with anyone who meant less to me.

Not that you asked or are even interested, but since I've got your undivided attention (I'm assuming anyway), I thought I'd tell you about Sable Thompson Greer. She's this old crank I've been interviewing and *have recently found out, of all things, is famous. I met her while out running one day, a fact that I'm going to count on you not teasing me about in your next letter. I know you asked me to go running with you tons of times during the summer and I wouldn't, but back then I wasn't puffing up on cafeteria starch. Anyway, the end of Sable's cane was stuck in the road, and because I helped her get it out, she decided to let me interview her.*

I didn't have a clue she was famous. I was just trying to find someone to interview for an English assignment. But now I know, only she's doesn't know I know, you know? Just joking. Anyway, so I've been meeting with her for a couple months now, and she never mentions anything about her life except for pieces of her childhood in Eureka, Utah, and bits about caring for her mother in her old age.

As you can imagine, what made her famous wasn't spoon-feeding her mom. The chunk of her life that everyone wants to know about is the part she doesn't mention. Sure, she tells me all about the benefits of putting horse manure around roses, but she never says a thing about her life in Europe. It's weird to think that a girl from a no-name town like Eureka even ended up over there, but from what I've read about her on the Internet, Sable knew early on in life she wanted to go to Europe and write. And when her parents said she couldn't, she stole the money from her dad (not that this makes it right, but he was very wealthy) and bought a one-way ticket to France. She wanted to be a journalist in Paris, but must have run into some roadblocks because she ended up modeling for a while. And, yes, she was a knockout.

The facts about how she was able to finally shift from modeling to journalism are sketchy, and even sketchier is how she became involved in the French Resistance, but by the time the Germans had occupied France, Sable, who passed herself off as French, was making German heads turn at the Parisian nightclubs (weird that they were still operating) and using whatever information they started spilling after a few drinks to help the Resistance.

Apparently one of the things the French Resistance did was help downed Allied airmen find their way to safety, hiding them in a series of safe houses along secret trails. Again, few details are known, but somehow Sable met this British pilot named Lawrence Glengarry, whose plane had been shot down near Normandy. All we know (I say "we" like I'm a member of a team of researchers) is that instead of hustling on down the trail to safety, Glengarry stayed behind. What happened to him after that is completely unknown. We do know, however, that Sable, when asked a few years after the war to have her portrait done, insisted that she have a cane across her lap. All she ever said about it was that it belonged to Captain Glengarry, and she still uses it today, even though her gnarled fingers have a hard time holding onto the shiny brass handle.

I suppose I should consider it an honor that I have the chance to get to know her. She really has lived an amazing life, but she's such a grump and tends to go on forever about plants and stuff. Speaking of going on forever, I've gotta cut this off. But I'm glad you're over there in Chile listening. Love, W

P.S. Assuming you're out there doing good work, which I'm sure you are, I'd just like to say, keep it up!

* * *

I was beginning to think there was something wrong with my brain. It seemed like historical facts and math formulas (you know, the kind of info destined to end up on a test) had to be continually pried from the caverns of my memory, but humiliating moments large and small were always fresh and ready for retrieval. Truth was, they tended to pop up on their own, for no reason at all, leaving me mortified anew when I least expected it. As I headed into finals week, fear started mounting inside me that perhaps at the end of four years at BYU, all I'd be able to remember about my collegiate experience would be the stupider things I had done. And if that were the case, one thing was certain: there'd be no escaping the memory of Miss Snell's final exam.

I know it sounds like I blew off studying for Snell's exam, but honestly, that wasn't the case. Colin and I spent a lot of time together getting ready for that final (happy sigh). So much time, in fact, that I was convinced signing up for a class I didn't need was one of the smartest moves I'd ever made—until, that is, I looked at the final. It was a pretty straightforward test, I have to admit. Trouble was, when Snell had told us to be sure and study our notes, I had thought she meant the parts that dealt with the class material. However—and rude she didn't make it more clear—Snell had meant everything, even the random info she had annoyingly prefaced throughout the semester with "Write this down." The same stuff, in other words, that I had completely ignored.

As a result, there were eleven questions that had me completely stumped. And as I tried to wrack my brain for the right answers, the classroom became as loud and distracting (at least to me) as the trading floor of the New York Stock Exchange. Pencils scratching on papers, chair legs squeaking against the linoleum floor, the occasional cough, Snell's irritating "adieu" as students handed in their completed exams, and even Colin's sniffle all seemed meant to distract me and jar my nerves. However, Colin handing in his exam and leaving the classroom didn't help to settle things down in my head; it made things worse. I mean, not only was I then frustrated about those eleven questions, I was humiliated that Colin had finished his exam before me (after all, I was supposed to be the English whiz) and had most likely motored on out of the JKHB without looking back, happy to resume a life that didn't include English papers or me. It was no use trying to remember stuff I had deliberately ignored, so after struggling for a few minutes more, I wrote down some hasty guesses and was bid a Snelly adieu.

To my surprise (I was going to say "and delight" but figured that sounded lame), Colin hadn't bolted from the building. As soon as I walked outside the classroom, I saw him sitting in the hallway studying and (hopefully) waiting for me.

As I walked toward him, Colin closed his math book and smiled, and not to be picky, but it was a slightly irritating smile, especially considering what I'd just been through. It was the kind of smile that clearly said, "Hey, I just cruised through a test and couldn't feel better." "So how'd you feel it went, eh?"

"Fine," I said, sounding like I had something to hide. "And how'd it go for you?"

"Fantastic," said Colin as he got up off the ground, "and I am so relieved this is over with."

"Whew! I know what you mean," I said, and felt the beginnings of what I was sure would prove to be the Niagara Falls of humiliation begin to trickle down on top of me. After all, no way in a million years would Colin have taken that class just to hang out with me.

"Listen," said Colin as he pushed his hand through his hair, "I wish I could stay and talk, but I've got to go. My chemical engineering final is tonight."

Uh-huh, I thought. *Sure it is.*

"I just wanted to say thanks. You've been a big help to me, eh."

Yeah whatever, I thought, *just get to the part where you say "See ya later" and don't really mean it.*

"So I was wondering if over the holiday we could get together and do something."

"Are you kidding?" Durr! What I had meant to say was, "Aren't you going to be in Toronto?" But it had come off sounding like, "How dare you think I'd take time out of my precious Christmas holiday to be with you?"

Colin looked slightly worried. "Maybe you already have plans, but I was just thinking that since I'm going to be in Salt Lake for Christmas—my parents decided last minute to take a cruise to Panama—maybe we could meet up sometime."

"Sure," I said, wanting to quickly clarify things. "I'd love you—I mean, *to!* I'd love to, uh, do that." The one thing that was totally clear to me was that this was the kind of moment I'd never be able to forget.

Colin smiled and maybe even looked slightly relieved, making it occur to me that it takes guts for guys to ask girls out. "Great—but it will be my treat," he said, wagging his finger at me.

I don't know who first gave Colin the impression girls want to pay their own way, but I'd like to give them a piece of my mind. I mean, having a guy pay for my Slurpee or whatever doesn't make me feel like I'm indebted or anything. It just makes me think, "Cool, you're buying so this isn't costing me anything. That definitely works for me." But figuring it wasn't what he wanted to hear, I faked defeat. "All right," I said. "If you insist."

Colin slung his backpack over his shoulder. "And I do," he said.

I knew he needed to leave, and, of course, now I wish I would have just said, "See ya." But at the time, chatting a little longer seemed harmless enough, so I casually asked what his brothers and sisters were doing for Christmas, unknowingly setting myself up for yet another memorable moment.

"I guess I didn't tell you, eh? They're all married with families of their own. I'm the youngest."

And here it came. "Me too," I said like a complete idiot. "I mean, I'm the youngest . . . er, and the oldest." I managed to smile though I wanted to disintegrate.

"Aw, Whimsy, you sure make me laugh."

"Thanks. You make me laugh too," I said, returning what I'm sure he thought was a compliment.

But it was a lie. I knew it and was afraid Colin knew it, so I was majorly relieved when he said, "Thanks; that means a lot to me. Back in high school, I was kind of quiet. In fact, my senior year I was voted most likely to become a librarian, I guess because I didn't talk much. But my mission and college really helped me get out of my shell."

And I'm sure you'll be a lot more chatty once I've had a chance to pry open that shell of yours a bit more, I thought. *And besides, you couldn't have been too quiet if people knew you well enough to nominate you for something.*

As if sensing what I was thinking, Colin said, "Actually, not many people knew my name in high school, so they just wrote *the guy who wears turtlenecks* on the ballot. Funny, but I hardly ever wear turtlenecks anymore, I guess because you can't see my puka shells if I do."

"Gotta love those puka shells," I said, hoping it was just a puka phase he was going through.

Colin looked at his watch. "I've got to run, but I'll be giving you a call," he said.

"That'll be great," I said.

Colin started to walk away, then turned around one last time. "Oh, and thanks again for all your help."

"It was nothing," I said, knowing it was a good thing my name wasn't Pinocchio. "Really, it was nothing."

* * *

As unusual as it was for Mom to call in the middle of finals week and invite me to lunch, I did my best to sound uninterested. "I don't know. I'm really swamped right now," I said, hoping that stung just a little.

I wasn't trying to bulldoze her with my chilliness, just bug her a little, but for some reason she didn't seem strong enough for even a mild cold shoulder. "I promise it won't take too long," she said in a shaky voice. "Just an hour. We'll even stay on campus to save time."

"I really don't have an hour to spare right now" was on the tip of my tongue, and if she had sounded a little more peppy, I would have said it. But instead I let out a deep breath into the phone to let her know I was far from thrilled and said, "All right, just an hour."

"Terrific," she said, her voice rallying a bit. "Let's plan on the Skyroom at noon."

Trying my best to sound put out, I said, "I'll be there."

* * *

I had never been to the Skyroom before, but as I climbed the stairs to the sixth floor of the Wilkinson Center (elevators are for people who don't eat bacon for breakfast), I couldn't help thinking of Matt and the night he found me sobbing and miserable and determined to hike to the Y. Having just waited tables at some swanky reception in the Skyroom, Matt was dressed in a tuxedo, but that didn't stop him from getting in my car when I told him where I was heading. I realize (now anyway) that hiking alone at night wasn't the most levelheaded decision, but at the time, I really didn't care. I just wanted to get to a place where I could figure out my life, and I guess Matt just wanted to make sure I got there safely.

That night it had felt like I'd discovered my world had been built on a fault line, and everything that had once seemed permanent was shaking and shifting around me. And one of the things that definitely had me quaking in my boots was the realization that Mom and Keppler loved each other. I sensed that their relationship was going to rock my world, and now, less than a year later, I was walking into the Skyroom to have lunch with Mrs. Joan Keppler. Weird. Up at the Y that night, Matt had tried to tell me to keep my eyes on what he called the big picture (it's a long story). The thing is, when it came to Mom and Keppler, I just couldn't help feeling like all they wanted in their "big picture" was the two of them, regardless of how hard they tried to make me feel otherwise.

As soon as I walked in the Skyroom, I saw Mom looking radiant but tired in a red cardigan and talking to some dark suit. Their conversation ended, thank goodness, before I got over there. I didn't really feel like dealing with introductions. Not that I was in a bad mood. It was more of a mush mood, or whatever you call it when your brain is fried from cramming for finals. As soon as Mom saw me, she walked toward me, gave me a hug, and kissed my cheek while I stood as still as a totem pole. "Thanks for coming, sweetie," she said, and showed me our table.

We sat down and I shrugged a "whatever."

"I'm really glad you came," she said, the quiver in her voice making me look up with alarm. My mom was fighting back tears.

Why is it that when you're starving, waiters take forever, but when you're not really that hungry and your mom's on the verge of crying and you want to ask her what the heck's wrong, they're at their most efficient? Mom had barely a chance to blot her eyes with her napkin when the waiter sped over to take our order. Somehow Mom managed to look absolutely normal, even carefree. "Mom," I said as soon as the waiter was out of earshot, "what's the matter?"

The tears instantly started welling up again. "Sweetheart, I know my marrying Stanley has been a tough adjustment for you," she said, and then couldn't speak for a while she was so choked up. Well, I don't know about the rest of you, but when my mom sobs I listen, and what's more, whatever it is she wants is hers. "Sorry," she said, blotting her eyes again with her mascara-stained napkin and then smiling a little. "I had forgotten how emotional I get when . . . It's just been so long since—"

"Since I've been by to see you," I said. "I know. I've acted like a detached jerk, but I've missed you too, which is probably hard to believe considering the way I've treated you, but in a way it might actually be good that I've ignored you because it's given the two of you your space, which I'm figuring you both want—"

Our overachieving waiter trotted over to our table with rolls and pads of butter. "Is there anything else I can do for you?" he asked.

Yeah, you can beat it, I thought as I politely said, "I don't think so." As he sped off to dote on his other tables, I said, "Anyway, Mom. I didn't want to make you cry."

"Honey," she said as I handed her my napkin, "you haven't made me cry. I just don't want to upset you any more than I already have." Then her voice got caught in another flood of tears.

Trying to make her laugh, I said, "Mom, don't worry. I bought a yoga video the other day, and even though I haven't watched it, just owning it makes me feel calmer, more centered. So don't worry about me, just tell me whatever it is." Just then our waiter as he hustled toward us with a pitcher of ice water, "Look," I said, "could you just cut it with the quality service? We're trying to talk!"

"Very sorry to have interrupted," he said as calmly as a seasoned diplomat, then placed the pitcher of water on our table and left.

Mom gave me a disapproving look. "I know," I said. "I'll apologize to him later. So anyway, where were we?"

"You were just telling me how calm you are."

"Baby steps, Mom, but it's progress. So tell me what—"

"Sweetie, I'm pregnant."

"Oh," I said. Neither of us spoke for a while after that. I guess I was still trying to absorb what she had said, and Mom was caught up in another rush of tears. I looked at her and felt what I can only describe as pity. Poor Mom. I'd never seen her so unstable before, and it was hard to not get out of my chair and give her a hug (I'm not one for public displays of affection). Anyway, I did what I could. As calmly as I could muster, I said, "Mom, you should have come to me sooner. But don't worry," I continued as I patted her hand, "we can work this out. We'll call the bishop, get your life back on track. I'll even spring for a copy of *The Miracle of Forgiveness*—"

"Silly girl," she said, tutting in disapproval, but she was clearly amused.

"Oh, that's right, I forgot, you're married. Whew, problem solved."

Mom let out a deep breath, obviously trying to get a grip on her emotions. "That's true. But, I have an eighteen-year-old daughter whom I love very much, and she hasn't been too happy with—"

"Where is she? I'll give her a piece of my mind . . . oh, wait a minute, that's me. I admit I've been hard to deal with since your wedding" (Mom gave me a look that said, "You have no idea"), "but it really was rotten of you to get sealed without consulting me first."

"Sweetie—"

"It just made me feel—" Now it was my turn to fight back tears, and, of course, just then our drinks arrived. I looked up at our waiter, confident I had done a great job of holding it all in. "Sorry for losing my temper," I said, not realizing that I looked like the world's most contrite customer.

"No worries," said the waiter, scrunching down to look me in the eye. "I forgive you." He patted my shoulder before walking off.

As soon as he was far enough away, I rolled my eyes and said, "Well, that's a load off." But as much as it bugged me being mistaken for someone who gives tearful apologies to waiters, I didn't mind the fact that the whole misunderstanding had left my mom giggling.

"So where were we?" she asked with a smile.

"No, let's not go back to it," I said. "It's too nice to see you smile. Just promise me the next time you get sealed you'll let me know." Mom shook her head at my silliness, but promised all the same. "So you really thought I'd be mad you're going to have a baby?" I asked as excitement over this new reality started to grow inside me.

"I didn't know what to think."

"Mom, I've only been begging for a little sister my entire life."

"I realize that, but still, you're in college now. I was afraid it might embarrass you."

"Only if she has Keppler's comb-over."

"Wilhelmina."

"So, speaking of Keppler, what does he think?"

Mom looked out the window as worry crept over her face. "I haven't told him yet," she said.

"Whoa. This sort of outdoes Jill's mom not mentioning fender benders."

"I wanted to tell you first, to make sure you were okay with it."

"I'm okay," I said. "So okay that it even surprises me a little. But a baby, Mom. You're going to have a baby!"

Mom smiled, then cradled her head in her hands. "I know," she said. "I can hardly believe it myself."

"So when are you going to tell Keppler?"

"Christmas Day," she said. "It's going to be his gift."

"Do you think he'll want to take it back?"

Just that quickly, a look of concern crossed her face. "I don't know. I really don't know how he'll feel. He's fifty, sweetie. That isn't exactly the age to take on late-night feedings and changing diapers."

"So, not to pry or anything, okay so maybe just a little, but was this planned?"

Mom laughed. "A complete surprise. After you, your dad and I tried to have another baby but couldn't, and I just assumed getting pregnant wasn't even a remote possibility."

"So how does it feel, being pregnant after so long?"

Mom's eyes welled up with tears. "Even the worst of it I'm cherishing this time. Does that sound crazy?"

"Sorta."

"It's true though. Every moment of it is so precious to me. Poor Stanley is walking on pins and needles. I'm so edgy and emotional."

"Nothing his students wouldn't say he deserves."

"It's true he's not exactly a soft touch in the classroom," said Mom, and laughed. "But he's a good man, sweetie. I just hope he won't mind—"

"Not grilling the preschool teacher?"

Mom smiled, and her worries about how Keppler would take the news seemed to momentarily flit away as we began talking about stuff like whether butter yellow was a boy or girl color, which bedroom should be the nursery, and why in the world she liked the name Wilhelmina well enough eighteen years ago to stick it on me.

"It's a beautiful name," she said, "but I have to tell you right up to the end it was a toss-up between that and Ava."

"Ava? Okay, Mom, you are not allowed to name this child."

Mom shook her head. "Honestly," she said as if I were the one tossing around grandma names.

I knew we had talked a long time but was shocked when she said it was nearly two.

"I didn't mean to keep you so long, sweetie, and neither of us have eaten much."

I looked around. Most of the tables were empty, and our waiter stood in the corner, doggie bags in hand and ready to pounce. "No biggie, Mom. I'm just glad we've talked. It's helped."

Mom smiled and touched my face, making me realize all the more how much I had missed her. "It definitely has."

"Look," I said as the waiter came sprinting toward us to wrap up our leftovers, "I've got to race over to Sable's, but I want to know what I can do to help, and don't say nothing because I want to do something."

Mom thought for a moment. "Well," she said, pulling a large stack of cream-colored envelopes from her briefcase, "there is something. I need to get these Christmas cards mailed. Could you do that for me?"

"That's it?" I said, practically disgusted. I mean, I wanted to do something big to help her.

"That's it for now," Mom said, grinning as she handed me the stack.

* * *

In spite of the wind and snow, I practically flew to Sable's house, thoughts of my little sister—and don't ask me how I knew she'd be a girl, I just knew—giving me unseen wings.

"You're late," growled Sable as she opened the door.

"Not in Tonga," I said. I learned early on the best way to deal with Sable's crankiness was to just make a joke of it, but today it didn't seem to be working.

She hobbled over to the fireplace, where kindling for a fire was laid. "No thought for decorum, no thought for common decency. You saunter in here when the mood strikes you and expect me to open my door."

"I tried the cat flap, but my hips wouldn't make it. So what are you doing?"

"Building a fire. It's cold outside, and I'd like a strong fire."

"On the living room rug?" I asked as the unlit match slipped from her fingers. "Listen, sit down in your Aunt Ruth's rocker and I'll take care of this."

She grumbled but looked tired, more tired than usual, and seemed relieved to have me take over. I helped Sable to her chair, and, as always, she began complaining as soon as she was comfortable. "I didn't need your arm. I could have done it myself," she huffed.

"Hey, every now and again I like to take a walk over to Aunt Ruth's rocker, and this was just one of those times," I said, marveling that I not only put up with her crankiness, but that it kind of cracked me up too.

Sable humphed in disapproval, and I sat down by the hearth to light the fire. A small log and a few crumpled newspapers were already in place, and I quickly did with my nimble, eighteen-year-old fingers what would have been a major task for Sable—lighting the match.

As the little fire began to crackle, Sable said in a voice struggling to maintain its gruffer quality, "There's more kindling there on the hearth."

I looked and saw a stack of old letters, at least a hundred all together, yellowed and torn in places, all bundled in a faded pink ribbon. I thought about saying, "Interesting kindling you got there, Sable," but sensed something was going on, something you didn't make light of. "You mean this pile of paper?" I asked.

"Do you see anything else lying about on the hearth that would stoke the fire?" she snarled.

"I guess not."

"Now throw them in one by one. I want to watch them burn," Sable said, and leaned back in her rocking chair and shut her eyes, but not soon enough to stop a renegade tear from sliding down her cheek.

I knew better than to ask what was wrong. She would have just told me to leave. And, more important, I knew better than to burn anything that had to do with her past. "All right," I said, "just doing a little spring cleaning in December. I can handle that," and while her eyes were still closed, and before I really had a chance to weigh the pros and cons of what I was doing, I quickly opened the flap to my backpack, stuck Sable's stack of letters in it, and pulled out Mom's Christmas cards, praying as I did (I know technically I was stealing and destroying U.S. mail, but I still prayed) that Sable's eyesight was as bad as I thought it was.

She opened her eyes, and I threw the first one in. "How's that?" I asked, hoping she didn't sense the fear in my voice.

"It is what it is," she said, and closed her eyes as another tear fell. "It is what it is."

chapter 16

To: Jillybean@azhot.com
From: Whims1@byu.edu

Hey Girlie,

Glad to hear you got home safe, but I can't tell you how much I wish I had been a part of that road trip. Not that I particularly want to be squashed between Meals on Wheels, but at this point I'd pretty much put up with anything to get out of the snow and the cold. If Brigham Young would have just hightailed it to southern California before announcing "This is the place," I'd be outside right now wearing shorts and throwing a frisbee instead of stuck inside all morning because of a raging blizzard. Things like this should be considered before Zion is established, dang it. So don't take this personally, but I miss the sun more than I miss you. You're a close second, but right now, seeing the sun again is all I care about.

For some reason Hudson is making it his personal mission to get me to love snow. Can you say fat chance? He's convinced if I learn to ski it's gonna change everything for me, and even announced he's coming down on Christmas Day to take me up to Park City for a couple days of skiing. I don't think her royal nagness, Merriwether, is too happy about it. I could hear her in the background when Hudson called, complaining. Come to think of it, she sort of reminds me of Sable.

Speaking of Sable, I'm still trying to figure out how to tell my mom I burned her Christmas cards. Can I please just tell her you burned them? She won't get as mad at you because you're not her daughter. Plus, you're in Arizona right now, so chances are by the time you get back, she'll pretty much be over it. Come on, girl. I took the blame in the fourth grade for your spit wads. My hand is still cramping from having to write "Spit wads are foul things" over and over. You owe me, but if you bring me back chips and salsa from Guad's, it will even the score a little.

So Josh is really going to wait until after winter semester to turn in his mission papers? For some reason I think it's a bad idea, but hey, what do I know. It just seems like it's going to get harder to give up the lime-light. I mean, besides pigeons (yawn), Josh and his chances of winning the Sugar Bowl are all Keppler talks about right now. And the look of satis-faction on my mom's face when she says Josh is from our stake back home, I'm telling you, I have yet to receive that look from her for the bang-up job I do keeping the lions dusted. Speaking of the Sugar Bowl, I can't believe your whole family is going. That ought to be fun, just you and your six brothers and sisters jammed into the back of your family's Suburban. You always did love family trips.

Oh, and since were talking about the joys of children, Melanie's due date is coming up. It's either January twenty-fifth or twenty-sixth. She's hoping, however, he (she wanted a girl) comes a few seconds after midnight on New Year's Day. Apparently, the hospital is giving away a year's supply of diapers to the first baby born in the new year. Yip yip yahoo. Girl, if I ever care that much about scoring a year's supply of diapers, organize a group intervention. But getting to my point: Mel is going to need some help with Tyson and McKenner after the baby is born, and guess what, Miss Popularity—Tyson wants you to watch him. It must be that subtle way you yank him away from the drinking fountain at church that won him over. I know you're going to be swamped when you come back, but think of it this way, spit wads are foul things. Ouch, my hands are cramping up again. Better go. Call or e-mail soon. Loads of love, W

P.S. I can't wait to tell you what I can't tell you! I know you want me to cave, but I'm not saying a word. You're just going to have to wait until Christmas.

* * *

Secrets are weird, or at least they make me feel weird. I mean, it's not like I set out to know about Phil's canteen-filling ways, Sable's amazing past, or even my mom's surprise pregnancy, but somehow I did, and keeping what I knew from others made me feel sneaky and transparent, as if even strangers on the street could look at me and tell something was up. And to make matters worse, I started to panic (especially around Keppler) that I might accidentally let something slip, like refer to my mom's "flu" as morning sickness and give it away. Or even look at her with too much enthusiasm. After all, Keppler is pretty savvy. I mean, Melanie's husband, Steve, who took a class from Keppler his first year of law school, swears the guy can look at his students and tell who didn't do their reading, and the fact that he makes a point of calling on those students has helped him earn his warm and fuzzy reputation.

So when Colin asked me to go out on Christmas Eve, not only was I glad, I was relieved, majorly relieved. I mean, it felt—and I know this is silly—like I'd just escaped a night chock-full of suspicion and scrutiny. And even though my mom wasn't too happy to have me take off, it was with her best interests in mind (okay, and mine too) that I decided the right thing for me to do was make myself scarce until Christmas morning, which is exactly what I did.

By the time Colin arrived at Keppler's house, the sun had already begun to sink behind the bleary mountains. It had been a useless sun anyway, giving off little light in the cloud-covered sky and even less warmth, so I was glad to see it go. And I hoped, in spite of what the weather reports were saying, that Christmas day would sparkle with the gift of a clear sky.

* * *

Colin's knock was light on the door, as if he somehow sensed my mom was taking a nap at four in the afternoon. Very impressive. His face and neck had turned a rusty bronze, except where his sunglasses had been, making it clear he had spent the last few days skiing, and unclear which was whiter, his teeth or his puka shells. You gotta love those puka shells. "Hey Whimsy," he said. "You look great."

"That's exactly what I was going to say," I replied. Apparently it takes awhile for my brain to process info because several awkward seconds passed before I added, "I mean, I was going to say that about you! You, uh, look great." Oh, brother.

Colin smiled (his teeth were definitely the white winners. I mean, it looked like he gargled with Clorox) and looked inside the doorway. "So this is your home?" he asked.

Practically before he had even finished his sentence I said, "Not really," surprising myself with how embarrassed I felt. It was just that I was accustomed to Mom making our home look beautiful. She was constantly experimenting with paint, moving furniture around, or putting up decorations for whatever holiday was just around the corner. But other than unpack her clothes, Mom had added nothing to Keppler's home. She said she was too busy with law school to worry about nesting, and so had I invited Colin in, it would have been nothing but Edna and crushed-velvet couches. Fortunately, he didn't ask me to explain why I was staying at a house I refused to claim. He simply held out his arm for me, I shut the door (purposefully not locking it because a burglar, especially one who liked crushed velvet, would have been a good thing), and we headed to his car.

The plan was to go to Salt Lake, get a bite to eat, then head over to Temple Square to see the lights, and I was game for all of it until seeing became a problem, at least anything more than ten feet away. And the faster the snow pelted the windshield, the faster I seemed to talk. I guess it was just my way of keeping my mind off our chances of ending up in a forty-car pileup. Colin, however, was totally relaxed (Toronto does get a tad more snow than Phoenix), driving most of the way with one hand and sometimes just a knee. In spite of how worry-free he seemed, Colin didn't say much, which came as no surprise, but still, only fueled the fire of my endless chattering.

"Isn't it weird," I blathered, making a point to look at Colin instead of the snowy confusion outside, "how old some rock stars are? They just never seem to want to retire, and why would they when all they have to do is put on old jeans and a T-shirt, sorta shout-sing into the microphone and, bingo, they're no longer fifty. And it's almost like the scarier they look, the greater their chances are of having a supermodel for a girlfriend, which I completely do not get. I mean, those girls could date anyone. Oh, and speaking of dates, I just tried this cereal the other day, and it had tiny bits of date in it, which at first I thought, gross, but it was actually good. But what's not good are those Jazz. They just can't seem to get it together." *Just grab your sock,* I thought, *and stuff it in your mouth.*

All the way to Salt Lake and even well past dinner, I yammered on and on as Colin watched with this amused look on his face as if I were a clown with an endless handkerchief streaming from my sleeve. In fact, it wasn't until we crossed the street to Temple Square and Colin took my gloved hand in his that I finally managed to put a cork in it. In spite of the never-ending supply of big, fluffy snowflakes plummeting from the sky, Temple Square was packed with people, many of whom were not so lucky as to be out with a guy smart enough to bring an umbrella. No doubt he had been one of Canada's finest Boy Scouts.

We walked around looking at the myriad of lights shining through the chaos, just the two of us cozy and relatively snow-free under his mambo umbrella, and as we did it seemed almost as if the crowd began to melt away, leaving us with each step all the more alone with each other. There are some things in life you're ready for. I mean, I was definitely ready to start college, for Jill to live just down the hall from me, and even more than ready to get my first check from cleaning the Bean Museum. But when Colin pulled me close under the umbrella and whispered, "Whimsy, I think I'm falling in love with you, eh," I only thought I was ready.

Of course it took me awhile to figure that out. After all, there I was at Temple Square on Christmas Eve with the guy I had endured English 115 for, and he was telling me he loved me or was starting to! The way I saw it, it didn't get much better than that, but still, it was hard to believe I'd heard him correctly. "Um, could you run that by me again?" I asked, looking at Colin with the temple behind him blurred by the falling snow.

Colin smiled. "I said I think I love you."

"Wow," I said, bursting into a lame, schoolgirl giggle. "I mean, me too." With the distant clip-clop of a horse-drawn carriage echoing in the night, Colin kissed me.

* * *

I was awakened Christmas morning by the sound of a car stuck in the snow, and as wheels spun in vain outside, the wheels in my head slowly began to turn, enveloping me in a warm, cozy haze brought on by the memory of Colin kissing me. It had been a simple kiss, but its simplicity had made it perfect, and afterward holding hands came so easily. I hadn't told Colin this, but that kiss was a breakthrough for me. After all, it was my first real kiss. Sure, Josh had kissed me last year, but if I had to file a kiss under "Things I'd Like to Forget," that's where it would have been lumped.

Kissing Colin had just been so sweet, and all of it—his soft lips, my giggling and blushing directly after, the way he had brushed a snowflake off my nose and called me his goofy girl (okay, so to be honest, that term of endearment bugged me)—all of it I definitely filed under "Things to Think About When I Want to Smile." As I continued to replay last night over and over, another thought sailed across my mind's horizon: today was the day Mom was going to tell Keppler she was having a baby, and the fear that I might have missed the moment got me out of bed in a hurry.

I threw on a sweatshirt and my softest, oldest pair of jeans, and went to find them. The two of them were sitting at the kitchen table, sharing the morning paper and eating breakfast. "You haven't done it yet!" I asked. "I mean, opened the presents?"

Mom said, as casually as if all she had in store for Keppler was an electric razor, "Of course not, honey. We wanted you to be a part of it."

Okay, I thought, *how do I say this?* "So you're sure you just want to sit there," I tried, "and casually eat and read when right now we could all be finding out what we got for Christmas?"

The way Keppler and Mom smiled at each other left no doubt I had sounded about ten years old. Durr! And just last night I had felt so mature. But Mom quickly made it all better. After blotting her mouth with her napkin, she stood up, gave me a kiss on the cheek, and said, "Good idea, sweetheart. Let's go see what's under the tree."

My mom is a firm believer in real Christmas trees, and so the living room was filled with the fresh smell of pine. Like everything else, Mom's Christmas ornaments were still packed away, and so we made do with what Keppler had in the attic and what I tried to throw together. The popcorn garland was easy enough, but my gingerbread men had been a disaster, with most of their bodies breaking off once hung on the tree, leaving just the heads behind. It looked to me like a gingerbread man massacre, but to be honest, I was so sick of ginger-bread I didn't care. Why I hadn't just gone out and bought candy canes was a mystery to me.

Anyway, Mom and Keppler sat down on one of the crushed-velvet couches, and I sat by the Christmas tree to hand out gifts. "You go first, Whimsy," Mom said as she rested her head on Keppler's shoulder.

"Sounds good to me," I replied as my face turned a jolly shade of red, and I made a mental note not to act ten at Christmastime. But really, easier said than done. After all, I love getting gifts. I picked up a small present for me from Keppler (I already knew what my mom was giving me. What can I say, she's bad at hiding gifts), which Mom had obviously wrapped. The bow on top was practically bigger than the present itself, and the wrapping paper was almost as thick as wall-paper.

As I unwrapped a microcassette recorder, Keppler said, "I know you're done with your English class and interviewing Miss Greer, but I thought this might still be of use to you."

It was definitely not something I'd been hoping for, but cool all the same. "Thanks a lot," I said, and Keppler smiled a "you're welcome."

"Who's next?" asked Mom.

"You are," said Keppler, leaving me slightly bummed. I was wanting it to be his turn.

I reached under the tree and pulled out a present for Mom, which she had clearly not helped Keppler wrap, but it was a small present, and generally speaking those are the best. Mom, careful not to tear the paper (she's such a kook), opened her present, and inside a tiny box was a single key. She looked at Keppler for an explanation, and he said, "You said you missed having sand between your toes, and I thought we should do something about that."

"Stanley," Mom gasped, and wrapped her arms around his neck, burying her face in his shoulder.

"Okay, I don't get it," I said, referring to the key, but Mom at the moment was too choked up to say anything.

"I bought your mother the condo we stayed at during our honey-moon," explained Keppler as he stroked her head.

"Whoa—that definitely tops a desk organizer," I said, thinking of what I'd gotten her. Mom was still nestled against Keppler's shoulder, and figuring that a house in Hawaii needed to be followed by something a tad more exciting than a bow tie (this year I thought I'd play it safe), I handed Keppler—not even stopping to think if Mom was ready for it—a small present to him from Mom.

Mom instantly popped off his shoulder. "I don't know if you should open that just yet," she said, sounding a bit panicky as she shot me a look that clearly said, "Why did you hand him that one?"

Geez Louise, I thought, *what'd you expect, that I'd hand him his Uncle Lester's fruitcake?*

Keppler looked truly confused. "Well, all right. I'm in no rush," he said, making it clear that all that mattered was his new wife's happiness, which I have to admit was kinda sweet.

As he began to put the present on the table beside him, Mom said, with tears now spilling down her face, "Or perhaps you should just open it."

It was hard to read Keppler's expression. It ranged somewhere in between fear and curiosity, but there was no reading Mom's at all. She had buried her face in her husband's shoulder as if to protect herself from how he might react, which, when I thought about it, was kinda funny. I mean, she was taking refuge in the guy she was needing refuge from. Anyway, Keppler quickly tore through the wrapping paper, opened the small box, and pulled from it a single fortune cookie. Wasting no time, Keppler broke the cookie open and read the fortune inside. I'm not sure what my mom was expecting, but I'm guessing the we've-just-won-the-Super-Bowl! hug he gave her did much to calm her nerves. "We're really going to have a baby?" he asked, practically laughing with excitement.

Mom lifted her tearstained face and nodded. "Yes, honey," she croaked, "we're going to have a baby." The only dry eyes in the room were Edna's.

* * *

The rest of the morning just wasn't anywhere near as exciting. I mean, the bow tie just didn't quite get the same high-five reaction. Go figure. But I have to admit, it was kinda fun listening to Keppler alternately quiz and chide my mom, trying to find out everything she knew so far about this pregnancy and then scolding her for not telling him sooner. (His students only wish he scolded that sweetly in class.) But after a hearty Christmas lunch of glazed ham, cheesy potatoes, and garden salad, Keppler's stream of questions tapered off until, at last, he dozed off on the couch next to Mom with his hand on her stomach. His first loud honking snore made us both giggle and somehow signaled it was time for a mother-daughter talk. "So how do you feel now?" I asked.

"Nauseous," she said, "but happy."

"He seems happy too," I said, to which Keppler added what sounded more like a duck call than a snore.

We tried to stifle our giggles, even though we both knew it wasn't necessary—Keppler was clearly down for the count. "And what about you, sweetie? Are you happy?" asked Mom.

Instantly thinking of Colin, I said, "I'm good. No complaints over here."

"So this young man," said Mom, pausing a moment as Keppler called once again for all local fowl to come to the family room, "is a returned missionary?"

How'd she do that? How'd she know I was thinking of Colin? And why did she sound concerned? I mean, hadn't she always told me to date returned missionaries? "Yeah," I said, "he's back from his mission."

Keppler honked again, and had the windows been open, who knows what would have flown inside. "To be honest, it makes me nervous," she said. "Returned missionaries are sometimes in such a rush to get married, and sweetie, I just want you to have a fun year."

Conveniently forgetting for a moment Colin's declaration of love for me the night before, I shook my head like she was seriously out of touch with reality, and said, "Mom, don't worry, we're just friends," and to be honest, I sorta believed what I was saying, until for some reason Sable came into my head saying, "Only a fool believes their own lies. If you're such chums with this fellow, why then can't you relax around him and be yourself? You're a three-ring circus in his company, trying in vain to make up for his—" I had never been so grateful to hear a loud, honking snore. It overpowered the nagging in my head, making me feel, once again, carefree.

"Your freshman year should be fun," said Mom.

And thinking of Colin, I said, "It couldn't be more fun, Mom. I swear it couldn't be more fun."

chapter 17

Elder Matt Hollingsworth
Casilla 28, Las Condes
Santiago 10, Chile

Dear Elder H,
  Hi. Hope you had a nice Christmas. Keep up the good work.
  Sincerely, W

* * *

Okay, so I admit snow makes a little more sense when you're into skiing, which isn't to say I mastered the slopes over Christmas break, but after a few days, it did start to become fun. Hudson was a patient teacher, which completely surprised me. I guess I was expecting him to just leave me to figure it out on my own, but he didn't. He stayed with me on the easiest run, coaching me down the hill. Merriwether, on the other hand, didn't have the patience to deal with a beginner, and in that snippy voice of hers told Hudson she'd see us at the lodge at one o'clock for lunch. It became obvious to me that Hudson was a regular at Deer Valley. Everybody seemed to know him, and what surprised me was that when introducing me to his friends, he called me his sister without giving any explanation about how he'd suddenly acquired one. I mean, it was one thing for him to teasingly call me "sis," but it was stunning to realize that he actually meant it.

What also surprised me was Hudson's reaction to the news my mom was pregnant. He's such a sarcastic guy, I just figured he'd make fun of the situation, but he didn't. When he came down to get me, Mom and Keppler told him, and Hudson gave Mom a kiss. Merriwether, however, instantly went into this long explanation about how glad she was that at twenty-four she was not yet married and pregnant. "I'm not even vaguely interested in settling down right now," she said, which was a complete lie. Anyone could tell she was desperate for Hudson to ask her to marry him. And my guess is—which might have had something to do with the *Bride* magazine on the backseat of her car—she already had all the hoopla figured out. Hudson would just have had to put on a tux and show up.

So anyway, yes, when it was time to start school again, I did look at snow a little differently, and it was nice to hang out with Hudson and have a chance to figure out a few things about him, namely, that he was closer to his dad than Merriwether assumed, and a nicer guy than he let on. I mean, at first I thought he and Merriwether must be perfect for each other since they both seemed so snobby and pretentious, but Hudson—and this completely surprised me—deserved much better.

But if Hudson's reaction to Mom being pregnant was surprisingly cool, Jill's was no surprise. I waited until she got back to the dorms to tell her, partly because I wanted to tell her in person and partly because I was busy with either Colin or Hudson the entire break. So when she finally got back and it was just her and me in my dorm room, I sat her down and said, "Well are you ready to hear what I was going to tell you?"

"Yes, you've been keeping me in freakin' suspense all break. Some friend you are."

Without stalling any further, I said, "My mom is preggo!"

Jill stuck her fingers in her ears. "We hold these truths to be self-evident! Dang it, girl, thanks for the visual. Why'd you have to say that?"

"Wait a minute, you were just mad at me for not telling you sooner."

"Well, if you would have told me what you were going to say—"

"But then I would have said it anyway."

"You could have mimed."

"You could have grown up."

Jill took a deep breath, then said quite calmly, "You have to admit, the world made a lot more sense when babies came from a magic filing cabinet."

It wasn't worth arguing over, so in the hopes of getting the conversation beyond that point, I said, "At any rate, I'm excited about it. I mean, I think it's gonna be fun being a big sister."

"Just wait till it's 'Can you watch the baby, can you feed the baby, can you change the baby's pants? They smell like an overflowing outhouse, but can you do it anyway?' No lie, Whims, you're excited now, but soon enough you're gonna hate it."

"Well, aren't you a little ray of sunshine."

"Hey, I'm just telling it like it is."

"Which is exactly what I was doing when I told you—"

"Pudge!" shouted Jill, and I was certain she was just trying to cut me off until I saw Pudge myself. Over Christmas break she had easily lost fifteen pounds, maybe twenty, and she looked incredible.

"Whoa," I said as I stared at her.

She giggled. "Ta-da! Look, I have cheekbones."

"Girl," said Jill, "you look awesome. How'd you do it?"

Pudge chucked her suitcase through the door. "Drastic measures," she said as she shook her head. "The tastiest thing I've had to eat in a couple of weeks is a puffed rice cake."

"Gag, those thing taste like cardboard," said Jill.

"Cayenne pepper gives them a kick," said Pudge, but not very convincingly, "Okay, so they still taste awful, but it was just time to do something about my weight, especially if I want to date at all this year," once again sounding like a desperate freshman.

"Pudge, you need to relax and go with the flow," I said.

"This coming from a girl who just took a class she didn't need to hang out with a guy," said Jill.

This was the first time Pudge had heard anything about my English 115 saga, and the look of complete surprise on her face was all I needed to say, "Have I told you my mom is PREGNANT?"

Pudge smiled and said, "Oh my heck!" but Jill whacking me in the head with a pillow sort of cut short anything else she was planning on saying. I was busy chanting, "Pregnant! Pregnant!" and getting whacked in the head when suddenly I noticed (in fact we both noticed) a tall, slender, stylish woman standing in the doorway. I stopped my chanting, but Jill still had to get a few good whacks in. She is so competitive. "Aunt Sophie!" Pudge cried, and hurried to the door to give her a hug.

Sophie dripped sophistication. There was something about her jacket, the thick gold bracelet dangling from her wrist, even the way she did her hair, that said "I'm accustomed to being both successful and beautiful," and after I got to know her, I realized she was also accustomed to being way nice. "Hello, Pudgy," she said. "But look at you," she continued, indicating for Pudge to turn around. "You look terrific!"

"I still have ten pounds to go," said Pudge, sounding like she knew it was going to be an uphill battle.

"Don't be ridiculous. You're perfect as you are," said Sophie, which had an instant calming effect on Pudge, and I made a mental note to tell kind lies like that more often. I mean, sure Pudge looked great, but still, it was true she could've stood to lose another ten pounds. "I wish I could have been there for Christmas, but work was piled high and I couldn't get away. We'll cross our fingers for next year. So Pudgy," said Sophie, putting her arm around her niece, "introduce me to your friends."

Pudge hit her forehead. "So sorry. I should have—"

"No saying you're sorry," said Sophie. "We've been through this."

Pudge hit her head again. "Sor—I mean, this is Whimsy, and this is Jill."

The charm on Sophie's bracelet swung back and forth as she shook hands with Jill and me. "Whimsy and Jill. Pudge has mentioned the two of you in her e-mails." Then, looking around at our tiny dorm room, she said, "It doesn't feel like it's been eleven years since I stayed here myself. Where has the time gone?"

"Aunt Sophie lives in London. She works in advertising, has a great job, and a really cool flat." Pudge then added mournfully, "And isn't married yet."

This obviously bothered Pudge more than it did Sophie. "You can just call me her spinster aunt," Sophie said, and smiled.

"Sor—I mean, I didn't mean it like that," groaned Pudge.

Sophie put her hands on Pudge's shoulders. "You worry too much, honey. And besides, right now spinster life suits me just fine."

Looking out the window, Jill said, "Is that your Mercedes outside?"

"Yes, it's a rental."

"Still, spinster life looks pretty good."

"It has its perks," said Sophie. "Listen, I was hoping to take Pudge to dinner. Why don't the two of you come along as well, and if there's anyone else you'd like to invite—"

I knew Pudge was thinking of Chloe, and I was about to tell her Chloe wasn't back yet when I heard someone sing, "Where are you all going?" There was no mistaking Special Kay's voice, and its fake, hyper-happy quality made me grit my teeth.

Sophie introduced herself to Kay and told her what was going on. In spite of all the looks of warning we gave her, she invited Kay to come along. "Gosh," said Kay, "I wouldn't want to intrude."

"Okay," said Jill.

"She means it's more than okay," said Sophie. "You're not intruding."

"Well if you're sure, then that'd be darn nice," said Special Kay in that special voice of hers. "I'll go grab my wallet."

"Don't be silly, it's my treat," said Sophie.

"Oh, speaking of treat, Whimsy, there's a real cutie downstairs who wants to see you," Kay said.

I knew it must be Colin, and as I bolted out the door, Jill said, "Meet us at the rented Mercedes or you're toast!"

I shouted that I'd be there in a minute and ran down the stairs only to find Phil on a couch leaning real close to a brunette from the second floor. As soon as he saw me, he popped up, shook the girl's hand (which she found puzzling), and came toward me. "Whims, hey, I was hoping you were here." Brunette Babe looked at the two of us, and, apparently realizing her relationship with Phil had just ended, headed upstairs in a huff.

"I should have taken my time coming down the stairs. It looked like she was just about to kiss you," I said, still a little mad at him for kissing little Miss No-Name in the Wilkinson Center.

"Nope, nuh-uh, no sirree. Just a little friendly conversation, that's all." I was about to say, "You do realize *friendly* and *flirty* aren't synonyms," when Phil said, "I got my mission call."

"So where you going?" I asked, sounding like a friend again.

"Las Vegas, Nevada," he said, trying to sound enthusiastic.

"I take it you're slightly bummed?"

"I wouldn't say bummed. More like ho-hum. I was sorta hoping for someplace a little greener. I mean, the whole mission's a desert."

"But hey," I said, and shoved Phil softly in the shoulder, "at least your canteen's full."

"Oh man," said Phil, holding his stomach as if he'd just devoured a Thanksgiving dinner. "You got me, you got me."

"So when do you enter the MTC?" I asked in a kind voice.

"End of January," said Phil, and something about the way he said it let me know he was scared.

I was about to tell Phil not to worry, that I was sure he was going to love his mission. I mean, it just seemed like he could use some encouragement, but then I heard the faint sound of a horn honking. "Look," I said, "I've gotta go right now, but congratulations."

His disappointment was palpable. "Uh, yeah, sure," he said, trying to sound casual. "I'll give you a call and let you know about my farewell and stuff."

"Sounds great," I said, hoping my chirpiness would make less apparent his disappointment. I mean, Phil was my friend and all, but Jill was still laying on the horn and Sister Wauteever was starting to shout in Finnish from her desk. "I'll be in touch," I said as I started to walk away from Phil, and before turning around, glimpsed him stuffing his hands in his jeans and lowering his head in sadness. I thought about telling Jill and the rest I couldn't make it, but Sister Whatever was shouting, "Chu are this wan slow girl! Going!" And besides, a mission call wasn't a bad thing. I mean, so maybe he wasn't going exactly where he wanted, but what could I do to change that? Besides (and this was really the reason I hopped in the car and left), why should it have been my responsibility to make him feel better about things? His parents were there, he had lots of friends besides me, and, to be completely honest, I was still mad at him for kissing that girl. *Phil's not my problem,* I told myself as I opened the car door, but still, I couldn't shake the feeling that somehow or another, I had not done what I should have.

* * *

"Who was that?" asked Jill. "Captain Toronto?"

"No," I said, and poked Jill in the side.

All it did was make her say "Ouch!" real loud and proclaim it was time for me to cut my nails. (Have I mentioned she hates long nails?) "Whimsy has a boyfriend," she taunted like she did in the third grade when I got a valentine from Gavin Slappey. I knew that denying it would only egg her on, so I just rolled my eyes and acted like she was out of her mind.

"That's so special," said Kay.

"That's what I'd thought you'd say," Jill said, then nudged me in the arm to acknowledge her joke.

"So tell me about Captain Toronto," said Sophie. "He sounds interesting."

Jill could hardly control herself. "And he is, especially if you're into fishing."

All the poking and pinching I could muster wasn't going to stop Jill. I knew her well enough to realize that the best thing I could do was act casual and pretend like I didn't want to kick her. "He's just this guy—"

"She met in class. It was just one of those amazing BYU coincidences—they ended up sitting next to each other."

I briefly wondered what constituted justifiable homicide, then said, trying to sound completely casual, "We spent some time together studying and—"

"Gutting fish."

Jill was as dead as dog meat. "And just hit if off."

"That sounds sweet," said Kay, and crinkled her eyes. Gag. "I don't have a boyfriend right now, but I've got the feeling something's coming." Then, turning to Sophie, she said, "So are you married?"

"No, I'm Sophie the spinster aunt," said Sophie, and looked in her rearview mirror and smiled at us.

Pudge, who was sitting in the front passenger seat, said, "She's just teasing. Aunt Sophie has dated lots of guys. She's just still looking for Mr. Right."

"Well, Captain Toronto is still fair game, isn't he?" asked Sophie.

We all laughed together at this, and for the first time I felt some kind of comradery between Kay and the rest of us. Until, that is, she said, "Well, it wouldn't surprise me at all if next year I'm living in Wymount, snuggled up with my honey, admiring my new wedding ring. I'm telling you, something's coming. I just feel it."

"Not me," said Jill. "I've got plans, and they don't include snuggling."

chapter 18

Wilhelmina Waterman
D-3209
Stover Hall
Provo, UT 84604

Dear W,

Just received another one of your perfunctory epistles and thought I'd write you while I have a moment. I'm glad you've been as good as your word and have written me faithfully every week. Your letters—even the ones you've been sending lately—are a great help to me, though I have to admit I prefer the ones when you went on and on about something that was bothering you. Your letters now have a lot of white space on them, which is, like I said, okay. I'm really just glad to hear from you at all.

The mission hasn't been easy lately, which has a lot to do with my current companion, Elder Henderson. It's hard—and you know this isn't like me—not to pound his face in. If I try to wake him up in the morning, he goes berserk, and if I don't we don't get out the door until it's practically time to come back for siesta. He breaks all the mission rules he can get away with, and then talks forever about how smart he is. It wasn't a good day when I asked him why, if he was so smart, he found it so hard to obey simple rules. I'm telling you, right now things aren't easy for me, but the truth is, if I don't have him as a companion somebody else will. So I guess it's my turn.

The hardest part is that I can see how much we could be doing right now. Santiago is a great city, and the field is definitely white here. My first companion, Elder Alvarez, taught me so much by what he did, and I

suppose from Elder Henderson I'm learning too, only this time it's what not to do. Well, I hope this letter isn't too boring and miserable for you. I still love being out here. Life is good. Hard, but good. Sincerely, Elder H
    P.S. Please write.

* * *

Cody Jeff Johnson was born on the thirtieth of January, much to Jill's chagrin. With the gymnastic season in full swing, not to mention school, and spending more and more time with Josh, the last thing Jill wanted to do was to help Steve and Melanie. She tried, "I can't do it, I won't do it, I wish I could do it," but after some subtle persuasion (threatening to bring Tyson to her next gymnastics meet), she decided on, "I'll do it, dang it." So during the morning, when I saw Pudge picking the raisins out of her raisin bran, I decided I'd walk over to Wymount in the afternoon and while Jill helped Mel, talk to her about Pudge.

After waking Mel from a nap (oops), I found Jill at the laundromat with Tyson and McKenner in tow. "Hey," I said as I came through those all-too-familiar glass doors.

"Hey," grumbled Jill. McKenner was on the floor next to Jill contemplating putting a ball of lint in his mouth, but Tyson was nowhere to be seen. "Tyson!" she said over the droning of the dryers, "I don't count to three, I count to one, and if you're not here by one, I'm here to tell you you're going to regret it!"

"So things are going well?" I asked.

Jill rolled her eyes. "Business as usual."

Before she started to count, Tyson ran toward her with a stuffed animal in his hand and hugged Jill's leg. This, however, didn't do much to put Jill in a better mood. "Give me the bunny, Tyson," she ordered, but Tyson only let go of her leg to better grip his bunny.

"No, I won't."

Jill snapped her fingers at McKenner, who instantly put the lint down. "Tyson," she said, "give me the bunny now."

Knowing how little patience Jill had with her brothers and sisters, I knew this was only going to get worse. "Do you want me to do something?" I asked.

"Yes, look out the window. There's a cowboy!"

This was all Tyson, the world's youngest boot aficionado, needed to hear to lose his focus, and when he turned around, Jill grabbed the bunny and threw it in the washer, which was already filled with water.

"Swim, bunny, swim!" cried Tyson.

Before closing the lid, she looked in once more and said, "Nice backstroke, bun. See you after the spin cycle," then followed Tyson outside to the playground. It was one of those rare sunny January days, and Tyson and McKenner were not the only kids at the little playground just behind the laundromat. It was just after two in the afternoon, and already the sun was beginning to pack less of a punch, something the children didn't seem to notice, demanding again and again to be pushed in the swings. The swings were all full until Tyson asked a young mom for the twentieth time, "Hey, are you done?" and she finally took her kid out and left, but not before glowering at Jill.

Leaning toward Jill, I said, "I think she's trying to tell you to teach your kid some manners."

"Swing hog," shouted Jill as they left the playground.

"Just the sort of friendly good-bye the moms at Wymount usually give each other," I said, taking McKenner from her so that she could push Tyson.

"Hey, I call it like I see it. So why are you here?" she asked, and gave Tyson an enormous shove, sending his swing soaring.

I put McKenner on the ground and let him play with a shovel someone seemed to have forgotten. "I wanted to talk to you about Pudge."

"Why me?"

"Well, you're her visiting teacher."

"Big whoop, you're her roommate."

"Are you trying to bug me?"

"Sorta."

"Okay, then I say we just move on." Jill nodded, and I got to my point. "I'm kinda worried about her."

"The girl is finally getting asked out. What could possibly be wrong?"

"I think she's doing something. I don't know what, but I think she's forcing herself to be thin."

"Like that one girl in our stake back home whose knees were bigger than her thighs?"

"Maybe."

"Whims, there's no way. That girl was a bag of bones. Pudge looks good. Yeah, she doesn't eat as much as before, but that's only because she's still trying to lose a few pounds. She's nowhere near emaciated. How's that for a big word?"

"Not bad," I said, though still troubled about Pudge.

Tyson yelled for Jill to stop, and as soon as she did, he jumped off the swing and ran for the slide yelling, "Okay, everybody off!"

A few parents stared at Jill, demanding with scowls that Jill do something, so she did. "Please!" she yelled to him, "Next time say, 'Everybody off *please!*'" Then she leaned toward me to say while stifling a laugh, "Ten bucks says the guy in the blue jacket gives me a piece of his mind."

The guy in the blue jacket was probably three times her size and, yes, was fuming (the Wymount crowd tends to take parenting seriously), but instead of saying something to Jill, he went over to the slide to police the situation. But it wasn't like Jill was breathing a sigh of relief. I mean, nothing scares her in the first place.

With things under control at the slide (no thanks to us) and McKenner happily swatting the snow with the shovel, we got back to talking about Pudge. "Jill, I'm telling you, something seems wrong."

"Whims," she said, "remember that time you thought the Gerber's dog was a polar bear and you said we should call the zoo?"

"He was white, huge, and fluffy. It was a simple mistake."

"Or how in the fourth grade you thought the wart on your finger was cancer and wrote up a will giving me your bike?"

"That sucker was huge!"

"Look, all I'm saying is that you can blow things out of proportion. I mean, Whims, you're the girl who said her frog shed a tear."

"It seemed like the word *vivisection* made him panic. Okay, okay, so I admit my brain can at times embellish—"

"Well I'm telling you, this is one of those times."

"I don't know," I said, still convinced my instincts were dead-on.

"Girl," said Jill, "you know I'm right, and as your best friend I think it's my responsibility to tell you not to worry about Pudge. She's doing fine, and I say if she's okay with eating nothing but raw cabbage all day, more power to her." Jill waited until my face was completely white before she told me she was joking. "Seriously, Whims, Pudge is fine. I mean, if you want to worry about someone, worry about your mom. She's the one who's losing her lunch every day."

"You don't know the half of it!" I shouted to her as I ran to get McKenner, who had wandered over to the slide and was trying to climb up the wrong end.

"Good, I don't want to know that half of it," said Jill as I came back with McKenner kicking and screaming in my arms. "But in general, nondescriptive terms, how's your mom doing?"

"Fine," I said, "just fine." But I couldn't resist adding, "If you don't count that the smell of her textbooks gives her migraines and she's busting out of her shirts."

Jill cranked her fist back like she wanted to hit me. "You're the worst!"

"Don't you think you're blowing things out of proportion?" I asked. "I mean, I didn't even mention the Tahitian gum tree lotion she's using to prevent STRETCH MARKS."

I knew better than to expect no retaliation. Still, she surprised me. "LOOK," she said loud and clear and sounding completely serious, "YOU'VE PAID YOUR DEBT TO SOCIETY ALREADY. I DON'T THINK YOU NEED TO TELL PEOPLE YOU'RE A CONVICTED FELON. IT'S NONE OF THEIR BUSINESS."

I smiled weakly as the blue-jacket dad and a few other parents scrutinized me, no doubt wondering what crime I'd committed, and the worst of it was that a dorky laugh was the only comeback I could muster. But really, it was just as well. Once Jill got going in a who-can-embarrass-the-other-more contest, she could be ruthless. I mean, it took me six months to convince our Laurel advisor I didn't have a tongue-stud fund. No, rather than compete, it was far better to look at my watch and say, "Whoa, I gotta get going," which is exactly what I did.

"What, you're not even going to try? Come on, at least ask me about my hemorrhoids."

"No, I really need to go. Getting completely humiliated is not on my list of things to do."

"Darn," she said, then shoved me softly and smiled. And when I tried not to smile she shoved me again and again until I finally caved.

"Relentless, pushy gymnast," I said, trying to sound mad.

"I like the sound of that. Listen, if I don't survive watching Tyson and McKenner, would you put that on my headstone?"

"With pleasure," I said.

"I owe you one."

"Which brings me back to Pudge."

"Talk about relentless," she huffed.

"All I'm asking is that you watch her for a few days and let me know what you think."

"If it makes you feel any better I'll do it, but I can tell you right now she's fine."

I looked at my watch and panicked. "Dang, I gotta go," I said. "I promised Sable I wouldn't be late today."

"Okay, you're the one I need to talk to. I mean, why the heck are you still going over to see that lady? You've finished that stupid class."

Stupid class was right. Miss Snell—and there was no way I was telling Jill this—had given me a B+. Let's just say her final exam was not my friend. So, yeah, the class was over and, most definitely, it was a pain at times to fit Sable into my schedule, but for some reason I kept going over there. "Well," I said, trying to pinpoint my motivation not only for Jill but for myself, "for starters, she needs help. I mean, sometimes I go over there and a jar is on the counter that I know she's too proud to ask me to open, but has left out in the hopes I'll say, 'Hey, can I open that for you?'"

"Whims, can't her visiting teachers help her out with stuff like that? I mean, how fair is it that I gotta monitor Pudge when her visiting teachers won't even open a jar?"

"They probably would, but she told me the last time they came she threatened to turn the hose on them."

"Okay, then her neighbors."

"She's cut herself off from all of them. In fact, I'm pretty sure I'm the only person she hasn't kicked out of her life, so I guess I'd feel guilty if I stopped seeing her."

"I have the perfect thing to take away your guilt: ward boundaries."

"Huh?"

"Listen, when my dad was bishop a couple of years ago, I heard him say the easiest way to fix a problem in your ward is to have it move."

"Why?"

"Because then they're not in the ward boundaries, which makes them some other bishop's problem. So here's the good news: Sable isn't even close to being in our ward boundaries, so girl, you don't need to worry about her."

Jill had a point, but still, something didn't feel right, and before I really had a chance to figure out why, Josh came through the laundromat's back door. "Jilly!" he said. "Man, I've been looking all over for you!" He kissed the top of her head, which Jill accepted but didn't reciprocate in any way. Until Josh, I thought Jill only gave off the vibe of your-affection-is-something-I-could-take-or-leave to her parents, but I had noticed that she was the same way around him, and instead of it discouraging him, it only seemed to make her more endearing. Who would have figured?

Josh was in the middle of saying, "Hey, Whimsy," when Tyson spotted him and came running over shouting, "Hut one! Hut two! Hut three!" The two of them growled at each other, and then Josh scooped up Tyson (who, by the way, was laughing his head off), tucked him under his arm like a football, and headed for an imaginary end zone.

Soon McKenner was waddling his way over to Josh too, flapping his arms in excitement. I watched Josh as he—with Tyson still under one arm—took McKenner by his snowsuit and turned around and around, making McKenner howl with laughter. "Oh, please," said Jill as she rolled her eyes at the three of them. "I'm gonna go check on the laundry real quick."

"Well, I'll just see you back at the dorms," I said. "I really gotta go."

Jill waved good-bye and as she opened the laundry room door, then said, "Whims, ward boundaries. That should be your happy thought."

I gave her the okay sign and, as soon as she was back in the laundromat, started running for Sable's.

* * *

Sable was in a crusty mood, which came as no surprise. "How ya doin'?" I asked as she opened the front door.

"*Ya* and *doin'* are not in my lexicon. Don't be so sloppy, girl," she said, and motioned for me to come inside. As usual, the curtains were drawn and her living room dark. I walked over to a pile of dirt she had started to sweep together and, without asking, finished the job.

"I didn't ask you to do that," she snapped.

"But I love sweeping. That and . . ." I quickly scanned the room, "folding laundry."

"You're an odd one," she grumbled, and I got to work sweeping ash into the dustpan.

"Did I tell you what I got on that paper I wrote about you?" She didn't say anything, which I knew meant, *No, you haven't told me, and I'm dying to know.* "I got an A, but next to your name, she wrote in the margin *Very funny.*"

"Why'd she do that?" asked Sable, completely incensed.

I gulped. "I guess because she figured you'd never talk to me."

"I'll talk to whomever I want!" she snapped as if Miss Snell were the one folding her laundry.

I gulped, trying to get a little more courage. "And maybe she assumed that you'd have more to say than where to plant hydrangeas." Sable huffed and I—which had to be the bravest thing I'd ever done—said, "I mean, you've told me everything you know about roses, but you haven't told me much about your life. I mean, your adult life."

"Maybe there's nothing to tell," she hissed.

Again, I gulped. "Maybe there is and maybe there isn't, but can I ask you some questions?"

Sable turned her head to the side and tutted as if trying to keep from smiling. "Such an odd girl."

"Okay," I said, "I'm gonna take that as a yes. Just let me put these dish towels away." As I walked toward the kitchen, I reached into my open backpack and pressed "Record."

chapter 19

To: Chiarissima@italnet.com
From: Whims1@byu.edu

Just came from Phil's farewell. Chiara, you missed a major sob session. I've never seen a guy cry so hard. Come to think of it, I've never seen a girl cry that hard. You would have thought Phil was heading to the guillotine, poor guy. He started wiping away tears during the opening hymn, and from then on it only got worse. To be honest, I couldn't understand much of what he said when he gave his talk because he was wailing so hard. At one point, the bishop did what I think we were all wanting to do: he went up to Phil, put his arm around his shoulders, and asked him (I think anyway—that bishop is a good whisperer) if he'd rather skip the rest of his talk. Phil smiled and shook his head, and the bishop patted him on the shoulder and sat down. But the rest of his talk was just as big a sob session, and by the time he sat down, there was a mountain of used tissues next to the microphone. And I guess Phil's mom (I like her) couldn't stand the fact he left them there because she started cleaning them up during the closing hymn, which by the way, Phil cried through as well.

I'd love to say more, but Colin is downstairs waiting for me. We're going stargazing, and by the way, I am the world's worst stargazer, but then again I hated connect-the-dots as a kid. (Did you have those growing up in Italy?) I know you like Matt a ton, but I'm telling you, Colin is a great guy. He's real cute, thinks I'm hilarious, and besides, Matt told me to enjoy myself. So that's what I'm doing. I'll write again later. Ciao, W

P.S. I'm glad Luca swings by to say hi sometimes on the weekends, but he realizes you're not going to get serious with him, doesn't he?

* * *

To: Whims1@byu.edu
From: Chiarissima@italnet.com

Carissima Whimsy,
   You must tell me quickly Whimsy if you know this is true. We just in our city get a new missionario, Anziano Cole, who is at BYU before he start his mission. I ask him if he know Phil Fitzsimmons and he say yes, they are friends. This make me so happy, but then Anziano Cole say Phil say to everyone at BYU is good to kiss many girls before the mission. I am in shock. Yes, when I did leave Utah I tell him we cannot be boyfriend and girlfriend. Problem is, when Phil say we can, I wanted to believe him. I know BYU is big school, but if you know anything, please tell me. Con tanto affetto, Chiara
   P.S. Luca did come to church with me last Sunday. He say it surprise him we are so small. I wish I could take him to Salt Lake City and show him a part of the Church that is more significant than our small chapel in Rimini.

* * *

For me, Valentine's Day turned out to be as unbelievable as the front page of a tabloid magazine, but for reasons that didn't involve tap-dancing aliens or cows that curse. It was the kind of day that shifted continually from amazing to gag-me, and the fact that the day started out on the gag-me side of the scale was entirely Jill's fault. I mean, I was just walking out the door to school when she leaned toward me and said, "I see London, I see Iraq."

"What?" I asked, and as I quickly scanned the lobby to see what she was talking about, I saw the fix-it guy bent over his work and didn't need her to say a word more. "Dang it, girl!" I said once we were outside. "I could have lived without seeing that!"

"Me too!" cried Jill. "But if I catch a glimpse of something like that, I'm taking you down with me."

I walked for a moment with my hand covering my eyes, trying to get out of my head our PG-13 lobby, when Jill tapped me and said, "Uh, Whims, you gotta see this."

Cautiously, I spread my fingers and saw what looked like Colin and Kay walking toward us, chatting pleasantly about something. I would have preferred it had been an army of fix-it men crouched and working. I mean, they just looked so comfortable, which especially bugged me because in the back of my mind, I knew being completely comfortable around Colin didn't come naturally for me. But hey, I wasn't afraid of a challenge.

"Hey there!" said Kay, as the two of them walked toward us. "We were just coming to find you."

We? Why did that make me want to kick her? "Hi goof," Colin said, and then kissed my cheek. *Take that!* I thought, glad to have Colin show Kay (and me) who he was interested in, though really, I was gonna have to do something about the "goofy girl" thing.

"Hey," I said back, not that he could hear me over Kay.

Kay looked at Colin and crinkled her eyes. "We ended up coming out of the Cannon Center at the same time, and I said, 'It looks like you're headed to Stover Hall. Who are you coming to see?' And he said, 'Whimsy,' and I said, 'Whimsy! Why, I'll take you right to her!'"

More like, "from her," I thought.

She continued. "And he said he was from Canada, and I said, 'Then you must be Captain Toronto!'"

Colin smiled and didn't look the least bit bothered. Still, my knees buckled under the weight of the humiliation I felt. And thankfully, before Kay could say anything more, Jill said, "Kay, I just remembered, there was a girl looking for you, wanting to know if she could have a . . . What was it? Oh yeah, a pet iguana in her room."

"Doesn't anyone read the bylaws?" moaned our resident assistant. "Well, gotta run. Nice meeting you, Colin. See ya, ladies."

As Kay walk-ran the rest of the way to Stover Hall's front entrance, Colin said, "Happy Valentine's Day!" and pulled out a heart-shaped box of chocolate from his backpack, a moment which was highlighted by Jill making oinking noises.

"As if I'm gonna eat them all at once," I whined.

"Oh," said Jill, "speaking of eating, that 'thing'—" she made quotes with her fingers just to be annoying, "we were talking about the other day, you know, at Wymount? Well, 'it'—" again the finger quotes, "looks fine to me."

"Okay," I said, knowing Jill had brought up Pudge right then just so I wouldn't be able to hammer her with are-you-sure's. Instead of going up to campus, Jill was going to the Smith Field House for a meeting with the gymnastics team, and as she waved good-bye and walked off, I said, "We'll talk about it later!"

"No we won't!"

"Yes we will!" I shouted, not the least bit surprised to hear Jill shout it with me.

"Jinx!" she said while I was still on "ji—" and then turned around triumphantly and trotted off to the Smith Field House, while I made a mental note to tell her I would no longer play that game. We were in college now, and besides, I hadn't beat her since my short winning streak in the eighth grade when she had her braces tightened.

"She sure is competitive," said Colin.

I rolled my eyes. "Tell me about it." The two of us began walking toward campus hand in hand. Already worried that silence would set in, I quickly said, "Darn, I feel bad. I haven't gotten you anything for Valentine's Day yet."

"No worries," he said, and kissed my head.

Please, I quickly prayed, *if it's not too much to ask, inspire Kay to come with a telescope to one of the third floor windows facing east and have him do that again.* Just then, Colin's cell phone rang, and he chucked my hand to answer it. Apparently heaven was swamped at the moment.

Colin's conversation didn't take long, but it was clear something was wrong. "That was my Aunt Henny," he said. "The one who lives in Heber." (As president of the bad name club, I could sympathize with Henny.) "She said my Uncle Horace just finished the paint-by-number mural of Hiawatha he's been working on for the last seventeen years and has lost the will to live."

"How horrible," I said, nearly bursting with pride that he had set me up. I mean, Henny, Horace, Heber, Hiawatha. It was a joke, and his serious tone had made me fall for it! Deep down inside, Colin was funny!

"Well, Uncle Horace is Hungarian," he continued, and it was all I could do to keep from laughing, Colin's delivery was so good. I mean, he sounded dead serious. "And has had a hard time since he closed his hat shop . . . in Halifax."

Oh, this is too beautiful, I thought, and in as serious a tone as I could muster said, "Has he a harmonica? Playing one might help."

"I can't imagine that it would," said Colin. "Uncle Horace doesn't like noise, which is why I think he likes to paint, but I'll pass the idea on to Auntie Henny."

"Huh?" He was losing me. I mean, now he was sounding like this wasn't a joke.

"No offense," said Colin. "A harmonica might be just the thing. But for tonight, instead of going out like we planned, I think I'd better head up to Aunt Henny's to cheer him up. He is, after all, a hundred."

"So we're really not going to do anything tonight?"

"Hope you're not hurt."

Okay, this conversation was starting to get on my nerves. "And this whole thing about your uncle isn't a joke?"

"Why would I joke about Uncle Horace's health?"

It was clear that now our conversation was starting to get on Colin's nerves too, and I knew I needed to say something to smooth things over, but what? "Well," I started, "um . . . it's just that I heard somewhere . . ." *Think!* I told myself, "that Canadians like to consolidate holidays, you know, celebrate them all at once and get them over in a hurry. I thought . . . I mean, it seemed for a moment like you were trying to merge April Fool's Day with Valentine's Day."

"How?"

Had Colin not heard himself? I mean, it had sounded like he'd bought the fix-it shop from Maria on Sesame Street and was introducing the letter for the day. Anyway, it was clear Colin hadn't thought what he'd said was funny, and so I tried to think of something other than the truth to explain myself. "Well, um, it's just that I've heard that Canadians generally don't live past ninety-nine."

"Goofy girl," he said with a smile. "You can't believe everything you hear."

I smacked my forehead with my hand. "Oops," I said, and shook my head at my gullibility.

Colin put his hands on my shoulders and looked into my eyes as understandingly as one of those all-wise TV dads. "Don't be so hard on yourself," he said. "Your naivety is part of your charm."

I did this weird smile-grimace thing, and bit my lip to keep from saying, "Hey, you're the gullible one, not me! I was just trying to smooth things over and you fell for it." Sure, it was great to hear he thought I had charm, but being called naive was about as comfortable for me as being strapped into a Victorian corset, which in my opinion, is just one of those things you don't have to experience first-hand to know you'd hate. And as much as I didn't want to let it happen, qualms about Colin crept into my head.

We crossed the street at the top of the hill and stopped for a moment. Looking at me, Colin pushed a hand through his thick, blonde hair. (Gulp.) The cold morning had turned his cheeks a bright, ruddy pink, and for some reason the longer I looked at them, the more my worries about us scattered like ticker tape in the wind.

"I'll call you tomorrow, eh?" he said.

"Sounds great," I said, feeling once again like all was right in the world. That, of course, was before he blew me a kiss (what good are those?) and said while walking away, "Bye, goofy girl."

"Bye," I said, faking a smile and feeling like the biggest chicken west of the Mississippi . . . and probably east of it too.

As we walked off in different directions, Colin to the engineering building and I to the law school for New Testament (and to say hi to Mom), I turned up the collar of my coat and mumbled to myself, "Geez girl, how hard could it be to say, 'Please quit calling me that. It makes me want to rip your lungs out'? Jill would have done it by now, and she also would have figured out a different name for Keppler than 'Um.' Why can't I be more like her? We've been best friends since grade school. You'd think by now her fearlessness would have rubbed off on me, but it hasn't. Then again, maybe that's a good thing. I'm more tactful than she is, most days anyway. I mean, if Pudge asks if a dress makes her look fat, Jill would not only tell her it does, but at which angle she looks the fattest. Maybe telling your boyfriend the pet name he calls you makes you feel like knives are being sharpened in your head is just one of those things I instinctively understand wouldn't be polite. So I'm not being a coward, I'm being considerate."

I was so deep in conversation with myself (weird, I know) that it took awhile for it to register that a *psst!* sound was closing in on me. But finally the noise caught my attention, and I turned around and saw Phil (sorry, Elder Fitzsimmons) walking toward me with another missionary contentedly chewing a candy bar. "What are you doing here?" I asked as I glanced around, half worried the president of BYU himself was about to stride across the snow-covered lawn and, wrongly assuming this little rendezvous was my idea, give me a piece of his mind. I could practically hear him say, "Elder Fitzsimmons has just started his mission, and you, little missy, need to leave him alone!" If only our trusted officials wouldn't jump to conclusions.

"Whims," said Phil as he walked toward me with Elder Milky Way, "I need your help."

His voice hinted of desperation, something I did my best to ignore. "And you couldn't have asked for it in a letter?" I chided. "How did you even find me?"

Phil pulled a candy bar out of his trench coat pocket and handed it to his companion. "I had my sister look up your schedule," he said. "And no, I couldn't have sent you a letter. They're not persuasive enough."

Handing the candy bar back to Phil, his companion said, "Do you have one with nougat? I sorta like nougat."

"Sure," Phil said, and reached into his pocket again and found a king-size, nougat-filled candy bar. Handing it to his companion, he said, "Just five minutes. Okay, bro?"

Nodding and unwrapping, Phil's comp went to stand by a frozen yew bush not too far from us.

Answering my question before I could even asked it, Phil explained, "My comp didn't want to ditch class, but the guy grew up in a home where baked wheat germ was as close as they got to candy, and—"

"All you had to do was dangle candy bars in front of him."

"More or less," he said as I glared at him. "But don't be mad, Whims. I wouldn't have dangled if it weren't an emergency."

"What is an emergency?"

"Chiara," Phil said. "Whims, she knows. My sister got an e-mail from her, and Chiara knows."

"Knows what?" I asked, just to make him say it.

Phil looked around, then lowered his voice. "About the . . . stuff I was doin'."

"Could you be more specific?" I asked. "I'm not really sure what you're talking about."

"Come on, Whims, you're killing me."

"No, you're the one doing the killing. I mean, the whole time you were out there puckering up with whatever girl was handy, did it ever cross your mind that maybe Chiara would be hurt by it?"

"But I wasn't planning on her finding out!"

"Well, that was thinking ahead, wasn't it?"

"Plus, she was the one who said we shouldn't be boyfriend and girlfriend while we're apart—that it wouldn't work."

"And you're the one who told her it would!"

"Okay, okay!" said Phil, taking a deep breath. "I admit it was stupid for me to say that, and I know I shouldn't have nicmoed."

"Huh?"

"Noncommittal make out. I shouldn't have done it. But I swear—and I know this is going to tick you off—kissing all those girls before my mish was a lot like sampling ice cream."

"How sweet," I said, but Phil was too busy making his point to catch my sarcasm.

"Each sample only made it more clear to me that Chiara is—"

"Rocky Road?" I offered.

"Quit joking around, Whims."

"Sorry, you were comparing girls to ice cream, and . . . "

"And trying to tell you that I know now more than ever that Chiara is awesome, and I don't want to mess things up with her."

"Phil, you've pretty much already done that."

"I know, that's why I need to ask a favor: lie for me." I swear the entire campus hushed to near silence as I contemplated that I was standing just a stone's throw from the Honor Code Office and an LDS missionary was asking me to lie for him. I suppose sensing my shock, Phil, or rather, Elder Fitzsimmons, said, "Okay, let me rephrase that. I'm not asking you to lie, just stall. Don't tell her anything . . . right now. Let me do it when I get back. Please, I swear I'll tell her then. Just let me wait two years. Come on, we're talking twenty-four months."

I groaned in frustration. "But she's already asked me if I know anything."

"And what have you told her?"

"Nothing yet. But Phil, I have to tell her! She's my friend."

"I'm your friend too!" he shouted, making a group of girls walking by look at us. However, it wasn't until Phil said, "Nothing going on here! Just a little friendly conversation between friends," and tossed his comp a candy bar that their look turned suspicious.

Phil waited a moment until the girls were past us, then said, "Whims, I swear I'll tell her down the road, but—"

"You sure weren't worried about who heard you a few months ago," I interrupted, "when you stood on that box and blabbed to the world about stockpiling kisses. Gotta fill your canteen, you said. Gotta prepare for the desert. Now look at you. You're bribing your comp with candy bars and begging me to cover for you!"

Phil looked down at the ground and, not that he deserved it, but my anger toward him melted. There was just such a sense of hopelessness in his eyes it was impossible for me to leave without helping him somehow. "All right," I said. "I'll think of something."

Brightening up considerably, Phil said, "Whims, I knew I could count on you," and then looked at his watch. "Whoa, we've gotta get back," he said, then, socking me lightly in the arm, added, "Thanks a ton."

"Don't mention it," I said as he and his companion hustled down the sidewalk. "I mean it!" Without pausing to turn around, Elder Fitzsimmons waved at me and all that was behind him.

* * *

Class was a short break from the weirdness of the day—so short, in fact, that the moment class was over and I had walked into the hallway, the first person I saw was Henry Spessard. "What have I done to deserve this?" rolled through my head as I smiled at Henry and said, "Hi."

"How you doin' there, kiddo?" said Henry, cradling a large bouquet of roses in one arm.

"Fine," I said, "and who are those for?"

Looking almost guilty, he asked, "Who are what for?"

The pencils in your shirt pocket, you moron, I thought, but still managed to say quite pleasantly, "The bouquet of roses, of course."

Henry looked at the bouquet with surprise, as if it were a total shock to discover he was carrying around such a thing. "Oh, that. Well . . . " he said.

He was obviously embarrassed, so just to help him out, I mean, motivated out of complete niceness, I said, "She's one lucky lady; they're beautiful." What he said in return nearly made me swear off ever doing anything nice again.

"Whimsy," he said as the hallway traffic continued to detour around us, "I can see where you're goin' with this."

"Huh?"

Henry took in a big whiff of air, scrunching up his nose as he did. "It's hard to let go sometimes, especially when somethin's so right you could kick it. Your mom and I were that way—just two peas smashed together in a kettle of soup—but I've moved on, and I have to tell you that I don't have those kind of feelin's for you."

"Huh?"

"This bouquet isn't yours."

I opened my mouth to tell him what he was thinking was groundless, illogical, and completely whacked, but Henry put his hand up to stop me and said, "You see, these flowers belong to that fair flower." Just then, Olivia Q. Snell—of all people—walked up and put her arm through his.

"Oh . . . my . . . gosh," I said.

Leaning slightly forward as usual, Snell said to me, "Fancy meeting you here. It's such a small campus."

"You two know each other?" I asked, completely stunned.

"Yes," said Snell as she began to snort with laughter, "and write this down: *Henry Spessard is divine.*"

Henry looked at Snell with love and then at me with concern. "But there's no need to be embarrassed about your feelin's for me, kiddo. I just thought I should be straight with you."

Rather than say another word that might be misconstrued, I simply took off down the crowded hallway with Henry shouting to me, "Put mud on a bee sting, that's what I've done. One day you'll thank me!"

Mumbling, "This isn't happening to me," I made my way to the law library to look for Mom. The day had been so weird that when I saw her sitting at her study desk, I half expected her to turn around and be a chimp with a blonde wig, but she wasn't. She was Mom, only she was nauseous Mom.

"Hi, sweetie," she said, pressing her fingers to her temples. "How's your day going?"

"You don't want to know," I said, but instead of asking why like she normally would have, she grabbed the garbage can tucked under her desk and bid her breakfast a fond farewell. No one vomits more discreetly than my mom, so it wasn't like it grossed me out or anything. I just felt sorry for her. She was four months along, hardly looked pregnant, but felt it to the core.

I was about to say, "Are you okay?" when Keppler materialized out of nowhere, took the garbage can from his wife, and said, "I'm taking you home."

"Stanley," she soothed, "I'll be fine now."

"Whimsy, could you tell your mother she needs to go home and rest?"

"Whimsy, could you tell my husband I'm fine now?"

"Whimsy, could you remind your mother that her doctor said to not overexert herself?"

"Whimsy, could you tell my husband—"

"Whoa, whoa, whoa," I said, "As much as I like being included in a conversation, I've gotta go . . . prior commitments, the whole nine yards. So, call me and tell me how it ends because I'm really interested, but see ya." I ran out of the law library and bolted from the building.

* * *

I needed a brisk walk, a chance to clear my head, and Sable's seemed like the place to go. I mean, if it hadn't been for the perfect score I got on my New Testament quiz, I might have thought I'd been kidnapped by aliens and transported to a replica of BYU where, if you unscrew a student's left ear, you see nothing but a jumble of wires, a place purposefully designed to freak me out, monitor my stress levels, and report any interesting findings to the mother ship. Good grades can definitely give one some peace of mind.

Anyway, by the time I got to Sable's house, I was still addled (one of Sable's words) and almost didn't want to knock on her door. I mean, if she greeted me pleasantly and asked me to stay for lunch, I might collapse in a heap on her front step. Tentatively, I knocked.

I waited with my eyes closed as she fiddled with the locks. "Just when I'm wanting a bit of peace and quiet," she said as she motioned for me to come inside, "you come banging on my door!"

I reached forward and, to her surprise (and a bit to mine), kissed the top of her head. "Thanks," I said.

"For what?" she demanded.

"For making my world normal again. Let's just leave it at that."

chapter 20

To: Chiarissima@italnet.com
From: Whims1@byu.edu

Dear C,

Hey, got your e-mail, and all I can say is wow. I mean, that doesn't really sound like the Phil I know today. In fact, I recently bumped into Phil on campus, and he made a point of telling me how awesome he thinks you are. That much is the truth. I'd write more, but I've got to head over to Sable's. Take care and don't worry about Phil. W

* * *

If I've given the impression that Sable suddenly transformed into a fountain of never-ending information about herself, I apologize. It wasn't that way at all. Yes, she was now at least willing to answer questions about her past, but they had to be good questions, both well worded and well-informed. "I'm not here to teach you history," she'd snap at me. "If you have a good question I'll answer it. Otherwise, we can talk perennials."

I hate to admit it, but as I launched into asking Sable the kinds of questions that for so long she had shunned, Merriwether was a big help. Not that Merriwether knew it, and I definitely had no intention of telling her, but the way she had yammered on and on at Thanksgiving about Sable, telling me more than I really cared to know, allowed me—especially at the beginning—to sound competent. "It's often assumed Thompson is her maiden name," she had said (among a million other things), "but it's not. It's her middle name. She once said that if parents go to the trouble of giving a child a middle name, that child should go to the trouble of using it. Always quick with the cheeky response, Sable is, which is a big part of why I feel a kinship with her." Hudson and I both gave each other a look that said, "Oh, please," and I had to bite my lip to keep from laughing.

Merriwether kept on talking. "Sable Thompson Greer was a pioneer of modern-day womanhood. She put career before companionship, and duty to country before career. When she came back to the United States to care for her mother, she'd already done so much with her life, she chose to embrace the one thing she had enjoyed so little of in Europe: solace. And if I never marry or have children, I envision I shall be like Sable, content to live my life alone, spurning the inquisitive busybodies who want to know about all my accomplishments. I shall be as private as her."

"I'll be sure not to stand between you and your dream," Hudson had said, and then we both burst out laughing, greatly vexing that future stoic spinster herself, Merriwether Huff.

* * *

The first question I asked that had struck gold (meaning Sable gave more than a one-sentence response) was about the cane, and to be honest, the question was a total guess. I mean, all I had done was remember that Merriwether said the cane had belonged to a Lawrence Glengarry, and so I said, "Why did Mr. Glengarry carve those pictures into his cane?"

I had braced myself for her to say something like, "You actually think a man of Glengarry's importance had time to carve pictures into wood! He bought it as is at a cane shop!" But she didn't. Instead, she stared at me, a look of astonishment in her dim blue eyes and her mouth agape with wonder. "You've done your homework," she had said, and then raised her chin with an air of satisfaction.

The cane, as it turned out, was originally given to Glengarry by his grandmother at the time he left Cornwall to join the RAF, and if you already knew that stands for the Royal Air Force, good for you. I didn't, and was panicked Sable would sense as much, which most likely she would have, given a little more time. All I can say is, it pays to carry a pocket dictionary. I quickly pulled it from my backpack, turned to the Rs, found the info I needed, and said, "Why did his grandmother think he needed a cane as a member of the Royal Air Force?" And that was a question Sable deemed worthy of an answer.

"Already Cornwall had seen so many of its men die in the war," she had said, leaning back in Aunt Ruth's rocker and nearly closing her eyes as she remembered. "The cane was meant to give him hope, hope that he would live through and well past the chaos and peril consuming the world. That he would one day, with cane in hand, tell his grandchildren what he had seen, what he had lived through. It was his idea, not his grandmother's, to carve the pictures. He saw incredible, breathtaking sights as an aviator before he joined us in Paris, and the images he wanted to remember he etched into the cane.

"He delighted in seeing the world from his plane—absolutely reveled in it. Of course, Cornwall was all he'd known before the RAF, so everything amazed him, absolutely everything. And it was this sense of wonder that made it so easy for me to spot him as an evader that June in the Paris station. He was so busy looking at the mosaics on the ceiling he didn't see the German soldiers walking toward him, eyeing him suspiciously.

"The Germans were generally as thick as planks when it came to spotting evaders, or rather, downed airmen trying to escape. But we in the Resistance knew, for so many little reasons, who was an evader. Glengarry wasn't being helped by our line. In fact, I was at the train station simply to buy a ticket to Marseilles for the next day. But the crowd was thinning, and I knew something must have happened to the helper meant to meet him. And so that day in Paris, I did for him what I had done so many times before to throw off the Germans: I rushed toward a young man I didn't know and kissed him," she said as a smile threatened to stretch across her face.

"You little tramp," I said, knowing somehow she'd find it funny. "And ten bucks says he was handsome as well as curious."

"We all had to do our part to win the war," she said, and laughed behind a gnarled hand.

It was the first time I had seen Sable laugh, and rather than being odd or out of character, her laugh was so natural, so infectious, it made it easy to envision her as she once was: young, beautiful, high-spirited, and above all, happy.

It looked like the smile on her face was going to be hanging around for a while, so I thought it might be a good time to ask if I could have a closer look at the cane. It was propped up against an end table near the rocker. "Do you mind if I pick it up and look at it? The cane, I mean."

"Of course I mind," she snapped, looking as if I had just asked to use it as a makeshift bat for Tyson's T-ball game.

Shrugging off my embarrassment, I said, "Then do you mind if I ask you another question about the cane?" She didn't say anything, which I knew meant she'd hear the question first and then decide if she'd answer it. "*This burden lifted,* the phrase etched in at the bottom of the cane, what does it mean?"

Sable closed her eyes and said in a voice that sounded faraway (not to mention Scottish),

"This burden lifted
I will not walk away
Though others sifted and sorted
The reasons not to stay
This burden lifted
In face of bitterest squall
I'll do that thou asked of me:
Be friend to all."

This was one of those moments when my guilt about taping Sable on the sly nearly evaporated. "That was beautiful."

"It's not beautiful," she snapped, with tears brimming in her eyes. "It's a pile of rubbish."

"What makes you say th—"

"Because you can't be friend to all!" she yelled. "It's impossible, but Caswell never could understand that."

"And who was Caswell?" I asked, though I figured she'd probably tell me to go to the library and figure it out for myself.

But she didn't. "Hamish Caswell," she said as she took the hand-kerchief tucked at her wrist and wiped away the tears sliding down her weathered cheeks, "was a Scottish minister who was an important link in the Summit Line. Caswell carved that poem above the door of the seamen's mission he operated. His little chapel at the edge of the sea was the last safe house on our line before the Pyrenees Mountains and the relative safety of Spain. Caswell was a dear man, a gleeful man, and a true friend, but I knew his kindness was bound to make him careless, and I should have done more . . . "

Sable stared straight ahead, looking at nothing and somehow everything. Her eyes were dry now, but the glint of intensity in them made it seem as though she was attempting to reshuffle, like a deck of cards, certain events in her life, trying to arrive at some answers about how things could have been different, at how she could have ended up with the winning hand. Questions I wanted to ask her came rushing to the tip of my tongue, but thankfully, something told me if I just stuffed a sock in it and didn't say anything for a while, she'd start talking about those images rolling around in her mind, and boy was I right.

"Of course, Caswell and Glengarry were as opposite as could be. Caswell's boundless enthusiasm was likely to leave you with spit in your eye, especially when talking about yet another one of his elaborate plans involving the line. I doubt there was ever a man who enjoyed clandestine work more. Don't misunderstand me—he was well aware of the risks, but for him, duping the Germans was enormous fun.

"As for my Glengarry, he was steady. Never rejoicing or despairing, just steady. A rock for all of us, really, from the moment he became a part of the line. It was Caswell who asked him to stay and persuaded me to approve it. Of course, London was reluctant to let Glengarry stay, which I understood. After all, they needed their aviators. It was an expensive undertaking to train a man to fly, and with the number of raids increasing, more and more of their men were getting shot down. Still, I hated losing to London, and knew if I told them that with Glengarry we'd be able to help more airmen return home, they'd agree to it, and they did.

"So Glengarry stayed. His French was decent, which was enormously advantageous for us, but what a surprise it had been for me. Indeed, the whole point in kissing him that day at the train station had been to keep him from talking. If the Germans had decided to

210   LISA MCKENDRICK

ask him their usual questions, either his lack of French or the presence of a shoddy accent might have given away his true identity. So I
had kissed him and, thinking myself quite clever, even said in
between kisses as the guards walked past us how good it was to see
him again, that it had been too long and what have you, and then
quickly carried on kissing him so that he couldn't reply. But then—
and I shall never forget this—he pulled away just long enough to say,
'I got here as soon as I could,' in French so perfect it made my knees
buckle. It was so unexpected."

I wanted to laugh but stopped myself. I didn't want to do
anything to stop her from remembering, and so I sat there as quietly
as I could as Sable continued to talk.

"The Germans were always trying to mess up our work, find a
way to infiltrate escape lines, which was a constant worry. Most of the
lines experienced arrests, but none as massive as the Shelley Line. The
entire line folded after the arrest of Erneste Dujon and over a
hundred helpers. It was stunning news. No one was sure, at least at
the cafés where we gathered our information, who had been the
traitor. No one suspected Gallo. Henre Gallo was a known member
of the Resistance who was credited with helping many men escape the
Germans. And when he arrived at the seamen's mission, bedraggled
and hungry, Caswell didn't question his story. Gallo told Caswell he
had been a part of the Shelley Line and had narrowly escaped arrest.
Caswell took him in, clothed him, fed him, and then tried to recruit
him for our line.

"Glengarry tried to tell me he sensed something was awry. He
tried to warn me that Gallo shouldn't be trusted. It was too soon after
the Shelley arrests, he had said. We needed to lie low, let things die
down a little. Easier said than done! The collapse of the Shelley Line
had created a backlog of men trying to escape. Countess LeComte's
summer chateau alone had thirty men in it just waiting for us to help
them. I didn't know if it was the right thing to do, but I was the
leader, not Glengarry, regardless of how much he fussed over me. I
was the leader. It was my decision, and I chose . . . I chose that Gallo
should become part of us."

"So what happened?" I blurted, stupidly saying exactly what I was
thinking. *Quick!* I told myself. *Act casual.* "I mean, not that I care

what happened." *Durr! Casual, not bored.* "Not to say I don't care, because I do. I mean, I care a lot . . . just, um, not enough to twist your arm . . . or leg, heh heh heh." *Somebody shoot me.*

Sable didn't laugh. She grabbed the knob of her cane, wobbled to her feet, and said, "I haven't time to listen to you prattle on. I need to turn my needle-point ivy to the sun, among other things."

"I completely understand," I said, though I wanted to scream, "Tell me right now this has a happy ending! Gallo was a skank, wasn't he? But you guys were able to figure that out, right? Tell me he didn't hurt the line! Tell me he didn't hurt Caswell or Glengarry! Please tell me he didn't hurt you!"

Sable shuffled over to the kitchen to fill the watering can. She was done talking for the day, no doubt about it. I watched her as her frail and clumsy hands steadied the can and turned on the faucet. No wonder, I thought, it was hard for her to accept help. Once she had been the one to lift others' burdens. Her hands had been strong and capable then, unspotted by age. No wonder she hated being reminded what they had become.

Still, her amazing past didn't change the fact that right here right now, the kitchen garbage was piled high, and it was tons easier for me to carry it outside than it was for her. So I did what I had become accustomed to doing: I made a joke of it. "Look," I said as she turned off the faucet, "I know you're fond of taking the garbage out, but so am I. And since you're watering plants, it's only fair I get to do it."

Water slopped to the floor as she made her way to the ivy in the front bay window. "Suit yourself," she said with a shrug. "You can take it all the way to the curb for all I care. Today is garbage day."

"Good, I'll do that," I said as I tied the bulging bag shut.

I was on my way out the kitchen door with garbage bag in hand when Sable said something to me, or at least I thought it was to me. "Wh—" I said, stopping quickly as soon as I realized she wasn't speaking to anyone but herself.

"It shouldn't still hurt this much," she said, shaking her head. "After all this time, it shouldn't feel like yesterday."

I didn't say a word, just quietly walked out the back door to take out the trash. But all at once I knew that regardless of what Sable wanted, I was going to find out what had happened so long ago. After all, it was "public information," as Merriwether would have put it, and I, as a member of the general public, was entitled to know. What's more, the budding journalist in me had to find out regardless of whatever promises I had made myself. I had to know what happened.

chapter 21

To: Chiarissima@italnet.com
From: Whims1@byu.edu

Hey, I know you're massively busy getting ready for that vet school exam, but I'm wondering if you could help me out by answering a question. Here's the situation: yesterday in New Testament class we got into this huge discussion about the parable of the good Samaritan and what Christ meant when He said, 'Go and do thou likewise.' The question we started battling over was how much exactly are we expected to actually do as we get out there and "do likewise"? This one guy in my class (and don't let the fact that he bugs me influence you) went on and on about how unless we're inconvenienced and uncomfortable, we're not doing enough to help our fellow man, blah blah blah. I shot my hand in the air, and said (before I had actually been called on—oops), "Whatever happened to man—and for that matter, woman—is that they might have joy?" How the heck are we supposed to have joy if all we do is bog ourselves down taking care of others? Be glad you're in Italy. There are some real bone-heads walking around BYU. I mean, that guy actually said to me, "Selfishness is a great fault," and then I said, "So is self-righteousness."

So before the whole thing got more out of hand, our professor assigned us to take a survey, asking five people we know the following question: As we strive to be good Samaritans ourselves, who are we expected to help? A) Everyone we see. B) Those people we have the time and means to help. C) Those who are most in need. D) Not sure.

Jill's answer to the survey question was E) Everyone who doesn't bug me, which is essentially no one. Anyway, I don't usually get so bent out of shape (mad, just in case that term is confusing for you) in class, and I suppose I probably should have just ignored what he was saying, but lately I'm getting stressed trying to juggle everything in my life. I've been going over to Sable's as much as I can because I know she needs me, even if she'll never admit it. Plus, she's been talking (when she feels like it) about her past, which I'll have to tell you about sometime because it's completely amazing. So anyway, it's sort of like a win-win situation: she needs me, and I need to hear what happened next in the story of her life.

But there are other things I have to factor into my schedule that I think are a complete waste of time, like visiting teaching Athena Croward and her fan of a roommate. They obviously don't need me, or for that matter, want me to bother them. Athena always takes a moment to discreetly roll her eyes when I ask if we can visit teach her. Sure, it's usually close to the last day of the month, but hey, at least I'm trying, unlike some people (think Jill).

Well, I've gone on long enough. I know that you, of all people, do not have time to deal with a survey, but I also know you, of all people, will take the time to do it anyway. I should be more like you, Chiara. I'm such a whiner, except when I'm around Colin. I swear he brings out the best in me, even though Jill says he brings out the fake in me. It's true I try harder to be nice when I'm around him, but isn't that a good thing? Anyway, got to go. Love, W

P.S. Oops! I almost forgot to thank you for the HUGE box of Italian chocolates you sent for my birthday. They arrived this morning, and all I can say is, truffles beat bran flakes for breakfast, hands down. Thanks so much! W

* * *

To: anglertomax@mapleleaf.com
From: Whims1@byu.edu

Dear Colin,

Just wanted to drop you an e-mail to thank you again for the lovely fishing gear. It was such a sweet birthday present and totally unexpected. I just hope you didn't spend too much! Still, I can't wait until we can go fishing again and I can use my new pole, not to mention gutting knife.

You really are so sweet. It'll be great to get back in the river again, and I swear this time the only thing that's gonna get soggy are the sandwiches in the cooler. Have fun in D.C. interviewing, and I'll see you when you get back. Smooch smooch. Whimsy

"Smooch, smooch," said Jill, sounding ready to gag.

I turned around to see Jill and Josh standing behind me in the Cannon Center computer lab, and it was all I could do to keep from jumping up and covering the computer screen with my raincoat. "Hey," I asked, doing my best to sound casual, "what are you guys doing here?"

"You mean besides reading over your shoulder?" asked Jill, plopping down in the chair next to me.

"Yeah, besides that," I said, and gave her a look that told her, "You're toast." She gave me one back that said, "Smooch, smooch, I don't care."

"Well, *cumpleaño* girl, we came by to give you your present, but since you've already gotten your heart's desire, a gutting knife—"

"Yeah, I tried it out on Spot and it works great."

Jill was in the middle of giving me a how-dare-you-say-that look when Josh said, "Jilly, be nice and give Whims the present." For a guy who didn't mind brawling over a football, Josh sure hated a fight. And it wasn't like we were really even fighting. I mean, we were just goofing around.

Jill pulled a small box wrapped in colorful paper from her pocket and gave it to me. "We were going to give you a bunch of fish hooks and a couple of buckets of worms, but this was easier to wrap."

"Ha ha," I said, and started to unwrap the present. Jill is a big gift-giver and receiver, which has its good points and bad. Sure, she gives good gifts, but if she doesn't like what I give her, she makes me take it back and try again. In fact, the year she turned sixteen, I made so many trips to downtown Tempe I not only overcame my fear of parallel parking but was voted downtown patron of the month by the Chamber of Commerce. I opened the box, pulled away the tissue, and saw a gorgeous sterling silver charm bracelet with a single, stupid charm in the shape of a trout dangling from it.

"Read the inscription," she said.

I turned the fish over and read, "Jill does not have gills." I looked up just in time to see Jill opening and closing her mouth like a fish. Calmly, I turned to Josh and said, "This is one of those times when I don't know whether to thank her or strangle her."

"I told her to go with the gymnast charm," said Josh, sounding as if he feared Jill and I were about ready to take this outside.

"That was a mud-flap girl, not a gymnast," said Jill.

"Still, she looked kinda sporty," said Josh.

"Besides," said Jill, "I ran into Captain Toronto at the bookstore and he told me what he was getting you, so I wanted my present to tie in."

"Well, that was thoughtful of you," I said. "Demented, but thoughtful."

"Speaking of thoughtful," said Jill, "I've got your entire birthday weekend figured out. Meals on Wheels' parents have a cabin near Brighton, and a bunch of us, including Chloe and maybe Pudge, are heading up there to go skiing. And here's the good part, *cumpleaño* girl. I'm covering the cost of your rentals and Josh is springing for your lift ticket, so the only thing you're gonna have to worry about is showing up. Does that make up for the trout charm, or what?"

"It does, but I've got one problem."

"Okay, fine," said Jill as she stood and handed Josh her backpack to hold. "Sable can come if she pays her own way. After all, it's not her birthday weekend."

I smiled at the thought of Sable, fragile and stooped over as she was, skiing down the mountainside. "It's not Sable," I said, "it's my mom. Keppler is going to be out of town this weekend. He's speaking at some conference in New York, and he asked me to stay with my mom, sorta keep an eye on her."

"Whims, this is the kind of situation for which cell phones were invented. I'll bring mine and you can call her at the top of the mountain, in the lodge, even while we're sitting on the lift, if you promise not to drop it."

"I can't. My mom hasn't been feeling too great, and the only reason Keppler was willing to leave was because I told him I'd stay with her."

"Bum—" she started.

"—mer," I finished. "I really wish I could go."

"Yeah, yeah," Jill said, and gave me a birthday hug.

"Be good," I whispered in her ear, and she gave a look that said, "Duh, why wouldn't I?"

"Bye, Whims," said Josh as he gave me a brotherly hug.

I meant to say good-bye, I really did. But all at once this indescribable concern for Jill swept over me, and I said, "Take good care of her."

Josh looked directly at me and said, "I will."

* * *

As much fun as a weekend of skiing sounded (and it did sound fun), I really didn't mind staying behind to hang out with my mom. It was the first time in a long time it had been just the two of us. Well, the two of us, the baby kicking, and Keppler calling every five minutes.

"I promise I'll call you as soon as I wake up in the morning, honey," Mom reassured him after his fiftieth call that night. "And yes, I'll tell Whimsy happy birthday."

"Tell him I love the journal."

"Whimsy says she loves the journal. Yes, yes, I'll be sure to tell her that too. All right, I love you, honey. Good night." Mom hung up the phone, took a deep breath, and looked at me, causing us both to laugh.

"He sure is concerned about you."

"Such a good man, but he is a bit anxious."

"Mom, the guy tried to order your doctor to put you on bed rest. He's practically flipping out."

Mom rolled her eyes and smiled at the thought of that previous conversation. "But he means well," Mom said. "And speaking of bed rest, I think I'll head there right now."

She paused for a moment, as if trying to gather some energy to deal with getting ready for bed, and while she sat there, the two of us saw a jolt of movement beneath her T-shirt.

"Whoa," I said, placing my hand where the movement had been, "that was huge. What did it feel like?"

"Heaven," said Mom. "Absolute heaven. I remember you kicking inside me and what a stinker we thought you were. You'd kick and kick, but as soon as your daddy would try to put his hand on my stomach to feel you move, you always seemed to stop."

"I'm sure I had my reasons," I said as I helped her off the couch.

I thought about telling her about Dad and the whole lack-of-money thing, but decided against it. After all, I was into the groove of working at the Bean Museum, and besides, I was beginning to take a certain pride in the way I dusted rhino heads.

"So are you going to bed?" asked Mom as she turned off the kitchen light.

"In a minute," I said. "It's not every day you turn nineteen. I'm gonna stay up awhile and soak up every minute of it."

"Which reminds me," said Mom, standing in front of me, "Stanley told me to be sure and tell you thank you." She leaned down and kissed me on the head.

Not that I had been tempted by Jill's cell phone offer, but a flash of guilt went through me anyway at the thought of being at Meals on Wheels' cabin instead of with her. "It's no biggie," I said. "I'm always willing to clear my schedule for a free 'I heart New York' T-shirt."

Mom smiled. "Love you, sweetie."

"Love you, Mom," I said, and she went to bed.

I waited until I heard her door shut and then reached into my backpack and pulled out what had been hidden in my top drawer for the past few months—Sable's letters. I swear I really grappled with the idea of invading Sable's privacy by reading them. I mean, I tried and tried to get her to tell me more about Gallo, Caswell, and Glengarry, but she wouldn't. She talked a lot about other people in the escape lines, some of whom she said she still keeps in touch with, but when it came to the story that had so intrigued me, she wouldn't budge. "I've told you all there is to know about that," she'd say. "Quit pestering me!"

Yes, it did bother me that I had pulled one over on Sable, but two things made me feel better: first, that the letters were in all likelihood important historical documents, and second, whatever Sable wasn't willing to tell me, I was certain the letters could.

I untied the faded pink ribbon and carefully opened the first letter to read it.

My Dearest One,

You are lying here beside me and yet I'm compelled to write this letter. Silly, I suppose, but I want you to know—always know—what a vision you were today as you came through the chapel doors. You couldn't have looked more beautiful, that pink ribbon in your hair and the small bouquet of daisies in your hand. My eyes well with tears and my heart nearly bursts just thinking of it . . . and everything that's happened since then.

Our world, the way it is right now, dashes to bits so much that once seemed permanent, but this it can never destroy or diminish—my love for you. From that first moment, that first kiss in the train station, I knew it was no use—my heart was yours. And so it is, and so it will ever be, come what may.

All my love, your husband, G

I really haven't done a lot of gasping in my life, but after reading that first letter, that's exactly what I did, I gasped. "Oh . . . my . . . gosh," I whispered. "Sable was married. But to who? How?" Then, as if in answer to my question, I noticed one envelope that seemed different from the others. It was the same size, but the paper was thicker. I pulled it out of the stack. On the front was written *Official Document* in the short, choppy script of what looked like a fourth grader. I opened the letter and inside was a marriage certificate stating that on 14 December 1943, Sable Thompson Greer and Lawrence Glengarry were married to each other by Hamish Caswell in the seamen's mission on a moonless night. And in the lower left corner, in that same somewhat sloppy writing, was written, *Until that time when order has again been restored to Europe, only God, His angels, and delighted servant of Scots descent shall know of this union.*

"Why the secrecy?" I asked, a question that grew inside me as I read letter after letter from Glengarry jam-packed with gushy sentiments. I mean, he obviously was nuts about her. Why, then, was it important that no one know they were husband and wife? As I read a letter toward the bottom of the stack, I started to understand.

Dearest One,

Out of my mind with worry over you. I know you're capable of running the lot of us, but as my wife I simply cannot allow you to be there when Gallo comes. Terrible thing to forbid one's wife. One almost instantly feels the ineffectualness of it, and so instead of forbidding let me then plead. I beg you, darling, please don't be there. My misgivings about Gallo are growing. Yes, he helped the last group safely make it from Paris to Marseilles, but Caswell mentioned in passing today he had been expecting seven men and Gallo brought four. It's possible that Caswell botched the number, but other things are possible as well. And so, my love, I beg you, I plead with you, stay away. And may the Protector of us all be ever mindful of us, especially now.

All my love, your husband

As if I had a say in how things turned out, I whispered, "No!"

I didn't want to read the last two letters, and in a way I didn't need to. My heart was already breaking because of what I knew they'd say. Holding one in each hand, I stared at the letters, wondering why things had to end the way they did, why they couldn't have been granted a happy ending. In fact, I was so consumed with what had happened so long ago that it took me a while to realize my mom was calling my name.

"Whimsy honey," she said, a note of false calm in her voice, "something's wrong." To be honest, the only thing I can remember from that point until the blinding lights and sobering paperwork of the hospital was the sight of my mother standing in the hallway with bright, fresh blood staining her nightgown and the look of fear on her face.

chapter 22

There are some people in this world who flat-out shouldn't be nurses. With hearts as cold as their hands, they barge and shove their way through their workday, never pausing to consider the enormity of what they touch or what they say. And when Nurse Speck shoved a wheelchair under my mother and said, "Did it even cross your mind to wear a pad?" I knew we were dealing with one of them.

"How long has she been bleeding?" snapped Speck as she looked at me while taking Mom's temperature.

I cleared my throat and tried not to sound intimidated by her. "She went to bed at ten," I said, "and was fine until, I guess, around one-thirty."

"And how far along and how old is she?" she asked in the same brusque way.

I wanted to say, "Why don't you just ask her?" After all, the thermometer had been in Mom's ear, not her mouth, and the whole preferring-not-to-speak-to-the-patient-directly thing was beginning to bug me. Still, I answered the question. "Twenty-two weeks along, I think," I said as Mom nodded lightly in agreement, "and forty years old."

"No wonder," mumbled Speck, making me want to take the metal tray in front of her and whack her across the head, but instead I took a deep breath and told myself Mom's doctor would be coming soon. "So where's hubby?" asked Speck as if she were doing what was probably her true calling in life, serving coffee at a diner.

"He's in New York," I said, "but he's on his way."

"Hubby's in New York and your doc's in Barbados. Not exactly the best timing."

I watched Mom close her eyes in pain as if Speck's little observation had been the prick of a needle. *That's it,* I thought. *It's time to tell Florence Nightingale that she's as short on tact as she is on height, and to keep her trap shut before I—* There wasn't time for me to finish my thought, let alone say anything, because just then another gush of blood came from my mother, followed by a rush of nurses, including Speck, wheeling my mother behind glass doors on which was written in bright red letters, *DOCTORS AND NURSES ONLY BEYOND THIS POINT.*

I stared at the statement on the doors for a moment as I said to no one in particular, "And prayers. It should say, *Doctors, nurses, and prayers.*"

* * *

My guess was whoever ran the hospital had worked their way through college as a lumberjack. What else besides a love of trees getting chopped down could explain the mounds of paperwork required for a single patient? I wrote my mom's personal info down so many times on so many different forms that, in spite of my best efforts to keep it from happening, a song of all that info formed in my head, plaguing me for the next couple of hours.

I waited for some news about my mom in a room far too cheerful for my mood, and passed the time by praying and looking down the hallway for Keppler. Aunt Helen had been the one to call Keppler. "Don't worry about anything but taking care of your mom," she had told me. "I'll take care of the rest." Why did her saying that make me feel as confident as if I'd just been asked to land the Concorde? I mean, sure, I had helped Mom before, even comforted her, but never in a hospital and never about something this big.

Bogged down with feelings of inadequacy, I mumbled to myself, "Whimsy Waterman, compassionate service leader," thinking about my calling in my ward. "Talk about your oxymorons."

As desperate as I was to hear what was happening with my mom, it was hard not to run in the other direction when I noticed a doctor in pale blue scrubs walking toward me. His face was expressionless, as if he'd seen too much as a doctor to ever be shocked or saddened again. A mask was still dangling around his neck, and he tugged one of the strings as he said in a steady voice, "I take it you're Joan's daughter." When I nodded my head, he continued by telling me exactly what I didn't want to hear. Obviously he was more experienced at giving bad news than I was at receiving it. I covered my ears with my hands and cried, "No!" as he told me about my mom's placenta previa becoming acute (whatever that was), the baby being too small to save, and their needing to perform an emergency hysterectomy to stop the hemorrhaging.

"Stop it!" I shouted. "Don't tell me my mom is dying and make it sound like you're ordering a pizza!"

The doctor and I stared at each other for a moment. He tugged even harder now at the string dangling from his neck, and in his eyes I thought I spotted the kindness he had learned, for whatever reason, to hold back. "I'm sorry," he said quietly but sincerely. "I wish I had something better to tell you."

I gulped hard as stupid tears (I hate crying in public) spilled down my cheeks. Reaching out with one hand, the doctor patted me awkwardly on my shoulder. (Geez, and I thought I was bad at the comforting gig.) "You can go in and see her now, though she'll still be groggy." I nodded my head and we walked together down a sterile hallway.

"Be strong for her," I whispered to myself as I pushed the door open. "Be strong for her." But that was easier to say than do. She opened her eyes as I walked into her room with a stiff, hopeless smile hammered to my face. I was nearly knocked backed by how frail, how vulnerable she looked. This may sound weird, but she looked like a child in that hospital bed with her hair all messed up and the color drained from her face.

"Hi, Mom," I said. *Be strong,* I thought. *And not sad, definitely not sad.*

"Hi, sweetie," she said as faintly as a gentle breeze.

This is okay. I'm good. I'm handling this.

Mom swallowed, and I knew that her throat was sore, but from what I wasn't sure. She took my hand and said, almost whispered, "You should have seen her. She was so perfect, so tiny . . . and she had Stanley's nose. I love his nose."

Comfort her, I told myself, and started to say something like, "That's great, Mom," but the words got all jammed in my throat as tears again filled my eyes. *Comfort her!* I tried to tell myself, but it was no use. I slumped down in the chair next to my mom, put my head close to hers, and sobbed and sobbed.

"Sh-sh-sh," she soothed as she stroked my head. "Sh-sh-sh. It's all right, honey. It'll be all right," she reassured again and again until my tears subsided and I drifted to sleep.

* * *

A few hours later when I awoke to the sound of Speck yakking it up in the hallway, my mom was asleep, her hand heavy on my head. The door to my mom's room was held slightly ajar by a tray Speck was planning to wheel into Mom's room after she'd finished talking, or to be more precise, hollering. Not that she was mad. She was just talking so loudly it seemed likely she was either trying to compensate for or give someone hearing loss. The tray banged against the door, and instantly I was on my feet. This was one of those moments when I didn't need to think things through. My objective was clear and had been clear from the last moment I had seen Speck. "I need to speak with you outside."

"All right," she said, making no attempt to lower her voice.

I waited until we, the tray included, were in the hallway and the door to my mother's room was completely shut, then I said through gritted teeth, "I don't want you or your loser personality anywhere near my mother, do you get that?"

She moved forward a little as if she could brush me and what I was saying aside. "I don't have time for this," she said. "I need to take her vitals, and—"

I was shaking with anger. "Take your own decrepit vitals for all I care, but you're never going near her again."

This time she made a sorry attempt at kindness. "Honey," she squawked as she moved toward the door, "if I've done something to—"

"Beat it," I interrupted as I stepped in front of her with a glare that most definitely said, "I'm seven inches taller than you, twice as strong, and while I've never actually taken someone down before, right now looks like a good time to start."

"I'll come back later," she scowled, obviously unwilling to admit she was backing down.

"Another nurse will come back later," I informed her as she stormed off. "We're done with you."

My heart pounded with what seemed to me to be victory as I watched Nurse Speck storm off to the nurse's station. Maybe Mom hadn't noticed Speck's rudeness, but I had, and keeping her away from my mom made me feel as if in some small way I had taken care of her.

Adrenaline was still pouring though me from my "chat" with Speck when I spotted in the distance Keppler walking—make that running—toward me. His bow tie was undone, with the two ends flipping about like Colin's catch of the day (not a happy thought), and his hat was crushed in his hand. "Keppler!" I yelled as I ran toward him. "Keppler!" I said again, not thinking for a moment that something remarkable had just happened. I had actually called my stepfather something other than "Um."

We met in the middle of the hallway, and I couldn't stop myself from giving him a hug, I was so glad, so relieved to see him. "Thank heavens you're here," I said as we hugged, certain he would instantly take control of things. And I was about to tell him all about rude nurses, emotionless doctors, and so much more when I realized that Keppler was shaking, crying, and clinging to me as if the world had collapsed and I was all that was left of stability.

I'm not going to lie to you, I felt like a total idiot. Not because of him, but because of me. I mean, I wanted to do something to help him, to comfort him, but couldn't think of what—at first, anyway. But after standing there for a while, letting his tears fall on my shoulder, my mother's voice came into my mind, and I said—or at least tried to say—as soothingly as she had to me, "It's going to be all right."

* * *

I didn't want to leave Mom, but by four in the afternoon both Keppler and Aunt Helen were at the hospital, each with a different description for the dark circles under my eyes. Keppler thought I looked like I'd been smudged with football grease. Helen thought I looked more like a runway model. "But the difference is," she had said, "they get paid to look drained, you don't. So get some rest and come back in a few hours."

"All right," I had said, and after hugging them both (Mom was sleeping), I drove to the dorms with only one thing on my mind: falling into bed.

As I climbed the stairs, each step seemed to take me that much closer to realizing how tired, how worn out, how sad I was. I didn't want to talk to anyone and was glad no one seemed to want to talk to me. I just wanted to sleep so deep that for a moment I'd forget everything, especially my worries.

I flung the door open to my dorm (we hardly ever lock), and my mouth fell open at what I saw: Pudge sitting in the center of our room with little brown papers strewn everywhere, an empty box of Italian chocolates in her lap, and her finger down her throat.

chapter 23

Carissima Whimsy,

I hope my English is good enough so you comprehend what I want to tell you. I am very worry for you. You sound tired, and I think you do too much. A few weeks ago you ask me question about good Samaritan. At time, I not sure how to say what I feeling about question and had so much studies that I quickly give answer, "We must help everyone we see," and not explain how I want to change answer.

It impossible to help everyone we see. Still, I think of all answers I pick best one, because of the word everyone. *Is important that word, because I think our Father Celeste need us to be, how you say? Willing to help everyone. If we can be willing, He can be guide, to let us know who out of everyone we can help.*

Each day when I walk across piazza to university, I have many children come to me and beg for money. Is sad, some are so small. Still, I cannot help this way they ask. I do not have much money, and what I have I need to live and to study. I have peace when I say no to the children because I know Father understand I would help if I could, but I can't. And I know He will show me who I can help, if I am this word: willing.

It is good you try to help your mother. Is so sad what happen, and I know she need you. And is good you help Sable too, and your roommate who you say is not well. But be careful, amica mia, to do what you can, and not, how I say, empty your pockets to children on street. Con affetto, C

* * *

Amy Hope Keppler was buried on a cloudless March morning with a chill just strong enough to make our breath hang about us like ghosts. It was a small family service (so don't ask me why Merriwether was there), and my eyes blurred with tears as I held my mother's hand and watched as Keppler and his sons gently placed the tiny casket over the grave. The rest of the service—the grave dedication, the bishop's words of comfort, even the hymns—dissolved into a murky haze as I stared into the distance and thought of my little sister and all that I wished we could have seen: her first smile, her first step, her pigtails and love of pretty things, her skinned knees and shouts of joy over simple things like popsicles or the sound of the garage door opening at the end of the day. "Good-bye, Amy," I whispered too quietly for anyone but her to hear. "I'm going to miss you."

In the weeks that followed, I tried with a vengeance to make life normal again: I dusted and polished the Bean Museum, laughed at even the slightly funny things Colin said, and tried to remember to put a bounce in my step. (When a complete stranger says you look like you're carrying around a couple of bowling balls, you know you're dragging your feet.) But the truth was, it wasn't working. I didn't feel normal, but then again, how could I, considering the stuff I was trying to juggle, like Mom, Sable, Pudge, and even Jill.

For months I had worried about Pudge, wondering if her dieting was out of control. Jill didn't think it was any big deal that she ate only granola on Monday and soup on Tuesday, and salads (or was it sandwiches?) on Wednesday, but I did.

"Hello?" Jill would say, "Soup and granola are food, aren't they? I mean, not to me, but most people consider them food."

"Yeah," I'd tell her, "but she's so edgy. I swear she hasn't said 'I'm sorry' since before Christmas."

"And weren't you the one willing to pay her a buck for every day she didn't say 'I'm sorry'?"

"No, that was you."

"Whatever, but you thought it was a good idea. Whims, I honestly don't see cause for alarm. Pudge looks better, guys are asking her out, and—"

"And she's not happy," I had said.

"Sure she is," she had said, "She's got every reason in the world to be happy," and that had been the end of it.

* * *

Under normal (there's that word again) circumstances, I love getting the chance to run up to Jill and shout, "Ha! I'm right," but that afternoon when I found Pudge in our dorm, the look of desperation in her eyes made it clear that this time there would be no victory dance.

It was one of those rare moments when, faced with something difficult, a calm disposition came over me, almost like a gift.

"Pudge," I said as I shut and locked the door, "you can't do this to yourself."

"I'm so sorry," she cried, "I'm so sorry," and she buried her head in her hands.

I sat down next to her on the floor, those little papers all around us, and said, "We're in a mess."

Pudge said as she cried, "No, I *am* a mess, and I'm so sorry. I'll buy you some more chocolates, and I promise this will never happen again. I promise," and again buried her head in her hands.

"I don't care about the chocolates," I said, wadding up one of the papers and tossing it in the trash. "Most of them were cherry filled anyway." I gave her a nudge. "What I care about is you," I said, too tired to worry whether that sounded sappy. "I mean, if you can promise me anything," I said, noticing the fatigue in my own voice, "promise you'll never devour a box of chocolates—or anything else for that matter—and try to cram your finger down your throat."

Pudge winced, which I have to admit, I took as a good sign.

"I'm so stupid," she said, knocking her hand hard against her head. "I don't know how I let this snowball! All I wanted was to finally get control of my life and lose the weight that's been stuck to me since kindergarten. And at first I did it, and it was wonderful. I worked out, I didn't eat, and the weight started coming off, but I got so tired of rice cakes and water. I can go for days without food, I can be so good, but then I get hungry. I shouldn't, but I get hungry."

"But you're supposed to get hungry," I said, amazed that I needed to state something so obvious.

"You don't understand what it's like," she snapped, which was a rare thing for her to do. "Forty more pounds and I become invisible, at least to guys. My whole life I've been the girl they couldn't see, and I'm tired of it. I'm tired of feeling—and I know this sounds pathetic—like no guy could ever love me," and her voice broke with emotion as she said it.

"That does sound pathetic," I said, and wadded up a wrapper and chucked it at her head, making her smile just a little. "You're the only person in this entire dorm who can make their own terra cotta. What's not to love?"

"Around forty extra pounds of fat—if I'm not careful," she croaked, looking absolutely desperate.

My head throbbed with fatigue, sorrow, and the clear under-standing that Pudge's problem was bigger than I was smarter. "But Pudge," I said, "if your idea of careful is throwing up, then—not to offend you—I think you might need some help."

"Will you help me, Whimsy?" she pleaded, making me say, *Huh?* in my head. I mean, what could I possibly do? She was quick to tell me. "If you just asked me every day if I've had any slip-ups, I promise I'd tell you. And I know having to answer to you will keep me from losing control."

I was too tired and too sad to think of the many reasons I should tell her no. All I could think was that she needed help and I was her friend, and so I lay down on my bed, closed my eyes, and said, "All right, but I'll be watching you." That night, I dreamt of little children running from me, their pockets full of money.

* * *

As March moved into April, I began to notice the first signs of spring shooting from the earth and growing on the trees, but my mother's countenance remained for me the embodiment of winter. "She is giving up on everything," Keppler said to me as soon as Mom left the room to lie down. It was a beautiful Saturday afternoon. Sun streamed into the dreary avocado kitchen, where the two of us sat at the breakfast table. "Even school can't pull her out of it. Heaven knows I've wanted her to give it up in the past, but not like this."

Keppler rubbed his eyes and looked very much like the last month had taken a toll that only his concern for Mom could overpower. "What should we do?" I asked, thinking of something along the lines of talking to her.

"I think we should take her to Hawaii," said Keppler, and I looked up to see if he was joking. He wasn't. "I know you'll have to clear your schedule, and that's a lot to ask, especially this close to finals. But she needs you near her, and she needs to relax. She can't do that here, not in this house. Let's take her where she can do that."

I have never been known to turn down a free trip to Hawaii. Still, I said, "But the tickets are going to be so expensive."

Sounding as if he were talking about springing for dinner, he said, "Absolutely not a concern. I'll take care of it." I liked him all the more for it.

After a couple of phone calls, everything was arranged (amazing the things you can afford when you don't dust dead animals for a living), and though Mom made a weak attempt at protesting, in her voice I thought I heard the faintest hint of excitement. "We'll pick you up at seven Monday morning," Keppler said as I began to make a mental list of all I needed to do.

"Great, I'll be waiting for you," I said as a wave of what should have been excitement washed over me.

* * *

Work and school were easy enough to square away, but I was seriously stressed about leaving Pudge, Sable, and even Jill (maybe it was just my imagination, but lately Jill had seemed kinda distant). Pudge insisted she'd be fine. "I'm doing better. Yesterday, like I told you, I had an episode after breakfast. But I swear, I'm feeling better, stronger. I know I'll be fine."

I tried to tell myself she was right. I wrote down my mom's cell phone number and handed it to her. "I'll call you every night to see how things are going, and if you feel the slightest bit tempted to, you know, vomit, call me, and I'll just, I don't know, work some Hawaiian magic."

"I promise I'll be fine, really," she said.

I smiled and headed out the door to see Sable. "Sure," I mumbled to myself as I walked down the hall, "just like you promised you'd never throw up again."

* * *

It wasn't until I passed the bell tower on my way to Sable's that I remembered Colin had asked me to meet him under the bells at five-thirty. He had just returned from interviewing in Little Rock and said he wanted to take me out someplace nice. "We'll start our evening under the bells and see where we go from there."

A part of me wanted to say, "What's with the bells?" but I just giggled and said I'd be there with bells on. Just joking. I said I'd be there.

Suddenly aware I was pressed for time, I ran the rest of the distance to Sable's house. It was nearly four, and if I was going to have time to get dressed up like Colin had asked, I needed to cut Sable short. As I ran I rehearsed what I was going to say to her, "Sable, I'm going to Hawaii for a week. I'll send you a postcard . . . even though you can't see well enough to read it." No, definitely not, but I knew I'd think of something.

Sable's front door was ajar, and I walked in as I shouted her name.

"Good!" she cried from the top of the stairs. "I'm glad you're here."

"That's a first," I whispered, and shut the door.

"There's something I need you to do," she said as I walked up the stairs. "The ladder to the attic is a bit unruly for me, but you can manage it, and I want you to go up there and clean. No one's been up there for twenty, maybe thirty years and it's high time the cobwebs came down."

"Sable—" I started.

"And there's one chest in particular, a large one. You'll see it. I'd like you to bring it down so I can have a look at what's inside. I haven't looked in it for at least . . . "

"Let me guess, thirty years."

"Thereabouts," she said, ignoring my sarcasm.

If I had been wearing a stress-o-meter (assuming such a thing exists), it would have been spouting smoke and losing springs. "Um," I said, trying to sound calm, "I have a problem, actually. Now's not a good time for me to do, uh, quarter-century cleaning. I'm sorta crunched for time. Colin, my boyfriend," (Why did she always say, "Pish posh" when I called him that?) "is taking me out tonight, and I've got to get ready. I came by, though, to tell you I'm going to be gone for a week. My mom is still real sad about Amy, and Keppler thinks she needs to get away. He's taking us to Hawaii. I just wanted you to know."

"Fine," said Sable as I started to breathe a sigh of relief, "I'll do it myself."

As she put her little foot on the first rung of the ladder, I wanted to shout, "Stubborn old bat!" but counted to ten quickly in my head and tried to reason with her. "I'm not saying I don't want to help. I'm just in a hurry right now, and I can't—"

"Scamper off then," she snapped. "No one's stopping you!"

The ladder wobbled, and I knew it scared her. Still, she climbed to the next rung. "You haven't seen this stuff in thirty years, Sable. What's another week? I'll come back and we'll work on this together. But my mom isn't getting better and—"

"She needs to be told to get over it," she interrupted. "What's done is done. Weeping won't change anything."

I told myself there was no way I was going to steady that ladder for her, but edged a little closer to it anyway as she put a foot on the next rung. "She doesn't cry because she thinks it will change anything. She cries because she's sad. She can't help it."

"Of course she can help it!" she shouted, "You can do anything you put your mind to!" Just then, her foot slipped and her cheek hit the edge of the ladder, making a small cut in her loose, paper-fine skin.

"If that were true, then why can't you figure out how to be nice!" I growled, and scooped her in my arms (marveling at how light she was) and put her on the ground, and at that point should have walked out, not saying another word. But my stress-o-meter was blowing gaskets and fuses, and I just couldn't seem to stop myself from giving her a piece of my mind. So as she dabbed her cut with her finger, I said, nearly shouting, "For months now I've been coming over here, tiptoeing around your ego while trying to help you out. I've been bringing in your mail, taking out your trash, and doing whatever you needed even though you haven't asked me. In fact, you've gotten angry and told me to leave stuff alone, especially when I tried to throw out a dead plant. I mean, who knew you were making seeds? I don't really care that you never acknowledge what I do for you or bother to say thank you. But what does bug me is the one time I tell you I can't stay and help, you get bent out of shape. I don't know why I even care about you. You're a mean, cranky, unapprecia-tive old lady who has totally cut herself off from everyone except me. And after this, I'm sure you'll cut me off too. I've seen your neighbor across the street sprinkle ice melt on your sidewalk when he thought no one was looking. There are people who want to help you, and you push them all away.

"Yes, you've lived through stuff I can't even imagine facing, but instead of it giving you an understanding heart, it's left you warped with anger. My mom is dying inside, but instead of showing some sort of concern for her, you say she needs to get over it. Well, why don't you get over it, whatever it was that left you so bitter and detached, so that you can start caring about something other than your stupid plants!"

Sable took in every word with a look of absolute calm. "It's my vision, not my hearing, that's giving me trouble," she said, "and I'd appreciate it if you—"

"Go," I finished. "I know, I'm going. I'm out of here," I said, and slammed the door hard as I left.

chapter 24

I sat at the bell tower knowing I should have gone back to the dorms to change. I had promised Colin I would, but at the moment I didn't feel like doing a single thing, including primping. I just sat on a bench, my eyes dry and my head spinning as everything I had just said to Sable played over and over again in my mind. "She deserved it," I told myself, but still couldn't shake the feeling that I had just yelled at an old woman with a closetful of medals for her commitment to humanity, and that, no matter how you slice it, is not a good thing.

It's hard not to feel like scum when you've read the riot act to a national treasure, but as Colin walked toward me looking handsome in his freshly pressed khakis and button-down shirt, I slapped on a smile and did my best to seem chipper. But I didn't have to pretend happiness for long. After all, it was good to see him again, and his hug scattered my thoughts of Sable like leaves in the wind.

"Sorry I'm not dressed up," I said as I pointed to my jeans. "I've had a bad day," I continued, pouting just a bit.

Colin stroked my cheek with his hand. "No worries," he said. "My goofy girl looks pretty as always." I smiled as I reminded myself he had meant that as a compliment. I mean, he had no clue how bad my skin crawled when he called me goofy.

Evening was just beginning to fall as the bells above us sounded the half hour. The sky was clear, making the mountains around seem even taller, like a bunch of ancient, inquisitive aunts all standing on tiptoe to see what was happening.

"I was going to wait until dinner," said Colin as I thought about how much I loved his ruddy cheeks, "but maybe I should do this now."

Later, I mean once I'd had time to think about everything, the fact that I had no idea what he was talking about helped me dodge a heap of second guesses. "What?" I asked. "Do you want to take an antacid? There's a water fountain over—"

"No, goofy girl," he laughed, smoothing aside the strands of my hair caught in the breeze. "I got the job in Little Rock," he said, beaming with happiness. "I wanted to make sure it was mine before I said anything about . . . making you mine. The truth is," he said as he pulled a small box from his pocket, "I could be totally happy married to you."

"To me?" I asked, feeling certain he must have meant someone else.

"To you," he said as he got down on one knee and opened the box. "Whimsy Waterman, will you marry me?"

I didn't know what to say, which had nothing to do with the fact I didn't like the ring. Don't get me wrong, it was pretty enough, I'm just not into heart-shaped diamonds. Anyway, I stood there with my mouth open, much like I had when asked to spell *vociferous* at the fourth grade spelling bee. (The whole thing was totally unfair. I got *vociferous* and Jill got *beetle,* but we won't get into that.) I knew I needed to say something. After all, Colin was probably uncomfortable kneeling down like that. *Say something! What do you want? Why are you hesitating? Colin is awesome. He's smart, funny . . . okay maybe not funny, but he's kind and considerate, and this is the time when you're supposed to say . . .* "Yes?" I said at last, and he stood up and swung me around in his arms.

* * *

Getting engaged was completely exhilarating for about five minutes. The trouble was, after kissing and jumping up and down, we started talking logistics. Colin was sad to know that I was going to be leaving for a week. "I wish you didn't have to leave, eh," he had said. "I'm going to miss you a lot, goof. But when you get back we'll start telling everyone and deciding on things like our apartment in Little Rock and the wedding colors. I've always liked hot pink and black, what do you think?"

"Me too," I said, feeling strangely like I'd just been snapped in the face with a cold, wet towel. Hot pink and black? We're talking wedding colors, not how to decorate the gym for a high school dance. And Little Rock? Wait a minute, I said I'd marry him, not move to the Ozarks! But suddenly, I was realizing that the two went hand in hand, and I had just agreed to pack up my life and move it to a place where I wouldn't even want to take a vacation. I mean, who cares about the Clinton Library? It was all I could do to keep from screaming, "I'm not ready for this!" And that feeling stayed with me until . . . let's just say until it didn't need to anymore.

* * *

Colin wanted to go to Salt Lake to have dinner, and on our way there, we stopped at a gas station in Lehi. My nerves were ricocheting off my skull (not a good thing), and I thought it might help if I got out of the car and walked around. There wasn't much to see, but out of the corner of my eye I noticed a beat-up van parked off to the side. I walked a little closer to the van so I could read the license plate. "Maine," I mumbled. "Geez, you're a long way from home."

I looked past the smudged and cracked windshield and saw a family with lots of kids crammed inside, and everyone was asleep. I didn't want to keep looking (something told me not to), but a part of me couldn't help it, and my eyes focused on the mom in the passenger seat just long enough to see that her shirt was unbuttoned and, uh, well . . . Little Johnny was apparently done nursing.

"You're not ready for this," I said to myself as I stared at her.

"I'm ready!" said Colin as he gently honked the horn. "I'm ready!"

* * *

By the time we got back to my dorm that night my head was practically exploding, but I still managed to playfully pout as I got out of Colin's car. "I'll miss you," I whined, and walked over to his window to kiss him once more. "Bye," I said as I waved him away. "Bye."

Instantly taking off the ring and putting it in my pocket, I started to head inside when I heard someone say my name. It was Josh. He was sitting on the hood of his Mustang with his cell phone in hand.

As I walked toward him he pressed his sleeve to his eyes and said, "Whims, man, I'm so glad you're here. It's Jill. She won't talk to me. I've been trying all day. You gotta talk to her, Whims. Tell her I need her. Tell her I need to talk to her. Will you do that? Tell her I'm out here waiting. Tell her I'm sorry and that I love her." Josh took a deep breath and looked up at the street light glowing in the dark sky, his eyes brimming with tears.

I had never seen Josh so upset. I mean, even when we lost to Utah because of an interception he threw, he didn't look this bad. "Sure," I said as I reached out and touched his arm, "I'll do that. Just wait right here."

Yes, a part of me wanted to stay there and grill him—just point my finger in his face and demand he tell me what was going on, but I didn't. I don't know, maybe deep down I was afraid of what he might say, but that's not what I told myself. I told myself there was nothing to worry about. After all, Jill was generally pretty tough on Josh. I mean, even something like not gunning it through a yellow light was enough at times to get her mad. "It's probably something stupid," I mumbled as I climbed the stairs. "He got her order wrong at McDonald's, clipped his toenails in front of her—"

"You should check on your friend," said Christine, a girl I didn't know very well, as soon as I got to the third floor. "She's been making a lot of racket." I sped past my room and the short distance from there to Jill's and found the door ajar and Jill inside punching the life out of Spot.

Stuffed animal innards fell like snow as I watched my friend destroy her oversized good-luck charm, something my walking into her room did little to slow. "Hey," said Jill as she briefly looked at me before burying her fist in Spot's stomach.

"Hey," I said, hoping to lighten the moment. "Need help?"

"No, I got this one," she said, and ripped off Spot's tail.

I watched her punch and rip a little longer before I said, "I just saw Josh in the parking lot."

"So?" she said as she continued to throw punches.

"So he wants to talk to you," I said a little more quietly.

"What's that gonna do?"

"I don't know, keep you from gouging out Spot's eyes?"

"I . . . hate . . . him," she said, punctuating each word with a blow to Spot's stomach.

"Which reminds me, he told me to tell you not to hate him . . . and that he loves you."

"That's not what I needed to hear! Not now, and definitely not at the cabin!" she shouted. "I needed to hear him say, 'No, we're not doing this.' Why couldn't he have done that for me? I needed that, not 'I love you.'"

"Tell me what's happened," I asked, my voice cracking a little with fear.

"I'll tell you what's happened," she said as she pounded Spot with even greater fury. "I'm off the team." Then she slumped to the floor and cried. As long as I had known Jill (and that had been forever) she had been on a gymnastics team. Gymnastics was a constant for her, and in some ways it was for me—the practices, the meets, the endless stomach crunches while watching TV. I knew that when it came to bad news, for Jill it didn't get much worse than this. What I didn't know, however, was what to do, what to say to her. I mean, there was my best friend as close to devastated as I'd ever seen her, and I just stood there, getting more and more angry—angry at myself for not being more of a natural at comforting, and angry at whoever let this happen to Jill. I sat down next to her on the floor, and with my fiery temper beginning to crackle and pop (it didn't help that it was late and I was tired), I waited for her to tell me more.

After a while, Jill reached across strewn kangaroo parts and grabbed a tissue. "This is so stupid," she said, rolling her red eyes. "I've just had one of my best seasons ever. I'm nailing my dismounts, worked new components into my floor and beam, I'm injury free . . . and I'm off the team." Her tone made it clear she was still having trouble believing it. Jill blew her nose hard, then said, "You could say BYU takes real seriously . . ."

"Messing around with your boyfriend," I offered, saying for her what I sensed she didn't want to say herself.

Jill lowered her eyes and nodded.

"Everything is so messed up right now!" I said, uncertain whether I was going to laugh or cry. "It's just too much—you of all people in trouble for *that*. You can't even hear the word *sex* without drowning it out with the Pledge of Allegiance. How in the world did this happen? I mean, duh, I know how it happened, but how did you let it happen?"

Jill grabbed a handful of kangaroo innards and let them sift through her fingers. "One kiss at a time," she said with regret darkening her face. "I let it happen one kiss at a time."

Somebody is to blame, I thought, and closed my eyes as my temples throbbed with anger. *This was so avoidable. Somebody should have been there to stop them. Somebody—*

"Hey," said a familiar voice. I opened my eyes and saw Chloe standing in the doorway, looking at the two of us sitting on the floor, surrounded by kangaroo carnage. She was dressed in jeans and a black T-shirt as usual. This one had *Hazardous Material* scrawled on the front. *Stupid shirt,* I thought. *She's always wearing those stupid shirts.*

Jill reached for another tissue. "Hey," she said to Chloe, somehow managing to smile. Then she turned to me and said, "She already knows."

Chloe cleared her throat and stuck her thumbs through her belt loops. She looked uneasy, as if it were difficult for her to see Jill a wreck and Spot reduced to fluff . . . or was it that she looked guilty? After all, she had gone to Meals on Wheels' cabin that weekend too. She had been there! She could have done something!

"The truth is," she said, stifling a yawn, "I need to go to bed. Whimsy, you don't mind if—"

"I'll tell you what I mind," I snapped, certain I had everything figured out. "I mind the fact that you're a crappy friend!" It was hard to say who this statement caught more off guard, Jill or Chloe. Both were speechless, which was fine. After all, I had a point to make and I wasn't finished. "You could have kept an eye out for her! You could have, for once, been a friend!"

Chloe rolled her eyes. "I can't believe I'm hearing this."

"Whims!" said Jill, but I kept going.

"But no, all you care about is you and your idiotic T-shirts. When was the last time you did something—anything—for someone other than yourself!"

Chloe clenched her hands into fists and gritted her teeth, making it appear as if she were ready to take this outside. "I'm the one who has looked out for her!" she yelled. "This has been building for a while, but have you noticed? No. Have you stayed up till two in the morning waiting for her to get back from a date with Josh so you can make sure she's okay? No! You've been so wrapped up in Bland Boy that you've dropped everything, including your best friend!"

"That's not true!" I yelled.

"It is true. If anyone is to blame, it's you!"

"Stop it!" shouted Jill. "Stop it! This is stupid. As if either one of you could have done anything. It's no one's fault but my own. It's my fault, mine and Josh's. And the fact that I have to live with the consequences is just . . . proof BYU doesn't accept bribes." This lightened the tension in the room a little, but not much. "The only thing yelling is going to do is make Special Kay come running, so knock it off," she said. "Just knock it off."

Chloe took a deep breath. "Look, I came in here to ask if I could sleep on your bed, Whimsy. Someone told me you were with Jill, and I thought the two of you might want to talk for a while."

"Uh, yeah, sure," I said, wading in humiliation. "Go ahead."

Chloe took a deep breath, grabbed her toothbrush, and said, "Good night."

As soon as the door was shut, Jill did what I least expected her to do—she grinned. "That was a nice touch, the way you attacked her T-shirts."

"Hey," I said, trying to keep my head above the shame rising inside me, "they're drab and depressing and why the heck does she always wear them anyway?"

"Free advertising."

"Huh?"

"*Hazardous Material, Pulled from the Wreckage,* and whatever else are the names of her friends' bands. She wears their T-shirts to help them get recognized. Not bad for a crappy friend," Jill said, and gave me a nudge.

"Oh," I said, flooded with embarrassment by the conclusions I'd drawn.

"But thanks," said Jill. "There's nothing like a good catfight to lift my spirits."

"Glad I could help," I said, wanting to roll over and die. Jill grabbed Spot's tail off the floor, and I watched her smile began to fade. "I'm sorry," I said.

"Don't worry about it," said Jill. "If there's one thing I've learned about Chloe, it's that she gets over stuff real fast. I mean, yeah, she's as chipper as your basic undertaker, but—"

"No," I said, gulping hard as I fought back tears. "I meant I'm sorry to you. Chloe's right, I haven't been there for you."

Jill whacked me in the arm with Spot's tail. "Will you quit it with the I-failed-you spiel! You're here right now, with me in the middle of this huge mess. Whims, you're here right now."

I wiped my eyes on my sleeve. "Thanks," I said.

"No really," Jill said. "Thank you."

* * *

We talked until morning, neither of us bothering to look at the clock (which was just as well because it was covered by a decapitated kangaroo head) or out the window. But as the first rays of sun started to appear in the sky, I asked Jill, "Do you think he's still out there?"

"Maybe."

"Do you want him to be out there?"

"Sure, if he's frozen to death," she said with a trace of a smile. "Seriously though, right now I've gotta deal with me, my life. Josh can wait."

"You know how much I love to give advice," I said, making her roll her eyes. "But right now I don't know what to tell you . . . other than we should try to get some sleep."

"You gotta point there," yawned Jill as she pressed her head to her pillow and closed her eyes. "But think of it, Whims."

"Yeah?"

"We're finally roommates. I told you I'd take care of it," she said as she drifted to sleep.

I smiled. "Even at the worst moments, you crack jokes."

Jill didn't say anything. She was already asleep, and it wasn't long before she was yelling at me to snip the parsley.

"It's snipped," I told her as I stared wide-eyed at the ceiling and fingered the ring in my pocket. "Stupid," I said, trying to chide myself for even thinking it, but it was no use. The thought came to me again. *If only I had been Jill's roommate this year, everything would be okay right now. I would have noticed things were getting too tight between her and Josh and would have done something about it. I could have made the difference. Chloe was right,* I thought, as I put my ugly (hey, at five in the morning, I call a spade a spade) engagement ring on my finger, *I have been a bad friend. I have been too wrapped up in Bland Boy, I mean, Colin. If only I'd been at the cabin, things would be different right now. And yet had I been there I wouldn't have been able to help my mom.* "I can't do it all!" I whispered. "I can't do it all!"

* * *

There was no prying Jill from her bed to go to church, and to be honest, if I hadn't agreed to teach the lesson in Relief Society, I probably wouldn't have been there either (for a saccharine-sweet Relief Society president, Special Kay could be persistent). I hadn't slept more than an hour, which may explain why it felt like my nerves were tossed into a vat of boiling oil when, as we walked to church, Pudge whispered in my ear, "I almost threw up after breakfast, but I didn't. You see, I'm getting better."

Yeah, it was good news, and I gave her a thumbs-up, but the truth was, her words made me feel like barbells (the kind used by Mr. Universe, not Mr. Spessard) had just been dropped on my shoulders. After all, right now not throwing up seemed as difficult and precarious a task for her as crossing a circus high-wire several times a day, and even in my sleep I was beginning to be plagued with thoughts of Pudge.

* * *

Sacrament and Sunday School didn't register in my head. Looking back, sure it's easy to say I probably should have closed my eyes and tried to rest, but that doesn't change the fact that I didn't. In fact, I couldn't. All I seemed capable of doing was staring at the wall as I thought over and over again, *I'm engaged, Jill's off the team because she broke the law of chastity, Sable hates me, Pudge needs help, Mom needs help, I NEED HELP!*

The lesson in Relief Society was on food storage, which you have to admit is a real yawner of a subject anyway. Not to give the impression I wasn't prepared, because I was. And to be honest, at first everything was going fine. I stood up when Kay turned the time over to me and launched into the lesson. It wasn't until hands went up that I started having trouble.

If Melanie would have kept it short when I called on her, I'm sure I would have been fine. But no, she started yammering on about everything from wheat grinders to powdered milk, and as I watched her mouth continue to move, my mind drifted to her kids—Tyson, McKenner, and Cody. The next thing I knew, her three kids had multiplied into an army of three hundred, and they were all walking towards me, surrounding me, tugging at my pockets and begging for help. Again a tug, only this time it was harder, and then harder, until I finally yelled, "I can't help all of you!"

"Sister Waterman," I heard a kind voice say while the children continued to pull at me, "Sister Waterman."

I opened my eyes and saw the entire Relief Society staring at me in disbelief. I smiled weakly as I tried to discreetly check for drool. No doubt about it, when it came to humiliating myself, it didn't get much worse than falling asleep while teaching Relief Society. Yes, this was one for the books.

Kay stood up quickly and began to sing the praises of seventy-two-hour kits as the bishop, with his arm around me, escorted me to his office (which was actually the Dean of Communications' office— apparently they had an understanding).

"Sorry," I said as I sat down on the other side of his desk. "Food storage is boring, but it's not that boring. Heh heh."

The bishop didn't laugh, and soon the fake smile on my face was gone.

"Sister Waterman," he said with a look of true concern on his face. "What's wrong?"

Well, that was the wrong question to ask if he was pressed for time because I immediately dove into telling him EVERYTHING, even about Jill and Pudge. He didn't say whether he was already aware of those two situations, and the look on his face revealed nothing (which was fine, but seriously, how do bishops do that?). So anyway, by the time I was done, Relief Society was long over with. It seemed like I should have felt relieved after unloading like that on the bishop, but I didn't. I just felt blank, maybe even a little hopeless. I guess deep down I felt like, in spite of everything I'd done, it hadn't been enough . . . *I* hadn't been enough.

"Wow," said the bishop as he put his hands behind his head and leaned back in his chair. "It sounds like you've been juggling a lot."

"Yeah," I said as an image of me scorching my hair and burning my fingers while trying to keep flaming batons in the air rolled through my mind.

"Do you remember the conversation we had at the beginning of the year when you were called to a position in the Relief Society?"

"Pretty much," I said.

"I remember mentioning to you at the time the good Samaritan—"

"Don't get me started!" I cried, interrupting my bishop (probably not a good habit to get into). "I have 'gone and done likewise' and look what happened—I fell asleep standing up! I'm a wreck. I can't help everyone. I'm sorry. I've tried, I really have. I'm sorry," I said, and put my head in my hands.

"Sister Waterman," he said, and as I looked up he smiled. "If you only knew how refreshing this is for me."

"Huh?"

"As a bishop, at times I have conversations—sad conversations—with people about the choices they've made. Often the problem is essentially they haven't tried hard enough to be good. But with you, Sister Waterman, the problem is quite the opposite: you've tried too hard to be good. I mentioned the parable of the good Samaritan not to bog you down with guilt, but to point out something crucial the Samaritan doesn't do: he doesn't stay." My guess was I looked as confused as I felt and was glad the bishop continued to explain.

"The Samaritan knew his limitations. Yes, he helped the person he saw who was in need, but he didn't try to stay and nurse him back to health. He took him to where he could get help, he did his part, and then he left."

"And someone couldn't have pointed that out to me sooner?" I asked, making the bishop chuckle.

"You've done what you can for your friends, and now it's time for others to step in and help them." I thought of how happy both Pudge and Jill would be if they somehow figured out I had confided in the bishop and breathed a sigh of relief I was on my way to Hawaii. "But thank you, Whimsy."

"For what?" I asked. "That beautiful Relief Society lesson?"

He smiled. "For caring about others and trying to do the right thing."

"You're welcome," I said, shrugging a little as if it had all been no big deal, but as I left his office and began to walk home, I couldn't help feeling lighter, happier, and for the first time in who knows how long, at peace.

* * *

I was glad my fiancé (why was it that word made me feel like I'd just downed a tall glass of tap water in Tijuana?) had to go to his Aunt Henny's that Sunday afternoon. I needed to pack, I needed to think, and though I didn't realize it right away, I needed to write Matt a letter. And so with my suitcase half packed, I sat down at my desk, writing quickly as thought after thought flashed through my mind.

Dear M,
Tell me what you want to do, I mean, before everything is set in your life. I know all you do is think mission right now, but after it's over and you're not wearing a tag, what do you want to do and see and try, before you can't do anything else, before you make choices, before there's no going back? Please write quickly. W

chapter 25

In my opinion, sitting on the beach sipping a fruit smoothie (complete with its own umbrella) is not a bad way to study for finals. Admittedly, I didn't do a lot of studying (okay, hardly any) while in paradise, but that which I did do was a perfectly pleasant experience. In fact, everything about Hawaii agreed with me: the balmy weather, the lush plants (Sable would have loved it), and a nice lady named Noni coming in to cook for us every night. Yes, this was heaven, and even the ring in my pocket couldn't stop me from enjoying it.

Why two people who owned a sleek, professionally decorated condo in Hawaii would opt to live full-time in a dumpy, dark, avocado monstrosity in Utah was beyond me. Still, Keppler had been right about one thing: Mom did need to get away. At first she just slept a lot, either in the house or in the shade on the beach, but after a couple days she started taking walks with us, looking in shops, and even smiling a little.

We had been in Hawaii just a few days when one afternoon while Keppler was out getting groceries I decided to peek in on Mom. She had been taking a nap in their bedroom, but when I opened the door she opened her eyes and gave me a groggy smile. "Hi, sweetie," she said as I walked over and lay down next to her.

Propping my head up with my hand, I looked at her and said, "How are you feeling?"

"Good," she said, still sounding half asleep.

"Food tastes *good,* Mom," I corrected her as she had me a million times before. "You are *well.*"

Mom smiled and closed her eyes. "And I thought you'd never remember that."

"Every now and again I pay attention to what you say," I said.

"Hmm," she said, her eyes still closed. "If only I knew exactly when."

"When what?"

"When you're going to listen."

The blood was beginning to drain from my arm, so I leaned back on her pillow and, while looking at the ceiling, said, "Hmm . . . when do I listen to you, let me see. Well, for starters, there's Flag Day, Hanukkah, Spring Equinox, the third, seventh, and eleventh days of Christmas, and Elvis's birthday. Not that I'm a fan, but I tend to listen to you better on the day he was born."

Mom smiled and opened her eyes. "Such a kook," she said.

"Oh, and today," I said. "I'll listen to you today."

"Sweetie," she said, "I'm fine." I gave her a skeptical look. "Okay, I'm healing. But I don't want to talk about me. I want to talk about you. I can tell something is bothering—"

"Some things," I corrected.

"Very well," she said. "Some things are weighing on my daughter, and I'm wondering if she'd like to talk about them."

I sat up and looked at her. "Your daughter," I said, referring to myself as a third party just to be silly, "who, by the way, loves Hawaii and hopes to return often, would like to talk about a couple of things. But there are other things she can't talk about, well, without hyperventilating." Worried I had said too much and she was going to start asking me pointed questions, I said, "Not that you would hyperventilate if we were to talk about them. No, you would breathe deeply and normally. There'd be no need for a paper bag."

"Silly girl," she said, still sounding groggy. "Just tell me the things you can. I won't pry about the others."

She was, hands down, the best mom ever. "All right," I said. "For starters, there's Sable. Um, I sorta yelled at her before we left."

Mom suddenly sat straight up in bed. "Sweetie, you yelled at Sable? You can't do that. She's—"

"In her late eighties and world famous. Trust me, Mom, I know."

"I was going to say she's your friend," said Mom, instantly causing guilt to well up inside me, "and apparently she doesn't let that happen often—friendship, I mean."

"I know I shouldn't have lost my temper, but I swear Mom, you should have been there. She was being so stubborn. I told her I didn't have time to help her with her attic, and she got all defiant saying that she was going to do it herself. And she probably would have if I hadn't . . . well, pulled her off the ladder."

Mom shook her head. "Oh dear," she said, obviously concerned about her daughter's conduct.

"I was afraid she was going to hurt herself," I said, trying to defend what I had done. "You should have seen how wobbly that ladder was. I probably saved her life, but can she see that? No. She'll probably never talk to me again. I'm sure she hates me."

"Whimsy, she doesn't hate you."

"Mom, we're talking Sable here. I mean, she has a general disregard for everyone. So if someone yells at her—even if they've gone out of their way in the past to be helpful—my guess is she's gonna hate them."

"Sweetie, she doesn't hate you. You just need to talk to her, apologize maybe."

"Mom!"

"After all, you did lose your temper."

"Even if I tried, she wouldn't listen to me. She's like that. I mean, she wouldn't listen to Glengarry, so why would she listen to me?"

"Who is Glengarry?"

"Her husband," I said.

"Honey, everything I've ever read about her says she never married."

"She did, though. She married Lawrence Glengarry. They worked together during the war. She wouldn't listen to him about Gallo—"

"Who's that?" Mom was now sitting crossed-legged and leaning forward with a look of slight anticipation on her face.

"A guy who's golfing with the sons of perdition right now."

"Wilhelmina," she chided.

"Mom, Gallo was a traitor—only he was the worst kind. He befriended people, weaseled his way into situations, gained trust, and then turned on everyone."

"Oh dear," said Mom.

"And Glengarry knew something was up with Gallo. He sensed it, but Sable wouldn't listen. They needed him, and she made the decision to bring him into their circle, and because of that, many people in the Resistance went to jail, even Glengarry and this Hamish Caswell guy."

"Were they okay?" she asked with a hint of anxiety. "Did they survive?"

I shook my head slowly. The truth of what happened back then was still hard for me to accept, let alone say.

"From the Fresnes prison, where Glengarry and Caswell stayed before they were executed, Glengarry sent Sable two letters that he managed to smuggle out of prison through a minister who came to visit Caswell. Both letters told Sable again and again not to blame herself about what had happened. 'Chin up, old girl,' he told her. Kinda funny he called her that since she was only in her twenties. But he said, 'Chin up, old girl. I can manage death, but not the loss of your smile.'"

Mom wrapped her arms around her knees and rested her chin on top of them. "That's so sad," she said quietly. "I wish she would have found a way to do that—smile again, I mean."

"Me too," I said. "She didn't know Gallo was a creep. If she had, she never would have trusted him. But because she did, people died, including her husband, and I imagine that's not the sort of thing that washes quickly off your conscience. And Mom, they were so in love. You should read his love letters to her. Sure, they're jam-packed with goo, but they're so swee—"

"And she let you read these letters?" Mom asked, putting on her reading glasses as if to read me better.

Quick! I thought. *Tell her something, just not the part about burning her Christmas cards!* "Well, um, uh," I started.

"You read them without her permission, didn't you?" she said, sounding ready to ground me.

"Mom," I whined. "I went over there one day and she was about to burn them."

"So you talked her out of it?"

"In a very general, very broad sense . . . you could say that."

"Wilhelmina," Mom said in a way that told me in no uncertain terms it was time to fess up.

"She's stubborn, Mom. I mean, she was going to burn the letters. They were stacked by the fireplace, ready to be chucked in. It was just one of those split-second decisions you make in life. She had to see something burn, and, well, um, there is actually a reason you didn't get a lot of Christmas cards this year."

"Darling, what are you saying?"

"That she sat and watched while I burned your Christmas cards, the ones you asked me to mail."

Mom was speechless, but hey, at least a bit of color had returned to her face.

"I'm really sorry I set fire to your Christmas cards," I said as I nudged her, trying to get her to snap out of her daze.

She shook her head as she smiled. "Unbelievable," she said.

"I promise I'll make it up to you," I said.

"Trust me, darling, you will," she said, and poked me in the side. "So where are the letters now?" Mom asked.

"In my bedroom at your house. I was reading them the night . . . I mean, when—"

"I understand," she said, and smoothed my hair with her hand. "I understand."

Tears welled up in my eyes as I thought of Amy. "Why is life so hard sometimes?" I asked, my voice cracking with emotion.

A tear slid down my cheek, and Mom wiped it away. "I've been asking myself that a lot lately," she said softly. "Asking why things couldn't have turned out differently, and I really don't know." Mom didn't say anything for a while. Looking weary and somehow vulnerable, she just stared out the window at the pale blue sky. Then, just as I was about to say something, anything, to make her smile, she did what I hadn't thought possible: she smiled on her own. "But one thing is certain," she said, her face looking lighter again. "At least when it comes to my life, good things eventually happen."

"Like snazzy beach condos in Hawaii and finding out your friends didn't write you off, they just never got your Christmas cards because your daughter torched them?"

Mom rolled her eyes and smiled. "Not exactly what I was thinking of."

"What were you thinking of?" I asked, pretty certain she was gonna say me, and that wouldn't have been bad to hear.

"A daughter like you," she said, and I smiled with the satisfaction of knowing that when it came to Mom, I could pretty much read her mind. "And a husband like Stanley."

Not that I was bugged to share the spotlight or anything, I just felt like teasing her about what could have been. "But to think you could have had the grand rodeo prize. You were that close, Mom. You could have married Henry and you didn't. It was like missing a million-dollar free throw."

Mom tutted at my silliness. "Then I suppose I should thank my lucky stars I've never been good at basketball," she said.

I pretended to look shocked and told her that was unkind.

"Whether he realizes it or not," said Mom, "I did him a favor saying no to his five hundred—"

"Six hundred," I corrected.

"Marriage proposals," she continued. "I'm all wrong for Henry, even if he couldn't see it himself."

"I think he's beginning to see it. But still, you broke his heart when you turned him down for the six hundredth time and told him you were going to marry Keppler."

"You can't marry a man who proposes to you just to keep from hurting his feelings," she said, not realizing that inside my head it was as if the lights just went on at Dodger Stadium.

"You're right!" I said, jumping off her bed. And as I ran down the hallway and into my bedroom, I shouted, "I told you today was one of my listening days!"

In my room, I quickly wrote a letter to Colin. And, yes, I probably should have put a little more thought into the letter to sorta soften the blow. But hey, my adrenaline was pumping, and besides, I was doing him a favor by being honest. He'd thank me years from now when he married the right girl and looked back on this with a sigh of relief.

Dear Colin,

Hey, I can't marry you. We're not right for each other. Someone else will be right for you, but it's not me. Here's the ring. Thanks a bunch. Whims

I folded the letter, put it inside the small box with the ring, and raced out the front door.

"Where are you going?" asked Mom just before the door shut.

I poked my head in long enough to say, "Just gotta go Fed Ex an engagement ring to a guy. Be back in a moment!" knowing as I ran down the stairs she'd have plenty of questions for me when I got back . . . not to mention a four-course dinner.

* * *

It's a little quirk of Mom's, cooking massive meals when she's worried about me. So I wasn't at all surprised to find her mincing garlic in the kitchen when I got back to the condo.

"Where's Noni?" I asked.

"Well, I decided to give her the night off," she said as she continued to mince.

"No kidding. And Keppler?"

"Just out," she said, mincing harder.

It was obvious Mom had orchestrated a little mother-daughter time, so just to freak her out I said, "Speaking of out, I think I'll go back to the corner market and—"

Simultaneously cutting off me and the head of a fish, Mom asked, "So what was that you were saying about an engagement ring?"

Sitting down at the bar, I picked up a peeled carrot and took a bite. "Engagement ring . . . engagement ring," I said as I munched, trying my best to look like I was jogging my memory. I'm not sure whether it was the look on her face or the knife in her hand (hey, everyone has their breaking point), but I knew it was time to tell all. "Oh that," I said. "Well, as it turns out, Colin proposed to me."

"And you said yes?" she asked, her voice cracking a little with fear.

"Yes and no."

"What do you mean?" she asked, sprinkling finely minced garlic on the poor, beheaded fish.

"First I told him yes, but now I'm telling him no."

Hearing this did little to unknit her brow. "And you told him no in a letter?" she asked.

"It was more of a note than a letter," I said. "But Mom, I sent it Fed Ex. What could be faster or kinder than that?"

"A phone call," she said without hesitation.

I instantly shook my head. "Mom, I can't do that."

"Why not?"

"Because you've never bothered to learn CPR, and calling him might give me cardiac arrest," I said, hoping she'd relent. She didn't.

"Young lady, there is a great deal I want to talk to you about, but first you need to give Colin a call and explain to him what you've decided."

"But Mom, I—"

"He deserves to hear this from you. And besides, not running from an awkward situation is a sign of maturity."

I let out a deep breath, wishing she hadn't said that bit about maturity. I mean, either she had a window into my soul and knew exactly what would motivate me, or she just rolled the dice and got lucky. "All right," I said as she handed me her cell phone.

I walked into my bedroom and shut the door. Dialing slowly, I began to wonder if it was such a good idea to make the call. I mean, it was one thing to send Colin a letter—okay, note—letting him know we were through, but to say as much over the phone just seemed messy. "I don't know about this," I said to myself as I continued to dial. "And besides, if I don't call him and just let him find out through the mail, it gives him time to work through most of his shock and despair before we talk, which in its own way is humane, isn't it?" One digit away from calling Colin, I put my finger on the button, but stalled when it came to actually pressing it. "But I guess I could call him, just to say hi. Yeah," I said, pressing the last button, "I can handle hi." I gulped hard.

After a few rings, Colin picked up. "Hello?" he said.

"Hi," I said. "It's me."

"Hey goof," he said. "I was just thinking about you."

Hey goof. Either he had a window into my soul and knew exactly what would motivate me, or had just rolled the dice and gotten lucky, but at any rate, hearing those words was all I needed. "Good," I said, suddenly imbued with courage, "because, Colin, we need to talk."

* * *

If I lived by the beach, no doubt I would accomplish nothing with my life. It was too easy for me while in Hawaii to sink into one of the overstuffed couches and take a nap or just sit in a deck chair and watch the waves. It worried me (when I actually summoned enough energy to think about it) what a natural I was at loafing. I mean, yeah, I had been through a lot the past year and deserved a break. But hey, three naps a day is a bit much.

Anyway, it was during one of my daily loafing sessions that I woke up and overheard Mom and Keppler talking. The two of them were sitting in the huge hammock on the balcony, watching the sunset. The doors to the balcony were open, and I awoke from my nap on the couch with gentle ocean breezes tickling my face.

"That's not how it happened at all," was the first thing I remember hearing Mom say, which in itself wasn't remarkable, but what was remarkable and good and even a miracle was the sound of her laughing—and laughing hard. "I cannot believe you remember it that way!" she cried. "I did not bat my eyes at you the first day of class."

"Then you should have," he said, "because I would have appreciated it. My heart was pounding so—"

"I was so worried to meet you," she said, thinking back. "I'd heard from so many of the students about stern Keppler."

"Tell me who they are, and I'll flunk them all."

"Stop!" she cried as if he'd just tickled her. "And you were stern. The day you made an example of me in front of the class, I thought I'd die from embarrassment."

"Yes, well, sorry about that," he said as they both laughed.

"I thought my life was over when I walked out of your office after having yelled at you."

"No, I thought my life was over. More than anything I wanted you to stay, even if you were yelling."

"Stanley, that's not true. You're rewriting history. You didn't fall in love with me until later."

"That's the official story, but the truth is I looked at you when you came into my class and thought, 'There she is, there's my wife,' and all I wanted to do after that was quickly jump the hurdles that lay between us. Nothing else mattered but getting here to this point."

For a while they didn't say much (my guess was things were getting smoochy), and as I closed my eyes and listened to the waves crashing in the distance, I thought of Mom and Keppler, their wedding day, and how mad I had been when Hudson had spilled the beans about them getting sealed. It had taken me awhile to work through it, no doubt about that, but as I thought of Mom and Keppler and Amy and even me, I knew there was something in there that was worthy of permanence, and though I didn't know exactly how all the pieces would fit in the end, I was glad to know that their love had ties to eternity.

"That's it!" I yelled, nearly making Keppler and Mom nearly tip over in the hammock. "That's it!"

The two of them stood up as I hurried toward them. "What is it?" Mom asked.

"It's Sable and Glengarry," I said. "I just realized it's not the end for them, it's not the end." As Keppler and Mom looked at each other in confusion, I looked out over the balcony and shouted the good news to the evening sky.

chapter 26

Wilhelmina Waterman
D-3209
Stover Hall
Provo, UT 84604

Dear W,

Run the bases at Yankee Stadium, play the guitar in a subway station and see if anyone throws me a coin, sail in water clear as glass, figure out how to graciously tell a telemarketer to beat it, walk at night through Paris after a fresh rainfall, make a stock pick by throwing a dart onto a board, learn how to choke down tofu since it's so good for me, write a poem and read it in a place where people will snap their approval, swim with the dolphins, backpack through Europe for six months and not cut my hair until after I've come home and said hello to my mother, take Wilhelmina Waterman out for tofu and listen to her complain. M

* * *

It's not like I had expected Spessard-like sorrow from Colin when I broke off our engagement. Sure, one sad country music song written about his broken heart would have been nice, but it wasn't the sort of thing I was anticipating, which, as it turns out, was fortunate. Consequently, I am pleased to announce that my ego, though far from bubble wrapped, survived quite well what happened next, which was simply Jill jumping over my suitcase, grabbing me by the shoulders, and shouting, "I kid you not, Captain Toronto and Special Kay are engaged!"

Granted, love blooms quickly at BYU, but come on.

"I just spoke to Colin five days ago," I said, somewhat dazed but not dazed enough to reveal what it was I had said to him.

"She's such a special snake. I saw the whole thing happen. Colin came over here while you were gone, and from the look on his face he was missing you big-time. I was just about to go over and comfort him," she said.

I rolled my eyes.

"Okay, wave. I was just about to wave at Colin when Special Kay wormed her way over there and started asking him how he was doing and why he looked so bummed. She was, of course, the perfect listener, nodding her head and patting his shoulder, the whole bit. Anyway, they went on a walk that night, and by the time they made it to Baskin Robbins—where he ordered a scoop of boring vanilla— they were already engaged."

I looked at Jill, waiting for her to get back to the truth.

"Geez," she finally said, "you're no fun to tell that someone has stolen your boyfriend."

"He wasn't my boyfriend," I said, sounding dead serious. "He was my fiancé."

Jill gave me a pathetic look. "And you think I'm a bad liar," she said, slowly shaking her head.

"He was!" I said, though deep down, in a very small way, I was pleased she didn't believe me.

"Look," said Jill, "if saying that makes you feel better, fine."

"It's the truth."

"Sure it is."

"He gave me a ring and everything."

Jill patted me on the shoulder. "Just keep on dreaming that bland dream," she said. "Keep on dreaming."

* * *

It did sting to hear about how quickly Colin and Kay became Colin and Kay, but I had no regrets, which was a major help because with finals in full swing, I didn't have time for them anyway. In fact, it wasn't until the day of my last final that I actually saw Colin again.

I was just about to walk into Stover Hall when suddenly Colin walked out.

"Whimsy," he said as his naturally ruddy cheeks turned even more red, "how are you doing?"

"Fine," I said, and bit my lip to keep from adding, "Of course, I'd be even more fine right now if you didn't look so handsome, but thanks for wearing your puka shells. That helps a little."

Colin shifted his weight from one foot to the other and rubbed the back of his neck like he'd just been rear-ended. "I was going to call you," he said.

"That's okay," I said, and smiled, glad to see that the conversation between us still didn't flow well. In its own way, it was reassuring proof that I had made the right decision. "But I'm glad," I said, half wondering if I had the guts to finish what I had started to say, "I mean, I heard you and Kay had . . . found each other."

A group of girls filed between us as they left Stover Hall. "You're not mad, eh?" Colin asked as they passed us.

"Surprised, sure," I said. "But not mad."

Colin quaked from what looked like a jolt of relief. "Can't tell you how glad I am you're not mad. It's crazy almost the way things have worked out. I mean, I came over here after you called me from Hawaii because I was down, eh. But then Kay saw me in the lobby, asked me what was wrong, and well, we've been together ever since. Whimsy, I know things have moved fast between Kay and me, but when something is . . ."

"So right you could kick it?" I offered.

This was clearly not an expression Colin was familiar with. "I guess you could say that," he said with a shrug. "But I think what it comes down to is Kay and how special she is."

"She definitely is that," I said.

Colin smiled. "I'm glad you think so. Well, I'd better get going."

"Me too."

"Take care, Whimsy," said Colin as he gave me the brotherliest of hugs.

"I will," I said, then stood there on my own and watched him walk away.

But before I could begin contemplating everything that had happened, I heard a cackling Finn. "You, this one Whimsy girl!"

shouted Sister Wauteever as she walked outside, smoothing her skirt. "You stay-ing here! One golf-ing car coming!"

"Huh?" I said as I turned around and saw a golf cart in the distance.

"For you!" said Sister Wauteever, who was now standing right next to me. "This one car com-ing for you!"

It's hard to say how I felt when I finally realized what was happening. After all, it's not every day you see an official-looking guy driving toward you in a golf cart with Sable Thompson Greer in the seat next to him. Of course, I was stunned and even happy, but more than anything else I think I was ashamed.

Sister Wauteever poked me in the arm. "Here is the one Whimsy girl!" she said.

"Thank you, Sister," said the official-looking man. "Whimsy Waterman, Miss Thompson Greer has honored us today by visiting our campus and, as it turns out, she has come to see you."

Sable looked tired, and I gulped back emotion as I understood what she had done: she had walked the distance from her house to somewhere on campus in search of me, and with only her dim eyes to guide her and Glengarry's cane as support. Since Hawaii I hadn't yet worked up the courage to go over and see her, and to my amazement and horror, she had instead come to me.

"Apparently when you're as old as I am and you walk onto these grounds, they insist on taking you around in one of these contraptions," she huffed.

"BYU is so into rules," I said, hoping to pacify Sable but not offend the official-looking guy, and was glad that he gave me a knowing grin.

"Could have made it myself. I was nearly here," she mumbled.

"So was there something that you wanted to tell me?" I asked before she could complain any more about BYU hospitality.

"Yes," she said, shifting uneasily in her seat, "as a matter of fact, there was something I needed to tell *you*."

Instantly catching on, Official Guy said, "Sister Wauteever and I, we'll be right inside if you need us."

Wauteever wasn't quite as insightful. "Why we go-ing inside?" she demanded as Official Guy held the door open for her. A smile was the only explanation he gave her, which I don't think she appreciated because as the door began to close behind them, I could hear her grumbling what I'm sure were some choice Finnish words.

Official Guy had parked the golf cart on the grass under a large tree, and as I sat down in the seat next to Sable, a gentle breeze came by, rustling the leaves above us. Trying to sound casual, I said, "So what was it you wanted to say?"

With her weathered hands resting on the cane's brass handle, she looked straight ahead and said, "You once asked me if there was anything I regretted."

"Yes, I did."

"And I believe I told you it was planting my lilac bush too near the house."

"That was it."

"Well, that wasn't a very good answer I gave you, was it? *Regret* is a powerful word, a powerful emotion. It makes you reconsider again and again the way things turned out, and wish till you're half mad that you had it in your power to change the outcome. It gnaws at you unceasingly, and like dandelions in a summer garden, crowds out everything else, every other thought. It can leave you desolate. Most certainly it can do that."

A few tears slid from Sable's stern eyes, and she brushed them aside quickly, as if unwilling to claim them as her own. "But it's not my lilac bush that I've regretted," she said, gripping tight on the cane's brass handle. "Not really."

"Sable," I said, certain she was about to open her soul to me. "You don't—"

"It's my daylilies," she said brusquely.

"Your what?"

"My daylilies. They've never bloomed as they should, and I highly regret it."

"Daylilies," I said, trying hard not to grin. "I know what you're talking about. Those flowers stress me out too."

"Well," she said, straightening up in her seat and still looking straight ahead, "I feel better now that I've said that."

"Me too."

"And I suppose I'll see you on Saturday as always."

"Of course, but can I bring my mom?"

"Whatever for?"

"One of her favorite pastimes is cleaning attics," I said, more than bending the truth.

"Her mind must be dodgy," said Sable. "But you can bring her along if you'd like."

"Great, I'll plan on it," I said, and reached over and gave her a hug, which is never a safe bet, but I did it anyway.

"Nonsense, silliness, absolute tomfoolery," she said, but in her voice there was the hint of a laugh. That settled, her naturally gruff disposition quickly returned. "Now where is that man?" she snapped as she looked around in vain. "Such incompetence. I suppose these days they allow just about anyone to be vice president of a university."

"He seems nice enough," I said, trying not to sound surprised that her chauffeur was such a bigwig.

"I suppose," she grumbled. "But he keeps going on about how grand it would be if the school could honor me with a dinner. Just the sort of pomp and nonsense I abhor." She smacked her lips together hard as if to make it even more clear she wasn't interested.

"Why not let them do it?" I asked.

"Why should I go there and mingle with people I don't care about?"

"Hey!" I said, suddenly struck with a brilliant plan, "You could go there and mingle with people *I* care about!"

"What are you prattling on about?"

"Let BYU throw you a party," I said, "and let me take care of the guest list."

"Why should I do that?

"Well, for starters, it'd be nice for you to meet all the people I care about, and besides, even if I live to be your age, chances are slim this school is ever gonna whip together a dinner in my honor."

"Well," she said with a shrug, "it's no skin off my nose if this university wants to cook me a chicken dinner."

Jumping out of the golf cart, I went to find Sable's chauffeur to tell him the good news.

To Do List:

- ☐ *Write Matt and tell him no way are we ever going out for tofu.*
- ☐ *Write Phil and tell him Chiara deserves to know he embarked on a one-man mission to get mono.*
- ☐ *Write Chiara and tell her, miracle of miracles, Chloe bore her "budding" testimony (as she called it) in Relief Society and made us all cry.*
- ☐ *Wrap stupid, oversized, stuffed platypus Jill picked out for her birthday, and somehow convince her not to transfer to Arizona State.*
- ☐ *Put together guest list for Sable's party.*
- ☐ *Call Hudson to find out what day we're going mountain biking next week.*
- ☐ *Look at apartment on south side of campus with Pudge and Chloe.*
- ☐ *Finish writing one hundred "Happy Spring" cards for Mom.*
- ☐ *Tell Mom she's going to have to take a small break from remodeling Keppler's house because I just signed her up to help Sable on Saturday.*

About the Author

Currently a resident of Florida, Lisa Kathleen McKendrick was born in Phoenix, Arizona, and later attended Brigham Young University, where she received both her bachelor's and master's degrees in English. She served a mission to the Italy Catania Mission.

She enjoys photography, running, shopping for deals, and dates with her husband (not necessarily in that order). She serves as Primary president in her ward.

Lisa and her husband, Richard, live in Lakeland, Florida, with their four children—Samuel, Julia, Caroline, and Victoria—and their dog, a Rhodesian Ridgeback named Deezsha. *A Life of My Own* is her second published novel.

Lisa enjoys corresponding with her readers, and they may write her in care of Covenant Communications, P.O. Box 415, American Fork, Utah 84003-0416